REbirth

Book One of the "Rain Experience" Series

Thomas W. Everson

This is a work of fiction which takes place on another world. Names, characters, businesses, places, events, and incidents are the products of the author's imagination or used in a fictitious manner. Any resemblance to real persons, living or dead, is purely coincidental.

DEDICATION

To my wife, Brandi, and my son, Bubby: Thank you. Without you, I wouldn't be who I am today, and this story would not be at all.

CONTENTS

ACKNOWLEDGMENTS

I would like to thank my editor, Dean Fetzer for his attention to detail and guidance, my illustrator Jake Murray whose hard work was to have the elasticity to take what I was looking for, and make it his own, and my friends and family who have supported my efforts.

1 SALVATION

I pant for breath and my chest hurts. There is a house in front of me, unfamiliar in many ways, and I cannot put my finger on it but I do not think I have seen anything like it before. When I look down my hands are covering my stomach. Removing them reveals that I am bleeding profusely, my hands covered with sticky red blood oozing from my abdomen. My thoughts are unclear and fuzzy. Both my head and my stomach are throbbing with an incredible amount of pain and I feel my throat lump up. When I attempt to walk forward, my legs collapse under me. As I fall to the ground I notice the door to the house is opening. My face meets the dirt with a heavy impact and I turn to curl into a fetal position just trying to get the pain to go away.

While the pain still exists, my mind becomes distracted but is put at ease when a torrential downfall of rain begins. Even though I should be anxious right now seeing my own blood mixing into the mud, the rain calms me. My hot body becomes cooler and I moan, feeling my life force begin to leave me. A scream pierces the air but it is not my own. It is feminine. Two distinct feminine voices emanate from the direction of the house, one youthful and the other soft, but I do not have the strength to move my head to look, let alone open my eyes.

"We must get him inside."

"He's bleeding quite a bit…I don't know if…."

The voices begin to sound strange, blurring together. I feel two sets of hands on me and as I am lifted up my body cries out in more pain, and my mouth follows suit. My vision goes black and I feel myself drifting, floating away, and then there is nothing.

This must be the end of my life.

I wake on something soft and padded that supports the length of my body, my head resting on a pillow and a raised portion of whatever furniture it is I lie upon. On my left side is a backing, which leads me to think it is a padded bench of some sort. To my right sits a tan woman, probably in her late thirties or early forties, hovering over me while placing a washcloth across my forehead. Her hair, brown with signs of graying near the sides, is neatly wrapped up in a bun. Her eyes are dark blue, accentuated by her high cheekbones, and her smile is thin and caring. She seems motherly, like a nurse or a maid in a long blue dress and white apron.

My abdomen burns like a wildfire from the pain. Looking down I find it has been bandaged. White mesh cloth is wrapped around my bare torso a few times along with a few metal clips to hold it in place. I cannot help but wonder what kind of wound is hidden, but I recall how terribly it bled and it almost seems too gruesome to think about.

Where am I?

My surroundings do not look familiar in any way, nor does the woman aiding me. As I look past the woman sitting on the edge of a table next to me, I find I am in an open, oddly shaped room. The left side of the room is closed off with portraits hanging on the walls in between a couple bookshelves. On the right there is a hallway and a set of stairs leading up. Where the woman sits is a dark brown, polished table that holds a bowl of water and some blood caked rags.

I try to remember anything at all, but find that I cannot seem to pull up any memories. Nothing comes up. No names, no faces, no places, nothing at all. It is as blank as a fresh sheet of parchment. I become frantic because the more I try to remember the more the emptiness swirls around my mind. I become anxious, and questioning everything.

Why do I hurt? What happened to me? Who am I?!

Startled by being in this unfamiliar place and having no recollection of anything, I attempt to get up quickly, but instead groan in pain and rest back into position reluctantly when the woman gently places her hand on my shoulder and shushes me.

"W...What h...happened?" I manage to wheeze out.

"Don't talk. Please lie still. You'll be all right dear," she says in a very sweet tone.

I notice a figure in the background shuffle about in the dark hallway. Nervously, I squint trying to get a better glimpse of who is there, but only see shadows moving about. Perhaps it is my imagination or my eyes playing tricks on me, but for all I know my wound could have come from someone in this house. I cannot help but feel unsafe.

"Who are you? I cannot...I cannot remember!" My voice elevates.

There is shuffling in the background again, but I cannot focus my eyes. Weary of the pain, my mind begins to drift out. Trying to stay awake and alert is proving useless. My eyelids are heavy, and droop.

"My name is Agatha. You've lost a fair amount of blood so please rest. You are in no danger here." She gets up and leaves through a white swinging door next to the stairs just inside my peripheral vision.

With my vision blurry and my eyes so heavy that I can barely keep them open, I feel like I am slipping away again, to that dark place. But that movement is there in the hallway once more and I am positive someone is lurking in the shadows. I am unable to keep focused on them. As the shadowy figure comes closer I can tell they are about to reach the bright light within this room, but I can no longer bring myself to open my eyes.

~~~~~~

Abruptly awoken, I find myself in a sitting position, slightly hunched over and slouched against the back of the furniture. Becoming aware, I am in that foreign place so eloquently built. Turning my head to the left there is a large window, and it is dark outside. My neck is stiff and it feels like I have been out for hours, but I am not really sure how much time has passed.

Instead of the older woman tending to me, this time a young and very beautiful woman sits to my right side on the padded bench. Her slightly curled, long brown hair flows freely over both her back and her chest. Her lips are pouty and her nose is small. She wears a knee-length pleated blue skirt and a white sleeveless shirt with a lone pink flower near her right shoulder. Trying to see her eye color through my blurred vision proves impossible while she keeps her face pointed downward, focused on replacing the bandages around my bare torso with her soft touch.

She is magnificent.

"Who...are...you?" My voice comes out as a raspy whisper.

She yelps in fright and covers her mouth with one hand, not having been aware I was awake and observing her. She looks at me nervously then over her shoulder at the white door.

"Shh." She cautions me to lower my voice putting her finger to her lips.

"Where...am...I?" I whisper.

"This...house is my mother's, and mine," she whispers back and then looks over her shoulder nervously.

"What happened to me?"

"We don't know. I saw you collapse in the mud in front of our house and there was blood everywhere. My mother and I brought you into the house, dressed your wound and cleaned you up," she explains pointing out the window.

"I...I cannot remember...my name. Do you know me?" I become frantic. I cannot remember anything and it is terrifying.

"Shh! You have to be quiet!" She turns around and looks over her shoulder again. "We don't know who you are. You don't remember anything at all?"

"I do not. Your accent is strange." I cannot help but notice her speech is different than mine. Most of her words make sense, but some seem to slur together making it difficult to comprehend everything.

Heavy footsteps approach from that white swinging door which Agatha had disappeared through previously.

"Shh. We didn't talk!" She becomes quiet, and continues about bandaging me up.

"I heard voices!" The white door bursts open with a loud thud as if hit or kicked hard from the other side.

Agatha has entered the room, but to my surprise she acts very differently than she did with me. The woman who was calm and gentle with me has apparently gone into a fit of anger as she storms over to where the girl and I sit.

"Why were you talking to him?!" she yells abrasively.

Not wanting to get the girl in trouble with her mother I reply.

"I...I spoke." Pushing my voice from my throat at a normal range causes a strange itch inside my throat, and am forced to cough quite violently.

"You shouldn't be talking! You're hurt. And if you were talking, that means *she* was talking!" She lifts her hand to strike the girl.

"No!" I manage to yell out between coughs and gasps. Despite the pain in my abdomen I stand to intervene, grabbing Agatha's wrist.

I stand a few inches taller than her, and find my arms are not exactly frail. My palm meets her wrist and I take care not to grip too tightly, to avoid harming one of the people who appear to be helping me recover. I am strong enough to stop her, but at the cost of severe physical pain and cracking of the scab binding my wound closed. My initiative to save the young woman is rewarded by being struck across the face with Agatha's other hand, rather hard.

The pain of being struck, along with the pain burning me up from the inside is too much and I collapse to one knee, resting my hands on the wooden table. My coughing worsens and bloody spittle appears on the hardwood floor. With every ounce of energy being sapped, I can barely hold myself up. The effort was all for naught when I hear some tussling and a slap.

"Go clean the kitchen," the motherly figure's tongue lashes the girl.

With my remaining strength I look up briefly and watch as tears roll down the side of the young woman's face while she gets up and slinks off to the white door. She pushes through as Agatha glares at her. Agatha turns in a huff, storming out a door behind me. Collapsing onto the cold, bloodied, wooden floor, the solitude of darkness finds me again.

I dream of nothingness. Though I think my eyes are open, I see nothing. I do not feel anything physical supporting my body, like I am floating in a vast nothingness. There is a sense of very slow motion, though I cannot discern the direction, as I tumble through the darkness in a fetal position. It is quiet and calming, sort of like the rain that washed over me. The vastness of the darkness is astounding. Eventually I can feel light appear in front of me but I cannot see it yet. It is that feeling of when someone draws the drapes open while you are still asleep and the sun is out. The light hits your face and you do not really want to wake up because you are at peace. But that ends. I am shocked awake with severe pain in my abdomen.

~~~~~~

My bandages are being changed again, and when I open my eyes I find my chin in the crook of a shoulder. Whoever it is sits on the wooden table. Through peripheral vision I can see the color of the shirt covering the soft shoulder I am nuzzled against. It is a frilly and soft blue cloth. A light perfume radiates off my attendee's body, a sort of spring, flowery smell. It relaxes my mind a little, and before I can restrain my mouth I speak.

"So warm…" I blurt.

"Mmm, you're awake." It is Agatha, and she sounds happy.

I am pulled away from her warmth, and leaned against the arm of the furniture. Agatha gives me a motherly smile. I blush and look away not having meant to actually say what I was thinking.

She has removed the bandage. My wound pulses, torturing me with searing pain. I look down, and there is blood crusted on my chest and abdomen in a very sporadic way. I can feel it on my back also. As it is the first time seeing the damage, it appears to be a stab wound. When I move I can feel in my body that whatever it was, it ran completely through, but by some miracle it seems to have missed my vital organs. Through the thick scab I note a few pieces of black string are protruding, one at the top and one at the bottom.

Is the string holding the wound together, like two sewn pieces of cloth?

"Since you're awake, let's see if we can stand you up and make this easier," Agatha suggests pleasantly.

She slings my arm across her collarbone and over her shoulder. I grip on and while standing up with her help, I can feel the scab start to crack and the string trying to hold the two sides of the wound together. It opens enough so that blood begins slowly seeping from the wound in the front. She lets go of me so that I am standing on my own, and moves with great speed. Placing clean pads on both sides and wrapping me tightly with the white mesh bandage, she then uses the metal clips to hold it all together. Finally, she grabs a cloth from behind her on the table and wipes up any blood that rolled down.

"Shh, now. You'll be fine," she says, her voice innocent and quiet. She grabs under my armpits, helping me lower myself down to the edge of the padded bench.

"How long have I been here?" I ask, while hunching over.

"Half a week now, but you must still rest. Though your healing is progressing well, you have a long way to go." Agatha stands there vibrantly smiling, hands crossed in front of her.

"Half a week?" I ask, surprised.

"You need to eat. Let me get you some fresh baked bread," she redirects the conversation and leaves through that white swinging door. I briefly see that there is a very fancy and clean kitchen on the other side.

There is shuffling in the background of the hallway again, but it is too dark to tell if the shadowy figure is the young woman from before. My attention is refocused when Agatha returns with a fresh loaf of bread on a platter and some butter on the side. She sets it across my lap, and I eat as if I have not eaten in months. I ravenously consume the bread and butter. As it hits my stomach, I can feel a sense of satisfaction that I am full for now. She sits down on the table, placing her hands in her lap.

"I am sorry if I sound ungrateful, but I am alarmed. Am I safe here?" I ask, shifting nervously and tightening my muscles.

"Of course you are. Why would you ask?"

"You seemed to lose control of your temper whenever I was awake last, and struck both the younger woman and I."

Agatha looks away for a moment, and then back with a sincere smile.

"I'm sorry for that. It's a very complicated situation here, and probably best not to worry you with all of the details. But I will try to keep it from happening again."

Though it seems a bit strange, I choose not to pursue it and take her at her word, as I am a guest in her home. My mind quickly moves to the beautiful younger woman, and hope to catch a glance of her again.

"What is the other person's name?" I manage to get out with only a small coughing fit.

Agatha's eyes widen for a moment, and she seems a bit flustered about the question. Her smile is gone and she has turned slightly pale.

"Whom do you mean?"

"The younger woman?" I question, very puzzled about her response.

Agatha sighs and her genuine smile returns as if somehow a disaster was just averted.

"My daughter's name is Ami."

"She seems very lovely – she is quite beautiful."

"Thank you," she replies earnestly.

Overall Agatha seems like a very calm person, and I have no explanation for why her personality would so drastically change. Perhaps it was just a bad day.

"Would you be able to show me to a chamber pot?"

"We don't have any of those. We have something called a 'bathroom'."

"I would be much obliged if you could lead me to this bathroom you have."

Setting the platter on the couch, she helps me up and leads me down the dark hall where the shadowy figure was previously. It has gone. She opens a door on my left and I enter. It is dark, with the only light coming in from a small window at the top of a wall in the back of the room. But the window goes dark as the room is completely illuminated in an instant. Looking around at the now well-lit room, I am amazed. The room is filled with extravagant items. A marble counter with wooden cupboards is on my left, with a white sink, pearl colored handles, and a shiny metallic spout sticking out over it. Above the counter is a large full wall mirror. In it I see a stranger standing with Agatha. To my right there is a white tub with a flowery curtain, and against the back of the room is a pure white seat that looks like a glorified chamber pot permanently affixed to the floor.

"This is your bathroom?" I turn to her and give a questioning look.

"Yes, this is a bathroom. That's the toilet," she points to the fixed seat. "That is where you can relieve yourself. When you are done just push the silver handle, and be sure to wash up at the sink afterward."

She exits and closes the door behind her. Taking a moment, I look at the rest of the room around me. There is another closed door on the left just past the edge of the counter with the sink. When I investigate the tub I find a setup that seems unfamiliar. Inside are two knobs and a spout attached at the top of the tub, and above that there is a strange round device with many holes hung overhead with a coil that comes out from the wall.

Moving to the toilet, I touch the ceramic top. It is cold and smooth. There is a metal lever on the top left of the tank as described by Agatha. After relieving myself I pull down on the lever and am amazed to watch the water swirl down, taking everything with it and then refilling with clean water. I stand there in awe of it, this strange contraption, and it comes to my attention that being so transfixed on such an amazing device that it seems impossible that I have ever seen anything like it before.

Over at the sink, I play with the handles to adjust the water flow. I notice that there are two of them, and after some trial and error find that one is hot water and one is cold. At a comfortable temperature I stop playing with the handles, and wash. There is a towel hung from a wooden ring attached to the wall adjacent to the mirror, and I wipe my hands dry.

I look in the mirror. The person reflected is a stranger. I take the time to study myself.

I have semi-short, chocolate-brown hair and green eyes. When I smile so I can see what it looks like I find nothing abnormal, and my teeth are for the most part straight. I look the way I feel, battered. On the left side of my pale face I have a black eye, and a bruise on my cheek. They appear to be healing, indicated by their yellow-green borders.

I appear to be in fit condition, and stand at a fair height. I examine every part of me, except my covered abdomen. Touching the bandages, I want to see the wound underneath, but a knock at the door startles me.

Agatha is waiting patiently outside, and proceeds to lead me back to the padded bench. As I sit back down I realize that I was not paying attention to how many doors down the hall the bathroom was, in case I need to relieve myself again.

There were a few, to be sure, but the number eludes me. I suppose she will help me again when the time arises.

"I'm going to tend to some chores. Please relax," she says cheerily.

She seems to smile a lot. Is she genuinely so happy?

She leaves and walks up the nearby flight of stairs to the right of the hallway and quiet falls over the room. With nothing going on I try to remember anything about myself while staring out the window to the tree line. While searching my mind, I find that I can recall facts like: wood burns, metal melts, there is a sun in the sky and it is bright, but memories fail to surface.

It is as if that entire part of my mind malfunctioned and flushed it all.

I notice shuffling around the hallway yet again, and Ami emerges from the darkness, her head not bowed as much as the last time. As she gets closer I finally get a glimpse of her eyes; pale blue.

It is like staring into a crystal lake. And she has the kind of face any young woman would love to have, smooth, flawless, beautiful.

"Ami?" I whisper to get her attention.

She stops dead in her tracks mid-stride with her eyes widened, but is motionless for only a brief moment. She walks quickly over to me and sits down. When she speaks it is in almost a normal volume voice.

"How did you find out my name?" she asks.

"Your mother told me."

"My…mother…told you?" She looks around frantically. "Look, the things here aren't what they seem. As soon as you are better you must leave from this house, otherwise you will become part of it. If you don't leave the first chance you get, you will be stuck here."

"What is that supposed to mean?" The enigmatic statement confuses me.

"It's best if you don't know the details. I have to go. She could change without any warning." She gets up and hurries off into the kitchen.

Though Agatha says I am safe, I cannot help but feel uneasy and perplexed at the situation, but after a few minutes of trying to contemplate it my mind becomes fuzzy and I feel that darkness coming again to take me away. I close my eyes and rest.

But the rest quickly turns to unrest as I dream. When I open my eyes everything is hazy and gray. It appears I am in the forest. Moving on its own my body propels me to a clearing in this forest but before I reach it I feel my body scream in pain. It feels like I am on fire both inside and out. Wiping my forehead, I am sweating profusely. My hand it is smeared with a vibrant red. Looking down I see a long, curved dagger pierced through my abdomen, and blood soaks my white shirt as the dagger is retracted. I clutch the wound trying to stop the bleeding, but I am unsuccessful. The blood gets all over and then the familiar darkness comes for me.

~~~~~~

My body does not startle me awake. Instead I slowly regain consciousness, lying there for a few moments with my eyes shut. I wonder if the dream that I just had is was what really happened. When I feel awake enough, I open my eyes. Everything is fuzzy, but blinking clears my vision.

I actually feel a little better; more refreshed than the last time I was awake. I wonder how long I have been out this time.

My stomach grumbles deeply, telling me that it needs sustenance. Struggling to get up, I stiffly walk over to the white door, shuffling my feet across the cold wood floor to the kitchen. I trip over my own feet a couple times but make it without falling face first, and knock politely to announce myself before slowly pushing it open.

The kitchen is rather large with a grand dining table and half a dozen chairs around it to the right. To the left, about the center of the room, are cooking utensils and various pots and pans hung on a rack from the ceiling, above an island counter with a bowl of delicious looking apples on it. I hear rummaging from the far left, and I press onward.

"Hello? Agatha?" My voice comes out a little shaky.

"What do you want?" A harsh tone rings out from behind a pantry door that is open to my immediate left. "You should be resting on the couch."

"I was wondering if I could get something to eat. My stomach is gurgling like I have not eaten for days," I explain myself.

"Well it's no wonder. You've been out cold for about a week now. We couldn't wake you if the world were imploding," her tone rings like a schoolmaster scolding a child.

She moves to the island counter, picks up an apple and throws it at my face. Fearing the impact, my instincts kick in. With lighting reflexes I catch it, avoiding being pelted in the face with a rather firm red apple.

How did that happen?

"Thank you," I reply politely, and back out while she glares at me.

Returning to the living room I notice Ami, head bowed, carrying a basket full of laundry up the stairs to the right. When I smile at her she pays no attention to me. An inquisitive nature kicks in.

I follow her up the stairs on tip toe to see what she is doing, making sure to stay several steps behind her. Cautiously, I look behind me to check and make sure I am not being followed. I hear Ami open and close a door. About half way up the stairs one of the boards creak and I am sure that I am going to be caught. Waiting a few moments while looking both directions I expect one of them to come ask me what I am doing, but when no one shows up I climb the rest of the steps. I tread lightly in this new dark hallway, not knowing where she has gone, and I wonder if I should just turn around and eat my apple on the soft furniture below. But my curiosity piques, and I try to figure out which door to put my ear to.

There are two doors only a couple steps past the stairs; one on my left and one on my right, and it could be either one of them, or neither of them. Making a quick judgment I put my ear to the one on the right and listen for a moment. When I hear nothing from inside I grab the knob on the door and twist as gently as I can. Slowly pushing it open, I find a very musty and unused room. There is a heavy drape covering the window and a dusty bed under it, but there is not much else of interest to me in there.

The door creaks a little as I pull it shut and release the knob. To my left there is my other option. I grab the knob and slowly twist, but as I do I hear a noise from inside. My heart leaps into my throat and I am sure that I am caught now. But I am not confronted. The door is not pulled open from the inside and Agatha has not come up the stairs to scold me. The noise continues. It speeds up and slows down, beating softly over and over. I push slightly and the door open with ease. Though I hear a faint squeak from the hinges the rhythmic clacking noise covers it and I am still not noticed. With the door only open a crack I can see in.

The curtains on the windows are pulled back, and light pours into this room. Ami is there, sitting with cloth draped across her lap and she is pushing it up across a platform where multiple pieces attached to a base structure move rapidly. This strange contraption stabs the cloth over and over with a needle with thread attached to it. As it pumps up and down Ami directs the cloth.

What in the world is she doing and what is that thing?

Feeling a tickle in my throat come on I try desperately to hold back a cough, but it happens involuntarily and Ami looks up. I have given myself away as she looks back at the door and sees that it is cracked open. Before I can move back down the stairs, she is up and at the door pulling it open and the knob slips from my hand.

"What are you doing up here?!" she whispers frantically.

"I am...I am sorry." I have no rational response for why I came up here. I was curious, but I have apparently invaded an area of their home at least Ami wished not to share.

"She isn't my mother right now! You need to be in the living room or else we're both going to feel her wrath again."

"She is not your mother right now? What does that mean?"

"I told you that it's complicated. It's best just to stay on her good side." She grabs the door with both hands and looks at me with fear on her face.

"What is going on?"

"We can't talk about it! Back downstairs!" She points her finger swiftly toward the stairs.

Reluctantly, I turn and head to the stairs. Looking over my shoulder I see her standing in the doorway watching me leave. She apparently was not expecting me to look back because I catch her smiling a little. As she sees me look, her face becomes straight. She brushes a lock of her wavy hair out of her face and retreats into the room, closing the door behind her.

A very odd situation indeed.

I tiptoe down the stairs and find my way back over to the couch without being caught by Agatha. As I sit down, I eat my apple and relax. The apple is so juicy and delicious that I consume the entire thing including the core, and lie down again. I run my hand through my hair, and note a lack of contusions. It leads me to wonder about my loss of memory.

There must be a rational reason that I cannot remember anything, but I have nothing to go on.

Though I have not exerted much energy since I woke, my eyes are getting heavy again. Sitting up I try to keep awake, but the room is warm and I feel cozy. My eyes droop and there is nothing I can do to fight it, so I stop trying.

Finding myself in a dream state once again, I find fog within the woods and I am running. My body feels like it is on fire because of the piercing pain in my abdomen from the stab wound, and my hands are smeared with red. Blood spills out onto the ground and then the blackness envelops me.

~~~~~~

I wake on the floor on all fours by the couch, my entire body burning like a wildfire. When I stand up I try to take it slow, but no matter how slowly I move, the pain and heat are excruciating.

"Aaargh!"

Bathroom! I need cold water.

As I wander through the downstairs hallway I remember that I do not know which door on the left is the bathroom. The hallway reaches far and eventually fades to blackness. Checking the first door on the left, I push it open. I realize by the interior that it is not what I am looking for. Instead I have stumbled upon a girl's room. The drapes on the window are pulled back so that light enters, illuminating the light blue walls and ceiling. The color reminds me of Ami's eyes. There is a bed in the far left corner, a wooden mirror with a desk on the right wall, and beyond that is a door in the far right.

That door must be the one that leads to the bathroom.

"What do you think you're doing?" a semi-cheerful whisper in my left ear startles me.

I nearly jump straight into the room, and let out a sigh of relief when I see that it is Ami. She is standing there, smiling a little.

"Are you getting cabin fever? You seem to be finding your way to other places of the house. The two I've caught you peeking into happen to be my rooms." She titters a little.

"Maybe it is cabin fever, but I think I have a real one too and I needed some cold water. I was looking for the bathroom." I grimace at the heat.

"Hmm, just when we thought we'd broken your fever." She presses her hand on my forehead and it feels nice. It is soft and cool to the touch, and I am disappointed when she pulls it away. "But you are a bit warm."

"Your mother led me to it once, but I was not paying attention to which door it was." I become distracted with conversation.

"When was that?"

"I do not know. I have no sense of time right now. It could have been days, or more."

"Well, you have been here for a little over two weeks now."

"I have been here that long already?"

The amount of time is unreal to me, since I have only been conscious in limited amounts. It does not seem like it could be that long.

"Yeah. Your wound is healing nicely, but you will have a decent size scar. We'll see about removing the stitches soon."

"Really? It is amazing that I have survived this far on whatever healing abilities you have, and only having eaten some bread and an apple."

"Well, that's not exactly correct. We kind of had to force feed you a variety of nutrient enriched and slightly medicated broths and water while you were passed out. And because you've had a fever most of the time you would just sweat the liquids out or…well never mind." She quickly drops the subject and leaves me wondering about what was about to come next.

"Never mind what?"

"Let's get you into the bathroom and get some cool water on that head of yours."

She avoids my question and takes me by the arm, pulling me into the luxurious room and over to the far right side door. Opening it she flips a lever against the wall on the inside, illuminating everything in an instant. The next thing I know I am in the bathroom, having been pushed in by Ami, and the door is shut behind me.

"When you're done, I'll be waiting out here to take you back to the couch," she says from the other side of the door.

I turn on the water and feel its refreshing qualities as I splash it on my face and pour it over the top of my head, draining it back into the sink. Cupping my hands I begin to trickle the water down my forearms and I feel the heat subsiding. When I feel that I have sufficiently cooled enough I use the towel hanging by the mirror and dry myself.

Before leaving, I examine myself in the mirror again and look closely at the bandaged wound site. It is not as thick as before, now only seeming to be a few layers thick. Removing the bloodied bandages I stare in the mirror with eyes transfixed on where the wound is. As the final wrap falls off I peel the pad which has stuck to my crusted scab. It is as Ami said it was, healing. The wound is growing quite small and little pieces of the scab have begun breaking away from the main piece.

With no warning, my vision blurs and my mind flashes with images. Fully awake, I appear to have left my body and am elsewhere. I see myself standing in front of the house clutching my chest as blood spurts out, but from the outside and hovering above my body. My attention switches to a glimmer and when I focus it looks like it could be the long dagger a few feet behind the image of me. It is covered in fresh blood. Mine. As the image of my body collapses, I notice some rustling of a shady character in the trees not far off, someone walking or maybe running away.

I return to the real world, and I have unknowingly collapsed in the bathroom, groaning in pain. Ami has rushed into the room. I see her lips move but I hear ringing instead. When I look at my hand I find I had been clutching my wound so hard that the front had begun to bleed again. She helps me up and replaces the padding and bandage wraps around my chest before moving me into her room to sit on the edge of the bed.

"What happened?" I hear her concerned voice as the ringing dies down.

"I am not sure. I think I saw a piece of my past, of me standing in front of your house...but not in my body." I talk slowly and in fragments, wincing due to the sharp pain ravaging my torso as I breathe. "I saw the weapon that stabbed me. And somebody leaving in the distance, but I could not see who it was."

"Hmm. Well, try not to move any more right now. You might lose more blood." She runs into the bathroom, returning moments later with a few dark towels. Laying them down across the comforter she then eases me onto my back. "You can lay here on my bed and I'll go tell Mother."

I sink into the soft mattress trying not to yelp in pain as she rushes out. Lying there, it is only a few moments before Ami returns with Agatha.

"Oh dear. What happened?" Agatha asks, her sweet tone rings as she enters the room.

"He had a fever so I brought him to the bathroom. The next thing I know he's collapsed in there in pain," Ami replies.

"I think my body reacted negatively to seeing a fragment of what happened," I whisper.

"We will just leave you here until you feel well enough to move back to the living room," Agatha tells me.

"I will watch over him, Mother," Ami offers.

When I nod weakly Agatha turns and leaves the room. Ami sits down on the bed with her back against the headboard, her legs running parallel to my upper body.

"I hope you don't mind if I sit next to you," she says quietly, trying to break the tension.

"It is your bed after all." I try not to sound awkward.

We become silent and soon after that I feel sleep calling me.

~~~~~~

"Hey! Wake up! Wake up!" I hear her close to my face.

Upon opening my eyes I find Ami sitting on her knees next to me, gently shaking my shoulder, and I have been taken from what seemed to be peaceful sleep. As I open my eyes, I notice the lights are out, and it is dark outside. I feel the warmth of Ami's hand on my shoulder as she continues to gently shake me.

"Are you awake?"

"I am awake. What is wrong?" My voice is a bit raspy and rumbles a little out of its normal range.

"Who is Drake? Do you know?" she inquires. "You called out his name a few times in your sleep."

"Drake?"

Though I have no residual memory of dreaming I become bewildered as an image comes to mind. I picture a man, six feet tall or greater, with spiky dark red hair. His face is contorted and I cannot tell if he is angry or something else. Dressed in a knight's armor he wears a black breastplate, along with spiked silver gauntlets, and black grieves. His hazel eyes burn my soul as he stares intensely at me. With two scabbards on his leather belt, one longer and one shorter, I wonder if one of the blades within stabbed me.

"Hey! Are you listening to me?" Ami whispers.

"What? Sorry, I think I had another reoccurrence. I remember this man, Drake. I think he is the one that stabbed me." I try to figure out what is going on.

"Why do you think he might be the one who stabbed you?" Ami asks.

"He was eerie, even in my own thoughts. It felt like he was malicious. If he is the one that did this to me he may come back if he finds out I am still among the living."

"You don't have to worry. You're in our care now and Mother and I will hide you until you are well," she comforts me.

"I feel that once I am better I may have to face him again. If he comes looking for me here then I will not hide."

"Oh." Her voice sounds sad.

Though it is dark, my eyes have adjusted enough to see that she has bent her head downward more to my face. She seems to be examining me to see if I am all right but she jerks back to a sitting upright position after realizing she was getting kind of close. Returning to her previous position where her legs parallel my body, she stays quiet and the only thing left to hear is her breathing. Not knowing if she's still awake or not I speak a little above a whisper.

"I hope that my memory returns before he decides to show up, so I will know what I am up against."

Closing my eyes again the sleep world calls me.

~~~~~~

Awoken by daylight pouring in, my eyes flutter open. I attempt to get up. My body is stiff, but after a little struggling and several small steps I manage to make it to the bathroom without collapsing. Looking in the mirror, staring into my own eyes, I cannot seem to tear my gaze away. I am entranced, searching for any idea of who I am. It is several minutes before I finally break the stare with myself, coming up empty for that one question that I desperately want to know the answer to. When I exit the bathroom back into Ami's room, Agatha is waiting for me, but her demeanor is harsh.

"What're you doing out of bed? You want to get better or worse?" She becomes irate with me even before I can give an answer. "Lie down now!"

Ami enters and is immediately attacked by the angry Agatha.

"You slept in the same bed as him last night, didn't you? Just because we're helping him doesn't mean you can get friendly with him." And with that, Ami is slapped again.

This time I find I have enough strength to stand up to her. Swiftly walking over to Agatha while she readies to strike Ami again I grab her hand from behind and spin her around.

"What is wrong with you?" I yell out as she attempts to strike me with her other hand. Having learned my lesson from the last time, I catch it mid swing. Both of her hands are now locked in my fists I am free to continue. "You have been very kind to care for me, so I apologize for intervening, but I sense there is something seriously wrong here. It is like there are two of you; a gentle and harsh version of you."

Agatha's face literally changes right before my eyes. There are subtle shifts which indicates there is a definite difference in personality, but also in person. It is as if two souls inhabit one body. A surprised Ami lifts her head from the ashamed bow she had it in.

"Oh dear. This is no good," Agatha begins.

Feeling no more hostility from her I let go and she collapses to the ground with her palms to her face, and begins weeping heavily.

"Ami, what is wrong with your mother?" I ask, shaken.

"This...she...," Ami starts but becomes too choked up and darts out of the room, shutting the door hard behind her. I want to go after her, but decide I should get some answers from Agatha first.

"I am sorry for attacking you Agatha. You have been very kind to me, but I find it a little disturbing that you seem to have two very separate personalities with one that gets angry and violent easy."

I kneel down to her level. She continues to weep, but manages to begin talking.

"It's a very long story that we wanted to keep quiet so that you wouldn't become involved. Our situation is confusing and we had thought it would be best that you heal and be on your way."

"Well I am clearly involved now, so please tell me," I urge her.

"My sister had a special ability and when she died in this house it bound us all here. She inhabits this house as a spirit who can take possession of my body. We are at the center of a break in time," she slows her tears a bit.

"I do not understand."

"We are not from your time."

"Not of my time?" I inquire, puzzled.

"We are considered from your future. You probably hadn't noticed because of your memory loss and sleeping schedule but we have things modern to our time, which is about two thousand years after the time you come from." Her tears slow. "My sister's ability was traveling through time, and when she died in despair it shook the entire house, sending us spiraling uncontrollably throughout time. Every time we are transported it is a different day, different month, different year, but the same house in the same place."

"This is insane. How can such a power exist?" I am completely baffled.

"We were just as shocked as you at first. My sister had just died and we were in the same place, but everything around us had changed. We weren't even sure what had happened so we stayed put in the house."

Having noticed things seemed a little odd, even with my memory loss, I had found things that I just did not recognize or understand. Her explanation sheds a little light on my confusion.

The exterior of the house was first, then the luxurious bathrooms, the fancy kitchen, Ami's contraption, and the instantaneous lighting. All things that I failed to even have a remote hint of knowing. I suppose it makes sense or perhaps no sense at all.

My mind is spinning trying to take things in that I cannot seem to comprehend.

"How do you survive if you cannot stay put?" I ask.

"We were self-sufficient from society in our time. We collect energy from the sun to power the house and we have a plumbing system connected to a large metal container in the ground. We grow most of our own food and what we can't, we barter for with the locals of whatever time we're in."

"How does one gather energy from the sun?"

"It's a very complicated system, but it provides us electricity to power the house."

"What is uh-leck-tri-city?" My curiosity gets the upper hand of the conversation.

"That is also a complicated thing to explain. It's very similar to lightning, but people learned to harness such a power from many different places and put it to use. That lamp has a glass bulb that illuminates when electricity touches it."

She reaches over to a night stand and pulls a string attached to an item which I can only describe as a vase-like piece of artwork with some metal brackets and a cloth pyramid that has its top chopped off. Light instantly appears from it and I sit in amazement.

Overwhelmed, I wonder how I had even come across the house. Then it hits me ever so subtly. I was at the edge of the grassy field when I felt the searing pain shoot through my body. The house was not there, but there was some wind and my vision went blurry. Then when my eyes came back into focus I saw the house. When I tried to walk forward, I collapsed and that is when I heard Ami scream.

"I am remembering a little. I think I saw your house appear and I bet it scared off my attacker," I tell her.

"For you to have been wounded as we were appearing seems like fate. Perhaps this is some sort of destiny for us, so we could save you," she says looking up.

I sit quietly trying to take everything in, but I just cannot absorb it all. It all seems so unreal that I wonder if this is not some bizarre dream. I drift into my own thoughts, but before long Agatha has called me back.

"The times that I seem angry aren't me," she directs us back to the original conversation. "They're my sister, Evalyn and I'm sorry for the way she is. She is a very angry individual."

"Is there no way for you to leave the house, leave her here and let it go on its own?"

"No, as a consequence of her power Ami and I are bound here with her. We tried a few times to get away but if we are not inside the vortex when the house begins to leave we will be dragged back in by an unseen force. Like hands grabbing us, refusing to let us go."

"How long does your house stay in each time?"

"About a month, give or take a day. We're nearing the time that it'll leave your era," she tells me, her voice very meek.

I wonder if there is a way to break this curse. Perhaps burn the house? I suppose that is the first thing I would have done, but could I even propose such an idea? To coax these women to burn their house down in an attempt to break this curse would be unthinkable. With no guarantees there are two rational outcomes. It either does not work and they are stuck traveling through time with no house, or it frees them and then they would have nowhere to go and I would have nowhere to take them.

"There is no way out? What about me? Since I am here now, does that mean I am stuck as well?"

"I don't think so. In ten years, we've had people visit, but we always made sure they were gone before the time came to leave," she tells me confidently and then pauses for a moment. "I would like to ask a favor."

"I am listening."

"Will you help me find a way to stop this curse? Or at least break away from it?"

"Are you asking me to stay with the house and be bound by the curse?"

"I believe that's what fate has brought us together for," she says with conviction.

"Considering that I cannot even remember who I am, and am wounded, I do not know if I would be of help or just a burden upon you. But I will contemplate your request," I say. "For now, how about we start one step at a time and go tell Ami that you are you again."

"That would be fine. I will search for Ami upstairs and you can search the rooms downstairs."

"I would not want to intrude, so I will ask permission now. Are there any restricted doors I should not be opening? Places I should not go?"

"Please feel free to check all of the rooms."

Agatha stands up, and then helps me up slowly, trying not to jar my wound open again. We exit Ami's room and Agatha heads for the beginning of the hallway, disappearing around the wall to her left where the stairs are. I walk slowly, listening intently for any noise that might give away Ami's location. The floorboards above me creak as I hear Agatha walk across them. She opens a door, there is silence, and then she closes it and moves on. I follow suit and begin opening doors, starting with the one across from Ami's room, revealing just a closet with racks of folded sheets, towels, and hung coats.

Closing it, I move on. Further into the dark hallway, only lit by a small rectangular window at the end of it, I begin to hear quiet crying nearby. Listening closely, I venture forth and find the noise strengthening. I open a door to my left to find a poorly lit room, with many sheets over furniture, but the sound is not coming from there. Several steps farther I open a door to my right, and find another bathroom but it too is lacking Ami. Finally, I pinpoint that the crying is coming from a room on the right just the next door down. I move to it and knock softly before opening it. It creaks loudly, more than likely alerting Ami. The sound of sniffling gets louder.

"Ami?"

I walk into the room to find a bed fit for a king, large with a canopy and white drapes covering it. The room itself is pretty devoid of any color, but the bed's polished mahogany radiates and makes the walls seem to shine along with it. She is on the bed with her back against the headboard, knees curled up to her chest and head planted firmly into them. I move into the room and stand at the edge of the bed.

"Please, let me be," her voice comes out a little muffled.

"It is okay now. Your mother is back to normal," I attempt to comfort her.

"It's not okay! I'm stuck here against my will with my stupid Aunt Evalyn who can't control herself, even as a spirit!" She slows her crying a bit.

"Your mother told me what is going on and thinks that I was brought here by fate to try to find a way out of here for you both. All of this is very strange to me, but I told her I would at least think on it."

"There isn't enough time for you to find a way to break the curse. We have no power over it and we have no idea what would work, save for maybe burning the house."

"Funny you should mention that. I actually had that idea." I jest.

"That's not funny at all!" She raises her head quickly and gives me a stern look. I hold up my hands to indicate that I was kidding. "We're going to be leaving your era soon, and Mother has never let anyone come with us. Between her and Aunt Evalyn, I have been denied a life of my own."

"Who is to say I am not bound here already?"

"We've had guests in the past but none of them were pulled with us."

Ami looks up, and her tears have halted, leaving the stains of streams down her red cheeks. Rubbing the palm of her hand across the bottom of her eyes she attempts to dry her face.

"Why did you say you'd think about it?" Ami inquires.

"I am indebted to you and your mother for saving my life and caring for me. If there is a chance I can repay you I must explore that," my mouth runs away from me a bit, and I feel I have just committed to their cause.

I hold my hand out for her to take. She hesitates. After a few moments she crawls to the edge of the bed and stares up at me with her beautiful blue eyes, and they glimmer with a hint of hope in them. Taking my hand Ami pulls herself up, but after finding the footing to stand on her own she realizes our hands are still coupled and quickly lets go. I notice her face flush a little more, and she seems to play it off by wiping her face again. Mine flushes also, and I turn away. Extending my arm toward the door, I let her take the lead out of the room, and I close the door behind me. Walking down the hallway to the living room quietly, we reach the stairs at the same time Agatha emerges from them.

"Ami dear, are you okay?"

"I'm okay, Mother. I know it's not your doing."

"Maybe we can figure this out together," I suggest as I move to the couch.

Very carefully and slowly I maneuver my body to sit down, and think. Agatha smiles weakly at me, acknowledging that I have agreed to her request. When they both disappear through the swinging door, I hear noises, including another door opening and closing. While I rest my back against the couch I process all the confusing information and the request for help.

I am here, I have no memory, and I do not know if I have anything to go back to. Why should I not help them? Someone tried to kill me and if I leave they could try again, so perhaps I would be safer going wherever they go, and leave the assailant behind.

Trying to process the information of their mysterious technologies brings me to a blank mind for a few minutes. Moving on from that thought, I notice that my time being conscious is increasing in duration, and I no longer have a fever. A good sign.

Being unconscious for large chunks of time is unnerving. Anything could be happening, including the attacker returning for me. And having them care for me while I cannot do so is somewhat embarrassing.

I rest my hands on my chest and lose more time just watching the scenery out the window to the left. A noise in the kitchen catches my attention, and when I look to the white door I see Ami enter the room with a tray full of food items on it.

"I brought us something to snack on."

I take note of everything that is on the tray. Sliced apples, a plate of crackers, a bowl with some creamy brown spread, and a couple slices of bread. There is also a pitcher of juice that has the color and consistency of juice made from apples, and a couple of glasses.

"Mother has gone out to tend to the garden. We'll be having vegetable soup for dinner tonight, providing you're not out cold again." Ami gives a half smile and I can see that she is trying to lighten the mood, despite the very dramatic day so far.

"Is there anything I can do to help? You are doing so much for me when others would have let me die or given me minimal care to keep me alive."

"Well, if you help us figure out a way out, we can call it completely even, but in the meantime I could use some company later taking some clothes down from the lines if you're feeling well enough."

She lathers some of the brown spread onto a cracker and hands it to me.

"I think I could manage that." Even though the wound had cracked open the night before, I feel my strength returning to me. Turning my attention to the spread on the cracker I smell it. "What is this?"

"Peanut butter on a cracker."

"Peanut butter?"

"Peanuts crushed until they're a creamy texture, essentially. It's a very common and handy source of nutrition in our time and goes well with an assortment of different foods," she explains.

I lick the peanut butter from the cracker to see if I like it. Its taste is much like its raw peanut form but slightly sweeter. I eat a cracker while watching Ami devour several, as well as slices of apple slathered with it. The texture is sticky and the taste is delicious as it makes its way around my mouth, causing me to salivate heavily. Copying Ami, I sit up, serving myself several crackers with peanut butter on them and quickly find that its thick quality has overwhelmed my mouth. Nearly choking, I reach for the pitcher and glass, pouring hastily and guzzling it down. It clears my mouth enough for me to continue eating. My hands and mouth drive me. Before I realize what I have done, most of the food and half of the pitcher of juice are gone. Not having left Ami much, my face grows red from embarrassment.

"I am sorry! I guess I did not realize how hungry I was!"

Ami giggles. "It's understandable that you would eat like that. We are in the past and I'm not sure how manners go around here."

"Hey! For all I know I do not know any better!"

"I'm kidding, I'm kidding!" She continues to laugh, covering her mouth while she chews.

Not knowing how to respond, I look out the window yet again and change the subject. "Thank you."

"For what?"

"Being this hospitable to me. You could have let me die out there and I would have been none the wiser."

"We were just phasing into your time when you collapsed onto the grass. I was coming out to investigate where we had stopped when I saw you. Why would I not help someone that I had just seen fall?"

"What if I was a bad person?"

"I didn't think about that. I just saw that someone needed help," she says with a small smile.

"Hmm."

After sitting silently for a few minutes, I stand and walk over to the window to get a wider view, finding a large yard filled with nothing but grass, and a well that is made of stone covered by an angled wood roof. The framing has a turning handle with a spindle of rope attached for pulling a bucket up. Beyond the yard are the heavily dense woods I was assaulted in, and I see the direction that I came from, and that Drake ran into. Curious, I almost want to look at that area for clues.

There has been no sign of Drake, at least not that they have told me. Perhaps he did come and they already hid me from him.

When I open the door to the left there is a small, wooden porch and stairs leading down to the grass. Beyond the grass leads to the edge of the woods, several yards ahead. Stepping out onto the porch, the smells of nature waft over me. The air is cool and serene, feeling a bit like springtime but there is no sound of wildlife.

Do the animals know to stay away because of the power?

Stepping down onto the grass I can feel the blades sink beneath my bare feet and the ground is dry, indicating that the day it rained has long come and gone.

Compelled by the intrigue of what has happened to me, I walk forward to the place I had fallen. Quickly I look back at the house in a strange fear that it all might not be real. But the house is there, and Ami stands in the doorway watching. I feel safe to continue to the edge of the grass. Looking at where my body fell, there is only a smearing of dried mud, and nothing more.

I peer into the woods but cannot see anything distinctive, finding nothing but trees and plants out there. With no trail of any sort I contemplate what I was doing in the middle of the woods in the first place. It is almost as calm in the woods as it is in the field, barely a noise heard. But when I think about entering, everything in my body tells me the woods hold nothing but bad omens for me.

"What're you looking for?" Ami asks, having come up behind me.

"I am not sure. I was just curious because of all the blank space in my head."

After a few more moments of looking in silence, we return to the house walking side-by-side. When we reach the steps, I allow her to climb them first. Once back inside I shut the door behind me, move back to the couch, and sit gently down. I feel the skin of my chest and back stretch, and it is almost like it is going to tear again, but blood does not soak through the bandage and I seem to be okay. Ami sits next to me.

"I would ask you to tell me about yourself, but with your amnesia I don't think it would do any good," she jokes.

"No, you know as much about me as I do. I am not even sure how I lost my memories."

"It's probably trauma amnesia. You know, where something so traumatic happens that your brain shuts everything down."

"I cannot say I have ever heard of that."

"Of course not. You have amnesia."

"I can remember *some* things, but only things that have nothing to do with my memories. It could have been something learned and retained."

After a few moments of silence Ami speaks up again. "So you are thinking about helping us?"

"Considering I owe you two my life and I have nowhere to go, it seems only fair that I assist you in breaking free of this cursed place."

"That would mean that you will be stuck with us until we do."

"I cannot think of any place better for me to be right now. Besides, other than the whole 'aunt possessing your mother' thing, this place is nice. Comfy."

"We have my father to thank for that. He built this house."

"Where is he?"

"Back in our original time. He was gone when Aunt Evalyn died."

"Have you never been back to your original time?"

"Not that I know." She shifts in her seat a little.

"I am sorry to hear that." I try to give a sympathetic smile.

"It's okay. We came to accept it long ago."

Again we sit in silence on the couch. Though I am unsure what to expect if I stay with them, it seems to be my best option for survival.

If I were to leave I would have nowhere to go, I would have no currency and it is likely that I would be hunted down again if I were recognized by anyone. Beyond that, I suppose adventure awaits me if I stay. I may not remember who I am but I do know that life in this time is dreary. Perhaps some excitement will jar memories loose in my head, but then will it really matter?

Ami gets up and heads for the door to the kitchen. Turning around she waves for me to follow. I push on the arm of the couch and ease myself up. My body, having relaxed a little, is stiff and uncooperative at the moment, but I hobble forward and follow. Once Ami is inside, she holds the door open so that it does not spring back and hit me. Through the doorway, she heads for another door at the back left of the kitchen that leads outside.

Making my way there is time consuming, but I am cautious not to open my wound again and use that time to look around a little more. Beyond the island counter lies another, longer counter with a sink that has two separate sections, and a rack with dried dishes in it to the right. To the left of the counter with the sink is a shiny metal box with four distinct spirals on top that appears to be a stove, but there is no chimney leading up from it. Past it, Ami opens another door to the outside.

Stepping out onto another small set of wooden stairs, I see Agatha tending a large garden on the left side of the yard, which has a wide variety of plants in it. One by one I take steps down the stairs until I am on green grass for a second time, and I note that this half of the yard seems cluttered compared to the other.

To the right are four large clotheslines set up in rows with washed clothes hanging to dry, and next to them are wash basins and an empty basket made from a strange material that is neither wood nor metal. Toward the far side of the grass boundary is an apple tree and it makes sense that they had an ample supply in the bowl.

Ami steps past me toward the clotheslines and I follow behind her. She picks up the empty white basket and holds it out for me. I take it, noting its lightness while holding it at my waistline. I follow her while she runs her hands over the clothes inside and out. It seems like it is every other one she pulls down, and places in the basket.

"Why are you leaving those? Are they still wet?"

"Yeah, they need some more time to dry."

Watching her work I cannot help but admire her beauty as her brown hair seems lightened by the sun, and her thin blue dress flows in a light breeze. Even while doing a mundane chore she moves with grace, and I find myself staring rather than just looking. As she looks over at me I look away to avoid feeling awkward. She brings a few more articles of clothing and puts them in the basket.

Looking at the next row through the clothing, I can see all manner of women's undergarments and I blush. Ami sees what I see, becoming excitable.

"Close your eyes! Don't look!" She puts her hand up to my eyes.

I do as she commands and close my eyes, blinding myself to my surroundings. I feel Ami tug on the basket. Trusting her, I allow her to lead me, presumably to the next row, and stand there awkwardly with my eyes shut. She rushes, moving faster than on the first row and the urge to peek is overwhelming.

I squint, just barely opening my eyes; in the basket are colorful pairs of panties and my mind tells me that they are Ami's. She pulls down a strange looking piece of clothing, two cloth cups held together by a tangle of straps which appears to fit a woman's chest. She tests it for dampness and decides it is dry enough. Grabbing and testing another she finds it acceptable as well and brings them over. I close my eyes completely so that she does not know I was squinting.

"Your eyes are still closed, right?"

"Yes." I do not lie as my eyes are in fact closed at the moment.

"Okay."

Agatha laughs a little behind me, and Ami grabs the basket's end and leads me to another stopping point. Feeling her put more clothes in, I crack my eyes open just a little again, and look. Normal clothes are now covering most of the undergarments, but Ami has not given me permission to open my eyes yet. She returns and places more in the basket.

"You can open your eyes now," she says, a smile in her voice.

When I do, the bright light of the overhead sun temporarily blinds me, forcing me to blink several times to adjust my eyes.

"So, what is your time like?" I ask.

"Urban for the most part, though these woods still half exist." She points out toward the woods past the apple tree. "Out that way is where the city is in our time and the direction you came from is all still uninhabited. My father built this house next to the woods to separate us from the urban environment."

"What do the cities look like?"

"Crowded with buildings packed close together and people like fish in cans," she says while returning to retrieving clothes from the lines.

"Do you miss that kind of setting?"

"I was young at the time when this all started, but I guess so."

She waves her hand at me and I follow her to the last clothesline.

Taking the clothes down which she finds dry, she returns to me, drops them in, and then takes the basket from me. Placing it at her hip she holds it with one hand.

"Thanks, that was starting to strain me a bit," I tell her.

"No worries. We can't have you doing heavy work yet."

"Yet?"

"Of course! You don't think we're going to just let you laze about once you're healed do you?" She smirks and shifts her hips to hold the basket better.

"I suppose that is fair." I smile back.

"Good. Because you didn't have much choice." She winks and moves past me, heading for the house, and I stare as she passes me. Looking back at me expectantly she catches me staring and stops walking. "You coming?"

"Yes." I follow and, as I pass Agatha again, she looks up at me and chuckles.

Entering the house there is a temperature drop, and my body sends a shiver down my spine, causing my shoulders to shudder. Following her back through the kitchen and into the main room of the house, she begins to head down the hall. Not knowing what she wants me to do I continue on behind her and when we reach her room she opens her door and turns back to me.

"You go ahead and rest in the living room. I have to fold and hang this laundry."

"You do not want my help?"

"For the same reason I made you close your eyes outside, there are just some things you shouldn't see! Now, go rest." She smiles at me and waves her free hand.

"Okay."

Turning around I make my way back. When I look over my shoulder I see Ami still standing there, watching me leave as if making sure that I am not going to stand outside her door and peek.

When I reach the couch, I turn around to sit, and see her enter her room, shutting the door behind her. Sitting for a few minutes causes me to grow restless. Seeing the bookshelves to the left of the hallway wall, my mind grows curious about what I could learn from the books they have. They are both filled from top to bottom on all six of their shelves, and from left to right the books increase in size, with a few stray books lying down on top of others.

Because they are from the future, I could probably learn a great deal about the future cultures. Perhaps even find out why they talk differently.

Standing back up, I walk over to the bookshelf and browse the titles written on each side. The first shelf appears to be filled with books of learning. 'Grammar', 'Literature', 'Linguistics', 'Mathematics', 'Carpentry', 'Economics', 'Sewing' and many others that seem like things one might learn in a schoolhouse.

The second shelf features other books with what appears to be story-based titles. Picking one up named 'Cold Nights,' I flip through it and randomly stop on page fifty-three. When I begin to read, I am embarrassed as the page describes a love scene between two characters in vivid detail. Placing it back quickly, I look around to make sure that I have not been caught snooping. I move back to the first shelf and grab the linguistics book to try and cover myself, even though I am alone.

Flipping the pages I am able to read most of the words in the book, but the content makes little sense to me. It discusses different languages and the study of them, but beyond that, it is difficult to comprehend. Shaking my head in confusion I place the book back and notice that there is no book labeled for history.

Hearing Agatha come into the kitchen, I head toward the white door and push it open slowly to peek. Agatha is at the sink and is washing some produce, taken from a wicker basket to her side. Once washed, she places it on the fireless stove. My stomach grumbles loudly, and I cannot help but think it has given me away so I push through the door to reveal myself to Agatha. She looks back and smiles.

"Is there anything you need help with, Agatha?"

"I could use some help cutting up vegetables for soup."

"I am not sure if I will be any good," I reply.

"It all goes to the same place anyway. Food doesn't have to be perfect."

I move over to the island counter in the kitchen while Agatha turns around and pulls out a wooden board and a large knife. She sets some washed potatoes on it, and motions for me to come around the other side. Doing as instructed, I pick up the knife.

"Cut it into cubes as best as you can, maybe an inch big or so." Agatha demonstrates with her fingers for me how big she wants them.

Cutting into the first one, I begin slicing it up starting from one end to the other and then laying the slices down side by side. I cut them into cubes as she asked which proves to be a time consuming task. Though she said it does not have to be perfect, I find myself being very cautious while cutting the first potato, and am slow about it.

"Would you like to see an easier method?" she asks.

I give her the knife and watch intently as she slices the next potato down the middle lengthwise, and sets each half down on the white board. She proceeds to cut each half down their middles and then lines them back up on top of each other. Making cuts all the way down she creates long slices and then cuts the slices into cubes. Looking back at me she smiles and holds out the knife.

"That does seem more efficient."

She relinquishes the knife again, with a smile, and I copy her technique. While I am busy she grabs a large pot from above me and moves away. Looking behind me she sets the pot on one of the dark spirals on the strange stove. While continuing to cut, I think to myself.

If I am to stay here there are many things I will need to learn. I am not even sure what I did for a living, let alone what skills I am proficient at.

"Agatha, if I am to stay, I will need training in everything," I voice my thoughts while continuing my task.

"What do you mean?"

"Well, since I am not of your time I will need to be brought up to speed on the world outside my time. And I will probably need to learn to speak like you if I am going to fit in."

"I am sure Ami would be more than happy to teach you."

"Why do you not have a book of history on your shelves?" I blurt.

"We prefer to not know if our interactions affect history. We did have a book once, but as we went the book changed just out of minor interactions so we figured it would be better not knowing if we adversely affected the timeline."

"An interesting idea," I move to the side to show her the potatoes. "I have finished."

"You have been up quite a bit. You should go rest a little bit while dinner cooks," Agatha suggests while taking the cutting board and pushing the cubes into the pot.

"Okay." Turning around I head to the swinging door into the living room.

When I get back to the couch I sit down a little too hard, and wince from jarring my wound, but I do not feel that it has opened. Closing my eyes I resolve to rest until the soup is ready. Sleep comes upon me quickly.

~~~~~~

I awake on my own. After sitting for a few moments on the couch, I head down the dark hall to the bathroom to relieve myself. When finished, I wash in the sink and stare in the mirror again, trying to find any sense of recognition behind the green eyes that stare back at me, but none comes.

Back to the main room of the home, Ami is waiting for me with two steaming bowls sitting on the short table. I sit down on the soft brown cushion and notice it has become dark outside. Looking at Ami she looks expectantly back.

Reaching down, the bowl has been warmed by the soup. Drawing it near, I inhale. It smells delicious. While I wait for it to cool, I make conversation.

"Your mother said that you might be willing to help me adapt, maybe teach me about the future and help me fit in," I tell her.

"We don't even fit in where we go." She snickers.

"I mean sounding more like you. Our speech patterns are different, but it is like you both slur your words together like a drunk man after too many cups of ale." I smile.

"Oh, I guess I don't really think about it, but you're right. I had a few years of school before we were taken but Mother picked up where it got left off, teaching me while we traveled through time."

"So then you will help?" I ask.

"Sure, I think we can get you up to speed," she says while taking a bite.

The soup has cooled enough to eat without scorching my mouth. I take one spoonful at a time and recognize the tastes of potato, carrots, celery and pepper. I chew, despite the vegetables being soft enough to squish with my tongue, and the flavor seems to be heightened by something as vegetables do not normally taste this good.

"What is in this besides vegetables?" I ask.

"A variety of spices that we've picked up over the years," she says while continuing to eat hers, leaning back against the couch.

The rest of the time eating is spent in silence as I fill my stomach, and when the solid pieces are gone I gulp down the broth thirstily. I let out an exclamation of satisfaction through a deep sigh, and wipe my mouth with my thumb and index finger.

"I am not sure why you helped me, other than being good people, but I will likely say this several more times. Thank you," I tell her.

"Lesson one; you can replace 'thank you' with 'thanks'," she says while putting her bowl down with a lighthearted look on her face. "Saying 'thank you' is formal."

"Thanks," I reply.

"So you've made the decision to stay?"

"I have." I nod while resting against the arm of the couch.

"Good, then I'm going to get busy and make you some clothes. It shouldn't take me but a couple days." She reaches for my bowl while taking hers.

Standing up, she heads to the kitchen with them, returning just a moment after to head up the stairs. Looking back at me I can see her demeanor has already changed for the better. I find myself happy because of it. She waves for me to follow.

"Are you coming? I can't make you clothes if I don't take some measurements."

Pushing up, I shuffle my feet until I am at the stairs, and she leads us to the top, to that door on the left that I had seen her in before. When she pushes the door open the whole room is revealed to me. Stray cloth is strewn about everywhere and patterns drawn onto a stack of papers sit disheveled on a desk to the left. In the middle of the room sits the contraption that I had seen her sitting at before, and when she moves off to the side to rummage, I move in. To my right I catch sight of many varieties of cloth in bolts hanging on metal frames. Beyond the bolts there lies a large closet with no doors, filled to the brim with endless clothes hung up.

"Ah, here it is," she exclaims under her breath and catches my attention.

She comes to me with a thick, flimsy white piece of banding with measurements printed on it. Beginning to move around me she places it against my bare torso in several locations, and in different directions. Turning, she scribbles several numbers with a writing utensil on an already drawn on paper. When she lifts both of my arms, she takes measurements from them. As I stand awkwardly with my arms out she scribbles and then gets down on her knees with the writing utensil in her mouth. As she uses the measuring device against the fabric of my flimsy pants, I feel her gentle touch and I become uneasy.

"Spread your legs," she instructs, patting the inside of my knees.

I blush hard and hesitate, causing her to look up.

"It's okay, I'm not going to do anything weird to you," she mumbles through the item in her mouth.

Doing as requested allows her to take more measurements of the inside of my legs. Just as quickly as she started she has finished, standing and writing down the final numbers, and I feel the muscles in my shoulders relax.

"Okay. Good. Now out, so I can work," she says with cheer and pointing her finger toward the door.

I take my leave from her room while shutting the door softly behind me. Moving carefully back down the stairs, I use the railing to support my weight.

I head into the kitchen. Agatha sits alone at the table eating her own bowl of soup. When I sit to join her she smiles brightly.

"It seems you have given Ami a new drive in her sewing endeavors," she says while sipping a spoonful.

"It will be nice to wear something other than bandages and these pants."

I look down and examine the bandage, running my fingers over its bumpy texture.

"I want to warn you now," Agatha says seriously, and my heart skips a beat. "Once you travel through time with us you *will be* stuck like us, so if you are having second thoughts you may want to leave soon."

"Oh no, I am not thinking that." I look her in the eyes.

"Okay, because we will be coming upon our time limit here and I don't want Ami to get her hopes up any more than she has that we will have permanent company."

"No ma'am, I will journey with you. I do not know if I will be of any help to you, but I will try," I assure her.

She nods and I stand to leave. Pushing through the swinging door, I return to the couch. Though my memory has fled to leave me feeling empty and insecure, I am able to find some comfort within this house and with these strangers who are willing to care for a dying man.

Their integrity is solid. I wonder if I would have done the same in their position. I do not know who I am, or what I did before here. It is possible that I could have been any sort of person but very little has surfaced to tell me about myself. Will it always be this way?

Then again, with no past to remember, I suppose I am left to decide who I want to be. I feel no bitterness or resentment to the situation, and I guess that would mean I am not bound to those kinds of tainting feelings. My actions from standing up to Evalyn might be indicators of my previous personality, a strong protector. But there is no real way to find out except for venturing into the forest to find what is there.

I do not think that it would be wise for me, though, to walk out there. Drake might be lurking to finish what he started. No, I seem to be safe here.

Again, I feel fatigue setting in, though my efforts have been minimal since I last slept. Knowing my body is still healing from its wound, I do not fight against rest. Instead, I get comfortable as I lie down on the couch lengthwise and turn inward toward the padded back. The cushioning is soft and sinking in a bit I am forced to reposition my legs and arms so that I am not consumed into the cracks between the back and the seat. Finally, with my arm positioned under my head and one leg bent at an angle I find myself comfortable and drifting to the sleep world.

~~~~~~

Feeling a little warm, I toss and turn, and it becomes hard to breathe.

Fumbling with my eyes closed, I have been covered up by something and I panic, jumping up and huffing heavily, but feel foolish as a blanket was draped across me while I slept. My wound pains me, and I feel that I may have caused some damage to it in my fright.

Seeing it is dark outside I tiptoe down the hallway, so as not to wake anyone that might be sleeping, to the bathroom. Pushing in, I close the door finding it completely dark but for a small patch of light beaming in from what I guess is the moon overhead. Flipping the little lever I had seen before illuminates the room, and I look in the mirror hastily to see if I have bled through. To my relief I do not see anything out of the ordinary. Unclipping the bandage, I spin it off of me and gently remove the padding that had been covering the scab.

It looks almost the same, and I do not know how much longer before it will be completely healed. Because I cannot remember if anything like this happened before, I look for more scar tissue to compare my current wound against. I cannot find anything significant.

My eyes become transfixed on the scab, and it itches. Scratching a bit, some of it flakes off and it becomes addicting, finding those areas that come off without causing myself to bleed. But I pick too much, finally tugging on an area that is still attached, and it begins to bleed. I pick up the pad and press it back to my stomach but when I look up a shadowy figure behind me has appeared. I can see its white teeth through an evil grin and when I look down a dagger sticking through the wound as it throbs.

Beginning to hyperventilate, the blood pours from the wound all over the floor and I cry out as the dagger is retracted. The shadowy form disappears from the mirror, and Ami bursts in from her room with an alarmed look on her face.

"What's wrong?!" she asks.

"He was here! I am wounded again!" I hold my hand over the wound.

"Where? Let me see." She moves to me and removes my hand.

To my surprise I am not actually bleeding. No blood has been spilt on the floor and the wound is still closed except where I had picked a little too much. She looks up at me and when I look over my shoulder for the shadow, I find no one.

"I...I swear they were here. I saw the dagger through my torso again!" I protest her look of confusion.

"Shh, it's okay. There's no one here," she says with a relieved sigh looking over my shoulder. "Let's put the bandage back on."

"But..." I am at a loss for words at what I had just seen.

"You were probably having a waking nightmare or some sort of hallucination," she says soothingly while wrapping my torso back up.

"I am sorry," I apologize while trying to shake it off, that feeling of dread. "I do not know what came over me."

"It's okay. You're still adjusting to the house and it can be a little spooky at night, but there's no one here that is going to hurt you. I promise," she reassures me.

Finishing with the bandage she clips it back in place and I move to the door, pulling it open while looking out into the dark nervously. She walks up next to me without hesitation, and leads me by the hand back to the couch. When we get there I sit and she tries to return to her room, but I make my nervousness known.

"Please, would you stay out here with me?" I ask.

I can see that she is tired when she turns back to me, but she does not hesitate to oblige to quell my fear. Returning to the couch she sits next to me and lies down with her head resting at the opposite side of the couch.

"Thanks, Ami," I tell her.

"Mmhmm," she mumbles as she drifts back to sleep.

Lying down on my side of the couch I leave my feet dangling over the edge, and while slightly uncomfortable, it is less awkward than stretching out and pressing our two bodies together. Despite my heart having been beating heavily only a few minutes before, her presence comforts me enough to find a restful state and I am able to sleep again.

~~~~~~

Sitting on the floor with the table in front of me, I comb through the book that Ami had picked off of the shelf while she retrieves us some breakfast. The book titled 'Language Arts' seems to have many lessons written out within it and I find that my reading skills are proficient enough to understand a significant portion of it. Near the back of the book I find a glossary of words called contractions that I find helpful in understanding Ami and Agatha's dialect.

Ami appears from the kitchen with a couple bowls steaming, and she has a disapproving look on her face. Setting my bowl in front of me I can see inside is some sort of porridge that has been doused in a liquid and topped with a brown crystalized powder that appears to be melting.

"I told you to wait for me." She sits down on the floor next to me and jabs her index finger into my shoulder.

"I am sorry. With so many voids in my head I just thought that I might get a head start." I frown.

She smiles to indicate that it is okay and begins to eat her bowl of soggy oats. Nudging her nose in the direction of my bowl she wants me to take a bite of the food, and when I do I find that the brown crystals make it sweet. I take a few bites at one time, and when I manage to swallow it all I cannot help but be excited with this food.

"What is the brown sugary stuff?" I ask.

"Brown sugar," she snickers while looking up at me from her bowl.

"Well then, I feel silly for asking." I chuckle.

"Don't worry about it. We're going to encounter many things you're unfamiliar with. I just thought it was a little funny that without knowing what it was called you called it by its name."

We finish our breakfast, and after she takes the dishes into the kitchen she returns to begin my lesson in how the language has developed from mine to theirs.

Hours pass as she runs through many nuances, and my mind wears thin even after several breaks. Resting my head back on the couch, I close my eyes to relieve some of the fatigue they are feeling. Ami makes sure to keep me awake with a few taps on the shoulder. Looking over, I smile at her. Her bangs fall across the side of her face, and I am staring again. She notices and looks away, her cheeks turning red a little bit. I find it pleasing that she has become flustered.

"Stop looking at me," she says while putting her hand up to the side of her face.

"I am sorry, I did not intend to embarrass you." I grin.

"'Didn't'," she corrects me on my use of 'did not' and peeks from behind her fingers. "You're not embarrassing me, you're being creepy."

"I am not creepy." I push her shoulder playfully, knocking her off balance.

She recovers by putting her hand out to catch herself and comes back at me by pushing with both her hands to shove me over. I counter and grab them, pulling her with me. She lands on my wound.

"Ahh!" I cry out in pain.

"That's what you get." She fakes apathy while turning her nose upward playfully.

"See, I am not creepy. It is not unnatural to look at someone that you intend on living with, is it?"

"You make that sound even creepier." She sticks her tongue out at me while pulling herself back up on the table.

"You are impossible," I tell her.

"'You're'," she corrects me again.

"You're impossible," I copy her and pull myself back up.

Until it is time to have dinner we practice over and over the newly covered information, but I feel that it will take me a lot more time than just today to master the language to the degree that they were likely taught from the time that they were children. Agatha appears in the doorway to the kitchen and motions for us to enter.

With my stomach growling at the savory smells emanating from the kitchen, I am the first to stand up, offering my hand for Ami to take. As she does, I find that it is easier to pull her up than anticipated, practically causing her to leap to her feet. She looks at me with a questioning look but a smile on her face. We release hands and she leads us into the kitchen to sit at the large table.

"You can sit wherever you'd like," Ami tells me.

Picking the chair at the end of the table, I pull it out. Before I can sit, Agatha snickers. Ami shoots her a playful glance, and I wonder what I have done to warrant that response. Questioning them with quirked eyebrows, I look at both Ami and Agatha to try and get an answer. When that fails I resort to asking out loud.

"Did I do something funny?"

"No, dear," Agatha replies. "That's just where my husband used to sit.

No one has sat there in the ten years we've been adrift in time."

"I did not know. I will choose another seat," I tell her.

"No, no. It's okay. It's just a little new having a man in the house again, and I thought it amusing that you would choose that spot," she says while moving about the stove as a searing noise crackles from a pan.

"Sit," Ami urges me while disappearing from my vision briefly, and returns with three glasses.

Sitting down, I feel like I am being waited on. It is both strange and familiar at the same time. While I wonder what it means, Agatha brings me over a plate, and the food on it makes my mouth water. On it lays a small, round steak, a biscuit, and what appears to be small cabbage.

"Thanks, Agatha." I look up as she brings me a knife and fork.

"You're welcome. How was your lesson today?" she asks.

"There is a lot to learn, but I am confident that Ami will be able to get it to stick."

I wait for them to sit before I start eating. Agatha brings over two more plates and more silverware while Ami pours each of us a glass of apple juice. When they have settled, Agatha is sitting to my left and Ami to my right at the table. Feeling like something should be said, I pick up my glass and raise it.

"Here is to new journeys and new friends." I feel a little cheesy saying it but I am sincere in my statement.

"Agreed." Agatha follows my lead and raises her glass.

"New journeys, indeed!" Ami raises her glass too.

Though they went along with my toast I still feel self-conscious about it and I turn my head downward to the meal. Devouring the delicious meal one flavorful bite at a time, I enjoy the silent company of my hosts while we exchange glances. I find, however, that I need to comment on the food to express my appreciation.

"You are a wonderful cook, Agatha. You certainly have a way of bringing the flavor out," I pay her a compliment.

"Thank you. I've had a lot of time to practice," she replies after clearing her mouth of a bite. "I try to pass some of that on to Ami but she's more creative with cloth."

"I'm not a terrible cook, Mother!" Ami proclaims.

"I didn't say you were, dear," Agatha giggles a bit. "Just that you're better as a seamstress."

"That reminds me. I'll have your clothes ready fairly soon." She looks at me while taking a bite of the biscuit.

"I will be glad for that. I have been a little chilly." I sit back and slouch a little in the chair, having finished my meal.

"You should have said something. I have a sweater you can use," Agatha mentions.

"Oh, it was nothing terrible. I am content in waiting."

"Okay, just let me know if you decide otherwise."

I nod and stand to take my plate to the sink however I am intercepted by Ami, who has also just finished, and she steals the plate from my hand. Somewhat dismayed that she has taken the plate from me I frown and stand there with my hand midair.

"I could have handled that," I protest.

"Oh, in due time I'll have you washing them," she winks at me.

Agatha laughs, and I cannot help but laugh too. Ami smirks at her own wit and I am left just with my glass on the table, still half full. I drink the contents down in one long gulp. When Ami comes for it I hold it up out of her reach. She tries anyway but is unable to take it from me. We spin around a bit near the table and she nearly topples me over onto the chair to get at it. But I keep it from her and she finally gives up by placing her hands on her waist. I grin and take it to the counter where the dirty dishes from the meal have been stacked, placing it defiantly on top of the plates.

"All right, then, now that you've exerted your energy for the day how about you go rest on the couch and read that book some more," Ami jests.

"Perhaps I will," I reply while moving to the swinging door.

Taking a seat on the cushion, I grab the book and begin reading over the same information that Ami covered earlier. Though as I settle, I find that my energy actually had been sapped. Ami heads through the door and up the stairs with a brief glance back at me before she is out of sight.

Finding my eyes getting heavy only a few sentences into the reading material, I close my eyes, resolving only to rest them a little. I quickly find I cannot open them back up. Instead of fighting it, I let unconsciousness take me.

A few days slip by with hardly a second thought about it, and I find that though I cannot remember anything about my former life, I experience no qualms leaving whatever life I had behind.

Examining myself in the bathroom mirror, I look at the neatly designed clothing that Ami has given me. Out of the couple sets of clothing she had fabricated so far, I decide upon some casual cotton garments. I fuss with the buttons on the light beige, collared shirt and then the ones to close the fly of the slightly darker pants. I find that they are comfortable enough, but that the color is not to my liking. On the right shoulder I notice an orange flower embroidered in and I wonder about it.

Ami knocks on the door, impatient to see how I look in the clothing I have chosen. When I open it she immediately begins testing different points in both the shirt and the pants to see how well they fit, humming as she does so. Standing back up from playing with the cuffs at the end of the pant legs she smiles at me.

"These look pretty good on you, I think," she says. "How do you like them?"

"They are nice, but I do not... *don't* think that this is my color," I correct myself to use a contraction.

"No, but that's okay because we're going to have plenty of time to figure out what your color is." She smiles and then heads out to the living room.

Following behind her, I head to the window to peer out into the calm woods. Though there are clouds hiding the sun, there is still enough light to see a fair distance into the thicket; not a living creature can be seen. Something calls me, however, an urge to step out into them and look about. Looking back, Ami is thumbing through the language book, no doubt planning the next lesson and I find that I need a little fresh air.

When I pull the door open, Ami's attention is caught. She closes the book and sets it on the table, accompanying me out onto the porch. Stepping down into the grass I slowly make my way toward the edge of the property, feeling the cool grass tickle the underside of my feet.

"Where are you going?" Ami asks from the steps.

"I just want to take a look at something," I look over my shoulder and tell her.

Standing near the definitive border where lush green grass meets the brown forest ground, I look at that area where I had fallen, and it is unrecognizable now, matted with a few sporadic leaves. As I am about to take a step out from the perimeter of the house, a quake shakes from underneath us and I am startled by a bizarre phenomenon in the air. As if painted blue with a paintbrush, the air around the house begins to kick up and swirl around.

Ami yells out for me, but I cannot hear what she is saying. Concentrating on keeping my footing steady proves useless as the quake launches me into the vibrant blue vortex that has surrounded us. As I connect with the vortex I feel a shock through my entire body, and I am thrown through the air, landing hard onto my back. I am forced to exhale all of the air from my lungs and my vision goes completely white for a moment. My body cringes in pain, both because of the impact and jarring my freshly-healed wound.

When my vision and breath return I cough and sputter, finding Ami kneeling by my side. She speaks, but my ears ring and I cannot hear what she is saying. I lie there dazed, but out of the corner of my eye, I watch the surrounding area change through the visible, blue swirling air currents, morphing our surroundings to something new and unseen by my eyes before.

"Ami, is this a shift through time?" I find myself able to speak.

"Yes, it is. Welcome to our world."

Monstrosities have surrounded us; unnatural and eerie, gigantic and blinding structures that tower far into the sky. I feel a little light-headed as it sinks in that I am now in this for good. I realize I have begun hyperventilating and I cannot slow my breathing down. My eyes dart around as the noise of this enormous city begins to overwhelm me, my mind trying to take in everything.

"Shh, calm down." Ami places her hand on my chest.

"I am...trying..." I huff.

While I had not doubted their story of spontaneous travel through time the strange reality of it actually hitting me, showing that it was true, seems a bit much to take in all at once. I have left a place that I cannot remember to a place I am completely sure I have never been to before.

"That was the grip that pulls you back if you're outside when the time shift happens. I tried to warn you, but I saw the quake knock your footing loose." She stares off at the changed surroundings.

"What are all of those towers?" I point at the structures beyond the more open field where the trees have thinned to near non-existence and people wander through the grass around the house openly.

"Buildings," her voice is slowed and she looks around also somewhat in shock. "We appear to have been thrown into the future."

~~~~~~

2 DEDICATION

The woods have disappeared, and the sky is now cluttered with these tall buildings. The majority of them have a multitude of windows on each face and they reach high into the sky. In between each building I can see something bridging them together, however I cannot make out what it is or what it is for.

My mind reels. There are strange noises coming from all around the house. As I bring my gaze down from the buildings to the ground slowly, noting the additional changes, the first being that the trees have thinned out so significantly that there are no woods anymore. It is replaced by a giant clearing in the center of these massive towers. The second is that a number of people have appeared outside of the invisible perimeter that is the barrier to the house. Some stand in amazement and begin talking excitedly while others scatter. The only thing I can think is that they saw what I had seen when I was about to die, and we have just appeared out of nowhere to them.

"We should go inside," Ami whispers and helps me to my feet.

The pain has mostly worn off, so I stand and stumble to the front door with Ami's help. We enter the house to find Agatha standing in the living room looking out the front window.

"Are you okay?" Agatha asks.

"He got a little jolt as he touched the wall," Ami answers for me.

"I will be fine," I tell her.

"I would like it if you two stayed inside until I can shoo the people who have gathered around, and find out a little about this time." Agatha smiles at us.

"I think we can manage that," I state.

"Good."

She retrieves a light jacket, as well as a closed small hand basket from a coat rack on the wall. She leaves through the door we just came through.

Ami lets me go, and I stand on my own now that the pain is only a dull ache. She slumps down on the couch with a loud sigh.

"Finally, she's gone. I only get a few of these days every once in a while to just relax and lounge about. She'll be gone for hours establishing contacts and people to trade with."

"What do you normally do in that time?"

"Normally? I read. We try to pick up a few books from each era. But when I don't have any new books I just sew."

"What should I do then?"

"You know how to wash dishes?" She grins from her slouched position on the couch.

"Surely you jest."

"You can clean the dishes from breakfast."

My heart sinks as I see that she is serious, and though I understand the concept, I am not sure I know how to do it effectively. Seeing her face twist and contort I surmise she is attempting to hold back a laugh watching my face twitch. Holding my arm out toward the kitchen, Ami jumps up and leads me in to the sink. She sets me up by filling one half of the sink with warm, bubbly water.

"Soak, scrub, rinse and then place it into the dish holder." She demonstrates with one dish. "It's easy."

I fold my sleeves several times in on themselves so I do not get them wet, and dip my hands into the water with a plate. I pick up the coarse round scrubbing pad she showed me. Washing my first dish I make sure I do well to clean it completely off, and Ami smugly stands there overseeing my work. Following the flow she set out, I rinse and then set it in the drying rack.

"Oh, I could get used to you doing my chores." She laughs.

Looking over my shoulder, I watch Ami disappear back through the kitchen door and hear her climb the creaky stairs. I continue washing the dishes while looking out the large window into the yard. I see Agatha move beyond the edge of her yard, talking to random people who stand about. As she finishes a conversation with a woman dressed in thin clothing, they walk together toward the skyscraping towers.

Looking in all directions that I can see from here, I wonder if this is a town square, just with grass instead of cobblestone. Past the grass and random trees is a border of trees. A barrier exists between this park and a deep gray ground area followed by the large buildings.

"I hope none of those fall over," I mumble to myself.

When I finish up the dishes, I dry my hands on a nearby towel and look around the kitchen, noticing a big pot with a lid sitting on the fireless stove. I am curious if it is vegetable soup again. When I get close I can feel heat emanating from it, and grab the towel I dried my hands off on to lift the lid. It appears to have the same color as the previous vegetable soup, but it looks as though it might have rice in it.

A little hungry, I wonder if a single spoonful would be missed as I take up the wooden spoon which lies next to the pot. Dipping the spoon in and swirling it around I see that I was correct that it has both vegetables and rice, but it also has meat, poultry from the texture of it. I blow on it heavily, and put a huge bite into my mouth. My cooling has proven useless and my mouth is now being seared.

"Ah! Hot, hot!" My mouth goes numb with pain and I open my mouth, emptying the contents onto the clean floor.

The spoon falls to the floor in my haste to turn the cold water on, and stick my mouth under the faucet. Hearing Ami burst in the door causes me to look back briefly before dousing my tongue with water again.

"What's wrong?!" she asks frantically.

"I buwnt mah mouf!" I attempt to talk through the water and over my swelling tongue.

Ami surveys the scene and puts the pieces together, bursting into a fit of laughter. When I am done gulping at the water I return to an upright stance, and she reaches down to grab the spoon, thumping me on the forehead with it.

"It huwts!" I blurt out. Everything inside my mouth feels like I drank molten metal.

"Well then you won't do that again will you?" Ami snorts with laughter.

"There's nothing I can do about it."

Ami replaces the lid on the soup and washes the spoon off, setting it in the dish rack. She hands me the towel, and I wipe up the mess I made. When I am done she takes the towel, places it on the counter and grabs my hand, leading me out into the living room. She removes her hand and waves it at the couch. I sit, and she begins showing me different colors of cloth that are laid out across the table.

"Okay, I need input if you want more clothes," she says

"All right."

She starts with the darker colors, holding a few pieces of cloth up for me. I shake my head, and point at the white cloths.

"I would like to see those ones please."

"How about this one?" She picks up and holds out a white piece for me.

I take it and rub the material between my fingers. It is not silk, but the texture almost gives the illusion that it is. I close my eyes and rub it against my cheek, picturing myself in a cloth like this.

Hard to wrinkle, flows well and seems airy. I would definitely wear a shirt made out of this material, but the occasion for it would have to be formal. It is too nice that it could not be an everyday occurrence and to treat a material as such would be wrong.

I realize my line of thinking is quite odd, as though I am familiar with different thread types and what they should be worn for. Opening my eyes reveals Ami waiting patiently for my answer. Handing her back that piece, I pick up something similar to the cotton base I am wearing now. It seems almost as soft, but a little bit more durable and less formal from the pile.

"This white material should work for me," I hold up the square for her.

"Good, now you need to choose some material for pants."

Again I am given a selection of cloth to pick from. There are quite a few choices, some I am not quite familiar with. I pick up a very thick material that is a blend of blue and white. It is stiff and seems very durable. It almost seems like it was dyed blue and then began to lose its color from use.

Could it be that this is recycled material from other clothing?

"What is this material?" I look at Ami inquisitively.

"That? It's a cotton-based material, specially treated to make it useful for a lot of different occasions. It's commonly used to make pants."

"Why is it faded like it has been used before?"

"I'm not sure why. When its inventor first started making the material it was a fashion statement to fade ones clothing to look well worn."

"How strange. Why would someone want something that looks worn out?"

"No idea, but it was popular in my time."

Returning to my current choice material, I hand it back to her. "Would this go well with the other material I picked out?"

"Not really. I'll show you some that would."

We go through a few more materials which I cannot seem to get used to before she hands me a more flexible cloth. It is dark blue, and not faded. It flows well as I hold it up, and fake wind by waving it through the air a few times. As I rub the material through my fingertips, I find that this texture is to my liking. She takes it back from me, apparently having noticed that I liked it, and begins to pack up her cloth. I reach out to help her and she slaps my hand down.

"I can do this."

"I should really help. Hauling all of this upstairs cannot be easy."

She looks at me reluctantly, and I know she does not want me to strain myself, but while picking up several piles of cloth she leaves some for me and nods. Quickly I gather up some stacks of cloth and begin to follow her. She looks back over her shoulder at me with her perfect blue eyes. I see a hint of a smile. When she notices I am looking, she focuses back on where she is going, but misses a step.

With all of the cloth in her arms she loses her balance. Cloth flies out in front of her, and she falls toward the heap on the stairs. I drop mine to the side and move to help her. Pushing herself up she grabs onto my arm, but when she pulls, she slips on a piece of material on the polished wooden stair and now we are both going down. She screams out as she falls again, sliding onto her backside against the rigid steps. I land on top of her. My chin hits her collarbone, and I cringe in pain both as the wound on my abdomen flares up, and my whole jaw aches from just being impacted. As much as I would like to curl up right now, I realize that I am in a very awkward position, my face next to the bare skin of her collarbone. My face turns red as I scramble to stand up, and she giggles.

"Are you okay?" She stands up and uses one hand to turn my face left and right, examining my chin.

"Yes. Are you?"

"Other than this pain in my collarbone, yeah. Just a little embarrassed that I was being klutzy." She turns red and removes her hand from my face, realizing she had been holding my cheek gently.

She flips around and begins to gather the dropped cloth. I follow suit. While we work together, our hands brush occasionally and I cannot help but wonder if she finds me attractive. When we have cleaned up the mess, we slowly, and carefully make our way up the stairs. Upon reaching the top, Ami fumbles trying to grab the doorknob to her sewing room. Cramming all of the cloth between her upper body and the door allows her to successfully reach and turn it without dropping anything. The door unlatches, and she quickly grabs the cloth, managing to keep hold of the stack. Inside the sewing room, she moves to the desk on the left and throws her pile down onto it.

"Just set it there." She points next to her pile.

"What is that?" I finally ask about the contraption on the table in the middle of the room.

"It's a sewing machine."

"How does it work? It moves so effortlessly."

"It's a machine." She moves to it and begins pointing at several points. "It's hard to describe, but basically instead of hand stitching everything, I can take a cut pattern of cloth, push it across this platform, under this piece that's called the foot, and this machine pushes and pulls the thread through the material for me."

"Is it powered by that 'uh-leck-tri-city' that Agatha told me about?"

"Electricity? Yes. When plugged into the wall over there the electricity provides power to it, which when I press this foot pedal down here makes the things inside the machine go and the needle goes up and down."

"It seems way beyond my understanding."

"That's okay. You'll get it as time goes on."

Moving toward the door she waves for me to follow, and we are soon back down in the living room. She motions for me to sit.

"We should change your bandages," she suggests.

Nodding to her, she moves down the dark hallway to the bathroom. Sitting on the couch to rest, my energy levels seem to be dropping, but I do not let it get the better of me. Removing my button-up shirt, I set it to the side and remove the metal clips. Beginning to unwrap the bandage to make it a smooth transition for her, she appears from the darkness and stops me.

"I'll do that."

She scoots the table forward and sits on it. I lean from the couch to make it easy for her and she, too, leans in, slowly taking the bandage off. She has to wrap her arms around my sides in order to pass the material from one hand to another. Each time she does we lean rather close together. I feel her warm breath on my bare skin, and I my face turns red against my will, making me wish that she or Agatha had done this while I was asleep to avoid embarrassment. She finishes unwrapping and slowly peels off the actual cloth that had padded the wound, first from the front, then she stands up and leans around me to take the one from the back.

"Your back is almost completely healed up, so we won't put a new bandage on that side; this should be the last one we have to put on the front," she says, while sitting back on the table.

I barely notice her actions anymore, but feel the softness of her hands as she works around me. I look down at the top of her head, admiring the smell of her hair; it is flowery. When she finishes fastening the bandage, she looks up and sees I have been staring intently at her. Our faces are close together, and she notices me blushing. We sit there for a moment and her face also reddens. An awkward moment ensues as an almost magnetic force slowly pulls us closer together. Our faces are mere inches apart, and the urge to lean in is becoming too powerful to control as I feel her breath close to my lips. However, I am startled as Agatha pushes into the room from the kitchen. She has a shocked look on her face.

"Ahem!"

Ami freaks out, leaning back too quickly and nearly falls off the table. Forced to over-correct she jumps to her feet and grabs the dirty bandages.

"Mother! How long have you been back?" she says while looking down nervously.

"Apparently just long enough, young lady." Agatha smiles and then shoots me a playful, dirty look.

"I…," is all I have to say in my poor defense.

"Well, I found the market out there. I met this adorable little girl who seems to be running a shop all by herself," Agatha tells us. "They use an electronic currency, but I think we'll do just fine bartering."

"That's good, because I have so many patterns to sell. I bet I'll make a killing," Ami says, while fiddling with the pads in her hands.

"Soup's about ready," Agatha says. "We can have an early supper and get some rest for tomorrow."

Standing up, I put my shirt back on and follow them into the kitchen. While Ami takes the cloth pads out to the washbasin in the yard, Agatha produces three bowls from a cupboard under the island counter and begins to dish up, handing two bowls to me. While I take them over to the table and set them on either side of my chosen chair, I turn around to get the last one from Agatha, only to find she has followed me with the last bowl and spoons. Nearly colliding with her, she backs up abruptly while trying not to spill. She lets out a sigh of relief as not a drop hits the floor.

"Sorry, Agatha." I smile and move out of her way so she can set the bowl down.

"No big deal," she says, as Ami reenters the house. "Would you like water or juice?"

"Water is fine. Thank you."

Ami hears the request and moves to intercept her mother, getting glasses from the same area as the bowls. Agatha puts her hands on her hips, defeated, and retrieves some bread from the pantry next to a tall, strange white box that I have yet to identify. She sets it down and retrieves a butter dish to compliment it. They sit and I follow their lead, feeling my body relax against the back of the chair. Still a little unsettled from the almost kiss, and its interruption, I let out a small sigh.

What in the world happened there? I barely know the girl and I am already subconsciously making advances at her. She is beautiful, no doubt. But is it wise to do such things?

We begin to eat our meal, and I start with a hunk of soft bread, slathering butter all over it and taking a bite. As the bread touches my tongue, I note a subtle hint of honey baked in. While I chew, I examine the dark-colored bread. I let out a satisfied grunt, as it nearly melts in my mouth, and I am delighted by the flavor.

"We still don't know your name, do we?" Agatha breaks the silence.

"I wish I had one to give you," I tell her, while taking another bite of bread and keeping my eyes averted.

I find my voice meek and I wonder if it is because I am unsure of whom I am, or if I am still feeling awkward after being caught nearly kissing her daughter.

"Well, since you can't remember, you should decide what you would like for us to call you, and that will be your name here." Agatha smiles at me while bringing a spoonful of soup up to her lips and begins blowing to cool it off.

I take time to think about it while I eat. Nothing but random bits about what happened in the forest come to my head, and the only name I know besides theirs is the one of my supposed attacker, Drake. My mind becomes distracted with thoughts of him.

I know that I am safe from him now, as whatever time I was in is far removed from where I am now.

His death, somewhere in the past, puts me at ease some and I return to the task at hand, thinking of a name.

"How about 'Burnt-mouth'?" Ami suggests and tries to stifle a laugh.

Agatha looks at her, confused. Ami sums the situation up for her, causing Agatha to laugh a little too. They continue eating while I stare into my bowl, swirling the rice and vegetables around with my spoon.

"I am not sure what I want to be called. Nothing is coming to mind." I take a spoonful of soup into my mouth.

"How about 'Rain'?" Ami smiles at me and I can tell her suggestion is sincere this time.

"Rain?" I inquire looking up from the whirlpool I had made in the soup.

"Sure, it was raining when we saved you. I figured it might be fitting."

"I suppose it does have a nice ring to it. So, I guess I am Rain," I introduce myself with my new name.

"Welcome to our home, Rain. Or should I say *your* new home?" Agatha officially receives me into their home.

We finish the dinner quietly and I ponder my new name, Rain, and who I will be as a new person with no past to influence me.

What kind of person is Rain? I could have been a bad person before, but does anyone ever really set out to be bad? What if Drake tried to kill me because I was worse than he appeared to be? Could I have been a criminal?

Normally one develops a personality from birth to adulthood, but I suppose whoever I was is gone now and I will find out as I go with resolve to do my best for the women who saved my life.

My soup disappears at a much slower rate than Ami or Agatha's. I eventually finish and stand up with my bowl to take it to the sink, only to have it stolen from me by Ami yet again. I squint at her, and give her a playful look, but she ignores it and washes up the few dishes we dirtied.

With nothing for me to do here in the kitchen, I retire to the couch and sit down, feeling exhaustion fall over me. My stomach full, my body clothed, and my head protected from the elements, I slip into a comfortable mindset and my body follows suit. Slouching against the arm of the couch, I feel my consciousness beginning to wane.

~~~~~~

Having fallen asleep leaning against the cushions of the couch, I awake when my body seems to spasm. Though the drapes are drawn across the window, I can tell it is dark outside now. Covered up with the blanket on the back of the couch by one of the women, I shift around trying to stay under it as the colder air threatens to drain my heat.

Curious though, I stand up and make my way over to the window with the blanket wrapped around me, and peer between the drapes to find that there are lights coming from all of the buildings. But what really perplexes me are the lights that appear to be hovering above the ground just beyond the border of trees.

Staring in awe at the sight before me, I think about electricity and all I can imagine is lightning bolts somehow making all of the lights illuminate. Turning back around, everything seems much darker because I had been staring outside at the lights. Carefully making my way back to the couch I sit down and pull the edges of the blanket tight.

But before I can get fully comfortable, I see Ami quickly and quietly creeping down the stairs with some items in her arms. My eyes have adjusted enough for me to see that she has some cloth draped over one arm and a small bag hanging from her shoulder. She is wearing a long white shirt with her shoulders covered by an airy shawl, and has on a long pleated skirt. Both look blue in color.

"Quick! Put these on!" she whispers while dropping some socks and a pair of shoes that had been hidden from sight into my lap.

Reluctant to uncover myself and be cold, I look at her with a quirked eyebrow, but she waves her hands for me to hurry. With the blanket still draped across my back, I slip the socks and shoes on and note that the shoes seem strange with thick padding on all sides. Shorter than I would have expected, the shoes only come to my ankles, and the lacing weaves back and forth up to the tongue. I pull the string tight and tie it off in a bow, finding that this mundane task is something I know how to do. When I wiggle my toes around, the shoes feel a little small on me, but the padding inside molds to my feet, and I quickly become comfortable in them. Finished I look up at her.

"Now what?" I question.

"Quickly! Let's go!" She grabs my hand with her free one and pulls me up.

Ami leads me through the kitchen, letting go only to open the door slowly and quietly. We sneak out and she closes the door in the same manner. I am confused by her actions. But I am compelled to go along both out of curiosity, and because she has my hand, leading me in a jog away from the house toward the edge of the field, and beyond that the buildings.

"Mother isn't the only one who can make connections. I'm pretty good myself," Ami's voice has returned to a normal volume, albeit a little labored as she huffs and glances back at the house.

"What are we doing?" I inquire, puzzled as to why we are heading toward the unfamiliar area.

"We're having a night on the town! I brought some extra clothes and designs to sell so that we can get some money to spend."

"Spend on what?"

"I don't know, whatever we want I guess."

We tear across the grassy field and through the tree borderline onto a hard grayish-black surface. Just from the looks of it I can tell it is a road of some kind, where people are walking to and fro en masse. Everything is strange to me at this point. I look up at the incredibly tall buildings and find they are more intimidating up close, in the dark and in person, than they were in the light and at a distance. But I can see now the supports spanning between the buildings are foot bridges with glass enclosures that connect the interiors of each building together as people are moving through them.

Light pours from windows and doorways in all directions, illuminating the street along with posts that have lights hanging from them as far as the eye can see, deep into the city. With my attention back on these completely solid roads, I find that they are the base of this massive city and they lead all along the outside edges of each building.

While on the outside perimeter of the buildings the crowd is casual; people walk at a slower pace. When I look in between the buildings the population increases significantly, and it is confusing that so many people would be out at this time of night.

Along with the loud noises coming from the bustle along the ground, I am startled by a loud clacking noise high above me and to the left, as a large snake like object with windows and lights flies along at immense speed across the top of the buildings. It comes to a stop on the building directly in front of us, and I can see movement inside the windows. Before I can point it out to Ami, it has sped off again, turning into the city out of my sight.

"What is this world?" I am in utter disbelief at this new experience.

"We will have plenty of time to gander later! Come on!" She tugs on my hand and begins to lead us into the masses of people between the buildings, stopping only briefly to talk to some people walking by.

"Hello! We're new around here. Could you direct me to a shopping area? Maybe some clothes shops?" Ami asks.

"You're on the edge of the shopping district now," a tall, skinny man responds, pointing off to our left. "If you follow this walkway down about half a mile, take a left where the road forks, and then keep straight. You'll reach an intersection a little farther down where there are several clothing shops. The first one you'll see has a big yellow sign with 'Anselmo's Place' written on it."

"Thank you!" She smiles at the man and urges me on. "Come on, Rain!"

She yanks on my hand yet again and leads us hastily in the direction that the man had pointed toward. I look over at Ami and find her joy is innocent and childlike. Her eyes sparkle under the lights as we follow the directions given to us.

Beyond the sea of people are stores and carts where merchants are selling numerous things. As we find our way through, all kinds of delicious smells assault my nose and the thought of food makes my mouth water. At one moment I smell something sweet, and another I smell something meaty. Ami seems to pay it no mind, but the smells are making me hungry despite having eaten only a few hours ago.

Ami forges forward, and when we find it, follow the left fork in the road where I find the buildings seem to be never ending, and the same can be said of the crowds of people. Before the numbers can overwhelm us, she pulls my hand, and we dart and dodge through breaks in between people, as if it were a game. I hold tight to Ami's hand. She looks back at me for a brief moment, smiles, and then continues to hustle our way through.

We finally reach an area of the road where the density of people has lessened and the bright yellow sign we were looking for lies several hundred yards in front of us, reading just as the man had indicated.

"All right, let's see if we can sell some clothes or patterns." Ami's excitement is intoxicating.

When we reach the glass store front she releases my hand to try and open the door, but I beat her to it and hold it open while she gives me a quirky grin. Immediately as we enter, we are greeted by another very tall, slightly husky man. He has longer brown hair, pulled back into a ponytail and a short goatee. He sports a very casual pull-over shirt with short sleeves and long blue pants.

"Hello! Welcome to my shop! I'm Anselmo and I sell 'Easy-Wear', your everyday clothing! Please come here!" The man lunges forward and hugs Ami, and then myself, his friendliness somewhat overwhelming. "How can I help you two?"

"Hi! So you're the owner then?"

"I sure am, young lady!" He steps back and smiles robustly, his teeth partially showing.

"I have come to negotiate the sale of my patterns and clothing styles!" She matches his enthusiasm.

"Negotiate?" he asks a little confused.

"Yes sir! I design clothes and I would like to sell you some of my personal designs!"

"What makes you think I might buy your clothes?" He crosses his arms over his chest, but shows he is interested by grinning and raising one eyebrow.

"Sir, you are obviously a man of good taste as I can see by the clothes in your shop," she sweet talks him, lathering him up with slick words, while looking about the many racks of clothing he has. "Why would you not want to expand that a little more and make a hefty profit?"

"Well, how can I argue with that?" His grin turns to a full smirk and he drops his arms. "Let's go to my office!"

Quickly he turns around and walks toward the back wall. As we follow him, I take note of many different designs and styles of clothing, but it is all a bit much to take in. Only able to see a fraction of the different clothes, we reach a door in the back, and Anselmo opens it. We enter into a smaller, but still fairly well sized room. There are pictures on the wall. Some are clearly paintings while others seem to be finely detailed images, glossed over.

There is a desk toward the back of the room, and it's cluttered with papers and writing utensils much like Ami's sewing room. To the left is a bookshelf half filled with books, and the other half filled with more fine detailed pictures of Anselmo with children in wooden frames. I stand there, staring at the confusingly sharp images while Ami takes a seat in front of the desk. Anselmo moves around behind the desk to sit down in an even more luxurious chair, propping his feet up on top of the mess on the desk.

"Please miss, tell me more!" He extends his hand as an invitation for her to begin.

"I'll get right down to it. I've designed a line of clothing that is comfortable any time. It's made from a light and airy blend of cotton that I've noted in my drawings. It's adaptable for both pull-over or button up styles and as you can see I already have people wearing the line."

She jumps up and pushes me toward Anselmo's desk and then spins me around.

"As you can see the clothing is unrestricting. One might say it's very 'primitive' because of its simplicity."

I shoot her a shocked glance, and she just winks back.

"I see," Anselmo smiles, clearly enjoying the show.

"I too am wearing some of my latest design." She removes her shawl to show off a short sleeve, pleated shoulder shirt. "This shirt is made in a similar fashion with the same material. The part around the breast area is a little thicker so that it is not see through – it gives women a little security."

Ami shows off her creation and spins for the man.

"Now, a key signature of my work is that I use this pink rose on the right shoulder to indicate my work on women's clothing, and an orange chrysanthemum on the men's clothing."

Looking at my right shoulder, I remember previously seeing the flower in the mirror.

"The pants are made from a slightly thicker material, and I have gone with a button system rather than the traditional zipper for closure."

She lifts up my shirt to show my pants off. Shocked again, I slap her hands away, and she slaps my hand back, lifting my shirt back up.

Anselmo leans forward slightly to take a better look, and then returns to his relaxed position. Appearing deep in thought, he rubs his chin, drops his feet back to the floor, and rests his elbows on the desk, clamping his fists together for his face to rest upon.

"You make a very good sales pitch and I like the clothing. Now how much is your asking price?"

"Make an offer. My designs are simple so I'm not looking for an exorbitant amount, but I want enough to have fun in town tonight."

"That's easy enough. If you'll leave your designs with me and enter into an agreement not to sell to anyone else, I think I can make a fair offer," he says clearly, despite his hands partially blocking his mouth.

"I'll do you one better. I brought sample clothing too." Ami lays out the clothing she's been holding and then digs into her bag to produce some rolled up paper.

"Very nice indeed!" Anselmo begins mumbling to himself, biting on his lip while unrolling the paper and looking over the patterns. "I will set a new trend with these simple garments."

"So let's talk payment. What would you offer for these?" Ami inquires.

"Hmm…One thousand credits." Anselmo's face becomes serious as they get down to actual negotiations.

"One thousand credits? That's not all that much." Ami sounds offended. "As I was passing by food stands I noticed that a small bowl of rice, vegetables and meat cost one hundred credits. Twenty-five hundred credits and you have yourself a deal."

"Twenty-five hundred?!" He leans back in his chair and I can see the surprise on his face. "You are a shrewd business person!"

"Twenty-five hundred, or I take my designs to the next shop." She smiles mischievously.

"Fine, fine. Take your money and leave the merchandise!" While he speaks like he is upset, he still smiles warmly.

Anselmo takes a strange-looking rectangular object with rounded sides, swipes it across a gray box on his desk with a black strip on the right hand side and taps a few numbers scribed on it. He hands the card over to Ami and she gladly accepts it, placing it into her bag and curtsies.

"It was nice doing business with you. I hope those designs bring in some good money for you."

Ami turns, grabs my hand, and we are on our way out the front door. We exit and stop for a moment while Ami pulls out the card to examine it carefully. She flips it one way, then another and I can see its top half is glossy with a gray tint, and the bottom half is black as night.

"What is it?"

"It's a piece of plastic. Mother said they use electronic currency so there should be twenty-five hundred credits allocated to this," she says with a shrug.

"That is currency? But it is only a card. Is plastic a precious item like gold or silver."

"There's a lot to learn about how currency changes. Most times we find that we don't have to worry about transactions of precious metals or gems. But right now you're going to learn about other things." She looks up at me and smiles widely. "The first thing I want here is ice cream. I haven't had it in over a month, and I'm dying to have some."

"And what is that, other than the obvious answer?"

"You'll find out when you taste it." She shoves the card back in her bag and grabs my hand.

Leading us back toward all of the food vendors, I squeeze her hand again when we reach the bigger crowds. Amidst the throng we dart and dodge until she locates what she is looking for, and hones in on it, finally coming to stop at an open vendor's counter.

People are gathered in front of the counter that runs adjacent to the two walls, pointing, speaking and then handing similar cards to a person inside. The person moves the card over the same type of device Anselmo had, hands it back, and then hands the person a checkered, tan, cone shaped item with two scoops of half circular objects on it that remind me of what might go inside a pastry.

Inside the counter, behind a glass wall there are rows of different colored and named flavors. Ami steps up to the person while I stand back and watch. I can see her lips moving, but over the loudness of the surrounding people I cannot make out what she is saying. She points, holds up two fingers, and then hands the card she received to the man behind the counter. He swipes it and then hands it back. While she waits, he turns away for a moment, returning with two of the cones topped with the cream. In her hands they are like gold as she cradles them carefully while walking back to me.

"Here." She hands me one. "I picked peppermint flavored because it's my favorite."

She begins to devour hers while I take a moment to examine mine. White and pink swirl together, and I can tell it is definitely a heavier texture than a pastry filling. I follow her lead and begin biting into the wet part.

Chewing the bite of ice cream I am shocked when I find it is much colder than anticipated. I fumble the bite with my tongue around until it warms up but as I do the sweet taste and recognizable peppermint flavor are not lost on me. After I get the first bite down, I proceed to take another bite, and then another.

"Wait! Take it slowly!" She tries to warn me but I just cannot help continuing to eat.

And then it hits me. My head becomes cold and begins to hurt terribly. Instinctively, I throw my free hand up to my temples and put pressure on to try and distract myself from the pain, but it fails.

"Ow!" I yell out in pain. "My head hurts!"

Ami begins giggling despite my pain, continuing to eat hers.

"Make it go away!"

"You'll just have to wait it out. It will go away on its own," she responds.

I move my left hand to my forehead and begin rapidly moving it back and forth to create heat, hoping to get the pain to subside by warming up my skull. She finishes hers, even going so far as to eat the cone. The pain finally goes away in my head, and I stand up straight from my hunch.

"Sorry, I should have told you what happens if you eat it too fast." Ami smiles as she puts her arm through mine and begins to lead us off to another area.

I finish mine slowly so as not to get that headache again, and try the cone as well. Its texture is like a thin cookie, crunchy and sweet. When it is gone I lick my fingers and look over at Ami, who is confidently leading us down a street. It is neither the direction we came from, nor toward Anselmo's shop. Instead there are more bright lights and more shops beaming from every direction into the street, and I liken it to daytime with the amount of light and people about. She appears to be leading us aimlessly, just taking in sights. While we walk, the large snake like thing on the top of the buildings speeds by again, I quickly point it out to Ami.

"That! What is it?"

"Wow. That's amazing! They have a train system on top of the buildings?" She's dazzled.

"What is a train?"

"It's a vehicle that carries a lot of passengers all at once. It looks like they've built one that runs on electricity because I don't see any smoke coming out of it."

I rub my forehead with confusion, and remind myself to ask Ami later about sitting down and catching me up on all of the things I should be aware of in this time to avoid asking about random and potentially ordinary things. She tugs at my arm and we continue walking the shopping district, just gazing into storefronts at the many varieties of items. We walk arm-in-arm for what seems like hours but she does not buy anything more. When she yawns I realize that she is just as tired as I am.

"We should go back to the house," I suggest.

"Yeah. You're right." She promptly does an about face.

It seems like hours had gone by while we walked. She turns us down a street. When we come to the open field in which our house sits in a matter of a few minutes, I figure that we took a different but parallel road to the one we came in on.

Through the tree line, into the field of grass, we find our way home soon enough, and I notice that Ami had been walking with her eyes closed while I led us. I am careful to open the door and lead her in. Removing my arm from hers, I close the door carefully behind us and turn back around to notice that she is gone. I enter the living room and find her collapsed, belly down on the couch and sound asleep. Not wanting to risk another outburst from the possessive Evalyn, I sit down on the floor with my back against the couch and stretch my legs out under the table.

While I relax I think about all of the new memories I am making in place of the lost ones. I revel at all of the things I have seen so far, and wonder what else I will see as I travel through time with this family. But questions soon overtake my mind.

Will I ever see my own time again? Will we ever find a way out, and live in one time? Will I ever fully recover?

Questions bombard my mind, but I am too tired to care about the answers now.

~~~~~~

I am abruptly awoken by Agatha's other half kicking at my foot sticking out from the other side of the table. I slowly open my eyes to see her staring, a frown on her face and her eyebrows curved downward to indicate she is not happy. Her shrill tone pierces my ears as she decides to lecture me first thing in the morning.

"Hey! Wake up! Since you've insisted on disturbing the peace around here by staying permanently, you're going to pull your weight!" She launches into a tirade. "First off, we are not your maids. I know very well that your wound is nearly healed up, and that means you're going to help with the chores. Second, you stink. Get up, take a shower, and then report to me for your list."

"Shower?" I am confused.

"Oh that's right. You're from the distant past. You have no idea what a shower is!" Evalyn sneers with sarcasm and spite. "Get up and I'll show you."

I stand and follow Evalyn down the hallway, and she turns a light on so we can see. When I glance backward to the couch, Ami is gone. Evalyn reaches Ami's bathroom on the left and opens the door. She enters and pulls the curtain back from the bathtub.

"This is a showerhead."

She points up to the bulbous, perforated item hanging from the wall and then turns the water on with the two handles near the base of the tub.

Flipping a lever stops the water from flowing out of the faucet, and instead it sprays out of the showerhead like controlled rain, and then moves to the counter by the mirror.

"Down here are clean towels, washcloths, and soap. You do know what soap is right?" She mocks me. "Make sure you clean up your mess when you're done."

She leaves, closing the door behind her, and I feel completely insulted so early in the morning. After retrieving the items she mentioned, I remove my clothes and bandage. Leaving it all in a heap to the side, I step into the shower, and it is cold as I get in. Adjusting the temperature, I turn it up to lukewarm, and lather up with the soap and rag. A lavender smell permeates the room. Quickly, I wash and rinse my body, taking care around my healing wound. I turn the heat up a bit, and let my muscles relax. Dunking my head in the water, I let it stream from the hair hanging into my face, finding this to be a rather enjoyable experience.

But not wanting Evalyn to get irritated with my taking too long, I turn the water off and step out from the curtain. The cold air hits me all at once and I grab up the towel I had left to the side, drying off quickly to get the cold to subside. I relieve myself, and then put my clothes and shoes back on. While looking in the mirror, I find facial hair has begun to grow. It is not rough as an old man's would be. It looks and feels soft, but I am aware that it will get thicker as time goes on. Determining to deal with it later, I adjust my clothing. My heart skips a beat when there is a loud knock at the door.

"Come on!" Evalyn hollers. "You've been out of the shower for a while now. You have work to do!"

I open the door to her standing there with her arms crossed, and tapping her foot. Before I can say anything she jumps back into berating me.

"Pick up that towel and wipe up any water you might have dripped, and then meet me out by the garden." She huffs and turns to leave.

What is her problem?

I do as she says, and when I pick up the bandaging, I determine that my wound does not seem to need to be bandaged again. Taking the dirty laundry with me through the house, I make my way to the yard through the kitchen, finding Evalyn has already started washing clothing in the large washbasin over a washboard.

The sun is out, and its beams warm my skin up quickly due to the moisture on it. The smell of soapy water and grass fill the air as Evalyn scrubs a towel over the washboard, wrings it out, and then places it into a smaller flimsy looking basket with holes. I look around and notice Ami is hanging the laundry up to dry.

"Hand them over, and start hanging clothing with Ami," Evalyn snaps, while motioning with her hand that she wants my towels. "And I don't want to hear a peep out of either of you."

I do as she requests and move alongside Ami to observe what she is doing for a moment. There are rows of clotheslines strung up, each one with its own set of items. Ami has a basket of clothing that she is working from, and I begin helping. They're shirts made for a woman. From the size I can guess that they belong to Agatha. Or Evalyn. I hang them up without thought, alternating with Ami. We end up taking care of the whole basket in no time, but Evalyn has finished the towels so we exchange baskets with her and hang those up also. Though it is repetitive work, with the three of us working at it, we finish quickly. But Evalyn sees opportunity in me and approaches with haste.

"Since I have someone else to do it now, take this tub and dump it out." Evalyn points off in a direction away from the house. "Don't dump it here, because it's too close to the garden. When you're done, meet me back here."

I nod, noting that while she is harsh, she has a way of effectively explaining things. I proceed to start hauling the tub, and as I pass within whispering range of Ami it crosses my mind to say something, however the likeliness of Evalyn hearing me is probably great and I decide against it for now. But Ami stops me anyway, motioning for me to set it down with her hands. I do so, and she grabs one handle while I grab the other. We carry it safely away from the garden together, and slowly dump the water out so it does not splash us. I am able to carry the tub back on my own while we walk, silently.

Evalyn is standing near the garden looking down at it. I can tell where the rows of different produce are, as the leaves and foliage change from one type to another, noting that each plant has a row or two dedicated to just that type. I visually recognize the leaves for potatoes, carrots, beets, tomatoes, onions, lettuce, strawberries and ground cherries, but there are others that I cannot identify. There comes a sigh from Evalyn's direction. Her demeanor has taken a lighter mood. She leaves and returns with a few medium sized baskets.

"What can we do to help, Evalyn?" I ask.

"Evalyn has left. She's quite agitated right now but I'm unsure why." Agatha has returned to normal.

"So Agatha, what can we do to help?" I let out a sigh of relief, no longer having Evalyn's negative presence looming.

"We are going to gather up extra produce to trade. Our stockpile of meat is running a little low. And I'd like some oranges," she says with a smile. "Rain, I'd like you to gather up at least three-dozen potatoes. Make sure to leave at least one potato on each plant so we can grow a new crop. Ami, please gather a basket of strawberries and ground cherries."

Agatha hands me a basket, and demonstrates how to harvest the potatoes. I follow her lead and do as instructed to dig them up, harvesting a couple off of each plant and leaving at least one. It takes me awhile, but I finally fill three baskets, each with a dozen fair-sized potatoes. I have worked up quite a sweat doing all of this manual labor in the sun. When heading to Agatha with one of the baskets, she informs me that my work is not yet done.

"Please wash them off and place them back in the baskets. We want to make sure they look good for the young lady I spoke with yesterday," Agatha says and points to the left of the house.

Rolling up my sleeves, I pick up two baskets and walk toward the side of the house to find a faucet sticking out with only a single twist knob on it, unlike the bathrooms and kitchen. As I turn the knob, the spout only sprays cold water. Being a little warm from the work and sun, I let it wash over my arms. I gently dump the baskets over, and begin washing the potatoes, placing them back in after they are clean. When finished, I return in time to see Ami has gathered her portion of the food, and Agatha has gathered up some heads of lettuce and a basket of carrots.

"During the daytime the city is mostly shut down," Agatha tells us. "It seems that they've developed a night life that turned into their main time of day to operate. But the girl I met works by herself and should be up right now."

"How far is it from here?" I ask.

"A few blocks into the city from here. It's a general food market area."

"Oh, we…" I begin to divulge information about the trip last night, but Ami swoops in and jabs me in the ribs. The impact is not hard, but it is enough to interrupt me.

"Hmm?" Agatha looks up from her baskets at me, while Ami gives off an innocent smile.

"I mean, we should be careful right? How can we be sure we are getting a fair deal?" I correct myself, keeping in mind our secret adventure.

"We'll find out how much she's charging and negotiate from there," she says making it sound simple. "Let's get going."

Agatha smiles while picking up a basket of potatoes along with carrying the one she filled. Ami and I take our baskets and follow her away from the house, toward the tree line that separates the field from the city. Upon reaching the road I observe what Agatha was referring to, as we find the roads nearly empty with only a few people moving about. Half way down a street very near where Ami and I entered the city she stops and turns left. A few more blocks in she stops at a storefront that has a wooden sign hanging over the street, painted pink, with the words 'Emma's Produce Market' printed on it.

Agatha knocks lightly on the glass, but peering in we can see figures inside and hear the sounds of a ruckus. A voice rings out from inside, and they seem to be getting very loud and belligerent. Slowly, Ami cracks the door, despite her mother's silent protest with a tug on her sleeve, and we all listen in.

"Yous don't wanna refuse boss's offer. He has been kind to yous cause he likes ya, but that don't make yous exempt from having ta pay for the protectin' of your shop. Yous gots 'til tomorrow."

There is some shuffling about by the two figures, and heavy footsteps toward the door. Ami attempts to back up quickly but the door is thrown open inward, and she falls forward at the feet of a couple men in clean cut clothing, and dome shaped hats with brims which circle all the way around. The first is tall and broad, his arms appearing to be as round as a small melon, where the other man is only an inch or two taller than me, but he is much skinnier. They stare Ami down as she gets back up out of their way, but pay no further attention to us as they push roughly past me, nearly knocking the baskets from my hands. Down the road a ways, the bigger one of them stops to look back, and then continues on his way.

We enter the shop only to hear a young voice ring out from behind a counter, "I'm sorry, I'm not open right now. Please come back at dusk and I'll have produce available."

"Miss Emma? It's Agatha," she says sweetly. "We spoke yesterday about produce."

"Agatha?" A blonde head pokes quickly up from behind the counter. "It's good to see you again!"

A young girl, maybe ten-years-old or so, with short blonde hair cut just above her neckline and hazel eyes has appeared, standing on something behind a counter. Wiping tears away with the sleeve of her white shirt, she adjusts some straps hooked to her shoulder that appear to hold up her long blue pants. She smiles, trying to hide the fact that she was crying due to whatever just happened.

"Who were those guys?" I ask.

"Oh. They're just a couple of Denis's henchmen. They do his dirty work in this side of the city. I haven't paid my protection fee the past month and if I don't, something really, really bad could happen to my shop!" she says with fervor.

"I bet that something bad would happen because of Denis. Denis is extorting you," Ami blurts out.

"Oh I know. But it's just better if I pay the fee when I can, and avoid the trouble," she says with forced cheer.

It strikes me as odd that a little girl is running a shop, and that she is being bullied by a man's thugs for money, but I keep my thoughts to myself, as this is all new to me.

"Well Miss Emma," Agatha says cheerfully. "Hopefully we have some produce you can sell for a good profit and not have to worry about that anymore."

"Ooh! Lemme see!" Her excitement reflects her youth as she comes around from behind the counter to inspect the baskets we're all carrying. After a few moments of poking around she speaks up. "These will do nicely! I can finally beat Laywin, my competitor!"

"Beat them?" I inquire.

"Yeah, they always get first pick from the produce suppliers because they have the money to bribe the delivery service. But this produce is a hundred times better than the stuff they get!" Emma disappears into a door toward the back and reappears with something in her hand. It's small, shriveled, and generally unappealing.

"What is that?" I ask.

"It's a potato, silly! But this is the lot I get." Emma's face abruptly turns sour as if she is going to cry again. "I have a few patrons who knew my parents who help support me by buying the produce I get, but when they think I'm not looking I see them go over to my competitor and buy his stuff too."

"Well, maybe they are just making a well-rounded meal by buying from different vendors," I console her.

"Really?! You think so?!" Her eyes light up and the smile returns to her face.

"Of course!" Ami plays into it as well while looking at me out of the corner of her eye, and smiles approvingly.

"Yay! Well now they'll really have a good meal with this food! You guys are the best!"

"Shall we get down to business?" Agatha holds out one of the baskets.

Emma runs back behind the counter, and we move up to it. Hopping back up on her stool, I see that she too has one of the strange boxes that handles the currency. She presses her finger on, causing it to illuminate, and waves for us to set the baskets down. Watching her diligently, her hand flies across the contraption while she taps on numbers like Anselmo had, and the illuminated numbers continue to increase.

"What is that you are doing?" I ask, genuinely interested in learning.

"I'm adding up all the totals for the vegetables you're selling me." She looks up with joy.

"How are you adding so quickly?"

"Where are you from?" She stops dead and looks at me questioningly with her innocent eyes.

"Not around here. I am from a place where such things do not exist."

"That explains why your accent is funny. You don't talk like anyone I know." She giggles. "That's so strange that you don't know about the PayPad."

"How does it work?"

"I have no idea. You have to keep it plugged in, and as long as you know how to work the keypad, that's all anyone needs to know. Everything else is handled digitally at the nearest bank hub." She is eager to share. "This one's a little out of date, but it works. It has multiple functions like exchanging goods for credits, keeping inventory, keeping record of how many credits you have in the bank, mathematics."

"Wow, my head is spinning. It all sounds so confusing," I tell her.

"It is. That's why I don't think about it and just keep my mind focused on making ends meet." She continues to smile innocently at me.

She returns to her work of taking inventory by moving all of the food to other baskets behind her counter, and continues to punch numbers on the PayPad. My mind tries to soak in the information, and I know that through just watching I am learning. But there are so many unseen things that are foreign to me, I find myself lost in her fury against the numbers. Emma finally comes to a stop.

"Ok. So from my calculations, if I offer you fifteen hundred credits for it all I can make a profit of an additional fifteen hundred credits if I sell all of it. That will give me the leverage I need to purchase some of the good produce from the supplier and I will be able to survive!"

"Fifteen hundred sounds fair," Agatha replies.

"Then it's a deal! Do you have your PayPad card?"

"No, we don't have one," Agatha tells her.

I look at Ami, pondering if she is going to say anything about hers, but she is silent. Emma grabs one of the cards from under her counter, and slides it across the PayPad, pushing several buttons as Anselmo had. When she's finished she hands it to Agatha.

"And we can use this anywhere?" Agatha asks looking at the card.

"Absolutely! All shops, stands and markets take these cards!" Emma responds excitely. "The markets will open about six o'clock."

"Thank you Emma," Agatha says while grabbing her two empty baskets.

Ami and I do the same, and Agatha begins to lead us out but when Agatha pulls the door open Emma stops us abruptly.

"Wait! What is your name?" she blurts out.

"Mine? It's—" Ami and I turn around and she begins to answer Emma but is cut off.

"No! Yours!" She points at me.

"My name? It is Rain," I tell her.

"Rain? I like that name. It was nice to meet you Rain!" She grins while leaning against the counter.

"It was nice to meet you too Emma," I smile.

When we are outside Ami looks at me, puzzled. I shrug. Agatha looks around, and because she is quiet I assume she is thinking to herself.

Instead of heading back toward the house, she starts to venture off into the large city. Ami and I follow her, and I assume that we are just out for some fresh air. The three of us walk silently as Agatha directs us randomly, and I enjoy their company while we all take in the sights of the clean and sleek buildings.

"So how close to six is it?" I break the silence after a good deal of time.

Agatha points up to a large circular object on the side of one of the buildings that reminds me of a sundial, but it is neither on the ground nor in a position that the sun would hit it continuously.

"It's about three in the afternoon now, so we have a few hours to kill," she replies.

"Are we going home, or going to walk until then?" Ami asks.

"Being that most people are sleeping, it's not a bad idea to explore," Agatha says, walking with her hands in front of her body.

We wander, observing the different buildings. I take notice that the building shapes, and materials used, start to vary. Along the inner edges of the city closest to our field, the buildings are all tall, and have four faces and multiple windows. While immaculate, they are plain in color, and other than their height there is nothing remarkable about them. But as we move farther into the city, away from the business and market areas, the buildings take on a more exotic look, and I cannot fathom having imagined them on my own. Pyramids, ovals, droplets of water; the architecture puzzles me as if someone had taken random shapes and made buildings out of them, and I think about the complexity needed to make such structures stable. These buildings too have many windows, some which seem to take up a whole section between supports, but most of them hold large, white drapes, which block what could be held within.

Having stopped to admire, I have lost track of how long I stood there. When I look down expecting to see Agatha and Ami, they are gone, having put a significant distance between us. Not quite specks in my vision, but very close, I panic. Not wanting to be separated in this monstrous city, I break into a sprint to catch up with them, pushing my legs as hard as I can. I contemplate calling out, but I am breathing too hard. Finally getting close they hear me coming and turn around. I see a smile on Ami's face, and the moment I reach them I slow and begin huffing heavily. My stomach and lungs ache, and I am hit with a witty remark.

"What happened? Did you forget how to walk and look at the same time?" Ami playfully jests.

"I…was…sorry, I…"

I am finding it hard to catch my breath, slouching over and putting my hands on my knees. They wait patiently for me. Finally after a minute I am able to stand upright, but I begin a coughing fit. Breathing in through my nose, and out through my mouth I get it under control.

"Sorry, I was distracted by the buildings. I did not know that you had kept walking," I labor to speak.

"It's okay dear, just don't get lost out here," Agatha warns.

"Should we restock on medical supplies while we're out?" Ami asks Agatha, while pointing at a sign that has a big red cross on the side of a lone building.

"Perhaps, after we have replenished our food," Agatha answers, but still takes a moment to think about it.

We circle back the way we came, and it appears that more people are finding their way to the streets. As we pass between buildings I catch a glimpse of the sun, and it has started to set.

Back in the market district, windows begin to open and doors begin to unlock. Agatha's random pattern of walking becomes more directed. She leads us to a building that has a large glass front, and inside are numerous shelves with what appears to be food lining them. Pulling the doors open, Agatha leads us in, but I follow behind Ami as she moves down an aisle separate from her mother.

Each item has an image on a piece of paper, which appears to clearly identify the contents within. Though I have questions about the perfect duplication of images, and perfect writing that labels the items, I save them and stick with assumptions. Ami however understands the system and begins loading her basket with numerous things. I pay little attention to what she is taking into her basket, but instead focus on not losing her in this store that seems rather large. Meeting back up with Agatha, she too has placed a significant amount in her basket, mostly meat items.

"We should check out now. We've probably reached our limit," Agatha tells us.

I follow behind her and Ami up to the unremarkable, yet well-dressed shopkeeper who stands behind the counter. When Agatha and Ami set their baskets up on the counter I watch closely as the man pulls each item out and presses some buttons on his PayPad, and then sets the items to the side.

"That'll be seventeen hundred credits," he tells us in a monotone voice.

"Would you take fifteen?" Agatha attempts to haggle.

"I'm sorry but prices are non-negotiable. I barely make a living as it is."

"Take out the mixed nuts and the pears. That will equal two hundred credits that you can take off the total," Ami offers up some of her selections.

"Ami, what about—" I start in, but am promptly jabbed again.

Agatha looks over to me with a puzzled look on her face and Ami just smiles sweetly.

The man removes them from the lot, placing them on another counter directly behind him, and types on his PayPad once again.

"Fifteen hundred credits," he holds out his hand expectantly.

Agatha hands him her plastic card, and he swipes the black part against the PayPad.

"You have zero credits remaining on the card. Would you like me to recycle it, or would you like to keep it to recharge it later?"

"I will keep it, thank you," she says with a smile, despite his lack of enthusiasm for his work.

We load our purchased goods into our baskets, spreading them out so we each have about an equal load, and begin heading for home. Making our way through the crowd of people that now bustles about the city, Agatha takes us on a direct route. In a much shorter time than I expect, we are nearing the border between the city and the field.

Into the grass just inside the tree line, where there are no lights, it takes my eyes a moment to adjust. I can soon see the outline of the house in the distance. My body begins to relax a bit when we finally reach the doorstep, and head inside. With my hands full, I use my leg to push the door closed, and then set my baskets next to the island counter.

"So, what is the point of trading one food item for another? It looks like we got less than what we traded."

"We did get less, but in a way we got more." Agatha smiles at me while unloading the baskets. "Being in these sealed cans, this food will last much longer than fresh produce. And we needed the meat."

"How does this food last longer?"

"There are canneries that process, purify, and seal them so that they stay fresh," Ami replies while helping her mother.

"Amazing." I am in awe.

Agatha takes the packaged fresh meat over to the tall, white, rectangular box next to the pantry and opens its bottom door. The inside is illuminated by one of the electricity-powered lights, and I can see a few things in there, including the soup pot from before. Curiously I watch, but with my brain overloaded from everything else today, I do as in the market, and keep silent.

There will be plenty of time to ask more questions.

My stomach grumbles, and it is loud enough for Ami to hear as she looks at me, shocked. Moving to the white box that her mother is reorganizing, Ami pulls out a white dish, and upon reaching the stove with it she opens the door and shoves the dish inside. Having caught a glance, I could only see cheese sprinkled on the top. She closes the door and fiddles with a knob, then turns her gaze to me.

"We're having lasagna tonight."

"What is in it?"

"Big noodles, cheese, ground meat and tomato sauce."

They move about the kitchen. Some things go in the pantry, some in the white box. For a few moments Agatha disappears into a door that when closed faces the side of the white box. Peering in for a moment I can see a set of stairs which go down below the house, however when I hear her coming back up I pretend I had not been snooping again.

After they are done putting the food away, we all sit at the table, and I place my head down on it to rest. My soft scar tissue aches, and I feel like it might rip open again. Slyly checking by pulling back a button reveals that it is still closed. Time passes and a smell begins to permeate the room. Breathing in deeply, the smell of cheese being melted causes my mouth to salivate, and my stomach growls heavier than last time.

We set the table and sit down for another meal together. I am quickly becoming accustomed to this new life. When I take my first bite of the lasagna and taste its salty flavors, I am soon shoveling it in. Ami looks at me funny, and Agatha just smiles. Involuntarily my stomach makes room and I let out a loud belch. My face turns red, and I cover my mouth.

"I apologize for my rude manners," I excuse myself.

"Don't worry about it. We're not all prim and proper here," Ami reassures me.

"Still, it is quite rude if I do not display some form of manners." I lean back and let the food settle.

Ami follows my sentence with a burp of her own, prompting a quick, stern glance from Agatha. Ami giggles gleefully, and I find her effort to belch funny.

"Perhaps it's time we taught *you* proper manners, young lady," Agatha scolds with a playful tone. "Rain seems to know a thing or two about them."

"Oh, Mother, when will I ever need manners?" Ami responds, and I assume she jests.

"Rain, while Ami teaches you, maybe you could teach her," Agatha teases Ami.

"He laughed." Ami points at me. "A burp doesn't count if it's after a good meal anyway."

"Well then! I shall leave you to your lack of manners, and we'll see what kind of man you attract!" Agatha winks at me for some reason.

Finishing our meal, we clean up in the kitchen, and I head to the couch to rest. Though the longevity of my consciousness has been steadily increasing, my body still seems to need a significant amount of sleep in order to finish healing. I lie down with the dark blue blanket under my head as a pillow and close my eyes.

~~~~~~

I do not remember falling asleep.

Ami drawing the drapes open on the window, and the light from outside hitting my eyelids, wakes me. Sitting up I groan and rub my eyes, and her backside comes into view. Wearing a long puffy pink shirt, and dark blue pants, I admire her…up until the moment she turns around.

"We're going to have to clear a room for you to call your own. The one across from my sewing room is a little dirty, and has a few things that need cleaned out, but it would be perfect for you," she suggests.

A room of my own would be nice, though I have been much too busy and tired lately to really care. I suppose at some point I will need a little privacy.

Pushing the blanket off, I find the morning still to be a bit cold. Though light is pouring in, I can see that the sky is clouded over, and even a little dark in spots that appear to be threatening rain. My attention is diverted when I notice a sweet smell wafting through the house. I am compelled by my growling stomach to get up and find what is causing my mouth to salivate.

Ami moves in quickly behind me, and Agatha is standing by the island counter with yet another strange contraption. Next to it is a stack of golden brown, bread-like squares.

"Take a seat at the table. I'll bring you some waffles," Ami offers.

"Is there anything I can do to help?" I offer eagerly, wanting to pull my weight.

"Nope. It's all rather easy, and Mother has it taken care of this morning," she smiles brightly.

I sit sideways in the chair, keeping my eyes trained on Ami when she is not looking. She moves about, collecting up the dishes needed for the meal, and I watch her hair flow as she moves elegantly through the kitchen. Agatha catches me and grins, causing me to reactively look out the window at the scenery. Ami sets the dishes down, and returns to where Agatha stands. When Agatha pulls another waffle out and sets it on the stack, Ami takes the plate they are on. Agatha joins us as Ami serves me.

"These are waffles," she informs me. "They are made from a batter created with flour as the main ingredient. Cooked up in the waffle iron over there, it creates this pattern."

"You know that you are going to have to explain just about everything to me?"

"Yeah, we'll have to do some more studying later. It's not like you're going anywhere," she says sounding almost as if questioning the fact that I am here.

I copy her when she puts a pat of butter in the middle of the waffle, and then drizzles a dark syrup over it. When I take a bite, I revel in its taste. The waffle is light, airy and sweet, while the butter gives it a salty flavor, and then to top it all off is the sweet taste of the syrup.

Will I never cease to be amazed at everything that is new to me?! It seems like every time something new comes to light I find myself in wonder of it.

After eating and cleaning the kitchen, I head upstairs to the dusty room across from the sewing room, ready to clean it. It appears it has been a storage area for a while; thick paper boxes stacked near the closet to my right have collected a significant amount of dust. Agatha had informed me that I could move the boxes down to the last room on the right in the upper hallway, but because it is their stuff I am hesitant to move it.

I pull the curtains open, and it sends a cloud of dust flying at me. Holding my breath while I struggle with the latch to open the window, I try not to inhale, but fail, causing me to sneeze several times. Finally, I get the window open and stick my head out, allowing my nose to calm itself.

I use the light coming in from outside to get a better look at everything in the room. Near the wall by the door lies my new bed, large enough for a single person to lie upon. It has no pillows or blankets and the mattress is dusty too. Next to the closet, behind the boxes, lies a dresser and coat rack.

Inside the dresser are a few random articles of clothing, none of which appear to be my size. When I turn back around I nearly topple a stack of boxes. I lift the flaps on one, and inside are some fine detailed images in wooden frames, which appear to show a much younger Agatha and a tall handsome looking man.

Must be her husband, Ami's father.

With a box in my arms, I move it down to the end of the hallway. As I approach, an eerie feeling sweeps over me. The hairs on the back of my neck begin standing on end. I cannot tell what is causing it, but a sense of dread falls over me, and I resolve to not linger in this section any longer than needed. Pushing the door open on the right reveals an unfurnished room filled with more boxes.

One by one I bring the boxes down to the other unused room, but when I go to leave it, my ears pick up what sounds like a growl coming from behind the door across from this one. My heart leaps into my throat, and I slam the door shut, hiding in the musty room with the boxes.

Could I have been this easily spooked before my memory loss?

Shaking it off, I slowly crack the door open and listen intently for the sound. Besides the door creaking, I hear nothing else and sigh in relief, pulling the door open completely. Lying to myself, I chalk it up to the floor settling under the new weight on this side of the house, but when I enter the hall the door and its knob begin to shake violently. Letting out a yelp, my heart leaps into my throat again, and I jump. The door continues to shake, and a light appears and disappears in the seams. The growling returns and I quickly race down to my room.

When I slam my door and put my body against it, I can hear the door at the end of the hallway fly open, smashing against the wall. Fast, heavy stomping makes its way down the hall, stopping right outside my door.

I wait and listen. It is silent now. I do not hear any breathing, or shifting of weight on the wood. Whoever is out there cannot have left without me hearing it, so I assume that they are still out there, waiting like a predator for me to drop my guard or open the door. But I realize whatever lies beyond the door will have to be confronted at some point, and so I shift my weight from holding it closed and grab the knob.

My wrist rotates only a quarter of a turn before the door explodes open, the corner hitting me square between the eyes, knocking me backwards off of my feet. Agatha roars and stomps around above me. Only it isn't Agatha.

"Bwa ha ha ha. What a little girl! I heard that yelp!" Evalyn mocks me scornfully. "Scared because of noises. I bet whoever tried to kill you did so out of mercy because you're so frail."

Her words sting, and my heart begins to ache. At a loss for words she takes the opportunity to continue to hound me.

"That's my door down there. Stay away from it," she warns. "If I catch you by my door again so help me…"

"You are a cruel woman." I jump back to my feet and point a finger at her, snapping angrily. "I was just taking boxes to the back room that Agatha told me to."

"I don't care what she told you to do. Don't come near my door again!" She takes a swing at me and I deflect.

"You need to calm down!" my voice gets a little higher.

"Don't you tell me to calm down! Who do you think you are? You aren't even supposed to be here!" Despite Agatha's smaller frame, Evalyn manages to throw a knee up at my gut, and I pull my stomach in so her aim is thrown off.

Her knee grazes my side, and in her imbalance I grab both of her arms, trying to be as gentle knowing it is Agatha's body. Spinning her, and pulling her arms around her back, I hold her there in defiance of her attack while she kicks backwards trying to hit me.

How did I just do that?

"Whether you like it or not, I was offered the choice to stay," I snap at her. "I think it would be best for us all if you became accustomed to the idea! Until this curse you have sent them into is broken, I am here."

"You know nothing about what you speak of. There isn't a way," she huffs. "All you've done is condemn yourself to endless, miserable, and random travel."

Releasing her arms, I step back, and she moves out into the hallway while fixing her hair. She turns around with an evil smirk, and we stare each other down for a moment before she moves toward me again.

"Better watch yourself in your sleep," she threatens.

"Why are you so bent on keeping them miserable?" Crossing my arms and glaring I ignore the intimidation.

"That's none of your concern."

"What did Agatha do to you? What about Ami?" I interrogate.

"They simply exist, therefore I have reason."

"What could you possibly have against their existence?"

She becomes irate with me prodding for answers, and moves to leave, anger apparent on her face. Disappearing from my doorway, she stomps down the stairs. I sit on the bed, my mind reeling with what just happened.

I accosted Agatha's body. I will have to apologize to her later, when she is herself.

Returning to my work of cleaning the room up, I manage to get most of it done and head downstairs in search of water. When I enter the kitchen, Ami is there prepping food, probably for lunch, but I notice her head is bowed and she does not appear to be happy.

Evalyn must have been through here too, and got in her face about something.

"Hey, Ami," I try and get a response from her.

All I get is a brief, fake smile from her before she moves to finish her task, taking three plates over to the table with tall sandwiches on them. Parched, I begin looking for a cup or glass. As I rummage through the cupboards on the island counter, it takes me a few tries but I find them.

I turn the faucet on at the sink to collect some cold water, and guzzle it down quickly. I let out a heavy sigh of satisfaction. The sandwich on the table is now extremely appealing.

"Would it be rude to ask if I could take this sandwich upstairs while I finish cleaning?"

"Of course not," she tells me.

"Great. Now I just need something to wipe the dust off of things in the room."

"Wash rags can be found in the hall closet just below the stairs, and I can get you a bowl of water if you like."

"That would be great. I will have the rest of that room clean in no time."

"You'll probably want to bring the mattress outside and beat the dust out of it later."

"Thanks Ami." I place my hand on her shoulder comfortingly, thinking she might need it right now.

Taking the meaty sandwich in one hand, I begin wolfing it down while pushing my way through the kitchen door. When I get to the closet she mentioned, I stuff the rest of the sandwich in my mouth, and wipe my hands on my clothes. Gathering rags from the closet, I head back to the stairs, and Ami comes through the swinging door with the water she offered.

I smile at her, but I can see she is hesitant to smile back. We walk up the stairs silently, and into my new room. I toss the rags down and take the bowl from her. Our hands brush lightly as I do, and she genuinely smiles a little bit, but abruptly turns around and makes a hasty exit.

I wonder if she finds me attractive or if she just is not used to having the opposite sex around.

Time flies as I scrub the room from top to bottom. After taking the dirty rags and bowl of murky water to the kitchen, I return to the room and pick up the mattress from the bed by two conveniently sewn on cloth handles. Dragging it down the stairs and out into the yard near the well, Ami joins me and gives me a long handled, woven wicker paddle that is self-explanatory.

After a hard day's work, I have a healthy layer of sweat and caked on dirt. A refreshing shower cures me of that. Putting on fresh clothes, this time in the white and blue colors I had picked out from the other night, and they are just as comfortable as my first set. With my room finished and my bed ready to sleep in, I sit on it with my back against the wall, reflecting.

Being from an era which was limited in knowledge, at least from what I understand, I find myself a little afraid of what I do not know. But I owe my life to these women and will do whatever it takes to help them in their journey.

I cannot help but wonder what my lost memories hold. Did I have a family? Are they mourning my disappearance or death? Am I, or I suppose I should say 'was I', even being looked for? Perhaps one day this family that I am not even sure exists will see me again.

Re-energized from taking a break, I head downstairs and into the kitchen. Agatha, or perhaps Evalyn, is there washing the few dishes from earlier. Looking past her, out the window, it is dusk already.

Has time always seemed so fast?

"Agatha?" I hesitantly question.

"Nope. Try again!" Evalyn's sharp tone shines for me.

"Ah, I see." My disappointment is clear.

"What's that supposed to mean you little twit?" She looks back angrily.

"Nothing. I was just working out if Agatha's body had been invaded again," I reply with a snarky comment.

"You little…" Evalyn scowls and hurls a soapy glass at me. I deflect it with my hand, causing it to shatter against the ground.

"How about for the sake of the dishes around here, you keep from throwing them at me," I tell her while moving around the far wall toward the door to keep my distance.

She glares at me the whole time while I head outside to drop my dirty laundry in the washbasin. When I return, it is obvious I have struck a nerve.

"Now, do you have something I can clean the glass up with?" I ask in a sweet but sarcastic tone.

"Do I have to show you everything?" She shoots a fiery glance over her shoulder.

"Yes, as a matter of fact, you do."

"Gah!" she exclaims while dropping a plate into the sink full of soapy water and drying her hands off

She shoves past me, around the island counter, and opens the pantry doors harshly. She waves her arms in a sardonic manner, pointing to where the broom is kept and then returns to the dishes.

When I have sufficiently swept up the broken glass, I hold it in Evalyn's peripheral vision with a cocky smirk on my face, finding that some part of me is getting pleasure out of irritating her. Though I am not sure if that is a good thing, or bad, I can tell she is about done with me as she looks at me with her dagger-like stare. She huffs loudly and pulls out a round metal bin from under the sink for me to dump it in. I do so and replace the broom and pan to their designated area.

My stomach growls.

"What can I do to help get dinner ready?"

"You can set up three spots at the table. We will need plates tonight, dear," Agatha says, control of her body returned to her.

"When did Evalyn leave?" I am a little surprised.

"After you dumped the glass into the trash bin." She looks over her shoulder and smiles.

"So suddenly." I cannot help but laugh a little.

"You really shouldn't provoke her. Her temper is nasty, and I would like to keep my dishes intact," she warns, but I see her smile turn to a satisfied grin.

"No promises. She cannot just bully people around."

I set up the table as best as I can, recalling from memory where the plates, silverware, and glasses are. Ami comes in, and proceeds to the tall white box next to the pantry. I move closer to it as she has the door open, and I can feel cold air coming from it.

"What is that?"

"This?" She holds up a glass bowl with a mixture of vegetables in it.

"It's salad and chicken, our dinner for tonight."

"No, that!" I point at the box.

"This is a refrigerator. It's best described as a place that cools things down so that they keep longer. And the top section is called the freezer. It cools them down even more, so that they freeze."

"That is amazing. How does it work?"

"Electricity." She shrugs.

"How is it possible that electricity can create light, but at the same time cool things down? If electricity is like lightning, how is it contained so that we are all still alive?"

"So many questions! I guess we need to sit down and do another lesson." She closes the door and heads over to the table.

"That sounds like a promising idea. Shall we start tomorrow?"

"Indeed," she agrees.

We have a nice and quiet meal. After cleaning up, I retire to my new room. I lie down on the bed and it is softer than the couch. Glad to have an actual bed to call my own, I fluff the pillow under my head, and pull the blanket up over me, only to realize that I have left the light on. I get up, flip the switch, and return to the bed, resolving to remember to turn it off before getting in bed next time. It is not long under the warm and cozy blanket before I am falling asleep.

~~~~~~

Time's passage is strange. One day feeling as if it is racing by and the next like it has come to a halt. Could it be an after effect of being displaced from time? Or maybe it has just been the couple days I have spent cooped up inside having Ami teach me about things that will likely take me longer to understand.

Resting on my bed, I stare out the window to the city, lit up against the dark sky by the innumerous lights. Though the day was spent only doing light work and learning, my mind is ready to shut down, overwhelmed with all the things Ami had shown me throughout the house, within our lesson plan, and studying the changes of our language.

I wonder if this feeling of awe at everything, and constant questioning how much I do not...don't...know will ever subside. No doubt she has only begun teaching me a miniscule amount of things I am unaware of.

But really, if someone would have told me without showing me that a small box that you can hold in your hand could capture sights instantly and perfectly in their moment, I suppose I would not have believed them.

Waiting patiently for Agatha to go to sleep, I think about Ami whispering in my ear after dinner, telling me we were going out again tonight, and how it excited me that she leaned in closely to do so. Though I am unsure if it was her breath on my skin, or the fact that she wants to spend more time with me, it sent shivers down my neck and caused my hair to stand on end.

I suppose that it could be loneliness, or just relishing the ability to go out and relate to someone about her age, but what if it is more than that? Could she actually be growing attached to me?

While I am unsure of her motivation, I am more than eager to oblige her, as I find her company captivating. My anticipation of leaving the house causes me to get up and pace, reminded that time feels like it slows when bored or in anticipation. I wonder if a nap might help me pass the time, however after a few moments I decide against it, not wanting to be left behind in case she sees I am asleep and leaves without me.

Tugging on my newest shirt, a dark green, wool 'sweater' as Ami called it, I find that it is a little tight, and I almost want to take it off. But at the risk of her becoming offended that I don't like her shirt, I try and stretch it out some. Becoming a little more comfortable in it, I stand near the window and notice that, while the sky is clear, I cannot see the stars very well. There is movement within the city, and a train passes across the tops of the buildings, stopping occasionally.

I wonder if I was an adventurer before. It seems when I am sitting still I feel like I should be moving. If the distant past that Ami and Agatha speak of was indeed a primitive culture, I cannot think of anything else that I might have done to obtain the excitement my mind seems to crave.

Finally, after a significant amount of both boredom and time, there is a light rapping on my door. I move swiftly and twist the knob. When I pull the door open, Ami is there with her hair tied off to the side in a braid, wearing a nice white blouse, and a very straight, white dress with a red ribbon tied around her waist in a bow. She catches me looking and puts her hands together in front of her hips, and shrugs while smiling coyly.

"Are you ready to go?" she whispers.

"Yes." I pull the door shut with the knob twisted so that the latch does not make any noise.

The stairs creak under our combined weight, so I let her go first, and then follow. The wood has no more complaints about being trampled on. Sneaking through the house, we slip through the kitchen, and out the door into the cool night. As if Ami had foresight, the sweater keeps me warm, and I am thankful I kept it on. She puts on a warmer top as well, and it appears to be of the same type of material, but it only has a single button in front in which to keep it closed. Though it has longer sleeves it only reaches half way down her torso, and I silently question the practicality of the top, regardless of how good it looks.

"What is that you're wearing?"

"What?" She looks down.

"The half sweater thing?"

"Oh, it's a midriff sweater. Do you like it?" She smiles while taking my arm in hers.

"While it seems a little counterproductive to what a sweater is supposed to do, it does look good."

"Thanks."

I can feel her skip a little as she begins to lead us into the city. Our pace is nowhere near as fast as the first time we snuck out, moving casually enough that I feel that she has no fear of getting caught tonight. While we walk toward the city line, I notice that people have continued to mill about in this large field around the house, some stopping to look no doubt in bewilderment at the house that only a few days ago was not there.

I decide not to ask her where we are going tonight and instead take in some of the sights while we stroll. She presses her side up against mine and pulls my arm in tighter to share warmth with each other. After a while of walking through the food market and not buying anything, to my dismay, we find our way a few roads over and near Emma's shop.

"Shall we go see how Emma's doing?" I ask.

"I suppose we can do that," Ami's tone is bland, and she grimaces a little.

The streets are familiar, but between day and night the city seems like two different places entirely. I take my time to observe everything, and notice that many shop signs are lit up, all in different colors. Many of them have a name and a greeting to try and get people to enter their shops. 'Welcome! Please Come In!' and 'Open for Business!' attempt to entice the masses.

I spot a familiar one, lit by a single lamp overhead. Emma's shop enters my view and she has the door open. When we reach her window there is a sign lit up in bright yellow that displays 'Welcome! Fresh Produce!'

People are bustling in, out, and all around her shop, and I find myself a little excited for her as it seems that this would be a promising sign that she is getting business. Upon entering her store we find little more than elbowroom to maneuver through, and people are raising their voices to be heard, wanting to be next in line. When we look around at her tables and shelves of produce, she has already increased her quantities and the quality of the produce she is selling. Catching a glimpse of her, I can see Emma behind her counter, her fingers flying at an incredible speed across her PayPad and swiping people's cards. The moment she has finished her transaction with one customer, she moves onto the next one and takes care of their needs just as quickly.

At the speed that the produce is snatched up, it does not take long for the heavy traffic to dwindle down when people either find what they are looking for, or that most of it is gone. Ami hugs tighter onto my arm as people brush past us to exit, and I find an opportunity to move toward Emma's counter, standing to the side. Emma briefly looks over and smiles brightly at us before returning to her attention to her last customer's needs.

While she finishes conducting business with her PayPad, out of the corner of my eye I see a boy about her age rush into the shop. As I watch him intently, he scowls while glaring at Emma. Shock enters my mind as the boy snatches an apple from one of her produce baskets, and turns to head for the door. My immediate thoughts are that he is a thief, and my instincts kick in.

"Hey! Come back here!" I start after him, releasing Ami.

Once outside the boy shocks me yet again, and lobs the apple at Emma's front window. I stop dead in my tracks and when the apple hits, it splatters, and causes the glass to spider-web. Ami shrieks and I pursue him.

"Next time it won't be an apple!" the boy threatens.

"Hey, get over here!" I yell angrily.

Seeing me heading toward him, his eyes go wide and he turns around, running to hide himself in the sea of people out on the street. Hot on his heels, I make a swipe at the scruff of his shirt and miss when he ducks between a couple people. As my arm over extends past where my hand was supposed to grab, I lose my balance a little bit and stumble, knocking into a couple and garnering a protest.

"Sorry!" I apologize and look for him again.

He is able to put some distance between us by running through the tight spaces in between the adults, and I am at a disadvantage. I am unable to keep up with him, and decide that scaring him off was enough heroics for the day. When I reach the door of Emma's shop, she and Ami are waiting for me.

"What was that about?" I inquire of Emma, trying to catch my breath.

"That was Denis. He's the son of the man in charge of the United Fighting Arts, Trevor Lindali."

"Wait. That was Denis?" I am shocked to find that this extortion ring is being led around by a little kid. "Why did he just destroy your front window?"

"He found out that I am earning more, and they want more protection money. I told them no." She sighs.

"That's pretty low," Ami says.

"Yeah. Thanks to the produce you sold me I was able to start a cascade effect, and begin to get better and better produce from the suppliers." She frowns. "Once I got better produce, more people started coming in and buying. That led to more money, and then the brutes heard..."

"Someone needs to stop them." I feel a rage inside at this injustice. "It is terrible that he would destroy someone's place of business, especially a little girl's."

Though I am angry with the child for breaking her window, I begin to seethe that one group of people is beating up on another for money.

"It can't be helped. He has the backing of the U.F.A. fighters and they are some of the best fighters in the world."

"Are you going to be okay?" Ami asks her.

"Yeah, I am just about out of produce now anyway. I'll just close up for the night and go contract a local window maker." Her disappointment is apparent. "This isn't the first time I've had a broken window."

"You are sure you will be okay? You are not worried they are going to come back tonight?" I feel compelled to make sure she's safe for the remainder of the night.

"Denis has issued his warning for the day. And because you chased him off I don't think he would come back anyway." She lets out a little giggle.

I don't feel reassured at all, compelled for reasons I cannot identify to help her by maybe confronting some of these henchmen, though I have no idea how. Remembering the large man with the much larger muscles, I realize that he would probably crush me. Ami hooks her arm to mine again and tugs, indicating that she would like to get going. Reluctantly, I cave in and begin to turn away but my mind and mouth run away from me.

"I will find a way to scare them off for good," I promise; something that I do not know if I can uphold.

"Really?!" Emma's eyes light up and a glimmer of hope shines.

"I don't know how yet, but I will think of something." Committed to what my mouth blurted out, I simply reaffirm it.

Ami elbows me in the ribs, and looks at me in disbelief. A smile is all I have to offer her.

"Thank you, Rain!" Emma jumps and hugs me around my waist.

It is an awkward feeling, as something in the back of my mind tells me that I have no past experience with children. Hugging into my stomach, she seems overly excited at my promise and I have to put my hand on her shoulder to break her away. Emma grins wildly up at me, and Ami tugs again.

"We'll come back and see you again soon!" Ami says cheerfully, but when her face is out of Emma's line of sight she grimaces and pulls even harder.

As we walk away, I look over my shoulder. Emma is watching intently. I wave to her and she smiles, intertwining her fingers and bringing them up to her chest.

How did I just let my mouth get me into trouble like that?

Walking, there is an awkward silence between us. Every time I look over, Ami has the same frown on her face. It appeared when I suggested visiting Emma, and has persisted since.

Why might she be upset at my suggestion to check up on Emma? Can I be so out of touch because of my memory loss that I am doing something wrong?

Ami directs us toward a sign which has a picture of people getting onto the train, and has an arrow pointing into a building. We walk into a doorway, and there is nothing in here but stairs and the one door we just came from. Hugging the right side of the stairs to follow the foot traffic, we make our way up and around to a door with no handles or hinges, split down the middle.

There are more stairs to the right, but Ami stops us at the doors where a multitude of others are standing and waiting for something. There is a ding, like the sound of a bell, and the doors slide open to reveal a very small, closed off space. People come out, people go in, and we move up in a line. We wait for our turn at the unknown, at least unknown to me. When the doors open again new people are there, and they exit as well, while more people move in.

Ami and I enter the enclosed space, and the doors shut behind us. Someone reaches over and presses a big white rectangular button with a symbol that looks to represent the train, and I let out a gasp of air when my body seems to feel heavier, and the box we are in makes noises. I suck in to catch my breath, confused at a sense of movement, and look at Ami in a panic. She tugs on my arm and the smile returns to her face. Pulling me close, she rests her face on my arm and I feel calmer.

The box stops moving and a ding can be heard again as the doors slide open. We exchange places with people waiting to get into it, and Ami deftly leads us out and to the side so we are not trampled. Back inside the stairwell, I breathe a sigh of relief.

"How did you like your first ride in an elevator?"

"What is that thing?"

"It's a mechanical device that uses electricity to control pulleys that lift the elevator up, or bring it down inside of a shaft."

"Wait, so we are at the top of the building? By the train?"

"Yep." Her eyes glimmer with delight.

She lets her arm fall, sliding her hand into mine, and our fingers intertwine. My heart beats faster as she leads me, pulling us up another set of stairs. The cool night air hits my face as we exit onto a flat surface, and we are on top of one of the buildings that looked so menacing before. But now we stand on it like conquerors, and when I look out over the city I see that it reaches far beyond what I could have ever imagined. It overwhelms me, and my legs suddenly feel unsteady. The height alone makes my limbs go stiff, and the wind that passes gently by does not help any. Yet somehow Ami coerces me toward where people are gathering near the edge of the building waiting for the train.

"Excuse me sir, what is the fare for the train?" Ami asks tapping a short elderly man on the shoulder.

"One hundred credits a piece missy. You can purchase tickets over there," he points behind us and we both look.

There is a booth with a person inside, and people in line out front of it. For purchasing tickets to get on the train, the line is rather small, in comparison to the number of people on top of the building.

"Thank you!" She lets go of my hand and runs off to stand in the line, leaving me feeling insecure.

I see it coming around a turn several buildings down. With two large lights on the front of it, it blinds me because I am watching intently. The speed it is traveling is just as unreal now as it was the last time I watched it. As it gets closer, I look behind me to find Ami is still in the line waiting to purchase tickets. Only a couple buildings away it speeds toward us. The train lets out such a large blast of noise that I am forced to cover my ears.

Squealing as it approaches, it comes to a halt in front of me, and the doors slide open to let waiting passengers out. There is a hustle as the people around me come and go, and I end up shoved in several different directions. Lost in the crowd, I look behind me to where Ami was. She is gone. I panic and begin to look around frantically, but with the sea of people still beating me around like an ocean, I cannot see her.

"Ami? Ami where are you?" My voice is nearly drowned out by the surrounding people.

Another large blast of noise sounds from the train.

"Ami?!" I continue to yell.

Grabbed by my arm, I am pulled in the direction of the train. Sliding in just before the doors close, we make it inside, and Ami smiles triumphantly at me.

I smile back nervously, trying to calm myself of the panic caused by mere moments of being separated from Ami in this absurdly-sized city, despite knowing she would not have left me.

The train begins to move, slowly at first, but then picks up. The platform where we were standing quickly disappears, and I watch in amazement as the scenery begins to change rapidly. She tugs on my arm and I am almost too entranced to move, but I realize that she's trying to get me to follow her to some open seats.

Though many people entered the train, the interior is larger than I thought, and we have plenty of room to move about. We sit down on one long seat that is facing the window opposite the door we came in. There is enough room for Ami and me to sit, but it leaves little room between us and other passengers on either side, making me feel cramped.

Ami pulls herself in close, and her hips and upper torso press against me. My hands start to sweat, and my body tenses, but looking down at her it seems she either does not notice or care as her attention is taken by the view outside.

We fly along at a high speed, and the buildings race through my vision. Then, as we turn, I see darkness followed by more buildings off in the distance. It seems like it might be the field that the house is in. We sit in silence, watching the scenery go by together. Her warm body pressed against my side makes my eyes heavy.

~~~~~~

My eyes snap open, and I am awake as the sun hits my face. I squint and see that it has begun to peek over some of the buildings' tops, and around one very large building that seems to tower over the others.

I shiver and groan, hating both waking up and the cold. Looking down, Ami is curled up on the seat, her head in my lap, and my hand across her collarbone. Realizing my hand is in a position that might be misconstrued

I quickly remove it, and notice that we are completely alone.

Where could everyone have gone? And why is the train not moving?

Ami grumbles and begins reaching for something, perhaps my hand that is no longer keeping her warm. When she cannot find it she rubs her eyes instead, and rolls over onto her back. She looks up at me and smiles sweetly. I smile back.

"Not to alarm you, but I think there is a problem," I tell her.

"What is it?" She groans while stretching her arms across me.

"It is morning, and the train is stopped." I point out the window.

"Oh no!"

Ami springs up, nearly smashing her face into mine, and presses to the window. She looks around, and begins mumbling to herself. I hear her say that her mother is going to kill her.

"So, what do we do?" I ask while getting up, and heading to where the door is.

She follows me.

"I have no idea where we are. All I'm seeing is city, buildings all around!"

The door is propped open partially, and we are able to slip out of it onto a rooftop. There is another train there in front of us, on the next building over, blocking us from seeing anything beyond it. As I survey the area, I see a few ticket booths and a stairway down.

"Over there." I point for Ami to see. "There are the stairs. I wonder if we could find someone to help us."

As I walk, Ami stops briefly to fuss with her hair, putting it up into a ponytail, and I do not recall her taking it down. She steps quickly to catch up, with a smile, and we make our way down the eerily empty walkway to the elevator. Ami reaches out and presses an arrow shaped button that is pointing down. When the doors don't open immediately, I listen intently. It starts out quiet, but eventually a humming noise resonates through the building, getting louder. The humming noise appears to peak, and the familiar 'ding' noise causes me to jump. Ami laughs.

"You okay?" she asks.

"Yeah, just a little unnerved right now for some reason."

"I guess hearing those noises in this quiet would do that to me too if it were my first time." She grins in a playfully mocking way.

"You are not going to pick on me now are you?" I poke at her side.

"'You're'," she corrects me while wrapping her arm in mine and poking me back. "And no, of course not! Why ever would I tell my mother how you jumped at the sound of a bell?"

The doors begin to close, and she thrusts her arm in between the two sliding pieces of metal. Alarmed, I attempt to stop her.

"Wait! Your arm!" I yell.

Ding. The doors open again and she giggles while jumping inside. My face turns red with embarrassment, and I enter. Turning around to face the doors, I cross my arms and look away from her.

"That is not funny! I thought you were going to be hurt," I protest her joke.

She presses a button labeled 'Ground', and then latches onto my arm once more.

"Of course it's funny. Because I knew I wouldn't get hurt, and you're cute when you're trying to be heroic."

The doors close, and we descend. I blush even harder, regardless of trying to ignore her comment. She promptly notices and points it out.

"Look at how red your face is!"

I release her arm, and turn to face the wall of the elevator. She jumps onto my back, wrapping her legs around my waist and pokes at my cheeks, squishing them together. In order not to fall over, I am forced to hunch and grab the railing that lines the interior.

"Look at Rain, everyone! Isn't he so cute when he blushes?!" She toys with me.

In the middle of trying to balance her while she pokes fun at my inability to control my blushing, the elevator stops. The doors slide open to reveal two men in blue and white striped uniforms, along with strange hats which have only a partial brim on them. They are toting around mops and an orange plastic tub with wheels.

"What're you doing here?" the taller of the two asks as he adjusts his wire frame glasses.

Before I can speak Ami buries her face in my hair and uses her hands to manipulate my mouth.

"We fell asleep on the train and when we woke up it was stopped! We were just leaving! Don't hurt us!" she deepens her voice, and jokes around pretending to be me.

"Well hurry on your way," the shorter and chubbier of the two says.

"Yes sir!" Ami continues the charade.

I haul her out of the elevator on my back, and we are in a building very similar to the one we entered to get up to the train. Heading down the stairs, we exit the building, and as we do the thought occurs to me that we should have asked one of the men where we were, and which way to go. But when I look back it is too late, they are gone. Stepping onto the road, I let go of her legs, and force her to stand on her own. Looking around, I become concerned about picking the right direction, and how far we are from the house. Without a soul in sight on this street I make a decision.

"I say we head to our left for now and see if we can locate someone," I suggest.

"That's fine. As long as we're together," she says.

"Hmm?"

"I mean, you know, as long as we don't get separated. That would be bad." She smiles innocently.

"Indeed it would." I smile at her and hold my arm out for her to take.

I am almost positive that she is not just hinting at liking me, but going out of her way to make sure I know.

As we walk down the street, there is something different. It is not a commercial area. There are no shops or welcome signs, but instead the buildings begin to space out, becoming fancier and nicer the farther we go. Their architecture is different, as their outsides are formed to look like large columns, and they have wide arches and carvings along their sides.

When I turn my head to the right, while passing an intersecting street, I can see the one building which reaches taller than the others. Though it is quite a ways down, I can see it clearly because it is separated from the other buildings. It has a similar style of this section of the city. I stop and stare at its majesty for a moment.

"I don't think we are going the right way," I tell her.

"I don't think so either."

Stopped, with four paths available for us to take, I look down each direction. When I turn my head to look back the way we came, I see two familiar figures off in the distance, and they are not friendly ones. Recognizing them as the two fighters that we saw coming out of Emma's shop the first day we met her, I pull Ami around the corner of the building as they head this way. I put my finger to my lips.

Did they recognize us as I did them?

Ami had not seen them, and is now giving me a questioning look, but it does not take her long to realize we are hiding from people as their voices can be heard. I strain my ear to hear what they are saying, but I am unsuccessful.

"Why are we hiding? Maybe they can help us," she says.

"They are the men from Emma's shop, the ones that were harassing her."

Her eyes widen, and she covers her mouth with one hand. I switch sides with her so I am near the corner, and peek around to see they are about a block away walking at a steady pace, not appearing to have seen us.

"Ami, go around the opposite corner of the building, and keep out of their sight," I whisper.

"What are you going to do?" She looks at me with confusion.

"Never mind. Just do it, please!" I whisper.

Ami lets go of my arm, and runs at full speed to the end of the building to duck around its corner. Seeing her peek her head out, I hug the wall near the building's corner pillar. I can hear their voices clearly now.

"I don't like the schedule. I wanna go back ta sleepin' durin' the day and bein' up at night."

I recognize the larger one's voice.

"Quit whining about it. It won't do any good, and frankly I'm tired of hearing it," his partner snaps at him.

"Didja hear what happened at lil' miss Emma's shop?" The big one asks.

"That Denis took things into his own hands, or that guy actually had the gall to chase him off?"

"Both I s'pose. Wonder who woulda had the brass ta run boss off."

They turn the corner, and I slink into the shadows of the pillar, hoping not to be noticed. I sit and bring my knees to my chest to make myself appear smaller, concealing the mass of my body as much as possible. They pass while continuing their conversation and I have the urge to follow them. When they are half a block up from me, I slink to a nearby doorway and continue to listen to their casual conversation.

"I wish they'd put in a day shift of the train to run us back and forth from the U.F.A. building and the market. I hate making the walk all the way to the commercial district," the skinnier one says while adjusting his dome hat.

For now, I find that I have gained a vital piece of information, discerning that the tallest building down the way is the location of the United Fighting Arts Emma spoke about. When there is sufficient space between us, I move up to the next doorway of this building, and hold my breath when they reach the corner I sent Ami toward.

Hoping that she too took refuge within a door way or something similar, I wait quietly to find out if they see her, crouching to spring into a sprint if needed. But there is no reaction from them. They continue on past the next intersection, toward the building with the arches more grand than the ones on these, and I hug the wall until I get to the corner. Turning around it, I find Ami is not there.

Ducking into another doorway on the new side of the building, I keep hidden to avoid detection on the chance that the two men look back. In the shadows I am attacked as arms wrap around my neck, and I now have a person on my back. I turn my head and see Ami smiling, as if nothing is wrong.

"Did you find anything out?" she asks.

"Yeah, first is that we are indeed going the wrong way. They just came from the commercial district, so we should head back the way we came," I tell her, and then point to the tall building. "Second is that I believe that is the U.F.A. building."

We wait until they are mere dots in our sight, and then return to walking arm-in-arm, following the building back to our original street and heading toward where we had exited from the stairwell.

Walking for a significant amount of time, I watch the building styles gradually change from the nicer style with a significant amount of thought put behind the architecture, to the simpler style. But that too changes and we find ourselves in a section of the city which is in disrepair.

The street turns at an angle, and we are heading in between two of the shortest buildings I have seen within the city yet. Their brickwork appears old, and their chimneys have all but crumbled.

A discomfort falls over me as we near, despite feeling like we are headed in the right direction. Walking through the alleyway between these two buildings, I survey and see the rectangular windows have all been broken out from the inside, as glass is littered all over the ground. That unease creeps up in my spine, and my muscles tense up in anticipation. I can tell Ami feels it too, as she clings tightly to my arm when we reach the corner of the buildings.

Our bodies have warned us with good cause, as a scruffy man appears hastily from our left wearing a long dark coat, its hood shadowing most of his face. He grits and bares his teeth while wielding a large knife in his hand. Whatever has caused his desperation, he now exacts it on us as he menacingly waves the knife in our direction.

"Give me any credits you have!" He growls.

Ami slinks behind me, her arms grabbing onto my sweater.

"Should you not be sleeping?" I ask him, trying to contain the fear in my voice.

"No, I'm a day walker. Now give me your credits!" He thrusts the knife in a threatening manner.

"We have none to give," I refuse his demand.

"Give me any valuables you have, or you'll be in the obituaries tomorrow!" he barks.

"Ami, back up," I whisper.

"But," she protests.

"Do it, now," I demand.

Her hands release from my sweater, and I hear her run a few feet back. The man moves to run after her, but I intercept and block his path to her. My heart begins to pump harder, and I get a boost of energy.

"Look, friend, we have nothing for you." I hold my arm out in front of my body to stop him. "We just want to go home."

"Well I'm *so* sorry, let me just give you a free pass through my territory this once," sarcasm rings through his voice.

"No heart? Cannot let us pass this once?"

"No, and no."

He comes at me with the knife held in both hands at his stomach level. As his arms extend outward to stab me, I dodge with ease, keeping me from being stabbed. Kicking his left shin as he passes, I cause him to falter. He grunts, turns around and tries again, this time holding the knife like one would a sword. With his right arm out too far, and his feet wide I notice several weaknesses within his stance.

Hurriedly he tries to assault me again, but switches methods. When he gets close he draws the knife up, and swings downward, trying to catch me in a shoulder, or the chest.

Resolving to show no fear, I wait for him to get just close enough that the metal nearly tastes my flesh, and then dodge down and lean my left side back so that his swipe misses me completely. Coming back up from the dodge, I plant my palm into his chin, and his teeth clatter together. He lands on his back. The knife is thrown from his hand, and spins across the ground. Ami hurries to step on it while he groans and spits out blood to the road.

My muscles loosen, and I find myself staring malevolently down at him while he wipes the blood from his lips. I cannot tell how much I have broken, but when he looks up at me I can see the spirit he had when he was attacking is part of it. He makes no attempt to get back up. When I look up at Ami I can see that she is still quite scared. Leaving the man, I move to her, retrieve the knife, and take her arm in mine to lead her away.

"Next time when someone just wants to pass, I suggest you let them." I wave the knife by the blade, showing him that I am taking it with me.

He starts to get up and I watch him carefully, but he retreats to the side of the building and leans against it.

Ami tugs on my arm, and we find our way through unhindered. The road turns slightly again, and several buildings down I toss the knife next to yet another run down building.

"I suppose it would do no good to ask where you learned to fight like that," Ami breaks our silence.

"Not really. It just came to me like second nature," I tell her. "That is not the first time I have noticed it though."

"Oh?" She looks up at me inquisitively.

While we make our way through the city, I tell her about Evalyn's attempts to assault me. She seems a bit disconcerted, but does not have much to add. We fall silent, and eventually I see a break in the buildings. Pointing it out to her brings the excitement back into her face.

"I will give you a five second head start," I challenge her.

"Five? I don't need one! I'll beat you there with ease," she scoffs with a smirk.

"All right. Ready?" We both prepare to break into a full sprint. "Go!"

I push off hard with my left foot and begin running at full speed, my arms swinging against my sides, and my lungs pumping. Pulling into the lead right away, and creating a gap of a few feet between me and her, I feel confident that victory will be mine.

Buildings seem to whir by us as we have our friendly contest. However, as I continue to run, my lungs begin to burn, starting out only as a little pain, but quickly increasing until it is hard to breathe. I struggle to keep running by breathing in through my nose and out through my mouth, but it is too late to mitigate the pain. Looking over my shoulder I see that my lead on Ami is closing rapidly as she keeps a steady pace.

Am I so out of shape that she is going to beat me?

My calves have started to burn as well, and I lose momentum. I cannot bear it any longer, my body forcing me to slow down while I watch Ami blow past me. Trying to get my rapid and painful breathing under control proves useless, as I instinctually breathe in deeply trying to catch my breath. My pride however convinces me that I am just being weak and I can go more. I attempt to run again, but this time my scar protests. Stopping dead in my tracks, I hunch over and rest my palms against my knees. While I wait for the pain to subside, Ami returns.

"Are you okay?" she asks while laying her hand on my shoulder.

"Yes. My scar is just hurting."

"Guess we'll have to finish our race later."

She props me up with her body, slinging my arm over her shoulder, and we find our way to the edge of the field together. We have come out of the city at a much different location than we entered it, now facing the side of the house which has the well. It only takes us a few more minutes to reach the door, and the moment we are inside the living room the kitchen door bursts open. Agatha jumps through it, wielding a knife at us.

"More knives?!" I protest.

"Where have you been? There are things that need to be done around this house, and I've been doing them by myself," Evalyn yells at us.

"We're sorry Aunt Evalyn." Ami looks down at the floor.

"I'd show you 'sorry' if it were still just the two of us," Evalyn snaps at her.

"Evalyn, enough! Did you die while menstruating?" It just slips out.

Ami snaps her head up, staring at me, and the shock on both their faces is quite apparent. The feeling of having crossed the line begins to nag at the back of my mind while silence ensues. But there is no backlash from Evalyn. In fact, I can see the change in Agatha's face that Evalyn has left, and Agatha is herself once more. Agatha looks down at the knife she's holding and lowers it, relaxing.

"I don't think that's ever happened before," Agatha says.

"What?" I ask.

"Her backing down and leaving." She taps her lips with her index finger a few times, appearing to contemplate while looking at me.

"She has likely gone to plot my demise while I am sleeping." I nervously laugh.

"Make sure to lock your door tonight!" Ami prods me in the ribs with her knuckles. I smirk and prod her back.

"So, what is there to be done today?" I ask Agatha.

~~~~~~

A month and a half ago I nearly died from a fatal stab wound and yet here I am now peacefully pulling weeds from a garden that belongs to my saviors. I may not remember what my life was like then, but this has to be better by far if someone wanted me dead. Somehow, manual labor just feels right. It feels good.

The sun beats against my back, and the heat feels nice because the past couple days have been overcast and cold. As I grab the base of a weed springing up between the ground cherries and strawberries, I am thankful for the pair of form fitting gloves Ami bought me with some of her money. I pull it up by the roots, toss it into the pile I have going, and move carefully down to the next weed that I can see.

While I am still unsure of the nature of my relationship with Ami, I cannot…can't help but think that we have become great friends. Friends who flirt? I suppose it can't be helped because we live together and the time we're actually near each other has been increasing. I guess I can thank Agatha for suggesting Ami teach me about things.

And it has been quieter since my brash but effective comment toward Evalyn. It's almost eerie that she has been so quiet, even when she has shown herself. I wonder if I should apologize to her.

I see Agatha returning from the city, still a distance away. She appears to be walking at a fast pace just short of jogging. Her flowing dress hinders her a bit. When I see urgency on her face, I stand up, throw the collection of weeds in my hand into the pile, and dust myself off. Moving to intercept her, she starts talking before we meet.

"Quick, Emma's shop is being destroyed by those thugs!"

"Now?" I toss my gloves on the ground.

"Yes! They're going to hurt her!"

"I will be back."

I begin jogging toward the city, pacing myself so I don't over exert like the other day. Finding a good pattern of breathing to the speed in which my feet hit the ground, I make my way across the trodden down grass toward the city line. With daylight dwindling, I do my best to remember the way to her shop. It takes me only a short while to make it there by taking a short cut down a few alleyways. As I come out between buildings, I find Emma's sign to my right.

As I get to the window, I look in to see the two thugs that seem to wander the city on Denis's command stirring up trouble.

The smaller one begins knocking baskets off of their stands, and stomps on her merchandise. I become infuriated. Swiftly walking toward the door, I am forced to jump into a roll to my left as a table comes flying through Emma's newly installed window. She cries.

"Stop! Stop! I'll pay! Just don't destroy anything else!" she pleads for their mercy.

"It's triple now. Denis's angry that you haven't paid him any of your protectin' money," the muscular thug hollers at her.

As I stand back up and move to enter the door, glass fragments crack under my feet, and there is no element of surprise now. Swinging the door open hard, I clear my throat to get their attention.

"You have one chance to leave," I issue a stern command as I see Emma beginning to swipe a credits card.

The big one turns around and glares at me from under his hat.

"Or what? You gonna teach us a lesson?" His rather deep voice gives the impression he's attempting to intimidate me.

"I just might."

I see Emma still continuing to issue her transaction on the PayPad.

"Emma, don't give it to them."

"But..." She looks up at me with tears.

"No 'buts' Emma. I'll take care of this."

I step in one more foot length. Emma stops, and now I have the attention of the smaller thug also.

"I think you better mind your own business, lest Driesen here has to see that you don't bother anyone ever again," the smaller man speaks.

"If you are going to threaten someone you better be able to make good on it." I frown.

Rather spry for someone with bulk muscles, Driesen lunges and swings at me with a ham sized fist. I duck it easily enough, but before I have recovered, his other set of knuckles are coming at me. I spread my legs with one forward, one behind and throw my hands out to brace for the impact.

When he connects, I use both of my hands to deflect. It throws his arm up over my head and past me, unbalancing him. I take the opportunity to throw a few quick jabs in on his exposed side, but he simply laughs as my punches hit solid muscle. Driesen recovers from being thrown out of balance, and begins throwing punch after punch at me. With each successful block or deflection, it becomes more difficult.

He pushes me toward the door, and as I feel my back press against the glass, I stand prepared to block another blow, even though my arms have become sore from blocking. He winds up and launches his left fist at me with great might, and being trapped against the glass I only have one option.

Things seem to go into slow motion while I spin my left shoulder and turn my back into him. Before his fist even hits the glass, I grab his wrist with both of my hands, secure my left shoulder into his left armpit area, and lurch my body down and forward while pulling.

Driesen's own momentum and weight work against him, and he is quickly airborne, flipped over and thrown into the door back first. The glass shatters, and the doorframe bends under the impact of his mass. Dropping to the floor, he lands with a thud and groans.

But before I can celebrate my victory against him, I am being repeatedly hit in the back. As my assailant hits me in several locations, it becomes crippling and I fall to my knees. Driesen reaches up and grabs the collar of my shirt, and the hammering against my back stops.

While Driesen gets back up, he tries to hold me from getting away, but I slip out of my shirt. Giving no warning to the smaller thug I turn around and jump into him, one knee forward.

He tries to block it but I connect with him in the gut. He's stunned momentarily, dramatically exhaling. I plant a right hook into his temple while he is hunched over, right before Driesen grabs me by the shoulders and swings me into the door frame, slamming my back against the metal.

I feel it dig into my bare skin, but somehow escape the shards of glass still stuck in the door. I lose my breath for a moment, but quickly regain composure.

Driesen switches from holding my shoulders to pin me by the neck, choking me. Against the door frame, between being choked and Driesen preparing to smear my face between his fist and the metal, it occurs to me that playing fair is not on their list of things to do, and neither should it be on mine.

I stick my leg out the doorframe to get better leverage, and tear my pants on a piece of glass. Driesen draws back his free hand. I grab the arm pinning me and, as his fist is coming at me, I swing my foot forward and nail him in the groin. The beast lets out a massive wail and drops me.

Back on the ground, I swing my foot into his shin. He wavers while dry heaving, and I kick him in the other shin. The pain caused by my first blow and the two to his shins causes him to collapse.

On the ground with his hands cupped over his precious area, he is vulnerable, and I make the final moves. Sitting on his chest I swing a left hook, and when my fist collides with his jaw I watch as he loses consciousness. I huff heavily, fury coursing through my veins, and when I look up to confront the smaller thug I find that he is already out cold, my temple blow had incapacitated him. I stand victorious over two bodies that I have no idea what to do with now.

"I…" Emma runs over, throws her arms around me, and begins crying. "I was so scared!"

"It's going to be all right. I will take them out of here and then I am going to visit Denis." I ruffle her hair a little and comfort her while she wails.

"You were so heroic!" she continues to talk through her bursts of tears.

I put my hands on her shoulders to separate us. She resists, but I finally pry her from my bare torso and kneel down to wipe her tears away with my palms. I shush her quietly and she sniffles, trying to calm herself.

"I am sorry about your broken door. I don't have any credits to fix it. But I am going to stop Denis from harassing you for good." I try to speak smoothly but the words come out somewhat unsure.

"Thank you! Thank you! Thank you!" She throws her arms around my neck and hugs tightly onto me.

It's rather awkward having her cling to me without my shirt on, only made even more embarrassing when a shrill voice rings out behind me.

"What do you think you're doing to that little girl?! What happened here?" Ami shouts.

Startled I jump up and spin around with my hands in the air.

"I was comforting her. And as for them, well, I had to stop them before they hurt Emma." I laugh, and scratch the back of my head nervously.

"So you're going to clean this up are you?" She puts her hands on her hips and gives me a blank look.

"In a manner of speaking. We need to bind their hands behind their backs before they recover."

I reach down and grab my shirt, putting it back on.

That boy Denis needs a good corporal punishing. Where are his parents?

"Well?" Ami asks.

"'Well', what?" I respond.

"What is your plan?" She frowns and pokes me in the chest.

"I am going to go find Denis, and I bet these two know where to find him. I don't know what I am going to do just yet but I intend on stopping Denis's terrorizing."

"You're going to do that with a cut leg?" Ami inquires.

"What?" I look down and find that where I snagged it on the door earlier actually cut into my flesh.

Pulling up my pant leg, I find that a piece of glass gashed me pretty well and my blood is running down my leg freely. Now aware that it exists, my body responds with pain to let me know it is damaged.

"I'll fix you up, Rain!" Emma's voice has returned to its normal cheery form.

Turning around, I find she has already sprinted for the door at the back wall. While Emma disappears into the back of the shop, Ami moves in through the broken door, and glass crackles under her footsteps. She leans in and whispers to me.

"Rain, what are you doing? You really shouldn't be exerting too much energy. You may be healed on the outside but we have no way of telling if your wound is fully healed on the inside," she says with concern.

I lean in a little to whisper back, "It will be okay. Besides, I cannot stop here. Something is compelling me to do this, and now I am invested, I have to see it through. If I don't something bad will happen to that little girl."

Emma reappears from that door in a hurry with a box in her arms, with a big red cross on it. Dropping down gently so she does not cut herself, she opens it and grabs a pair of scissors, cutting the bottom half of the pant leg clean off.

"Hey! I could have mended that!" Ami protests.

"They're only pants," Emma sneers and begins tending to the wound, first making sure there is no glass inside.

"Pants that *I* made for him!" Ami huffs loudly.

"Well then you can just make more," Emma titters.

Dabbing my leg with a rag, she soaks up the blood and then pulls out a metal can. But unlike the ones that hold food, when the top of it is pressed it makes a hissing noise and sprays me with something. I jump, startled – it feels like it is burning my skin – but as I watch, it foams up all around my wound. She uses some strange bandages to pull the gash closed, places a piece of gauze on it and wraps it up snuggly, clipping it in place when the roll runs out.

"There! All better!"

"Thanks Emma. Now we need some rope." I point at the two incapacitated men on her floor.

She disappears once more into the doorway, returning with a couple smaller spools of rope slung over her shoulder. Taking them from her, I move to the smaller of the two thugs as he begins to groan. I flip him on his stomach and bind his wrists together, making sure to tie a couple tight knots with the end so that if he attempts to free himself, he will at least have to struggle to do it, and give me a chance to knock him down again. I drag him over to Driesen, and proceed to double the knots for his bindings due to his size. The skinnier man comes to and begins to struggle.

"I would not do that. I tied your arms in a way that if you struggle too much the rope will sever your hands," I bluff, having done the best I knew how and made it look good.

"The U.F.A. will not take kindly to this," he snarls.

"Don't worry, Mister…?" I trail off waiting for his name.

"Grada. Anthony Grada."

"Well, don't worry Mister Grada, they will not take kindly to what I am about to do to them either, but nonetheless it will happen. Now, let's stand you up," I am firm with him.

I move around his back and tug on the rope that binds his hands together, forcing his arms to bend up behind his back unnaturally, and causing him pain. He stands up hastily, and I shuffle him out to the road. Noticing a few people have gathered due to the commotion, I watch them lean and whisper amongst themselves, prompting me to give them a show. I grin and wave my arm at them.

"Rain!" I hear Emma call from inside the shop.

I turn around and look to see Driesen rolling around, struggling to get free. Handing my end of the rope to Ami, I move to intercept Driesen.

"You just stay put Mister Grada, else I will have to chase you down and do unpleasant things. Believe me when I say you don't want that," I warn him sternly while entering the shop.

As Driesen squirms around, grunting and trying to break the ropes, I put my knee into a soft spot on his back and pull up on the rope's end until he hollers out in pain and stops.

"You and Mister Grada are going to take me to the U.F.A. building and we are going to sort this whole 'protection money' thing out with Denis. If you attempt to get away, I will incapacitate you again, and this time I will tie you up in a much more unpleasant way."

"Yous won't get away with this," he grumbles.

"What is there to get away with? Who is going to stop me?" I puff myself up to them, despite being injured and in pain.

Silence follows. I slowly stand up, and pull on the rope, coercing him forcefully to stand with me. As he climbs to his feet following my unspoken command, I twist his arms to get him to go where I need him to. We exit the building together and I stand him next to Anthony, both facing me.

"Now then, you are going to take me to the U.F.A. building, and I am going to speak with Denis," I direct them. "You will walk a few feet apart from each other and if either of you try to escape I will drop you both."

It is strange. The words coming out of my mouth are confident. Between the events that have been happening over the past couple weeks and now, the confrontations, I'm not sure if this change in me is good or not. But I suppose being able to assert myself to protect people is not terrible.

"I'm coming with you." Ami grabs my hand.

"You should help Emma clean up. I don't want to put you in any danger."

"Don't be silly." Emma springs to life from the door of her shop, and clings to my other arm. "We're coming with you."

"Your shop..." I start.

"Is destroyed," she finishes.

"What if *you* get hurt?" Ami asks.

"Then they would likely turn to hurt you and Emma next. I really need you to stay here." I turn my head, smile at her, and then whisper. "Besides, you are older: you should set a good example and keep her out of danger."

Ami lets out a loud 'humph' while crossing her arms, but after a few moments of me pleading with my eyes, she drops her arms to her sides and reaches her hand out for Emma to take. Emma protests, but I let her hand go and smile. She reluctantly takes Ami's hand, and I turn to the thugs.

"All right men, we have a long walk ahead. Best we get started now," I grab their ropes like the reins of a horse and whip them along.

They turn and begin walking, following parallel to the park, and though I cannot see the tower that is the U.F.A. building, I know they are leading me in the right direction.

~~~~~~

After walking at a steady pace for about an hour, we have arced our way through the city, past the run-down section, and found our way into the nicer area where Ami and I woke up on the train.

While they have been silent and cooperative for the time being, I keep my guard up to prevent any surprises. Looking over my shoulder every now and then nervously, I cannot help but make sure we are not being followed, by the girls or otherwise.

"So what is Emma to you? Why get involved in our affairs?" Anthony asks from my front left.

I see no harm in some conversation and it will certainly pass the time faster.

"I saw a little girl being picked on by grown men for money. If that is not morally bankrupt I am not sure what is. She needed help."

"So yous don't actually know her?" Driesen asks.

"Sure I do. We have a business relationship."

"I remember you. You were coming in with two women one day with all that food," Anthony recalls.

"That is correct." There are a few moments of silence before I speak again. "So what is in it for you to beat up on little girls?"

"We don't bother people that pay their protection fee," Anthony replies.

"It is not really a protection fee if you are the one that is tearing her down, is it? Back to my question: what's in it for you?" I ask a little more firmly.

"Boss pays our bills. Boss says ta do it, we do it," Driesen responds.

"So Denis, a child, tells you what to do and gives you money for it, even if it is wrong?"

There is silence again as we continue to walk, and I see the U.F.A. building come into sight. Getting closer than I had previously, it sits separated from the other buildings, a large perimeter of solid ground surrounding its base. I find its black exterior quite ominous and the dark windows make me feel like I am being watched from each and every one of them.

"We used ta be fighters. We were paid by the boss's dad ta fight each other. People would come from all over ta see us fight," Driesen speaks up. "The pay was better then."

"Well, what happened?" I ask.

"Denis's father went away on a business trip," he continues. "He's been gone for a while and only Denis gets ta talk ta him."

Message by bird? Or courier?

"I miss the ol' boss."

"Why not get him to come back? And what happens if he does?" I ask.

"We'd probably go back to the old ways, fighting each other for money," Anthony replies.

Our conversing stops when we near the entrance to the building. There is a large arch above the doorway with amazing and intricate swirling patterns covering it. Several doorways line the exterior, but I find that rather than traditional push or pull doors, there are pieces of glass hinged at one point and slowly rotating as if to let one person in at a time. Posted out front are two very husky, bald men guarding the doors in blue pants and red straps that are hooked onto the front of the pants, which strap up and over their shoulders to their back sides. When we reach the door the men speak.

"What do…" the first one speaks.

"…you want?" the second one finishes the first one's sentence.

"I want to see Denis. We have some business to discuss."

"Driesen…" first one.

"Anthony…" second one.

"What is…" first one.

"…going on here?" second one.

"Wow, that's extremely annoying. Can just one of you talk and the other be silent?" I bark at them.

"They could, but you'd only get half a what they're sayin'." Driesen's deep chuckle fills the air.

"This man has stopped us from collecting money and tied us up. He wants to see Denis," Anthony replies.

"Denis won't…" first one.

"…like that!" the second one finishes.

"Hey," I yell at them and point my finger. "I don't care what Denis will and will not like. I am going in to see him! Anthony, Driesen, show me in."

I advance with Anthony and Driesen still in front of me, and the two large men move into our path. My patience wears thin, my energy doing the same. I resolve not to show weakness.

What would be the best and easiest way to take down these two? Use them against each other?

"Move or I will be forced to make you move," I warn them.

"No," they speak in unison this time.

Acting impulsively, I push between Anthony and Driesen, and dart to the gap between them. The husky men quickly apprehend me between their two stomachs. I slam my foot down on one of the right one's feet and he squeals, loosening their belly grip on me. The one on my left reaches down and grabs me by the shoulders, lifting me up to his level and shakes me rapidly. Dizziness sets in, and the other one hits me in the back with his club of a fist.

Being up in the air provides me an opportunity. Leaning back as far as I can, and then swinging my head forward, I use my forehead to crack him right in the bridge of his nose, feeling it shatter. He drops me to grab his nose, but it does him no good the way the blood gushes to the ground. He wails.

"Last warning. Let me pass unharmed." I turn to the one who is not bleeding.

"Not going to…" he starts, but the other is too busy trying to control his bleeding and wailing to finish the sentence.

"Fine," I say, frowning.

A strange thought occurs to me when the fat man tries to grab me.

Why am I so adept at fighting? I seem to know just how to get what I want in a fight.

His girth works against him, and I am able to maneuver and elude his grasp. He swings around and tries to backhand me as I move under one of his arms and to his side, but he misses. I jab at his kidney, but his fat is too thick that I am not able to get in a solid blow. He swings around again and I evade his attack, switching places to find myself no longer in between the two of them.

The one whose nose I crushed seems to no longer care that his face, chin, neck and shirt are being completely soaked with blood, and joins his brother's side again. They move as quickly as they can to overtake me, but I back away, out of their reach. As the one who is still unharmed takes the lead, I get an idea and turn around, running away.

"Look at him run..." the one in front starts.

"...he's scared," the second one finishes.

Turning back around, having put a dozen feet in between us, I run at the one in front full speed. I see his legs brace and his arms outstretch to grab me, but leaping into the air I swing both legs out in front of me and plant my feet into his sternum. A look of surprise and dismay appears across his face while toppling backward onto his brother. He exhales all of the air from his lungs.

Falling onto my elbows and hip, I feel the abrasiveness of the solid ground, but I spring to my feet again, ready to go. Alert, my eyes dart around, and I find that while I have been tussling with these two, Anthony and Driesen have found the opportunity to disappear. Looking at the brothers, the one I kicked in the chest flounders on the ground, choking and gasping for air, while his brother stumbles around.

Should I be thankful that Driesen and Anthony didn't decide to add in to this already overweight fight, or uneasy about where they have disappeared to?

With the twins muddled, I move toward the doors. Without anyone to guide me, I realize I am stuck searching this ridiculously large and unknown building for Denis. Pushing on the glass as it moves around, I jump in nervously as it spins, closing me in between three pieces of glass for a brief moment. The door spins so quickly, that as soon as I have entered, I have exited.

Upon entering this building, I am met with a very different layout of interior features which I am unfamiliar with, but signs everywhere give me indications of what it is all for. To my immediate front is a row of a dozen small booths with doorways to what lies beyond in between each one. Blocked by walls on either side of the dozen booths, my way forward is through one of the entrances labeled 'Ticket Sales' on a placard hanging from the ceiling. Moving cautiously through, it opens up to an area which is slightly larger, but a wall runs left to right and I notice several areas of importance noted with more signs. Looking around nervously, the quietness begins to unnerve me, and I attempt to find my direction.

Directly in front of me lies a set of double doors, with more booths labeled 'Bidding Posts' on either side of it. As I move toward the wall, a hallway runs the length of the building and I find a couple illuminated elevator signs. Walking on tiptoes, I put my hand on the handle of one of the doors, but it will not budge. Noticing a little lever at the top of the handle I attempt to press it down, but find it locked in place. However, luck favors me when I try the other handle, and I hear an internal click. Looking around once more before pulling I feel as if I am a criminal creeping around, but I remember that my goal is noble.

Looking in, beyond the door is a dimly lit room with rows upon rows of seats which spiral around the room, all facing the center where a large fighting ring exists. I recognize its likeness to something floating around in my brain where men in suits of metal armor would swing swords at each other, and fight until one was incapacitated or dead.

A strange thing to remember at a time like this.

Off to my right, above the seats, there is a closed-off room with a large viewing window looking down into the ring. A light on inside piques my interest.

As I am about to enter, a familiar sound causes my heart to skip a beat. Ding! The sound of an elevator opening to my right startles me, and I move to hide myself behind the door.

Inside the arena, I close it quietly and rush down a set of stairs into the spiraling seats, ducking down in between two rows to my right.

My fear ignites when I hear the same door click open, and voices begin to echo throughout the arena. Crawling on my belly like a snake, my arms and legs swiftly carry me to another break in the seats and more stairs. Hiding as best I can amongst the seats I listen intently, gauging the distance of their voices rather than what they are saying. When they make their way down the stairs to the ring, I breathe a sigh of relief. They're dressed up identically, and in funny clothing. Each appears to be wearing a multicolored single piece that wraps all the way from their heads down to their shins, and I am reminded of a jester, dressed to entertain.

Every one of their steps threatens to expose me should they turn around. Crouching, I move as silently as possible to the adjacent chairs, and get down on my stomach again. I notice that I have inadvertently been moving closer to the room to the right. Hoping to take refuge within, I slink quietly along while they converse, and as I reach the door on the side of the booth I pull it open and slip in.

Locking the door behind me, I am alone again, and I can breathe normally. Keeping to the wall, so as not to be seen from the outside, I survey the room. It is decorated from wall to wall with large pictures of many different people dressed in fantastic ways. A dark brown, polished desk sits at the back of the room, and a comfortable looking, empty chair is beyond.

Moving along the wall to the desk, I finally exit the view of the window, and I take a seat in the chair. Scattered papers litter the top of it, and some appear to have not been touched in a long time, but a singular object has fresh ink on it. A book is sprawled open to a page which had been written in just recently, and I can see a list of businesses and credit amounts. Thumbing through, I find that Denis's extortion efforts are wide, as each page has a multitude of business names. Snooping further, I find a map of the city, titled 'Chas'. Its expanse on paper makes it seem much smaller, as beyond the borders of Chas, farmland is labeled and it spans at least double the size of the city.

Closing the book to take it with me, I am shook while sitting in the soft chair, and a deep hum fills the room. Watching out the window, the arena begins to move down and finally disappear, blocked by a solid wall. The whole room is moving upward, like a giant elevator. Though I think to exit at some point, I wonder where I might end up if I opened the door out of here now.

Where is this taking me? Did I press something I should not have?

The room arrives at the next arena floor, but continues to pass by. Walking to the window, the wall turns into another fighting ring beyond the window and there are more people on this second floor arena. They notice me and puzzled looks cross their faces, realizing I am not supposed to be here. But even as they start toward the room, there's nothing they can do about me because the room is in motion.

Floor by floor the room heads up the massive building, and with each level I pass, more people become alerted to my presence. Letting out a chuckle, I feel a bit smug that they cannot do anything about me being here. The room comes to a halt with a jolt, and the door flings open.

"What is he doing in there?!" Denis yells at two muscular bodyguards who are not dressed as outrageously as the others. "He has my journal!"

"I believe we have some things to discuss, Denis." I wave the book at him with a grin.

"That's mine! Give it to me! Make him give it to me!" he begins whining, and then looks at his guards for help.

A guard quickly takes a step forward, and attempts to snatch it from my hand. I step back out of the way, and as he oversteps into my reach, I drop my torso down and jam my shoulder into his ribs sharply shoving him to my right. He stumbles into the window and tries again, swinging his fist toward my jaw in a right hook.

With incredible instincts, I drop the book and kick it behind me a few feet. Then I grab his fist and his upper arm, and use his own momentum to swing him around and slam him into the glass again, shattering it.

I am too adept at this to have been a butcher or farmer in my time. Because I vaguely remember a fighting ring, does that mean I was a fighter?

As the first guard hangs through the broken glass, I turn my attention back to Denis, but he has begun running, escorted by his other guard, and heading for a door in the same location as the one on the bottom floor.

"You are not getting away from me," I mumble.

I grab the book and run after him. The door closes long before I can get there, but I race to catch up, running out into an unknown part of the building. The layout is similar to the bottom floor, with only a few notable differences such as stairs leading up and down to my direct front, instead of ticket booths. The elevator to the left dings and I see them duck in. Though I rush to make it, the elevator doors close before I reach them. Numbers light up above the elevator, and they climb from twelve to twenty.

Must not be trying to escape.

I press the button to go up, and wait for the elevator to return. When it is half way back to me a horde of fighters, the same ones I saw while riding up in the room elevator, have begun appearing down the hall in the opening where the stairs are. They spot me, and one of them points. Quickly they begin to move to intercept me. When I look up the elevator is still at sixteen. They begin to get closer, but when I hear a ding before expected, I look to the elevator door and find that this one has not opened. The one a few banks down has. I rush over to it to find the twins from outside looking at me, dumbfounded.

My chance to get away from the fighters massing and moving toward me dwindles, and I act impulsively.

"Get out! Get out or I am going to beat you senseless!" I yell and move my arms excitedly.

There is fear in their eyes, not wanting to deal with me again, and they do as they are told. Jumping in before they are out, I press the number twenty on the pad of numbers. The doors begin to close, and someone yells about stopping the elevator, but the twins stand in inaction.

When the doors have closed and I ascend through the tower, I sigh, relieved I have a moment or two to catch my breath.

For all I know there are more of these fighters waiting for me when I get to the twentieth floor. Hopefully he is not hard to reach.

It reaches my chosen floor, and I hide against the side of the elevator, preparing to assault anyone that comes through. The elevator dings, and the doors open. There is silence for a few moments while I wait patiently for any attacker who may also be making an attempt to be cautious. But no one enters. I poke my head around the corner. This floor is much different than the others. There is a small very nicely furnished rectangular room there to greet me. I take notice of a few chairs scattered about, a couple tables with flowers in pots, and a large set of solid wood doors, but there is not a soul in the room.

As I exit the elevator, I cautiously look around to find that only three elevators reach this high, and there are no apparent stairs up to this location. Making my way toward the big doors, the elevator closes behind me, and the other two have come to life. The situation becomes urgent and rather than being quiet, I psych myself up by breathing in and out a few times, puff up my chest, and kick the doors in.

They fly open, and I am caught off guard by Denis's other bodyguard rushing through and slamming two fists into my chest.

Exhaling violently, I am staggered, and he takes the opportunity to unleash a fury of punches and kicks that cause my body to scream out in pain. Aiming for the tender parts, he hits my ribs, sternum, my left kidney and finally my temples as he swings both of his fists into each side of my head.

Dry heaving, I fall to one knee. I block as much as I can with my arms, but he is relentless, and begins a series of kicks against my forearms to try and break my already weak defense. Desperate, I continue to block with my arms and the book while I move from one knee to crouching, preparing to spring up.

I time his kicks, and there is a brief moment of reprieve that becomes my chance. Pushing against the floor with all of my legs' strength and aiming as best as I can, I drop my arms from their defensive position and thrust my head forward. When my forehead connects with his abdomen, it catches him off guard and gives me an opportunity.

My turn.

He stumbles backward only a few inches, but I find it enough to throw the book at his face, and then a few blows at him. His abdomen is just as solid as my fists when I connect, causing my knuckles to crack and blare with pain. But despite the bruises forming all across my body, I continue anyway, distracting him with a light set of punches to his torso and abdomen.

He swings a left hook, but I turn my body sideways while lifting my leg. Overextended, and his knee exposed I bring my foot down directly into his kneecap as hard as I can.

A sickening crack can be heard, and he wails in pain, but his resolve is strong. He tries to keep going, putting all his weight on the other leg and swinging for a lucky shot. Now able to out-maneuver him, he misses again. I wait for an opportunity, ducking under and around missed blows, and when I see it, I clamp both hands together and swing them at his cheek. He collapses to the floor but looks up at me with ferocity.

"Stay down," I manage, panting heavily from the stress on my body and lungs.

"Or what?" he responds defiantly.

"I will make you regret it," I tell him.

He begins to get up, and I immediately take action, rushing at him and slamming my foot into his groin. His yell is so loud that it echoes throughout the room, and he collapses, rolling around in pain.

The first of the three elevators ding behind me and I turn to slam the wooden double doors shut before whoever is on the elevator can step off. With haste, I grab a couple chairs from within this room and jam them up against the handles. Banging ensues, but I have a moment to breathe.

This secluded room is much larger than the room that doubled as an elevator, but it has a similar layout. There are shelves and pictures lining the walls, and strange miniature statues and oversize belts on those shelves. A desk and chair block my path to a wide window that overlooks the edge of the city and out into the farmlands. The chair is turned facing the window, and from behind it I can hear Denis breathing as quietly as he can.

"This is over, Denis," my voice is firm.

"It isn't over until I say it is! My pops is going to get you for this!" He yells out from behind the chair.

"Does your father even know what you have been up to?" I ask him.

"Y...yes! He said that these guys would take care of me while he was away!" I can hear a quiver in his voice, despite his attempt to sound fearless.

"You are lying to me. I think I will just contact him," I bluff as I have no idea of how I could contact his father.

"No, don't!" he exclaims while spinning the chair around.

His sandy blonde hair reaches his cheekbones, and I can see the tears welling up in his eyes.

"Why not? If he knew what you were doing then it should not be a problem, right?" I cross my arms in front of me.

"Because he's on an important business trip and he will be mad if you call him!" The sniffling begins.

"Call him?" I am a little puzzled what this means, but play it off. "I was just going to have him come home and take care of this."

"No! No! No! I promise to be good! Please don't bring him home! I'll be in trouble." That breaks him and the bawling begins, a distinct look of fear on his face.

"Denis, you are in trouble anyway. The city is tired of you harassing them and they are not paying you anymore," I lie, continuing my charade. "Why not let your father come home and fix this?"

Two parts of me war inside. One laughs and urges me to torture the boy more with idle threats, while the other tells me to let it go and find a way to get his father to come home to straighten all of this out. It pleases me to make this child squirm, but I cannot understand why.

Perhaps because justice is prevailing, or could it be a darker side of me surfacing? I suppose with my past unknown it is hard to find what is driving me now.

"Fine, I'll call my pops." His tears begin to slow down and he looks over to some of the trophies on the shelf to his right.

The banging continues behind me – it sounds like the full horde of fighters is trying to get in here – but I wait patiently for him to do something, unsure of what.

"What? You want me to do it now?" Denis inquires.

"If possible, that is the idea."

"But…!"

"Don't try to squirm your way out of this! I am not leaving until it is done!" my voice raises a few notches.

Denis pulls out a small rectangular object similar to the PayPad, but it is slightly different. Instead of an area to swipe a card over, there is a circular device attached. Denis presses some buttons, and what happens next astonishes me. A small man sitting in a chair appears, see-through, with his back to me.

"Denis, I'm a busy man. What is it you need?" The little moving image speaks.

"Dad! I'm being picked on by a bully!" he complains.

"Now hold it…!" I begin to protest but am cut off.

"Must be a tough bully if he can get to you through all of my prized fighters there to protect you," he sounds annoyed.

"He beat them up!" Denis whines.

"If I could get a word in…" I try again.

The small transparent man spins in his chair and addresses me formally.

"And you must be him, since I don't recognize you and you're standing in my office." The man crosses his hands at chest level, placing his elbows on the armrests of his chair.

"Might I have a word?"

"Anyone that can break into my building and make it to the top without getting beaten, thrown out, or killed is worthy of a minute of my time. Say what you have to." He waves his hand, displeasure in his voice.

"Thank you. My name is Rain. I have recently come to this area, and become involved with some locals. Those locals are being harassed by your thugs…or fighters…whatever you call them. Denis has been extorting people of their money with the promise of 'protection' from him." I take a deep breath to continue. "Your men, Driesen and Anthony, recently ransacked a friend's shop, destroying it in the process because she refused to pay Denis this 'protection' money."

"That's a pretty wild claim. Do you have evidence of this?"

"Denis was keeping a log book of frequently hit stores and businesses." I pick the book back up and wave it around.

"My journal!" Denis exclaims.

"Denis, I'm coming home. I'll be there in a couple days and you and I are going to have a long talk. Keep that evidence safe, as I will require it when I get there."

"Yes, sir, Mister….?"

"Lindali."

"One more thing, Mister Lindali. Outside your office your fighters are trying to get in here, still pursuing me. How should I handle that?"

Mister Lindali turns back to Denis. "Activate the com-system."

"Yes, sir." Denis hangs his head in shame while pressing a few more buttons on the pad. "Com active."

"This is Trevor Lindali," his voice echoes through the room, and I assume on all floors of the building. "All fighters are to stand down, and the man who has breached the building is to leave unharmed. You are no longer to follow any of Denis's requests as I had directed before, except for basic necessities of food and care. I will be returning to the office within two days to straighten things out. End transmission."

With that, Denis hits a few buttons and sulks even more in the chair and the echoing stops. Mister Lindali turns back to me.

"That should take care of all the issues until I return. I will expect to see you here in two days time."

"You could send Driesen and Anthony for me when you arrive," I smirk at the thought of seeing their faces after all this. "I am staying at the house in the middle of the park."

"I wasn't aware there was a house there." He quirks an eyebrow at me.

"This has been a strange experience," I comment.

"Mmm. Indeed," he replies while rubbing his chin.

Removing the chairs from the doors, I pull them open. The once empty room is now filled with a variety of characters, all of which are giving me a dirty look. When I start to walk they open a path for me to the elevator. Pressing the number one for the first floor, I smile audaciously as the doors close, and I descend. At the bottom, Driesen and Anthony are there, unbound from my knots. I nod, and proceed to exit the elevator.

"Mister Lindali is going to have you come find me when he returns. I live in the house in the middle of the park."

"House in the middle....?" Anthony begins to question.

"Do not ask. Just know that I live there."

With that, I push by them, and exit through the booths and spinning glass doors at the front of the building. A long walk home through the city while my body aches leaves me worn. When I find that park, it is a beautiful sight. When I reach the door to the kitchen I push in to find Agatha there and she moves to aide me.

"Rain! What happened?" She looks at my face, examining it.

"Got in a few fights. I am going to go rest," I tell her with a weak smile.

"I should look at your wounds," she says in her motherly tone.

"After I sleep."

Moving away from her, my body hurts even more now I am coming down from my energy spike, and my muscles are beginning to relax. Climbing the stairs is a feat, but I manage to make it to my room. Without turning on the light, I gently lower myself onto the bed and close my eyes, the book squished under me.

~~~~~~

I hear a noise next to my ear, and it startles me. I open my eyes suddenly. In my peripheral vision I see a little blonde headed girl bent over, her eyes closed.

"What are you doing?" I ask her calmly.

Emma squeals and jumps up from a kneeling position and puts her arms behind her back while innocently looking out my window.

"I was just checking on you to see if you were okay!" she says slyly.

I sit up and rotate so my feet hit the cool floor. Smiling, I realize that after dealing with Denis the other day she has become infatuated with me, finding her hovering over me while I slept then, too.

I wonder, since we will be leaving here soon enough, if I should break it to her that she will have to detach herself from me, as well as from Ami and Agatha.

"What are you doing here?" I ask.

"I only wanted to make sure you were okay. You have a lot of bruises." She laughs nervously and retreats to the door to my room, but watches me intently.

I stand up, stretching my arms and legs, causing my body to protest with pain. I grunt. Though I have had a day to recuperate, my bruises tell me it will still be at least a week or two before my body starts feeling normal again. But normal seems to be an incorrect term to describe me. With violent tendencies and the ability to physically assert myself, coupled with a drive for justice, I am left plagued with wild ideas of who I used to be.

Moving toward the door causes Emma to retreat, and when I turn to head down the stairs she beats me to the bottom. Slowly and cautiously I take the steps one at a time while reflecting on the current situation.

I have not heard from Driesen or Anthony yet but the day is young. Mister Lindali said two days so I wonder how far he has to travel. Their technology and travel methods are so far beyond what I could have imagined. Two days walking is a significant distance, but how far is two days by their train system?

Emma was helpful enough yesterday teaching me a few more things about this time, but it still baffles me about their image technology. A miniature version of the person appearing out of thin air is baffling. But I suppose it all is still.

Reaching the bottom of the stairs, my bladder tells me that it is time to head for my morning bathroom routine. When Emma follows me down the hall I make sure to lock both doors, feeling a little bit smothered. After relieving myself, I wash my hands and take the opportunity to shave with a razor blade Agatha provided.

For the first time since my memory loss, I am growing a little stubble along the base of my chin and my upper lip. Though I cannot remember, I find that I am proficient at shaving when I lather my hands up thoroughly with a bar of soap, and then apply it to my face generously.

Rinsing my hands, I grab the single edged blade and place it carefully to my face while dragging it across slowly. It takes me a good fifteen minutes, and I cut myself a dozen times, but I manage to finish up. I wash up and dab my face with a dark hand towel, finding it difficult to get the bleeding to stop despite being minor nicks, but they eventually calm down.

Exiting the bathroom after cleaning up my mess, I find Emma has disappeared. I move to the kitchen door and the smell of fried eggs hits me. I salivate, and my stomach gurgles painfully. Pushing through, I am met with a waft of cool air from the open door, carrying that smell directly at me. Agatha, or perhaps Evalyn, is cooking, while Ami is lavishly spreading butter on a plate full of toast. Emma sits at the already set table, squirming in her seat as if she cannot control herself.

"Morning everyone," I announce myself.

Ami looks up and bursts into a fit of laughter.

"What happened to you? You look worse than when you came back from the U.F.A. building!" She continues to laugh at my bloody encounter with the razor.

"It is not that funny." I frown at her.

"Yeah! It's not funny! Rain is hurt!" Emma shouts at Ami. "Are you okay?!"

"Keep your voice down inside, young lady," Evalyn scolds her brashly.

"I am fine. Just cut myself a few times shaving." I pause before moving to the back door to toss my dirty towel out into the washbasin. "Is there anything I can help with?"

"No, sit down and wait," Evalyn snaps at me.

I do as she commands and Emma sits down in Ami's normal spot, right next to me, and I hear a small grumble from Ami as she notices the same attachment. But she does not speak out against her spot being taken. Emma crosses her arms on the table, and lays her head down on them, staring at me.

Is what I did worth such admiration?

"How's the cleanup of your shop coming?" I ask her.

"There's a lot of damage. It's going to take me some time to recover, but with not having to pay Denis anymore, I should be able to manage the losses to profit," she says while sitting back up.

"Glad to hear that you will be back on your feet soon." I smile at her.

I look over to see Evalyn and Ami heading our way with the food. We are all given two fried eggs, bacon, and a piece of toast to eat. While Ami, Evalyn, and I use our forks to eat, Emma folds the toast in half and places the two fried eggs inside, eating it with rapid speed before I have even put two bites in my mouth. Wide-eyed, I cock my head and give her a funny look, but while the rest of us continue to eat, she inhales the bacon, washes up, and cleans the dirty dishes.

"You could take a lesson from her, Rain," Evalyn taunts.

"Har har," I mock her with a fake laugh.

"Don't tease my Rain!" Emma protests.

"Your Rain?" Ami questions her.

"I...I meant Rain. Don't tease Rain!"

While I see her like a little sister, I know she has a crush, and I find it difficult to address the fact she will have to give that idea up. Feeling bad, knowing we will be leaving this time, and her, I soon wonder what the ramifications will be when she realizes we will not be coming back.

Will she grow up okay now that Denis is not harassing her? Will she resent us for having to leave?

The possibilities continue in my head as I gaze out the kitchen window toward the city, and am only brought back to reality by Ami prodding my arm. Apparently while I was so lost in thought, Ami and Evalyn have finished up and washed their dishes. I quickly finish my food, and wash my own plate and fork.

"Thank you for the meal." I make sure that Ami and Evalyn know that they are appreciated.

"Of course Rain," Agatha responds.

"Back again, hmm?" I ask her.

"Yes, Evalyn likes to remember the taste of things once in a while," she says.

"The drifting in and out must be disconcerting," I comment.

"It's been so long, and happens so frequently, that I've become accustomed to it." Agatha smiles at me.

I smile back and stand in front of the window by the sink, finding two familiar forms off in the distance. Anthony and Driesen make their way through the park, and I head upstairs to retrieve the journal from my room. Getting properly dressed, I change into a pair of blue pants and a light green shirt. When I turn back around, I find Emma has followed me into my room. I panic a little.

"How long have you been standing there?!" I ask.

"I didn't watch you change, I promise," she smiles innocently.

I frown at her and furrow my eyebrows.

"You should come live in the city, next to me," she suggests excitedly. "I could use someone to protect me full time!"

"I cannot do that Emma."

I continue to frown while grabbing the journal from my nightstand.

"Why not?"

Now seems as good a time as any.

"I have made a promise to Ami and Agatha that I cannot break." Smiling sadly, I turn back to her. "We are going to be leaving here soon, and we will not be coming back."

"Then I'll just come with you. I can make a living anywhere," she responds with just as much energy.

"That really is not my call, but you have to stay here, and live a normal life. Traveling would be bad for you." I put my hand on her shoulder and kneel down to her level.

"But...I want you to protect me!" I can see the joy drain from her face.

"There is nothing you need protecting from anymore. You will be fine."

"But..."

"Emma, it will be okay." I ruffle her hair a little. "I have to go meet Mister Lindali and give him this book so he can punish Denis."

The liveliness is gone from her face, and she runs from the room. She begins to cry, and I can hear her sobbing as she barrels down the stairs and into the kitchen. Though I feel terrible, it had to be done.

Protecting her from danger here is one thing, but traveling through time must have its own perils which I cannot even fathom. I chose this because I had nothing else, but she can live a normal life for her time here.

Stretching my legs, I stand back up and return to the downstairs area. By the time I return to the kitchen, Driesen and Anthony have reached the door. Before they can knock, I have opened it and stepped outside.

"Welcome."

"Yous can hand us the book and we'll be on our way," Driesen holds his massive palm out for it.

"Not a chance," I shake my head and tuck it under my arm. "I will deliver it to Mister Lindali personally."

"I'm afraid that isn't a possibility," Anthony retorts.

"Look, here is how it is." I point aggressively at Anthony. "For all I know Mister Lindali is not back yet, and Denis sent you to get the book before his father sees it. I am not handing it over. End of discussion."

"You...are a tough man," Anthony tells me with a grin. "Under different circumstances, I'm sure you'd be working for Mister Lindali and doing well for yourself."

"Shall we then?" I motion for them to lead the way.

~~~~~~

Our long walk through the city is quiet, uneventful, and though there are many fighters out in front of the towering building, including the two large brothers who had guarded it before, we are unhindered as Anthony leads me through. Driesen follows behind. Inside the building again, I do not feel the same air of tension I felt previously while entering the elevator and climbing to the twentieth floor.

Upon arriving at the top, the room before Mister Lindali's office is bustling with men and women, busy moving about, shuffling paperwork and conversing. The double doors to his office are wide open, and he sits, speaking with a woman. He waves her off as we walk into the room, and watches me intently.

He is wearing a brown-collared overcoat, and a white shirt underneath. Clean cut and shaven, I can see that the features in his face are strong, his jawline solid and rectangular. With his face propped against his right fist, and elbow on one of the chair's armrests, he watches me emotionlessly. I cannot tell if I am welcome or not. I quickly find I do not care, as I proved myself a formidable opponent and have evidence of corruption within his corporation.

Regardless of if I am welcome or not, he has to oblige me.

He waves for me to have a seat in one of the chairs in front of his desk, and proceeds to let out a rather loud yawn. He looks exhausted, and not in a particularly good mood. I take a seat directly in front of him, holding firmly onto the book.

"Be gone from us." He waves Driesen and Anthony off.

I briefly look over my shoulder, and see they have retreated out of the room and closed the doors on their way.

"Mister Lindali." I nod in acknowledgment of his stature, despite the lack of formal acquaintance.

"No offence, Mister Rain?"

"Rain is my name," I reply.

"No offence Rain, but I have just returned from a long journey. I have been up for forty plus hours, and I was hoping my men would be able to retrieve the book from you and we would be squared up."

"I apologize, but I insisted that I bring the book to you directly. I had to take a precaution that it was not Denis attempting to cover his tracks by getting the book before you."

"I can understand that. Denis is a bright child, he just lacks discipline. A problem that I am going to rectify."

"You should find all logs in here of what has been happening." I place the book on the desk and push it forward into Mister Lindali's reach. "I am glad that you will be putting an end to his unethical 'business'."

"Indeed. Now that you know that it's safely in my possession I must ask you to take your leave. I need some shut-eye."

"Thank you for resolving the issue." I stand up and nod again.

Turning to walk out, when I reach the door Mister Lindali speaks again.

"Should you ever need a job, Rain, your gall, resolve and strength impressed me. You would be well compensated for your services," I see a slight grin cross his weary face.

"Thanks for the offer." I leave out that I will not be here soon, and exit.

~~~~~~

Having had enough adventure within the city, I find myself back into a routine of chores while we wait for that strange vortex to rip us through time again.

With my wounds still healing, my body is a bit stiff, but I manage to help clean and care for the house. As I draw up a bucket of water to douse myself with after a hard day of trimming the yard using what Agatha calls a 'push mower', I think about not having seen Emma, as her free time not caring for her shop or sleeping, has been spent here. I pull the push mower back around the side of the house toward the kitchen. The warm sun overhead quickly heats my body again. Entering the kitchen, I find Agatha preparing vegetables for soup.

"Thank you Rain." She looks up.

"I have to make up for your hospitality somehow, right?" I smile. "Where's Ami?"

"Upstairs, sewing, I think," she says, returning her attention to chopping carrots.

"I see. Any sign of Emma today?"

"No. She was pretty upset the other day when you told her she couldn't come with us."

"Have you had to deal with that before; someone wanting to come along but having to deny them?"

"To be honest, you're the first person that wanted to stay. I can't imagine Emma would want to stay if you hadn't helped her."

"True, but she can have a life here. I had nothing, and wanted to repay my debt by helping you as you had helped me." I stand next to her with my hands on the island counter. "I *will* find a way to break this cycle for you."

Returning outside to the warming sun, I begin walking around the house while looking up and watching some light clouds slowly shift shape above the cityscape. Leaning against one of the posts of the well I look out to the monstrous, towering buildings, turning my attention to day walkers milling about the park.

Will Mister Lindali do as he said? When we leave there will be no way of finding out unless a historian writes something on it, and why would they? It's likely such a small thing within this city's history that it will eventually fade away.

Relaxing, I slide to the ground and sit in the freshly cut grass, its potent but soothing smell reaching me quickly. Out of the corner of my eye, I see the drapes in Ami's sewing room shift. Looking up, I squint through the sunbeams to find Ami looking out at me. I smile and wave to her which causes her to quickly disappear, and the drapes fall back into a closed state.

Though we share a connection which seems to extend beyond housemates, I wonder if I shouldn't just focus on stopping this curse before I let something like that get in the way. It's too late to block the emotion entirely because I have grown accustomed to both of them, but I seem to be fueled by passionate feelings. My actions now not just affect them, but apparently people in different times. I could end up making an emotional decision and hurting her, or others.

With the warming rays of light beaming onto me I find myself in the mood for a nap, and close my eyes.

~~~~~~

Waking to a gentle breeze and the sun falling to my right, my body is cooling. I get up from the grass and jog to the door into the living room. A nice heat wafts over me, along with the smell of soup when I get inside. Pushing through the swinging door, I find that the table is already set. The soup is gently simmering on the stove, and fresh cut bread lies on a cutting board on the island counter. The door that leads to the downstairs just past the refrigerator, a place I have not been yet, is propped open. I can hear voices below. Ami and Agatha are conversing, and I walk gently over to it and listen.

I should not be snooping, but I cannot help myself!

"He's a nice boy, right?" Agatha says.

"He's not a boy, Mother. He's a grown man," Ami protests.

"Figure of speech, dear."

"We've been out a few times, and of course I like him. But I've been sheltered here in this house. He's the first real male contact I've had since Father," she speaks with hesitation.

Oh, I should definitely not be listening to this!

"What happens if he doesn't like me that way? Then I'll look stupid, and we'll be stuck traveling together until we die, and it'll be awkward," Ami continues.

"Don't be so pessimistic. He will find a way to follow through on his promise, I can feel it. Then we can all settle down together in one time."

"Mother! For you to be making such assertions about my life! About his!"

"Sorry, just looking out for my only daughter. I want you to be happy."

At this point, footsteps begin climbing the stairs and I am in a compromising position crouched against the doorframe to the basement.

I cannot be caught here! If they knew I was listening...!

Swiftly and quietly I move to the back door, twist the handle, and pull. It creaks a little but I cannot care right now. Out the door, I spin and pull the door shut. To alleviate any possible suspicion to any sounds they might have heard, I head over to the garden, bend down on one knee and begin to pretend to examine our crop. The door opens behind me, and I can hear them talking still.

"You're not going to rush me into anything!" Ami pauses when she sees me.

"Good evening." I smile and play ignorant. "What's Agatha trying to rush you into?"

"I...er...nothing. Just a sewing project," Ami stammers and blushes while Agatha grins impishly. "I was telling her that I'm working on my own stuff, and that she can't rush me into doing something she wants."

"Ah, okay," I smile.

I turn my head back to the crop of food while Ami returns back inside, but I continue my charade while looking at the plants.

"Making an assessment?" Agatha moves up next to me.

"Yeah. Just wondering what we have."

"When we harvest, we always keep some and dry out the seeds or roots to replant. We've lost it before due to severe conditions, but we always bounce back," she explains.

"Smart."

"Anyway, soup should be done." She places her hand on my shoulder.

As I stand, Emma's small familiar figure appears from the border of trees between the park and the city, running toward the house. Turning to enter, Agatha waits for her, and I open the door for them both. When Emma arrives, she excitedly runs in, and grabs an extra setting of dishes.

I close the door behind us and turn to Ami.

"Bring your bowls over and I'll dish up," Ami says, and smiles at me coyly.

As we all get a bowl full of vegetables and rice, and sit down at the table, I get back up and grab the cutting board with the fresh bread and the butter dish. Before they are even on the table, Emma is grabbing some.

"Thanks for inviting me to breakfast!" Emma says, sitting down next to me.

"Well, dinner for us, but you're welcome," Ami responds, her mood lightening. "But you're going to have to scoot down. That's my seat."

The look on Emma's face could kill, but she does as requested and moves one seat farther from me. Understanding that they both have some amount of affection for me, it becomes apparent that they are going to butt heads all night, while one does something to antagonize the other. Ami has made the first move by forcing Emma down. The next move is Emma's. Though Agatha is settled, Emma interrupts her before she can even take a bite.

"Um, Aggy. Can I sit by Rain?" Emma frowns, and speaks hesitantly.

"Of course dear!" Agatha shoots me a glance, and smirks while moving down a spot.

Gleefully, Emma jumps up with her bowl and bread, moving hurriedly to the open spot to my left.

Unable to protest, I make a face at Agatha that tells her I know what she is doing, squinting my eyes and pursing my lips. Emma does not notice or care as she sits and eats, content to be near me.

As we eat, Emma proceeds to engage me in conversation about everything that is involved in her life. I genuinely listen as she speaks in her normal, hyper voice, nodding and smiling every once in a while to let her know that I am paying attention.

"One day I will move up in the world and change my business from a food market to an actual restaurant where I serve hot food to people!"

"That's a very ambitious goal," Ami tells her approvingly.

"I want you guys to come visit me all the time!" Emma looks directly at me, as if Ami and Agatha don't exist.

"I'm afraid that what Rain told you is right. We will be leaving soon," Agatha tells her.

"But you can come back, right?" She looks over at Agatha.

"We travel a lot." Agatha tries to let her down easy. "So much so that it's unlikely that we will be back."

"Can I come with you then?" Emma's tone drops a bit.

"No. That would be dangerous," Ami roughly tells her.

"Rain can protect us though!" Her eyes dart to me, pleading.

Leaving it to them, I lift the bowl to my lips and slurp the soup down, since the last time I tried ended with her crying. When I'm done with a mouthful of the soup, I set the bowl back down hoping that Emma's eyes have been directed elsewhere, but when I see she is looking between the three of us, I speak.

"I am sorry, Emma." my tone is gentle as I explain. "I don't know what we'll be expecting and there may be things that even I cannot protect you from. This is not even my house to say 'yes' or 'no'."

"It's because you really don't like me isn't it?! You like Ami more and don't like me in that way!" Emma slams her spoon down on the table.

Ami's eyes go wide and Agatha stifles a laugh.

My mouth is open, with nothing to say, but I can see she's about to cry again. Not wanting to cause this little girl any more grief, I scoot my chair back and stretching out my arms, I beckon her in for a hug. She leaps at the chance, bolting from her chair and latches onto my neck with her arms.

She begins bawling.

"Emma, I do not want to see you get hurt," I tell her. "That's why you cannot come with us."

She cries on my shoulder for a little bit longer, but eventually calms down. I try to pull away a few times, but her grip is locked.

"But who do you like better?!" she asks.

Oh dear. How do I get out of this? I have no other option to break this little girl's affinity toward me. She'll realize that it could never have worked because of our age difference when she's a little older.

"It's not a matter of who I like more. Ami's my friend and you're like my little sister," I tell her as nicely as I can.

"Your little sister?!" She pulls away and hits me in the chest, her eyes tearing up again.

"All right, Emma! You should come see what I do for fun." Ami intervenes while getting up to pull her away.

Emma resists, but finally goes with. Ami looks at me disapprovingly and takes Emma through the swinging white door. Left to wonder what I did wrong, I shake my head and Agatha laughs again.

"Hilarious, Agatha," I smirk at her.

"I think so. I think her crush on you is cute." She gets up to start cleaning.

"I certainly don't think so. It's awkward for me." I move to help her, picking up Ami's bowl and mine.

Cleaning up, the leftover soup goes in the refrigerator, the dirty dishes get washed and the table and counters get wiped down. Together we make short work of it, but I still find myself tired again, the nap not having been enough to recuperate.

When we are finished, I make my way upstairs to my bedroom. Though I can hear the two girls, I decide to leave them be, and shut my door. Undressing, down to my undershorts, and climbing into the bed, my eyes get heavy. My body melts into the soft mattress.

~~~~~~

When you have nothing but preparing to be ripped from this time, and learning, to keep you busy, time's passage seems slow, unlike those few days of adventure in the city which were over before I knew it.

I suppose that slow and quiet are good things, though. With daily updates from Emma that things are improving, I feel glad, but I wonder how long that will last in a city like this, especially with day walkers like the one who tried to assault Ami and me.

I pin washed laundry on the clothesline. Spared of the women's undergarments by a mutual understanding, I hang towels, and other regular garments up.

Though my being here changes things for them, I will do what I can not to complicate things any more than I already have just by being in their personal bubble.

Hanging up the last of the towels, I wipe some sweat from my brow and turn back to the house to get a drink of water. My thirst is powerful, and when I turn the sink faucet on I dunk my head under and begin to slurp noisily. The cold and refreshing water dribbles from my mouth, and down my chin to my neck. Once satisfied, I turn the faucet off and wipe the wet spots dry with my already wet shirt. When I stand up, I am startled by Ami standing there watching me.

"Good water?" she asks.

"Mmm, very," I reply.

"How's the laundry?"

"All but yours is done," I tell her with a smile.

Leaning against the counter and crossing my arms, our eyes meet, and her eyes sparkle in the sunlight. Despite my resolve to not complicate things, I find her beautiful, and it is hard to deny my own thoughts. Her lightly tanned face is smooth and flawless, and her large curls flow freely over her shoulders.

I suppose my mind is a safe enough haven to admire her from.

"See something you like?" Ami taunts.

"I…" I avert my eyes, embarrassed I have been caught staring. "I was simply marveling at your eye color. It is unlike anyone else's I have met so far."

"Remember to use 'it's' in place of 'it is'," she corrects me, as she has been for days now, and moves a step closer. "But besides that, you find my eyes attractive?"

"Er…" I shift nervously. "I was just thinking that they are unique."

So much for not complicating things. Who knew just looking at her would provoke her interest in me.

"'They're'," she corrects me again, and a flirtatious smile crosses her lips.

Slowly, she leans toward me, apparently trying for that interrupted kiss from before, but before I can lean in to meet her, she has stopped and is staring out the window with wide eyes. Puzzled, I turn around and see Emma off in the distance at the edge of the park; she is hauling a cart. Moving to intercept her, Ami throws the backdoor open. The earth begins to quake beneath us.

"She can't be here! Mother! We're shifting!" Ami yells through the house.

Springing out into the yard, I overtake Ami who has begun running toward the boundary between our plot of land and the rest of the park. The vortex begins to swirl around the house, and its multiple hues of blue air currents become visible as they slice that barrier.

When I reach the edge I stay on our side. Emma has drawn close enough, and I can see a scared look on her face. The earth quakes even harder, but I hold my footing. The buildings begin to fade and I wave my arms, trying to swat Emma away, but she continues.

"Go, Emma! Go the other way!" I scream out over the whirring noise permeating the air.

She stops dead in her tracks. I can see the tears in her eyes, but when she and the city disappear, it matters no longer as our new time comes into view and Emma has not become stuck like us. For good reason we had not let her come with us, and I am satisfied with that decision as our new time has come fully into view.

A heavy, dry wind blasts me in the face as the vortex dies down, and my vision blurs as gritty sand beats against me. Ami reaches me and we are both forced to hold our shirts over our faces to avoid being choked completely by the massive, arid desert that lies around us.

~~~~~~

3 DESOLATION

Even though the vortex has dissipated, the wind roars by us, and around the house, bombarding us with harsh sand particles. I cannot see far beyond my position, and even looking back at the house is blurry. My eyes are watering.

"What is this?!" I try to yell over the howling wind, and choke a bit.

Grit enters my mouth, and no matter how much I try to spit it back out I find that there is still more. Ami puts her back to the wind and sand to reply.

"A sandstorm! Get the clothes inside!" Ami yells back.

I do as she says, and run to the clotheslines. The wind pelts us with sand as we take things down, and it's like nothing I have ever felt before. As the grains hit my skin at this high velocity, I feel like it is going to tear through. Agatha joins us in this sand storm, grabbing everything she can. With a basket full of clothes and sand, I reach the kitchen door and toss the clothes inside. Turning to head back, Ami stops me.

"Stay here!"

She rushes down into the basement, only to reappear a moment later with a large wooden cover. Setting it down, she then grabs a small towel and soaks it with water from the sink. She pins it over my nose and mouth.

"This will keep sand out. You need to go cover the well! Just make sure to use these latches to cinch it down," she instructs over the howling, and demonstrates the latches on the two sides.

Running through the house, I burst out onto the small porch from the living room, and use the well cover as a shield to cut a path through the barrage of wind and sand. I stumble a few times. Reaching the well, I struggle to drop it in place between the two posts but finally get it in place. Using the latches, I find two hooks on the well to attach it to.

Once it is secure, I make my way back to the house, the sand whipping me across the back. When I am inside the living room door, I slam it shut and make it back to the kitchen, dropping sand all over along the way.

"What about the rest of the food?" I ask Ami and Agatha who have retreated inside, and are looking out the window of the closed door.

"We will salvage what we can after the storm has passed." Agatha looks back at me.

Though we are safe inside, it howls and rages against the wood panel siding. Removing the wet cloth from my face and placing it on the counter, I move to the window and stare out at this unlivable environment.

"This is terrible," Ami says while also staring out the window. "We've been in storms before, but never a sandstorm."

"How did you know what it was then?" I ask with a quirked eyebrow.

"Read about them happening in other parts of the world, but there has never been a desert here before," Ami replies, still transfixed.

"Shake these clothes off and start hanging them around to dry off," Evalyn chimes in gruffly.

The sandstorm continues on, and heat seeps in from outside, making it very humid while we shake the wet clothes off, sand landing all over. Draping items everywhere, everything has become a makeshift drying line. Not a space within the kitchen is showing underneath all of the laundry, even going so far as to take the hanging pots and pans down, and putting garments on the hooks. With the three of us working together, it takes a short time to accomplish our task.

"We'll have to wait for them to dry completely to get the rest of the sand off," Evalyn grumbles. "We already have a big enough mess to clean up. Check the house and make sure the windows are closed."

Heading off, I follow Ami along the hallway downstairs, leaving Evalyn to take the upstairs so I do not violate her rule of going near her door. Ami takes the left side while I take the right and we check the windows room by room. Finding the two rooms I am given to check are secured, I meet Ami back out in the hall.

"Find anything?" I ask.

"Nope. You?"

"All clean, thankfully. Evalyn would probably make me clean it up by hand." I snicker.

"Probably." She grins.

We return to the living room and stand at the window, watching sand shred through the air. The sound of it, and the wind, beating on the house is rather loud.

"With three mouths to feed, we're going to have to start rations immediately," Evalyn barks from behind us, startling us both.

"Of course," I reply while looking back outside.

"This would be easier if you weren't here," Evalyn sneers at me.

"Don't start with me, Evalyn," I bark at her, trying to not let her get under my skin.

"You know, if you died, Ami and Agatha would have more food and water," she snidely comments.

"We've only been here a few minutes and you are threatening me?" Angrily I turn around and cross my arms, scowling. "Back off – we will survive!"

"He's right, Aunt Evalyn. We'll get through this as we have with everything else." Ami backs me up.

Evalyn crosses her arms and we start a staring contest, but she quickly gives up, huffs, and retreats to the kitchen.

"So you've been through things like this before?" I sit on the couch and look at Ami.

"We've been through tough times before, but never anything like this." She sits next to me, crossing her legs. "This storm is going to tear our garden apart and I doubt there will be any apples left to salvage."

"Hmm. Well what now?"

"Not sure. Nothing important to do until the storm is over."

"That is, if it ends?" I question and rest my head against the back of the couch.

"If it doesn't, our electrical equipment on the roof will fail."

"Is that bad?"

"Yes, but there's no use worrying about it until we can get to it." She puts her hand on my leg and uses me as a brace to stand up. "I'm going to go take advantage of the light we have up in my sewing room. Want to come with?"

"I'm going to rest, actually. If we're going to be cleaning things up after the storm I'm going to need my energy," I stand up with her.

She nods and we head up the stairs together. As she turns left, I turn right, and I close the door behind me.

Taking off my sandy clothes, I head over to the window to peer out as the storm rages on. I throw my dirty laundry in the basket next to my door, shut the light off, and plop down onto my unkempt bed. The wind, though harsh, provides a nice blanket of white noise for me to drown my thoughts in as I stretch and close my eyes. My thoughts turn to this house and its curse.

What can be done to stop it? How can someone manifest such a power? Though I cannot remember, I have a distinct feeling that such an ability is beyond rare and no one from Emma's time exhibited anything like it.

Evalyn knew how to use her power while still alive, but would she be able to use it again even in spiritual form? Or in Agatha's body? I suppose she will not help since she is intent on making Ami and Agatha's lives miserable. Maybe I will find someone like her, with an ability that could help us.

~~~~~~

I wake to silence, and it's a welcome lack of sound, though at the moment I cannot hear Ami, Agatha, or Evalyn either.

Sitting slowly up in my bed with my feet on the floor, I look out the window to a very strange sight. I see the woods where I was stabbed, but I am on the wrong side of the house. I can see the well in the yard and the path I came from.

This isn't right. And what happened to the sand?

I can see shadows moving in the forest toward the house. I stand up and watch intently. They're running. As one shadow is about to hit the clearing, the other shadow is attacked from behind.

"Die!" I hear a voice as if whispered in my ear, and a sharp pain screams through my body.

I look down and see that familiar dagger through my abdomen, and I am no longer inside the house. Instead I have traded places with the shadow, and Drake is behind me gripping the dagger with all his might. I reach my hands up to the dagger, but before I can do anything it is ripped back out of me, and I am now trying to contain the blood with my palms. I stumble forward and collapse.

My eyes snap open, and I am in the house again, in my bed. This time I can still hear a very faint rhythmic noise coming from across the hall. Ami is sewing. I sit up slowly, afraid to look out the window, but as I do my eyes are met not with the sight of the forest, but with hills of sand, a rather large embankment of it not far outside the border of our plot of land. The sand has decimated the yard, and destroyed the apple tree, but our house still stands in defiance of the sandstorm.

Standing up my scar protests, and I check it. There is no blood, it has not reopened, but it burns as much as the day I first awoke. Looking for a fresh pair of clothing, I find the lightest clothes I can, a white button up shirt and a pair of thin green pants with a drawstring. But I feel warm, stifled by muggy air in the room. I open the door for fresh air, but the hallway is no better. Moving over to the sewing room, I knock, and the rhythmic noise stops.

"Come in," she says.

Upon opening the door I see something I'm unprepared for: Ami is in a loose, thin white top which hangs from her shoulders with small straps, her pink brassiere peeking out from the top and sides. With both her undergarment, and far more skin showing than I'm accustomed to, I avert my eyes.

"I…er…I'm sorry, I was not aware that you were not properly dressed. I will wait outside." I turn around and proceed to exit.

"What?" she asks.

"Your shirt," I reply, my back still to her. "If I had known you were in your nightwear…"

"Oh, it's not nightwear, just a tank top. It's meant for warm weather," I can hear the smile in her voice.

"Still, it's a little…exposing."

"I suppose it is, but you can't expect me to wear anything more in this heat." She laughs a little.

"I guess not. This heat is sweltering."

"Does it make you uncomfortable seeing me in this?" I can hear her voice take a slightly taunting tone. "Because I might just wear it more."

"Whatever comes out of my mouth will sound insulting, so I will instead keep my comments to myself."

"Well, don't worry Rain. I'm making up some more protective sets of clothing for the three of us so we can combat the desert." She becomes more excited.

"Protective? It sounds like you are preparing to go out into the desert."

"Perhaps we are. We need to know if there is anything out there, don't we?" She picks up her sewing again.

"Are we in trouble being here? I mean, will we be okay?" I ask, while looking out my window from her sewing room.

"We haven't faced a desert before, but I'm certain we will survive just fine." Her confidence is infectious, and I can feel my mental strength bolstered.

"I should head down and see if Agatha or Evalyn need my help with anything." I take a step forward but she stops me again.

"I make you nervous still, don't I?" The smile returns to her voice.

"Pardon?" my voice wavers a little.

"You've been here two months now, but you still act like we're strangers sometimes. You must not have had much female interaction in your previous life." Her machine stops.

"I…" I begin to respond, but words elude me.

She shuffles, and before I know it I have been attacked from behind. Her arms are thrown around me, and she squeezes, pulling her body into my back. I feel my face become hotter than it already is, due to the blood rushing to my cheeks.

"You may not realize it, but I'm glad you're here," she says quietly.

"I'm glad I am here too, Ami." I place one of my hands on her arms. "Without you and your mother I would have nothing to live for."

She removes her arms, and gives me a playful little shove from behind to help me out the door. As I turn around to see what that was about she smiles and closes the door slightly, sticking her face in the opening between the door and doorjamb.

"Go see what needs to be done."

She winks at me. I blush again, and this time I know she's seen it. Hastily retreating down the stairs, I find myself feeling awkward and comforted at the same time.

My stomach is aflutter, and I wonder why she makes me feel that way. Though I'm attracted to her, I have no experience from my past to guide me in the proper etiquette to that kind of emotion, but the attention is not unwanted.

Entering the kitchen, Agatha is leaning back in a chair with a crudely folded paper fan in her hand trying to cool herself down. She has changed into one of her gardening outfits, overalls and a thin shirt.

"Here to help finally?" Evalyn snaps.

"What is it that you need done?" I ask, without spite.

"Since the storm is over, go hang all the clothing back up," she barks her orders.

"Okay."

A couple pieces at a time, I haul items back outside. One of the poles has toppled, leaving only three usable rows to hang garments from. Though I imagine it will be easy to fix, with the possibility of another sandstorm I take a guess that it will be fixed next month.

Little by little, I accomplish the task, making sure to grab an even amount of clothes for each of us so that none of us will be left without. Though still damp, the hot air begins drying them even before I am done hanging the last.

Inside, getting a glass of water from the faucet, I guzzle it down as Evalyn struggles to bring up a metal ladder from the basement. Intercepting, I offer my assistance, and she obliges by giving me the tail end. She leads us outside and takes it from me, positioning it against the side of the house. Though the ladder looked fairly small, she somehow extends it so that it reaches the top of the second story. She begins to ascend the ladder, but it wobbles and I stop her.

"What are you doing?" I ask.

"I'm climbing up to the roof to see if there has been any damage to the solar panels. If we're going to survive, we need to keep them in working order."

"Is that something I can do? It looks rather unsafe."

"Do you know anything about electricity?" she berates me. "Just hold the ladder!"

"No, but at least allow me to help out," I try to calm her with a soothing voice. "What if the wind kicks up?"

Annoyed, Evalyn stares me down for a moment, and I can see a change in her. When the mood in her face lightens, I know she has not accepted me, but rather she has given Agatha control of her body again.

"She really does not like being around me." I smirk.

"You're getting good at knowing when it is me or Evalyn." She smiles in defiance of her sister's awful mood.

"Unfortunately. Can't you block her from taking over?"

"I used to be able to, back when all this had just started, but I just don't have the will to resist her anymore." She frowns briefly, but quickly changes the subject. "Look at you though. You used 'can't' instead of 'cannot'. Ami's teaching is working."

"I guess it is. It is also probably because I am immersed in your dialect of the language constantly." I smile and think of my time with Ami.

"Ready to go up?" she asks.

I nod with a smile, gripping the ladder tightly while she climbs. Planting my feet firmly on the ground, I concentrate on keeping the ladder upright. Agatha reaches the top of the house and disappears; it's my turn. Carefully I climb, calling up to her.

"Agatha, stay still until I get there," I yell.

When I get up there, she is sitting down, looking out over the desert. Even with the extra few feet above the second level, all that can be seen is a wasteland of sand, rock and occasional dead bush. Slick with sand, the shingles provide no help in holding our footing, so I stay low, practically crawling.

Agatha does the same, and turns toward what I assume are the solar panels. They are large, black rectangular pieces bolted on frames to the roof. A number of them line the roof with enough space for a person to maneuver through. Following closely behind her, I watch intently while she inspects each of them, occasionally leaning over to run her hand across them and brush sand away. Digging my toes against the roofing, I brace in order to catch her in case she slips, but I pay attention to the panels, each with a grid of multiple other rectangles, appearing to be black glass, and held together by a metal structure.

Following Agatha's lead I brush sand away as the setting sun continues to beat us heavily. We make our way carefully along, finally circling back to our starting position. I take her silence to mean she found nothing wrong.

"So, with all this sun we should not run out of power?" I break the silence.

"We'll see. For now they seem okay," she says, sitting down on the roof.

Slowly, I set myself against the wobbly ladder, and feel it shift as I begin to climb down, but Agatha grabs the top and holds it for me. I descend as steadily as I can. Upon reaching the bottom, I secure the ladder for her to come down.

Leaving it, we head back inside, and I guzzle down another glass of water. Sitting in my spot at the head of the table, I fan myself by lifting and dropping my shirt several times in quick succession. It works until I stop, and the heat fills around me again. Agatha opens the refrigerator, quickly pulls something out, and just as quickly closes it again. A draft of cool air hits me for a brief moment.

"Ahh, that felt good," I groan.

"The refrigerator?" she asks.

"Yeah. The cool air rushed over here and hit my neck."

I look behind me to find her at the island counter.

"If it wasn't storing our perishables I'd invite you to stand in front of it." She smirks at me while unwrapping some leftovers.

"Well then perhaps we should eat all of that food first so we can make use of it," I jest with her.

She laughs, and Ami pops in through the kitchen door, looking just as hot and tired as us.

"Were you on the roof?" She looks at her mother.

"Yes, dear," she replies softly.

"Everything okay?"

"It's all in working order for now, but we'll have to maintain a watch on them to make sure it stays that way," Agatha replies.

"How're the outfits coming?" I ask.

"They're nearly finished. They will be great for us when working outside."

"What about something to protect the head and face?"

"I'm building that into the outfits." Ami moves over to the table and sits down. "They will have hoods that will drape over the face and a shielding piece we can put up to cover everything but our eyes."

"Sounds like you've thought of everything," I compliment her.

"I've tried." She smiles.

Silence ensues for a few minutes, and Agatha brings over small plates with leftover turkey and bread stuffing for each of us. I nod at her in appreciation. While I eat, I find an opportunity to bring up Evalyn's power.

"What methods have you tried to stop the house from being sent through time?"

"Stopping it? Not a lot. The first time it happened we tried to escape but after the month was over we learned that we were bound here. I was hurt pretty badly," Agatha says sadly. "We also buried Evalyn's body in another time but that didn't work."

"Evalyn has done things to deter Mother from trying, so we just sort of accepted it," Ami chimes in while sipping a glass of water.

"Have you ever found anyone else with power like her? Or maybe she can reverse it while possessing you?" I ask the questions that have been burning within me.

"We have heard stories, but never found anyone. And Evalyn is not likely to help. We are at her mercy." Agatha shifts her gaze to stare blankly at the wall.

"That's a little unfair. Punishing you because she was miserable," I comment.

"I'll show you who's miserable!" Agatha's arm reaches up to strike me across the face.

Nearly caught off guard, I lean backward quickly. The chair tilts back too far and I slam into the floor.

Looks like I struck a chord.

"Why don't you let them go, Evalyn?" I hastily get up and right the chair. "Why can't you let your grudge go?"

"I don't have the ability to let them go! I'm stuck here just as much as they are! You have no right to come into this house and judge me! They should have left you to die!" Evalyn gets up, but instead of trying to strike me, she storms through the swinging door.

Her stomping up the stairs can be felt through the floorboards, and even after she's at the top of the stairs I can hear her grumbling, though I cannot make out the words. Ami and I sit in silence while finishing our small meal, but she breaks it.

"I'm sorry," she says.

"For what?"

"Two things really. Since you're here she has been taking her frustration out on you, not me." She laughs a little to break the tension. "But I know she won't say sorry, so I'm saying it in her place."

"Don't be sorry. She's miserable because she wants to be, but being caught between life and death does not sound like it was intended."

"I find it funny, but if you think about it, she played a part in saving you also." She smirks at me while laying her head on the table. "If she hadn't put us in this situation, you would be dead in the woods."

Nodding, I contemplate this notion and find she's entirely right.

Though I do not agree with Evalyn's behavior, I wonder if I should be a little more sensitive. Maybe apologize to her later and smooth things over? I never got around to apologizing for the last time I severely offended her, so maybe one of these days I will make one big effort.

For now though I finish the turkey on my plate and set the dish in the sink, finding no use in wasting our precious water washing one dish.

With Evalyn upstairs, I feel even being in my room might be hazardous, so I settle for the couch in the living room. With the shades drawn shut, it seems less warm here, and I stretch out, legs propped on the table. But despite being cooler than upstairs, I still find the heat sapping my energy.

~~~~~~

When I wake it is night, the room dark except for the moonlight seeping in through the cracks in the drapes. Lying on my stomach, my arm is draped over Ami's shoulder, and she is holding it tightly against her chest. I quickly yank my arm away, embarrassed that my arm was in a compromising position resting across her breasts.

"What are you doing?" she whispers.

"What are *you* doing?" I whisper back, a little uneasy.

"You were keeping me warm," she protests sleepily.

"I don't think that the way my arm was positioned was appropriate." I stammer a little.

"There wasn't anything behind it. I just needed the warmth and comfort."

"Comfort?"

"Yeah." She becomes silent for a moment. "It's so dark and quiet that it's eerie."

"Well since we're both up and it is cool now do you want to go for a short walk outside to see that there's nothing to be worried about? The moon will light our way." I smile.

"Okay!" she whispers excitedly.

Leaping quietly into action, she disappears up the stairs and returns just as quickly as she had gone with clothing in her arms. Handing me a set, I unravel them to find they are the ones she had mentioned earlier. She moves to turn the living room light on while I examine them.

"You got these done already?!" I whisper, astonished.

"Of course!"

The top is a white, very loose and shiny fabric I assume to reflect the heat of the sun. It's long sleeved, however the sleeves come off just by unbuttoning a few areas around the biceps, making it versatile for different situations. A hood is attached in the same fashion, but unlike a regular hood, I find a stiff piece of material embedded in the neck and top of it to keep it from flopping down into a person's face while still providing adequate protection from the elements. The pants are similar in design, both in the type of cloth as well as being able to shorten the legs by unbuttoning fabric around the knee.

"Very nice handiwork," I say.

"Thank you." She curtsies and waves her hands in an insisting manner. "Now try them on."

"If I'm going to try them on, you had best turn around. And no peeking."

"Oh! We're doing this out here?" Her eyes go wide.

"If we go anywhere else right now, we might make noise and wake your mother. You might as well change too," I tell her.

"Mmhmm. You're just trying to see me in my underwear." She crosses her arms.

"Turn around and change." I smirk at her and stand.

She quickly turns around with her set and I turn to face the couch, changing as quickly as I can. Stripping everything off except for my undergarments, I practically jump into the new pants, and throw on the new shirt. Pulling drawstrings on the pants and bottom of the shirt to tighten them up, I move a bit and feel there is minimal restriction. Thinking she had done the same, I turn and catch that she has only managed to get the pants on. Catching a glimpse of her pink brassiere, my face flushes, and I focus my vision back on the couch.

"Psst," she hisses to get my attention. "Are you done?"

"Yes, are you?"

Turning around I cover my mouth to choke back a laugh at the unflattering, baggy clothing, but she either does not notice or perhaps does not care. I slip my shoes back on while bracing against the arm of the couch. She's already put hers on.

"Ready?" she whispers cheerfully.

"Sneaking out seems to be our thing."

"You better believe it." She grabs me by my arm and leads us through the kitchen.

"We should leave the kitchen light on too," I suggest.

"Sounds like a good plan." She hits the light switch and the light comes on.

We exit the house as quietly as possible, closing the door slowly behind us. She releases her grip from my arm and grabs my hand. Leading me away from the house, we bathe in the moonlight while absconding into the night.

With Ami directing us, we set out toward the large embankment of sand several yards out from the decimated apple tree, but unlike before where our pace was fast, we stroll instead.

I find myself enjoying my time with her already as we quietly adventure toward the desert. Reaching the hill we step out onto it, and I find I am ill prepared to navigate the sand, as it sinks and shifts around me, causing me to stumble. She giggles, and I release her hand, hobbling forward as I try to climb the somewhat steep slope. Thankfully, after trying to climb up, I turn around and find she is also having a hard time.

"This is ridiculous!" I blurt.

"Definitely," she agrees.

Thrashing around in the sand, we do our best to stand up and I move to help her steady herself. I grab onto her waist, and hold her while laughing.

"Do we try and continue, or do we go back?" I ask.

"We can make this." I catch a glimpse of her brilliant blue eyes underneath her hood.

Nodding, we use each other as supports and begin to walk farther up the slope. Surprisingly the sand begins to firm up a bit, and our climb, though still difficult, becomes a little easier. Hunched over, our four feet work together and take it one step at a time, forcing our way up. The farther we go, the firmer it seems to get and we finally make our way up to the top of the hill.

The hill turns into a plain for what appears to be a few hundred yards before reaching more hills, or possibly valleys, and the beauty of the landscape under what little light we have leaves me in wonder. Because the moon fails to illuminate everything, I fear pitfalls or other dangers which might not be apparent. Ami taps my shoulder.

"Look." She points to our right where far off in the distance is a strange orange glow.

"That's not where the sun comes up. What is that?"

The orange gets brighter for a brief moment, and a ball of fire rises into the air, but from this distance it only seems like a flicker of a flame.

"What was that?" I ask.

"An explosion of some kind, I bet." She sounds eager.

"I think it would be best if we return to the house, and come back to check on it tomorrow. If whatever it is gets closer we may want to prepare to defend ourselves," I cautiously suggest.

"Agreed."

As we turn around, the hill is more intimidating looking down than it was while looking up. The house seems rather small, but I begin by leading the way. Putting one foot down as slowly as possible after another, I lean back to avoid tumbling forward and breaking my neck. Looking back, Ami does the same, and we slowly walk back down the side of the sandy hill. Taking about the same amount of time to get down that it did to go up, we make it back to the solid ground that the house sits on, and my legs burn heavily from the workout.

Finally back outside the kitchen, we remove our shoes and socks, dumping the sand out we had picked up on our short journey. My feet itch, but when I scratch them it begins to irritate the skin even further. It burns like pouring salt into a wound.

"I wish we could spare the water. I would rinse my feet off," I complain.

"I know, so do I. We're just going to have to bear it for now and rinse it all off on our scheduled shower times."

"Scheduled shower times?"

"Oh, that's right. You were asleep when Mother and I decided that we would have a designated time for showering for each of us. Because we don't know how long our water will last, we're going to each take a shower once a week and they'll be limited to ten minutes each."

"Well then. When's our next shower?"

"Our?" she questions me playfully.

"You know what I meant!" My eyes widen, and embarrassment sets in again.

"Of course I know." She pushes my shoulder, nearly knocking me from the top step at the kitchen door. "Six days."

"We should probably get some more sleep," I suggest.

"Yeah." She hesitates but stands up and shakes off her clothing as much as possible before heading inside.

A few moments pass, and the swinging door comes to a rest. Checking over my shoulder to make sure she is not there, I take off my shirt and pants, shaking them heartily to get as much sand out as possible. Standing outside in my undershorts feels strange, and after shaking the clothes for a few moments, I put them back on in a hurry incase Ami decides to return.

When she does not reappear, I pick up my shoes and tread softly, sneaking a glass of water before heading back to the living room. Instead of heading upstairs though, where I imagine the heat is still lingering, I plop down on the cool couch, and close my eyes.

~~~~~~

"Get up you lazy swine," Evalyn barks at me. "It's already mid-day."

"What is there to do but sit around and sweat and wait for this month to be over?" I retort, seeing how agitated she is already.

"You're going to collect some water from the well and store it in some jugs," she directs forcefully.

I wipe a large amount of sweat from my forehead, and stand up. My body is sore from the excursion last night, but I hide my discomfort from her for fear of her questioning me.

"So what are you waiting for?" she snaps. "Start hauling water around back where Ami is setting up a filter."

Shifting from one leg to another, I got more sand in my clothes last night than I had thought, and the skin between my legs is irritated. Chafing against my skin, I fight against scratching and head upstairs to change.

"Where do you think you're going?" she demands.

"To change. I have sand in my undergarments from yesterday." I sigh at her.

I bound up the stairs, two at a time, thinking getting there faster would be better, but the grit tears at my skin even more. Slamming my door, I throw off all of my clothes, and sand trickles out. I dust off, but due to my sweat, it's difficult to get clean. After getting most of it, I throw on new undershorts, and shake the new protective clothes out again before putting them on.

Finished, I make my way outside to the well, keeping my raw legs spread as far apart as I can, to avoid any more irritation. The wooden cover has a mound of sand on it, and the only way to remove the lid without getting it inside is to dig into the sand again. Scooping with my hands, I fling it away from me until I can lift the lid enough to dump the rest of the sand off the side.

Though the sun is scorching overhead, the white hood covering me with its protruding brim offers protection. Hauling the first bucket up with the hand crank, I am confused as to why we are not using the faucet out back to filter and stock up on water, but decide to let it go. When the bucket reaches me, I notice that a fair amount of sand made it into the bucket before I was able to get the cover on, but not wanting to waste anything, I take it anyway.

Unlatching the wooden bucket from its hook, I move around the house, trying to hide in what little shade is being provided, but a large pile of sand has gathered against the siding, and I am forced out into the sun. Though the hot, dry air causes my lungs to burn, the clothing does its job effectively otherwise.

As I reach the other side of the yard, Ami is standing next to a strange rigging setup. Four poles are planted in the ground just beyond the empty clothing lines. Draped across the poles is a cloth with a layer of sand across the top, and underneath is the washbasin.

"Why are we using the basin?" I ask Ami as I get there.

"It's the only thing large enough to accommodate what we're doing."

"Isn't it dirty?"

"I'm going to wash it out with the first bucket of water, and then the rest will get saved." She smiles at me triumphantly.

"Is it ready? There seems to be sand in the middle of the cloth." I tilt my head slightly to the side.

"I found an old survival book we had stored away. It had a method to filter water with sand that will help reduce bacteria in the end product. Then we boil it."

"Why can't we just run the faucet in the kitchen and bring the water to the store room downstairs?"

"If we run the water too much we risk sand getting sucked into the pumps, and then we'd be in bigger trouble. Though the well was covered for most of the storm, we decided to take a safety precaution."

"Time is wasting!" Evalyn bursts out the kitchen door behind me. "Why are you standing around talking?"

"Sorry, Evalyn." I shoot her a sideways glance. "Ami was just teaching me about the method we're using for purification."

"Well hurry up with it. I'm in here waiting to boil and store, and you two are holding me up!"

I smile at Ami out of Evalyn's sight, and dump the bucket of water as close to the middle as I can. As it filters through I watch it start off like a waterfall from the underside and trickle off. Heading back for another bucket, the moment I am around the corner, I overhear Evalyn scolding Ami.

"You need to get your head out of the clouds. Stop flirting with him and focus instead on staying alive," she barks.

Though she was talking directly to Ami, I know she intended for me to hear it because it came out as soon as I was around the corner. Though we were just scolded, I think about Ami flirting with me.

I may not remember any relationships from the past, but it does feel like this is the closest I have been to a girl before. Could the same be true for Ami since she's been in this vortex most of her life?

Back and forth, I haul buckets. After Ami has cleaned out the wash basin of dirt and soap residue, the real filtering begins. Each time I dump a bucket, I watch for a few moments as the delicious water trickles down. Feeling parched, I have to resist drinking from the bucket or the basin, instead forging ahead toward dumping that next bucket. Eventually I drain the well enough that the bucket hits bottom and the basin is quite full, but without Ami, Agatha or Evalyn around I wonder what I should do next.

Famished, I return the bucket to the well and place the cover back on, securing the latches. Upon entry to the house, I kick my shoes off and dump them outside the living room door, making sure to get whatever sand I encountered out.

With my shoes placed by the closed door, I head into the kitchen and find the table already set with a plate with a meaty looking sandwich and glass of juice. Upon closer inspection, I find there is a piece of paper with my name on it, and I find it likely that Ami had anticipated my needs.

After finishing the delicious roast beef sandwich, and downing the glass of apple juice, I lean back in my chair, satisfied. With every last crumb on the plate devoured, I set my dishes next to the pile gathering in the sink. When I look out the window, Ami has reappeared outside with several jugs that she is scooping cups of water into. Staring, I find it safe to admire her from here without fear of reproach.

"Rain?" Agatha speaks next to me and I nearly jump out of my skin.

"Oh! Agatha! How long have you been standing there?" I ask, completely flustered.

"How long have *you*?" I see her playful grin.

"I was just, uh," I have no adequate explanation so I move on. "I filled the tub with all the water I could get from the well."

"Okay. Ami's going to bring the water in and boil it. Would you help me check on the panels again?" she asks.

"Of course." I open the door for her and allow her to exit first.

~~~~~~

Lying with my head at the foot of the bed, I watch the light disappear outside my open window as the sun sets on the other side of the house.

A few days have come and gone, slowly and agonizingly. Though we keep ourselves busy surviving this dangerous desert, it has already begun to drain our sanity.

Our choices to keep cool are limited, and needing to cook most of our food to eat exacerbates the issue. With water rationed, and my shower still days away, I think of cold things to keep my mind from the heat. It is unbearable. I tear off my clothes down to my undershorts, and return my head to the pillow.

Though I have been thrust into bizarre situations since the attack and my amnesia, I seem to thrive in it. I like it. Whoever I was before must have been adventurous also, as I cannot see myself really settling down to a calm life. Have I traveled the world? How much have these eyes actually seen?

Drifting in and out while watching the horizon become dark grey, and then black, I am in a state between asleep and awake. I find myself less aware of my surroundings than I had thought when a whisper tickles my ear, and causes me to swing my arms wildly.

"Hey! Shh, calm down," Ami whispers frantically.

"What is wrong?" My eyes spring open, my voice in a normal tone.

"Other than you about to hit me? Nothing," she whispers again.

"Sorry, it was a reflex." I realize that she is whispering for a reason and copy her.

"I created some attachments for our shoes so we can walk on the sand easier!"

"We're going out tonight?"

"Of course. The explosion means that there are other people out here," her whisper becomes excited. "While explosions are generally a bad thing, it could have been an accident. I want to see if we can make contact with the inhabitants of this time."

"What if the explosion was intentional?" I ask. "And how will we get back?"

"We'll keep our distance until we scope them out. I have some binoculars. And for getting back, it shouldn't be hard to follow our footprints back with the attachments I made!"

"You have an answer for everything, don't you?" I turn my head and grin at her.

She leans in closely, grinning from ear to ear, and I have my answer. With her there, hovering so near, I stay hesitantly still as it looks like she might lean in to kiss me. Instead, she grabs my hand and yanks me out of bed. The blanket I didn't know I had pulled over me, falls off. She squeals while covering her mouth and turning around. Puzzled, I look down. I am in my undershorts.

"I'm sorry!" She shakes her head and covers her face.

"It is all right. Just don't turn around!" I scramble to grab my clothes and jump into them.

Once I am dressed, I find an opportunity to play a trick on her, and I tiptoe over. I position my hands near her sides and then poke her, causing her to let out another squeal, this one muffled because her hands are already over her face. She spins around and drops her hands.

"Ready to go?" I smile.

"Not funny! If we're caught, our trip is over!"

"Well then you and I could just stay here together." I smile, playing with her.

"I…uh…what are you…what do you mean?" She puts her hands back up to her cheeks and looks down.

"Are you blushing?" I poke at her arm.

"No...I..." She looks back up at me.

"Come on, we better get moving if we are going to find those people."
I wink at her.

"You!" She proceeds to hit me, but it only comes out as a tap.

She enters her sewing room and returns with some objects I cannot
identify in the dark, before moving down the stairs. I wait until she is at
the bottom before I follow, and taking one step at a time I minimize the
creaking of the floorboards. Once we find our way outside she talks
normally.

"These are binoculars." She hands me a small object that has two round
cylindrical pieces attached to each other, and fits into the palm of my hand.
"And these are the special shoe fittings that should allow us to walk more
steadily on the sand."

She lines up four circular objects with a weaving pattern that
crisscrosses and makes a hatch pattern through the middle. Handing her
back the binoculars, I pick one of the attachments up and examine it
closely.

"Oh. How did you make these?"

"I cut the handles off some old rackets we had and added some
strapping to hold them onto our feet." She's proud of herself.

"But, these are full of holes. How is this going to support us?"

"You'll see. Just put the back strap on the inside of your shoe under
your foot and the front strap on the outside."

I do as she instructed. With my shoes back on I attempt to walk, but
they are awkward and bulky. I trip. She giggles from behind me as I waddle
around, nearly knocking myself against a clothesline. Ready to go, she
waddles too, headed toward that hill beyond our yard.

When we reach the edge of the property, the shifting sand which leads
to our mountain waits for us to attempt to conquer it again. I take a step
out onto it, then another. Surprisingly, while there is still some give, I don't
feel like I am going to fall over like last time. Walking awkwardly toward
the hill, we quickly find ourselves working our way up the incline but with
much less effort than before. At the top once more, we scan the horizon
and she is quick to point out that same faint orange glow off in the
distance, in a slightly different area. Ami puts the binoculars up to her eyes

and stares for a moment before breaking the silence.

"I can't see anything from here," she says while putting her arm through a strap on the binoculars. "Let's walk a bit and see if we can get any sightings."

"Are you sure about this?" I put my hand on her shoulder. "I don't want to get lost in the desert and be out here in the daytime."

"You worry too much. We'll be fine," she says soothingly.

She takes me by the hand and we walk a good distance along this sandy plain. I feel apprehensive, but she's insistent, and I seem to be weak to resist her desires.

Reaching a dip into a valley, she boldly leads us down it, and the orange glow disappears from our vision. Crossing the small valley, and back up, we can see the orange glow again. I look behind us and by the light of the nearly full moon, I can see our tracks faintly in the sand.

"We are going in a straight line, right?" I ask nervously. "So we should be able to turn around and head back the way we came?"

"Of course." She squeezes my hand reassuringly.

After walking for an unknown amount of time, we near the orange glow, and I think there is movement within it. Ami grabs me, and pulls us to a small mound of sand, then throws us both down so we are lying flat on our stomachs. Putting the binoculars to her eyes, she studies the orange glow intently.

"There *are* people there!" she whispers excitedly.

"What are they doing?"

"I can see that they're moving about, but not what they're doing. There are tents and several fires though."

"Should we attempt to make contact?"

"We should wait and observe more. Here, take a look." She hands me the binoculars.

Pressing them up to my eyes, I try and see through them, but it causes my eyes to hurt for a moment while they forcibly readjust to the glass inside. I use them to look around a few moments and get my bearings before focusing on the orange glow. When I do, I can see the inhabitants of the area milling about. Their movement patterns suggest there is purpose, but they could be going about their daily routines.

"Let me see again." Ami taps my shoulder.

I hand her the binoculars, and only a few moments after she puts them to her eyes again, she is tugging on my arm and standing up.

"We have to get closer to learn about them," she whispers.

"What?" I almost yell out, but catch myself and whisper instead.

"I'm interested! Let's go!" She is already up, but crouching while moving forward.

Unable to sit idly by and watch, I follow after her, crouching and waddling. Though I may have some physical prowess, I am leery of creeping up on a camp full of people. Several hundred yards pass quickly, and she drops to her belly on the flat sand with the binoculars pressed to her eyes. I lie next to her, and after only a few moments she breaks the silence.

"They look like they've been through a war," she whispers.

"How can you tell?" I ask.

"Their clothes and tents are tattered, and from what I can tell they're really skinny," she whispers.

"I cannot imagine that it is easy living out in the desert like this. I bet the house would be paradise to these people." I frown, even though she cannot see it.

"Oh no! You're right!" I can feel the weight of the situation fall on her as she whispers intensely. "If they are raiders we could be in big trouble. Our tracks lead right back to it!"

"See! This was a bad idea!"

"We need to cover the tracks!"

Ami and I stand up and we begin to backtrack with swiftness. While she stays ahead of me, I do what I can to smear our checkered footprints, and that orange glow sits in my vision as a beacon of angst.

A hundred yards away from where we laid down to observe is not far enough, as a voice rings out and it is not one of ours.

Unintelligible due to the distance between us and the camp, I continue to try and erase the tracks, but a noise fills the air like thunder cracking despite there not being a single cloud in the sky. Ami pulls me urgently by the arm and we begin to run as quickly as we can with these attachments on our feet. Nearly making it back to a valley, we are cut off. My fears are realized as a group of shadowy figures overtake and surround us.

"Halt!" There is a clicking noise that comes from behind me that accompanies the voice.

Ready to take a defensive stance, I rip my arm from Ami and begin to spin around to swing, but she stops me, yelling out.

"Rain! Do as they say!"

In the man's hands is a strange looking object. It's nearly the length of his arms, and a small circular opening is pointed directly at me, with a knife strapped to it. Holding it by a wider area against his shoulder, I find it safe to assume it is a weapon of sorts, and I heed Ami's cautionary direction.

"I can get us out of this," I tell her calmly.

"Rain, don't," she comes back at me sharply. "We need to cooperate with them."

"You should listen to her. This rifle has the ability to take you out from three hundred yards away, and if you're close, I won't even waste the bullet." His tone is firm and confident while he waves the knife end of his weapon at me.

"Should we bring them back to camp and interrogate them?" Another voice comes from behind us.

"Bringing them back means more mouths to feed," a gruff feminine voice barks.

"Who says we need to feed them? Kill them now." Even more commentary from another shadowy person.

My instincts want to kick in, by choosing to fight them upon hearing the word kill, but I wait, grinding my teeth together.

"Shut up! All of you. We will take them back for Lady Eve to determine their fate." The one pointing his weapon at me silences them. "Back to the camp, now move!"

Reluctantly, Ami and I are forced by their numbers back toward the orange glow. When we get close, I notice two distinct classes of people within the encampment: those that are weak and broken, their clothes shredded, and those that are healthy, well-fed people, their light tan tents pristine. Each group appears to have a wide range of ages, with one exception – within the group that is weaker, there are no children.

We are hustled along through the dirty, ragged outskirts into the clean area of the tent city. The fires currently being stoked illuminate the dire situation the less fortunate are in, and it makes them look sicker. But my time to observe is short as we reach possibly the largest tent within the encampment, and I liken it to a war tent.

Reaching the front flaps, two muscular women dressed in tattered leather garments guard the entrance, their rifles resting upright against their shoulders. They recognize the group escorting us and nod, pulling back the flaps of the tent while Ami and I are shoved from behind, followed by the marauders who apprehended us.

The inside is luxurious for a tent. It's decorated with clean furs and pelts hanging around the perimeter, and laid out on the ground is a white rug that looks like it was taken from a bear. Sitting in a cross-legged position is a very tall and curvy woman with blazing red, curly hair. She wears nothing but a frilly green shirt that barely reaches below her breasts and leather shorts that ride high on her legs. I watch as her deeply tanned, freckled skin glistens against the candle light within the tent. Averting my eyes, I find myself quite embarrassed at the way she is dressed and instead focus on the shorter looking rifle at her side

"Lady Eve, we've captured two members of an unknown faction spying on the tent city. We brought them here to be interrogated," the leader of the group that brought us in speaks.

"What for?" She answers sharply. "If we don't know where they came from, kill them and dump their bodies."

"If I may object, Lady Eve, it may be a good idea to at least get an idea of who they, are and see if their clan is a risk to ours," he protests.

"We are just wanderers. We pose no threat to you," I feel compelled to say.

"Who said you could speak?!" I am abruptly hit in the back of the legs and collapse to my knees.

"As a prisoner, you'll learn quickly that around here you keep your mouth shut until someone addresses you," Lady Eve says while standing up.

She moves closer and examines Ami first. Keeping my eyes directly on Ami, Lady Eve circles her, playing with the fabric of her clothes. She gets in her face and runs a hand over her cheek, and then checks Ami's hands.

Lady Eve lets out a 'humph'.

"She's definitely not anyone in power in her clan, but it looks like she may have gotten into her leader's vanity supplies," Lady Eve scoffs. "Perhaps she's a permanent servant and her master is generous."

"Hey! What is that supposed to mean?!" Ami blurts out but is also hit in the back of the legs.

"What did I just say about speaking? I wasn't talking to you, therefore you should be quiet," Lady Eve smugly tells her.

Outraged, I look Ami in the eyes, seeking approval to counter them. Ami sees me and reads my face, shaking her head gently. Lady Eve moves over to me, leans down and grabs me by my cheeks. She forcibly moves my head back and forth, and then proceeds to stand me back up by grabbing under my arm and yanking. For a woman she has incredible strength. I feel intimidated by her clothing, and her show of dominance.

"This one is a fine specimen of a fighter. If they were indeed sent by someone, he is *her* guardian." She moves around me, running her hands over my body and I tense.

Massaging my arms and chest she grins seductively, but despite avoiding looking at her, she pulls my face down and we make eye contact. I squint at her in a questioning manner.

"I will interrogate him first. Everyone else, get out!" she orders them.

Ami is pulled to her feet by one of our captors and taken out of the tent. I watch as I am separated from her. I try once more to signal her that we need to do something, but she shakes her head, and I am left to follow along with whatever she is thinking.

"Now, it would be in your best interest to cooperate with this interrogation." Lady Eve buttons the flaps of the tent shut and then approaches me.

"What am I to be interrogated about? My companion and I are simply travelers and we happened upon your camp."

"Travelers from where? You don't appear to have any travel gear, food, or weapons. That's quite unlike any traveler around here," she speaks in a bit softer of a tone than before, hovering quite closely to me.

"I guess you could say we travel over great distances, and don't see the need to lug around a bunch of unnecessary equipment." I try to sound confident, but with her staring intently at me with her dark green eyes, I fail miserably.

"What's unnecessary about travel gear, food, or weapons?" She crosses her arms and leans all her weight to one leg.

"Our travel gear is what we're wearing. We make do," I tell her.

"What clan are you from?"

"None. It is simply my companion and I."

"That would be impossible. Everyone's affiliated with a clan, whether by choice or by being a prisoner."

"We are not from around here." I shrug.

"Well, then tell me about where you're from," Lady Eve takes a step toward me, closing that personal space I was hoping to keep open.

"Well, I used to live in a place that was green with trees and plants. There were buildings of stone—" I am abruptly interrupted by Lady Eve.

"Don't lie. Such a thing doesn't exist." Her face turns sour.

"Why would they not?" I question.

"Because there is nothing left like that. There hasn't been for a long time. So don't lie to me. I want to know where your clan is right now!"

"I am telling you, I don't have a clan."

"I would be willing to forgive those lies if you just tell me the truth. Where are they?"

"Fine, our clan was about one hundred miles south of here, but we were exiled. That's why we don't have a clan." I am left with no option but to lie to her and appease her growing fury.

"Exiled and not executed?"

"Our…execution was supposed to be to wander in the desert and die that way, but we found ways to survive." I perpetuate the lie, trying to make it sound convincing.

"Why were you exiled?" Lady Eve looks at me skeptically.

"Mistress Ami was the leader's daughter, and I was a soldier. We fell in love and when her father found out he was not pleased." I find myself crafting a story to keep her from questioning too much more. "I was not what he had in mind for her, and forbid us to be together. When he found out that we had been secretly meeting he exiled us."

"Ah, so that explains why the skin on her face was well cared for. I wonder, what would she think if I bedded her soldier?" She bites on her lower lip and presses herself against me.

"She would not like it and neither would I." I step back, blushing heavily.

This angers Lady Eve, and her face becomes sour again. Forcefully she grabs my hand and pulls me back to her, pressing us close together. I can feel her breath on my cheek as she whispers harshly into my ear.

"I'm the leader of this clan and that means I get what I want." Her breath is hot and I feel an urge to run spring up inside. "You'll do as I please!"

She swings me by the arm and proceeds to shove me toward a bedding of rugs. Finding my situation becoming more appalling by the second as Lady Eve attempts to force herself on me, I work quickly and try to pull my arm away from her. Tightly gripping my wrist, she holds me fast. I use my opposite forearm to push on her collarbone while ripping my captive arm away. Separating us, I stumble and hit against the main post in the tent while she hits the floor.

Her eyes begin to fill with tears as she becomes angry. Though I had no intention of letting her do what she wanted, I cannot help but feel bad because I knocked her down. Sighing heavily, I move to help her up and extend my arm out for her.

"Look, I am sorry I knocked you down. You left me no choice but to defend myself." I frown.

She grabs my arm and hoists herself up, but before I know what's happening she has both hands on my arm and is spinning me around like a rag doll. Letting go she launches me through the tent flaps, nearly tearing the entire tent skin down, ripping the buttons completely off. I land on my back in the sand a few feet from the tent, and Lady Eve and her personal detail quickly surround me.

"You could have had it good here," Lady Eve sneers at me, then looks to her guards. "See to it he gets assigned to daytime recon with gruel rations. And bring me the girl."

Surrounded, with the wind knocked out of me, I have no option but to stay put while she retreats back into her tent. The two muscular women hoist me up by my underarms, and drag me around her tent and further into the camp. Passing tents, I watch as Ami is led out of a nearby tent to my right and I have to act fast.

"We are just wanderers! We do not have a clan! We are just nomads from far away!" Pretending to rant like a madman while struggling against the guards, I try to give Ami as much info as I can. "We are not spies! This treatment of travelers is unfair! It's not enough that we are exiled from our own clan for loving one another that we have to become slaves to another clan now?!"

Once I am out of earshot of Ami I quit ranting, and hope she understood everything. Letting myself be dragged along the sand to the opposite side of the camp where another group of battered and beaten people are, I am already planning an escape into the night as soon as Ami and I can meet back up.

Reaching our apparent destination, I am put with a group that consists mostly of men in the same age range as I. Assuming that they are also captives here based on their malnourished and broken look, I cannot help but feel these people are being worked to a literal death. I am dropped to the ground by a fire where men are huddled, trying to stay warm in the cool night. Quickly, I attempt to stand back up, but that is quelled when they shove me back down onto my tailbone.

"Try to leave and you will be shot!" One of my escorts informs me roughly.

"Shot?" I question her.

"Yes," she replies exasperated, as if I should know already. "And our perimeter guards don't miss. If they don't cripple you, they will kill you."

My escorts find a place at the edge of the camp and proceed to patrol back and forth. I watch them from the side of the fire.

The rifles are the reason that Ami wanted to comply, I'm sure of it now. The man said he could hit me from a great distance, but how can it do such a thing? Can its projectile hit hard enough to actually kill? I suppose Ami warning me about it is proof enough, and I will have to go along for now. Agatha will be worried and Evalyn will be angry, though.

Waiting here, hoping to see Ami, plus the heat from the fire, is making me tired. Though people surround me, none of them are eager to speak, but just as well as I find my eyes closing slowly.

What could Lady Eve possibly be interrogating her about? Perhaps because of my rejection of Lady Eve she's giving Ami a harder time than she would have if I had not made up that stuff about us being lovers. But it was the best I could come up with.

My eyes are drooping, and I close them anticipating hearing Ami's sweet voice, but it does not come.

~~~~~~

I wake to find myself amongst other men strewn about in the sand and on make-shift beds made from tattered cloth. As I become more aware of my surroundings, the sun is just peeking over the horizon. When I search for Ami, she is nowhere in sight.

Jumping to my feet I begin frantically looking for her. There are a few guards strewn about, but when they notice me they don't seem to care that I am roaming around.

I find a group of women and girls huddled up asleep around a smoldering fire pit, but I do not see Ami's unique clothing and move on. Passing some tents, I peek in and find more women still asleep. She is not there either. I poke my head into another tent only to get an eyeful of a woman changing. Before I can drop the flap, she has noticed that light is pouring in and screams. Pulling her shirt on the rest of the way, she grabs a crude metal cup from a nearby table and lobs it at me.

"Get out of here, you pervert! Get out! Go!"

Having let the flap go, the cup hits it and I turn to leave, but she follows me out and begins berating me quite loudly.

"What do you think you were doing? You can't just go looking in tents as you please!" she barks.

"I am sorry, I—" I start, but am abruptly cut off.

"You're sorry? You think you're going to get off that easy? By just saying sorry? I've been violated and I'll be sure Lady Eve hears of this!" she threatens me.

"Look, it was a mistake. I was just—" Again I'm stopped mid-explanation.

"It doesn't matter if it was a mistake! There are privacy rules around here for a reason! Looking in on someone is unacceptable!"

"I don't know about the rules. I'm new—" I cannot seem to get more than a few words out at a time before being interrupted.

"Well consider this your first lesson. Now get out of this area. If I catch you here again, I'll have the guards take you out to the wastelands and leave you!"

With both hands up, I begin backing off and nodding at her. Though I have begun to turn around and walk the other way she shouts at me yet again.

"Watch where you're going!"

I trip over women strewn across the ground, fall onto them, and wake them. Jumping back to my feet I try to apologize to them also.

This is a nightmare!

"I am sorry, it was an accident," I tell them. "I was distracted."

Apparently I am not convincing enough, and before I know it the woman who I accidentally looked in on is waking other women, shouting about me being a voyeur and a pervert.

The women I tripped over believe her, and they too join in on waking everyone in the vicinity. An army of angry women closes in on me, all causing a commotion while yelling. They surround me, taking up arms in the form of sticks, clubs, pots, pans and cups. And soon, rifles are being wielded against me. Anticipating a brutal strike at any time through all the yelling and accusations, I ask myself just how much force should be used to escape. Putting my arms up in a defensive block, I know that they will only be able to take a certain amount of trauma before giving up.

"*What* is going on out here?" Lady Eve cries out, and everyone else becomes dead silent. "I was sleeping!"

"This man here was peeping in on me changing, then pretended to trip over some sleeping women so he could grope them!"

"That is false!" I yell out to Lady Eve from the middle of the crowd. "I wasn't peeping on her, I was looking for Ami. And I really did trip!"

A brief silence follows my defense before the crowd starts parting from the direction of Lady Eve's tent. Even though a sea of women surrounds me, Lady Eve towers over them while she makes her way to me, finally in full view when my original accuser moves out of the path.

"You haven't even been here a day and you've managed to give yourself a bad name, with both me, and the women of this camp." She crosses her arms and glares.

"Sorry. It wasn't intentional. Perhaps you should just let Ami and I return to traveling."

"Hah. Good luck with convincing me of that," she sneers. "Did you really peep on this woman?"

"Not intentionally. Like I said, I was looking for Ami."

"Did you feign an accident to grope women?"

"Absolutely not!" I protest vehemently.

Lady Eve looks hard at me for a few moments, then speaks loudly enough for the group to hear. "Let it be known that I declare this man innocent this *once* of the accusations that he intentionally violated the women of this camp, however he is forbidden from the women's side of the camp unless directed to be there by myself."

"Thank you…" I try to acknowledge her.

"Don't thank me yet," she barks. "Furthermore, the people who were violated accidentally, step up."

The crowd shifts some and the woman whose bare back I saw, and the three women I fell on step forward, each standing next to one another in a line.

"You each can have one shot at him with a fist if you still think he deserves it." A malicious grin crosses Lady Eve's face.

"Wait! What?!" I protest.

"Wait!" Ami's voice rings out from beyond the crowd, coming from the area of Lady Eve's tent. "Let me through. Let me through!"

Before Ami can reach me, and before Lady Eve can reply, I am cracked on the underside of my jaw by the woman whose bare skin I saw, causing me to bite my tongue and draw blood.

"How ish thish fair?!" I yell at Lady Eve with a lisp. "You shaid I wath innoshent."

"I said you were innocent of *intentionally* violating them. Intentional or not you still took something without asking. But you'll learn that as a servant of this camp, nothing comes free." An evil laugh escapes her lips as she enjoys my pain.

Ami shoves her way through the crowd, finding me dribbling blood down my chin. She wraps her arm backward around me, placing herself between my accusers and me, stopping the others from hitting me.

"We're new here. He shouldn't be punished for not knowing the rules yet," Ami defends me.

"He got a peep at my skin, I got a shot at his face. We're even." The woman scowls at Ami.

With Ami between us, I can see on their faces that they do not seem to want confrontation with her. They back down one at a time, and for my unintentional transgressions, I am only left with the one solid punch to my chin. I let out a sigh of relief. Ami grabs my hand. She and Lady Eve enter a staring contest, and neither budge.

"I thought we had the understanding that because we aren't spies we would be treated with respect here," Ami boldly snaps at Lady Eve.

"You and I had the agreement that *you* would be treated with respect here. He will still work as a servant on daytime recon, which by the way starts soon." She glances at me. "Don't worry Rain, we'll get you to the right person and he'll show you the ropes."

Ami huffs loudly and drags me off away from Lady Eve. Pushing through the crowd, we find our way back to the other side of the camp and stop near a fire pit where some elderly men continue to sleep. Turning around abruptly she looks beyond me at the place where all the women are still milling about, and then throws her arms around my neck. Hugging her back, I feel it's both right and awkward at the same time, but I do not let it concern me because I was truly worried about her.

"So, we're exiled lovers are we?" Ami whispers in my ear.

I laugh and pull away from her. Sticking my tongue out, I touch it with my index finger and I can tell it's swollen. Though still bleeding a little, it does not hurt nearly as much and I can talk almost normally.

"It was the best I could come up with when she would not accept the truth that we don't have a clan. I am glad you are okay," I tell her, releasing her from my grip.

"I'm glad you're okay too, but apparently I'm the only one who will get some sort of leniency here." She pulls away.

"It does seem like the women rule the roost here, but Lady Eve is likely still upset I turned down her offer to seduce me." I shrug.

"She did what?!" Ami's voice pitches high.

"Shh! Calm down," I urge her to lower her voice with hand motions while looking around. "She tried to bed me, but while resisting, I ended up knocking her down. She didn't like that, and launched me through the air."

"Well, you've apparently managed to aggravate the entire female population of this camp, save myself, all in a day." She puts her hand on my chest and pats playfully. "Good work, maybe they'll exile us."

"I would hardly call it good work. It was not intentional."

"It's the result that matters though, isn't it? We're going to have to find times to get together and plan…" She leans forward and whispers. "Plan our escape."

"We will need to do it when most people are asleep, either early morning or late evening." I keep my tone low while looking around tensely.

"Since you're banned from the woman's side of the camp, I'll come over to the men's side when I get a chance."

"Rain!" Lady Eve yells at me from across the camp. "It's time to start your recon training!"

I turn my head. She is standing on the top of the hill near her tent, posing like she is having a portrait painted, with her hands on her hips and hair waving slightly in the desert breeze. Looking back at Ami, I shrug.

"Looks like the mistress requires my attention," I spout sarcastically.

"Better go before she beats you up again," Ami jests.

"Very funny."

I find the most direct route toward her tent, and note a change entering into the center area of the camp. Examining as I walk, two groups exist within the camp. The first are the sickly and treated poorly, while the second are the upper class citizens within the center of the encampment who are somewhat healthier.

I find my way around the side of Lady Eve's tent. She is waiting with a burly man who is balding up top, but has a full beard of red hair. His clothes are tattered, but he appears to be one of the better-fed people I have noticed yet, next to Lady Eve. He carries a large bag on his left side, but I cannot identify anything within it. Lady Eve and the man take notice of me and I see a scowl cross both of their faces.

"Finally! When you're called, you need to put your feet to the sand and find whoever called you immediately," she criticizes.

"Okay," I nod.

"The proper response would be 'Yes, Lady Eve'," she smirks coyly.

"You like that power don't you?" My mouth cannot help itself.

"I do. Now say it or I will throw you across the camp again."

"Yes, Lady Eve," I mutter.

"We'll work on your delivery *later*." Lady Eve grins from ear to ear. "This is Kohan. He will be running you through the wringer on your first recon mission. A couple nights ago we took down a small caravan a mile or two from here. You will be doing recon and salvaging it."

"Let's go. Daylight is burning and I want to be back here before the hunting party returns," Kohan demands in a deep, scruffy voice.

"Lead the way." I pull my hood up to shade my face and begin to follow Kohan toward the north side of the camp.

"If you try to escape, Kohan will kill you," she calls after me gleefully.

"Do not worry, I'm not going to try anything."

Without Ami that is.

Kohan starts barking out orders to prepare for the excursion as we enter a new section, but they are not directed at me, so I ignore them. Half a dozen men and women stand, slinging either rifles or water skins over their shoulders. Joining Kohan and I, our group is led through yet another gathering of poorly cared for people. Though my group mates are from this area, they seem to be loyal enough to follow commands. I imagine they do not have much choice. Just beyond the border of the camp, heading north-northwest, Kohan barks out orders again.

"I want a standard checker formation. Those with water skins in the back. Those with rifles in the front. Someone hand him a water pouch," Kohan yells out, then points to me.

One of the men has both a rifle and water pouch. He removes the pouch from his shoulder and thrusts it at me. When I strap it across my torso by its leather belt, it is much heavier than I anticipated. I have to adjust it a couple times before I become comfortable.

Kohan moves us out in a formation, and I seek to find a spot for myself in the back. As I stride forward, I do my best to pick up my feet, but I end up dragging them more than not. While my reflective and airy clothing does me some good by keeping the sun out directly, indirectly the rays are bouncing off of the sand, and I can feel the heat on my face. Doing what I can to ignore it, my mind drifts in and out in this mundane march.

After walking for a significant amount of time, we come upon the wreck of material Lady Eve had instructed me about. Burned fabric and wood make up the majority of items, scattered about with hints of metal. As I wonder why Lady Eve's marauding band decided to attack whoever they were, Kohan starts instructing again.

"Take down wagon tarps and use them to drag everything," he barks out and begins pointing around the few wagons. "Gather wood with wood, cloth with cloth, and metal with metal."

I move to help pull the tarp off of the nearest wagon, but Kohan stops me by slapping his arm across my chest, and points me to a pile of wood instead. Grabbing a loose wooden wheel, it is heavier than I expect, but manage to drag it toward Kohan. The cloth tarp is brought over to the same area, and I roll the wheel on top of it, starting the woodpile. Back and forth I collect as many pieces of wood as I can before I am fatigued. Leaning over, I counterbalance myself against the weight of the water skin as it pulls on me.

"Hey, Kohan, I am going to need some water." I cannot tell whether it's dehydration or simply my personality that causes me to be so bold speaking out to him.

"Bring that pouch over here. Everyone gets one cup!" Kohan bellows out.

Pushing up off my legs I move to him and find that everyone rushes in behind me like a pack of wild animals. I lift the strap of the water skin up over my head and hand it to Kohan, who takes it easily and he pulls out a single cup from the bag on his back. He hands me the cup and proceeds to uncork the pouch, pouring the water carefully into the cup right to the brim. I guzzle it down, but find that it is not refreshing at all, warm and somewhat murky. Handing him the cup back he then passes it on to another person and rather than watching everyone take their cup, I get back to work.

When I have scavenged as much wood as I can, I collect scraps of metal and place them on a second cloth tarp. When most of the remnants have been broken down and separated I wonder how we are going to pull such weight. Though I know I will be rebuked I start to ask anyway.

"Kohan—" I barely get his name out before I am cut off.

"Hey, new guy, shut your hole," Kohan responds roughly.

"If I'm to be on this recon team, I would like to know how things work."

"The way things work are to do what I say, or you won't get fed when we get back," he says in my face.

Food definitely trumps knowing what is going to happen next, but I find an opportunity to bother him further. I do as I am told and wait for a command from Kohan, staring at him just to get on his nerves. He furrows his eyebrows and frowns at me but my face is expressionless, irking him a little more.

"What do you want?" he barks.

"Orders, sir!" I bark back, and smirk.

"A wise guy, hmm?" His glaring attempts to intimidate me, but he backs down and turns his attention elsewhere. "All right! Everyone is going to help haul these two tarps. It will be four to a tarp."

"Gather up for one last cup of water!" he yells out and produces the cup again.

Everyone lines up, and this time I am not first. I have to sit through everyone else drinking theirs, including Kohan who drinks two cups. When the cup gets to me, I wipe the brim with my sleeve before drinking. The warm water still does nothing to quench my thirst, but I am grateful to not being left out here for dead. Returning the cup to him, I move to pick up the end of the cloth tarp with the scraps of metal, along with ropes and an assortment of other items. Three others join me, but we wait for Kohan to take the lead.

Heading to the front, Kohan and the three other members on his tarp begin hauling the wood by dragging the cloth. As they hoist the cloth over their shoulders and walk, I copy them and work with my three to drag the heavy cache of items. The hauling is monotonous, worse than the walk out here. One step after another, my feet are becoming raw due to sand in my shoes.

Kohan looks back to make sure we are keeping pace. Though I cannot see his expression, I have no doubt he is scowling. Dragging our haul back takes what I estimate to be two to three times longer than the walk out.

Torches have been lit, and guards patrol the perimeter as the sun is descending. Kohan leads us into an open area within the camp, and my group follows, walking past people who pay us no attention. When he comes to a stop, he drops his cloth with a thud under the weight of the wood pieces. Laying ours down right next to his, we move up to join the rest while Kohan moves toward Lady Eve's tent.

One of the women guards leans into the tent flap and Lady Eve makes an appearance, standing with Kohan. We all watch and wait for our next directive. I am too far from them to hear what they are saying, but I continue to watch anyway. Kohan's face is quite sour while he speaks with her. She laughs out loud and slaps him on the back vigorously. I can only hope it is because I struck a nerve in Kohan.

Maybe if I annoy him enough they will stick me on some other work detail so I will not have to go out into the desert unnecessarily.

"All right recon servants, it's time for your food!" Kohan bellows out from the mound near Lady Eve's camp.

Upon hearing this, everyone I'm with rushes over to the other side of the camp. My stomach growls, and despite my feet hurting, I follow along, practically running to get whatever they are offering for food. Trailing behind, there is a large tent set up, and upon entering it is just as worn down as the rest of the camp. There are some makeshift tables and seats to my right and a counter with a crude metal pot over a fire to the left. A man ladles a gray, lumpy paste substance into bowls and then places a single strip of dried meat on it for each person in line. When my bowl is handed to me I catch a whiff of it. Its bland, bitter smell assaults my nose. The dried meat's origin is indiscernible as it's more like leather than anything.

With no silverware to be had, I take a seat in between my fellow reconnaissance workers who shovel the gruel into their mouths with their fingers. I stick my finger into the bowl and begin to play with the food. I try a bite of the gray paste and immediately spit it back out. Extremely bitter flavors hit my taste buds and I nearly gag. Looking around me, I see others having no problem with it.

How can anyone choke this down?

"Psst. Hey."

I look to my right and see a man trying to get my attention slyly.

"Hey. Break off a piece of the meat and take a bite of the gruel along with it. It won't get rid of the bitterness, but it will make it a bit more palatable." He smiles and nods eagerly.

"Thanks." I hesitantly follow his instructions.

I am still quite repulsed by the gruel, but his trick works well enough. I make sure to break up the meat as evenly as I can for each bite, so I do not run out of meat before gruel.

"How long have you been here?" He gets up and shuffles down to me, working his way in between myself and another person.

"A day." I chew vigorously and swallow with haste.

"Hmm. I've been here about four weeks. They raided my camp east of here. How about you? How'd they get you?"

"My companion and I were traveling, and we came upon this camp not knowing that it was hostile."

"Wow. Tough luck!"

"You're telling me. The whole women's side of the camp got rallied against me this morning," I half laugh.

"That was you? You're like a walking bad luck charm. Maybe we shouldn't be talking."

"Superstitious?" I quirk an eyebrow at him.

"A little bit."

Letting out a 'humph', more to myself than to him, I realize that I feel like a bad luck charm. I was stabbed and nearly died, then embarked on a permanent journey through time, I chased and fought a small army of fighters, and now I am a captive in the desert.

I may have a good home with Agatha and Ami to look after me, but I get into a lot of trouble. I think at least half of that is Ami's fault.

He asks no more questions of me while we eat. I finish off my food, if you could call it that and as it settles in my stomach, I slouch in my chair a bit and relax. The tent begins to clear out with people placing their dirty dishes back up front and I slowly follow suit. Just as I am about to leave the tent I bump into Ami.

"You're okay!" She exclaims.

"Yeah. Why would I not be?"

"'Wouldn't', we are going to have to keep up on your language skills," she corrects me. "Anyway, I've had my ears open all day and learned that recon missions are usually almost as bad as the actual battles because of the resources at stake."

"Well, nothing at all happened, other than difficult work in the desert with little water."

"Good. We can't have you getting hurt out here." She grabs my hand and smiles. "Come with me. Since we're not with any opposing faction, Lady Eve has shown a little leniency."

She leads me through camp to the other side, back to where the recon team came in at, and we enter the healthy section of the inner camp, on the men's side. We reach a grouping of tents and Ami crouches down next to a small two person sized tent. Pulling the flap back, she lets go of my hand and motions for me to go inside. There is a single piece of cloth laid out, and just enough room to sit up, albeit still hunched over. She climbs in after me and proceeds to remove my shoes and socks, before shaking the sand out of them just outside the door.

"What is this?" I ask.

"This is our tent. Since we are 'together' and neither of us are from an opposing faction, we've been given a tent."

"Seems a little unfair to the other people,"

"It won't matter much to us for long," she whispers close to my ear.

"Why?" I whisper back.

"Because in here we're going to plan our escape!" she whispers excitedly. "Then someone else can have the tent."

"What about the rest of these people? The others who are captives here."

"Rain, we need to look at this logically. This is how things are in this time period, and they will have to figure everything out on their own. You may have been the hero last time, but there's nothing you can do this time." Ami puts her hand on my shoulder. "We should get some sleep."

"Yeah."

I cannot help but feel pity for the people that are here, and the ones that will get abducted.

We lie down and I roll the opposite direction of Ami. Though we have a strong friendship which borders on something more, I feel uneasy about facing her.

I sigh and shift around a bit, trying to get comfortable against the cloth over the sand. I run through the events of the past couple days, and realize that just a couple days ago I was in a warm comfy bed with my stomach full of food which didn't taste like dirt. Despite the situation, I become sleepy and drift.

~~~~~~

"Hey, get up." Ami shakes me gently.

"Mmph," I reply to her.

"Kohan is looking for you."

"Gururuu, I do not want to go." My body aches as I feel the aftereffects of yesterday and a poor night's sleep.

"Come on!" She shakes me harder.

I wave my hand trying to shoo her off, but instead she grabs it and yanks me up to meet her face to face. She pulls too hard, and we nearly collide, finding ourselves mere inches from each other. As my eyes come into focus they are drawn to her eyes, and then her lips. The thought of stealing a kiss at this opportunity nearly takes over, but she notices the look I am giving her, blushes and turns her head away.

"You should probably hurry. Kohan doesn't look like a guy you want to keep waiting." She crawls to the entrance and exits the tent.

Following along, I put my shoes on and slide out of the tent. I pull my white reflective hood up and begin stretching my whole body out, one part at a time. As I do so, Kohan is making a direct path to me, going so far as to walk over people still lying about on the ground. The look on his face is unpleasant.

"You're late waking up! Get over to the food tent, eat and report back to me immediately at the sorting ground for your daily assignment!" he yells at me.

"Got it, Kohan," I reply, yawning.

"Lady Eve and a select few have the privilege of calling me Kohan. To you and all other servants I'm 'Sir'!" He roars it out loud so that all can hear.

"Got it…Sir." I sarcastically smile.

He glares at me while I walk casually around the hill near Lady Eve's tent. Looking at where we dropped off the materials yesterday, some has already been sorted, but I pay it little mind for the time being as my stomach grumbles.

Finding the tent from last night, it is the same situation as before: gruel with a thin slice of dried meat, but in addition we receive a small cup of water too.

With food in hand I take the same spot I sat in last night, but before I can sit I notice the guy I spoke with getting up from the table, eyeing me suspiciously. He returns his dishes to the counter while looking over his shoulder at me.

Could he really think I am bad luck?

Others around me look nervously in my direction, and I cannot help but wonder why. With the little that was given, it does not take long to finish. I tip the cup all the way back and suck up every last drop of water I can get before returning the dishes to the counter. As I move, the gruel sits heavily on my stomach, like sludge.

I wonder what is in it. I hope it will keep me healthy long enough to get out of here.

Back out in the sun that is already heating everything up in sight, I am glad for the clothing that I have to deflect some of the deadly rays. Leisurely, I wander over to the area of camp where Kohan and the piles of scavenged items are, and people furiously work to sort material.

"Finally done wasting time?" Kohan asks. "Grab some metal and take it over to the metal crafters."

"Where are they at?" I ask.

"Do you need a map of the camp?"

"A map would be quite helpful, thanks." I let my words out sardonically.

"It's not that big! Find it!"

"Don't have a fit."

"Watch it, wise mouth," Kohan warns while pointing his finger antagonistically.

"Or what?" My mocking grin returns.

Kohan moves to hit me in the mouth, but even with my clunky shoe attachments I duck under and dodge his blow. He tries again with his opposite fist, and misses yet again. Dancing ahead of him by at least a step, I taunt him and avoid a pummeling at the same time. Though he is better built than me, he moves in a predictable manner just swinging wildly and trying to land blows, but I evade and practically run circles around him.

"Stand still!" he bellows, his face turning deep red.

"And let you hit me? No thanks."

"I'm going to teach you to respect your superiors!" He spins heavily on one foot swinging his fist around to try and catch me.

Instead of dodging again, I throw my arms up, intercept the blow and throw him off of me. Kohan stumbles a few steps before recovering, but I am on him faster than he can swing again.

"There is one thing you need to know." My playful grin leaves my face, replaced by something more serious. "You are not my superior. I simply do what you say so that I get fed. That is it."

Not liking my attitude or response, his fist barrels toward me again. With a fluid motion, I use both of my forearms to block the blow and push him off to my right side, leaving him briefly open. With the attention of the camp garnered, I use the opportunity to show I am not some weak servant. Swinging an uppercut, I catch him right on the bottom side of his ribs and back away a few steps. He becomes enraged, fighting off the pain.

Kohan recovers quickly. He charges. I space my feet apart, and throw my hands up, ready to use his own momentum and weight against him. He thrusts his arm out to hit me. I pivot on my heels and grab his arm instead. With both hands I pull him into me, combining our two forces, and I jam my shoulder into his sternum knocking the wind out of him. He becomes dead weight, falling forward onto me. Rather than let him crush me, I squat and push back up, launching him over my body to slam heavily onto the burning sand. Kohan wheezes. I turn around to look at him lying there. Lady Eve and Ami are spectating.

Other than Kohan trying desperately to catch his breath, it is dead silent. Moving my shoulders around in a dominant fashion, that malevolent smile crosses my face yet again, and I am smug about my victory. Confused as to why I feel justified by violence, I try to play it off by turning toward the crowd blocking the metal pile so I can do what was expected of me in the first place.

I wish I knew what was lost in my brain so I could understand why I am so good at being violent.

Reaching the crowd they part for me, but behind them are guards. Their rifles are trained directly on me, the knives mere inches from carving out my chest cavity. Instinctively, I put my hands in the air to show surrender. From each of their weapons an audible click can be heard.

"My tent. Now." Lady Eve has snuck up behind me and her harsh tone is unnerving.

"Yes Lady Eve," those few guards reply in unison.

Turning around, I follow behind her, and am brutally shoved along. I am hit in the back with something hard, like wood, and I feel a knifepoint digging into the area between my two shoulder blades. Passing Kohan, he snarls and glares at me.

When we reach the tent, Lady Eve grabs me forcibly by the wrist but holds her other hand out to stop the guards from following. Yanking me abruptly through the flaps, I am led again into her tent.

"That was impressive," Lady Eve says quietly, while circling me. "I like strong men."

"I told you Lady Eve, I am not available." I sigh.

"Oh, I think you are." She stops in front of me and places both hands on my chest. "You see, nothing is unobtainable for the person in charge. You may have rejected me once, but believe me I don't give up that easily."

"What about the whole throwing me out of your tent bit?"

"I was just a little upset, that's all." She stares down at me and smiles.

"Look, if you must keep Ami and me here, then I suppose we will have to deal with that, but I am unobtainable to you."

"Are you? That's not what it looked like last night when you were in your tent with her, but had your back turned." She runs her hand over my face and I lean back.

"You're spying on us?!" I exclaim, outraged.

"You two sure don't act like forbidden lovers."

"Well, you will have to forgive us." I make sure my disdain for her is known. "See, we were captured and that is somewhat stressful."

"I'm going to make you mine, whether by force or your choice. It's only a matter of time." She slaps my face gently enough to be playful but hard enough to sting.

"Sorry, Lady Eve. You can threaten me, hit me, throw me, assign me to the worst jobs you have around here, but nothing will happen between us," my voice is firm.

Instead of getting mad and throwing me this time, she places her hands back on my chest and smiles deviously. Before I know what is happening one of her arms is around my back, the other hand around the back of my head, and I'm pulled into her, face-to-face. Our lips meet. I struggle to get away. Her grip on me is too tight and she takes her time kissing me passionately. She releases her grip and looks at me triumphantly but I stare at her emotionless.

Maybe if I show no interest she will lose hers and move onto the next person. Why am I finding myself in increasingly awkward and difficult situations?

"You're free to leave the tent. Report back to the recon team." She is still pleased with herself.

"Yes, Lady Eve," my tone is serious and I turn to leave.

"Don't forget, Rain. Nothing is unobtainable for me," she calls after me.

Without acknowledging her, I exit the tent to find the crowd has dispersed back to whatever areas they came from, and Kohan is waiting for me. I anticipate he will try and repay me for what I have done, but he simply stands there glaring at me. Upon reaching him, he turns toward the area currently holding the piles of material we brought back. I follow behind him silently, wanting to be fed again later. Workers are already about the business of hauling materials to several different locations within the camp.

"Metal to the metal crafters. Follow the people already hauling it there," he states bluntly, trying to hide his embarrassment underneath a stiff exterior.

I nod and move to grab some metal. Most of it is quite sharp, and bent in awkward directions. I do my best to not cut myself. Loading up as much as I can, pointy edges jab into my forearms and chest as I struggle to hold it against myself and not die. Walking slowly in tandem with other workers carrying the hazardous materials, we move toward the southern side of the camp. Three larger tents come into view. They seem to be in fairly good condition, and the center one has a little pillar of smoke rising from it. As we file into the open doorway, a wave of heat rolls past and I nearly choke.

The inside of the tent is elaborate, and I am in a familiar setting. What lies before me is a forge, set up with two slabs of stone and a small metal cauldron suspended by a metal frame chassis. Behind it a stone furnace smolders. To the right there is a workbench with small, long pointed items all over it, and tooling I have never seen before where a lone man works, fiddling with the items and a black powder. Several other people bustle about, working to cut up the pieces of metal with various saws and metal cutting scissors, and throwing them into the pot.

I follow the lead of the others and set the metal down in a pile to the left. After several trips back and forth the pile dwindles and Kohan redirects me to the pile of wood.

Though the labor is intensive, I trudge along and bring the wood to the tent next to the forge. Within is a collection of everything wooden, from scraps to wheels, and they are being broken down as well.

Finally, the materials are sorted, and following the lead of the others that I have been working with, I pick up an end of the cloth tarp and haul it over to the tent to the right of the forge. When I enter I am not the least bit surprised to see Ami there, amongst the various pieces of cloth and leather that Lady Eve's camp has collected.

She smiles at me while unraveling some thread from a woven sack, and I can see she is in her element. We shove the large piece of fabric in their storage area. While the others from the recon team leave, I take the time to sneak over to Ami.

The other people working in the tent look warily at me, but I pay them no mind. I lean in close to her ear.

"You need to hear it from me first because Lady Eve has not given up. First, she spied on us while we were sleeping and because we were not 'together' she now thinks I am fair game. If we are going to keep up this charade of being eloped lovers then we need to act like it," I whisper.

"Got it," she whispers back and I can see a glimmer of excitement in her eyes.

"Second, because she thinks I am fair game, and because I beat Kohan she decided she was going to force herself on me. She kissed me despite my struggling to get away."

"What?!" Ami looks at me with wide eyes then covers her mouth, realizing she had gotten loud.

"Shh!" I put my hands to my lips and look around at the peering eyes. "We just have to keep up our act."

She stares in disbelief as I turn to leave the tent, but smiling at her breaks jealousy's hold, and she returns the smile.

Out into the hot desert again, I search for Kohan and locate him standing near the hill by Lady Eve's tent, conversing with her. To annoy him, I move directly behind Kohan and stand there silently, hovering. They are talking quietly. Although Lady Eve has seen me, she allows Kohan to continue on, uncaring that I am listening.

"We need to head toward the mountains and take a cave. We've gathered enough supplies to try and take the stronghold and gain a permanent place with the clans again," Kohan tells Lady Eve.

"Do we have the manpower though?" She crosses her arms.

"I'm fairly certain that we do with the materials and supplies from the armored wagons we took the other night. And, if we put Rain with them we should have a fairly decent chance at minimal casualties. It takes a strong person to take me down."

"I'm not sure that I want him on the front lines." Lady Eve smirks while looking at me in an obvious manner.

"I assure you that with him being there it will be our best chance."

Kohan finally notices I am behind him and looks at me scornfully.

Since he is the one that seems to have been the strongest before I took him down, I am willing to bet that he was Lady Eve's favorite play toy, and that by putting me at the front of whatever battle they are planning, he is going to ensure I die so he can reclaim favor with her.

"If I may interrupt, what should be done now since we are finished with sorting?" I ask.

"Do you know how to use a rifle?" Kohan asks.

"No," I reply hesitantly. "I didn't even know such things existed until recently."

"We'll train you to use a rifle," Kohan blurts out, but instead of looking at me ends up staring at Lady Eve.

"Fine." She draws it out and sighs while looking at me. "But Rain, don't think that you'll be able to use it to get away from me."

"Let's go." Kohan turns and bumps into my shoulder on purpose.

We quickly walk over to where he gathered the others yesterday for our recon, and take shelter from the sun under a canopy. There, the members of the recon team sit at a bench, dismantling and cleaning the items I have come to identify as a 'rifle' with long black brushes. Kohan grabs one that is assembled, and a handful of the long, spherical, pointed objects I recall seeing in the blacksmithing tent.

"Grab that target and come with me." Kohan points at a wooden, man-shaped object.

I do as he says, and follow him around the back of the tent with the heavy and awkward target while he leads us out of the camp, several hundred yards from the edge.

"Set that up about fifty paces from here," he instructs brashly.

"Fifty? Did you not say these could reach up to a few hundred yards?"

"They can, if you're good enough with them and take care of them." He is already becoming annoyed as I see his face turn a little red. "But since you're green, you are getting the kid training and starting off with a short range. Now get moving."

Placing it as instructed, I return to where he is standing, and he begins to instruct me in the ways of operating the rifle.

"There are things you need to know about the rifle before you use it so that you know what I'm talking about. First is this entire thing is called a rifle. It fires bullets, round metal projectiles, at whatever you aim at and pull the trigger." He holds it up for me to see. "I'm going to quickly highlight the key points of the weapon. There is the barrel, where the bullet shoots out of. Underneath the barrel is the hand guard. There is the body where the breech, scope, grip and trigger are located. And this is the butt of the rifle."

"So how does it shoot the bullet?" I examine it closely, realizing that it is far out of my league of understanding.

"The trigger initiates a small explosion and sends the bullet down the barrel. But that is what you need to know for now." He hands me the rifle and points to the ground next to where he is. "Now stand here, and with one hand put the butt up to your shoulder area, and your other hand under the hand guard on the barrel."

I do, and wait for him to tell me what to do next, but he manually adjusts the butt of the rifle up further, digging it into my shoulder. Circling me like a hawk, he scrutinizes my stance, and then kicks at my feet so I have them slightly spread apart, with more weight on my back leg.

"Now bring your hand up to the grip and trigger, but *do not* touch the trigger," he barks. "Then hunch your shoulders up, tilt your head and look through the scope."

As I do, everything appears to get closer in that eye, but in my other eye everything stays the same. It's similar to Ami's binoculars.

"Aim the crosshair of the scope at the target and do your best to keep steady," he commands.

Trying to do as he says, I train the scope on the target. It is harder than it sounds because every time I breathe my chest rises and my arms move. Holding it in one place, my arms become fatigued and I allow my arms to relax and point it down.

"It is difficult."

"That's because you need to build up the right muscles in your arms from training, and learn to regulate your breathing," he scoffs. "Try breathing in through your nose and exhaling through your mouth."

Bringing the rifle back up and looking through the scope, I breathe as instructed. There is a small improvement in steadiness. He keeps me waiting for his next direction, standing in the sun as if to torture me, but my protective clothing helps me stay cool. In position for several minutes, my arms go a little numb, and I struggle to keep the barrel and scope pointed at the target, the breathing trick no longer working to keep me steady.

"I cannot hold my arms up much longer," I tell him.

"Well then I guess you won't last long in battle," he retorts.

"What about using the rifle?"

"Not until I say that you're ready!" he barks rather loudly.

My arms just cannot take it any longer, and I have to drop the rifle to my side once more. They ache from the stress of being in the same position for an extended period of time. Kohan looks at me displeased.

"Lift those arms back up!" he yells.

"I held them up for as long as I could!" I snap back.

"How did such a weakling beat me?!"

"I am faster and smarter than you. That's how." I turn to him, contemplating pointing the rifle at him, despite not knowing exactly how it works.

"Why you!"

Kohan lunges at me. I swing the rifle around and hammer him in the stomach with the butt, however he is unfazed. He grabs my right arm, and twists it around my back, causing my muscles and joints to blare with pain.

"Not so smart-mouthed now that you're caught, huh?" Kohan's tone is smug.

My arm feels like it is about to be torn off. I find myself in debate on whether I should attempt to get out of it, or just give in. While I am contemplating it he takes advantage of the situation and hits me in the back of the legs at my knees, forcing me to the ground.

"You come here and disrupt our way of life. You've only been here a few days and have effectively upset the entire camp. And my chances with Lady Eve are gone because of you!"

"I don't want her. Let me and Ami escape and you can have Lady Eve," I grunt.

"I'm afraid I can't do that. You have to die in battle, and I have to come out alive in order for me to gain favor with her again. That's how she works."

"Maybe you and I can work together to make her think I died, and then you can help me sneak Ami out of the camp so she and I can be on our way." I struggle against his grip.

Kohan is quiet, and while I cannot see him, I know he is contemplating my proposal. His grip loosens and my arm comes free, allowing me to bring it back around to the front of my body. Back on my feet I turn around, and Kohan's suspicious stare judges my words and face.

"How do you plan on coordinating such a thing?"

"Can you protect against bullets? With metal perhaps?" I question.

"We do have some shielding that can be used. We're not sure where it came from, but we're pretty sure it pre-dates the cataclysm from the sky in the past."

"I have no idea what you're talking about." I am confused by the combination of words he has strung together.

"It's the reason this area of the world is desert. But that's beside the point. This material is bullet resistant and is a lot lighter than metal." He scratches his red beard and looks off to the sky.

"So I would put this material on, get shot, and you could report to Lady Eve I died."

"It might work." He is deep in thought about this plan. "It would require your garment to convince her."

"I do not know how I will make it to my destination without it, but if that is my only choice then so be it." I nod.

"If Lady Eve finds out about any of this she will kill the three of us. Are you sure you want to put your friend in danger?" His eyes return to me and a scowl crosses his face.

"We have no choice." I shrug.

"We will be moving soon, meaning our chance of coming across a caravan to raid will increase. When we do, you will be with me and that's where you pretend to die. You will have to return to camp and stay outside visual range, but that night I will patrol and bring her out to release her with supplies which will get you far enough away from the camp."

"I like this idea because we both get what we want." I smile.

"For now, just continue as if this agreement doesn't exist. Make it look like we are close to snapping each other's necks."

"What are you talking about? I was this close to snapping your neck just now," I joke with him, while using my fingers to indicate a small amount.

"Don't do things like that." For the first time Kohan cracks a smile, but his face turns sour again. "Joking around will be suspicious. Back to training. Lift that rifle up."

Under the new mutual understanding, I find myself not feeling so antagonistic toward him, following his instructions.

"Now that you have the basics, put your finger on the trigger and just barely pull it back while aiming at the target."

Breathing in I hold my breath and pull the lever, hearing an audible click within the rifle, but nothing happens. I raise my head and drop my shoulders while looking to Kohan.

"Nothing happened," I state the obvious.

"Right. There was no bullet loaded." Kohan hands me a single bullet. "Now take this, open the breech and push it up until you feel it snap into place."

He hands me a bullet, and I insert it into the chamber.

"Now close the chamber and do what you did before."

Taking my stance and bringing the gun up to my shoulder once more, I hunch and look through the scope. My free hand slides onto the grip and finds the trigger. Barely pulling on it releases a deafening boom right next to my ear, and the rifle is forcefully shoved into my shoulder. Trying to keep my balance, I fail and fall backwards, landing on my tailbone. Even though it is sand, it still stings.

"What was that?!" I yell, trying to stand back up. My ears are ringing and Kohan smirks once more before going back to his sullen look.

"Let's see how you did." He stretches out his arm and helps me up.

We examine the target, and there is a large gaping hole directly in the chest area. As I marvel and fear the power I hold within my hands, he speaks.

"Not bad, but you will need more practice." He points to return to the original spot.

~~~~~~

After hours of practice we return to camp, and as he directs me to the outdoor bathroom at my request, we part ways. The bathroom they have set up is away from the camp, and it is a community bathroom. It is quite disgusting: there is a grouping of four walled enclosures near each other, and once inside one of them I see that the toilet is a hole in the ground. I shudder.

Finished, I have nowhere to wash my hands, and wipe them fervently against my outfit as I head to the food tent. Upon entering silence falls over the area and all eyes are on me.

Wondering what I have done to garner such interest, I nervously take my food and water rations, and sit down. When I do, I notice a shifting amongst the table I have sat at, and everyone moves away. I glare at them for fun while I eat. My solitude is broken when Ami enters the tent, grabs her rations and sits next to me. She puts her hand on my leg and we exchange smiles while eating our gruel.

"How've you been, dear?" she asks sweetly.

"Just fine, sweetie." I grin endearingly. "Kohan decided that I needed training on how to shoot a rifle."

"What?!" Her voice jumps in pitch and tone. "No, no, no. You can't be using those things."

"Why?" I ask.

"They are deadly!" She smacks my leg.

"I don't have a choice. Lady Eve and Kohan said that I was going into battle to help them capture something." I shrug.

"This is outrageous! I'm going to speak with Lady Eve right now." Ami starts to get up. I grab her arm, and pull her into my lap.

"It will be okay. I promise." I wink at her to try and give her a hint there is more to it than I'm letting on.

Without realizing it, I have put both of us in an awkward situation as my arm is wrapped around her, and she sits on my lap. She, however, does not miss a beat and throws her arms around my neck, and leans forward. Our foreheads touch and we gaze into each other's eyes. Even in the dim light of the candles and lanterns of the tent I can see her beautiful light blue eyes clearly. After a minute, she slides back to her seat and eats her food silently. Looking bashfully at one another while we eat, we play up to the idea of being together.

After we are finished, we head toward our tent. While walking, we see Lady Eve. Ami latches onto my arm and pulls me in close, giving her a dirty look. Though I do not know if she is just acting her part out, or if she is truly being jealous, I follow her lead and wrap my arm around her. Lady Eve catches sight of us and she scowls, but not a word is exchanged.

When we reach our tent, I pull the flap open for Ami and let her in first. Hoisting the flap up so that light from a nearby fire seeps in, I follow behind her. She looks at me, and I smirk.

I lean in close to her ear and whisper, "We now have a plan to get out of here."

"How?" she whispers back.

"I have made a truce with Kohan, and he is going to get us out of here. It will take some explaining though."

I tell her of my discussions with Kohan; why he has it in for me, and what we're going to do to fix the whole situation. She nods while I go over the details of the whole plan, and then is silent for a few moments.

"So you're going to be protected the whole time?" She sounds genuinely concerned.

"If we execute this perfectly, we will escape and head the opposite direction, and we can get back to the house."

"You didn't tell him where we were going right?"

"Of course not." I am a little offended at the thought that I might be daft enough to divulge that information.

~~~~~~

Days have passed, and they have begun blending together as the camp prepares to set out toward the mountains. Everyone works to load things onto armored wagons we finished assembling yesterday. In a moment alone, Kohan informed me that it will take a couple days with a caravan this large to get there, increasing our chance for the plan to work.

With no animals to do the hauling for the camp, the servants are required to do it instead. The armored wagons are tall enough to fit people under, and attached on the underside, between the axels and metal plated wheels, are large bars to grab onto and push against. Metal skirting is hung from the base to protect those pushing.

On the top is more protective metal shielding, and metal arches for cloth to be draped over to protect from the sun.

Joining the recon team, we load unused materials onto one of the armored wagons. While passing chunks of wood along a chain of people to be loaded, I look around and notice that the camp has become desert once more, save for the food tent and Lady Eve's abode.

With everyone in camp working together, the work is accomplished with great speed. When the wood is loaded, the other materials not in use follow suit.

Once everything is loaded, and I have a brief break, I find Ami up on the second armored wagon hand-sewing together the canopy with other women. I sit down on a wooden box next to her while she works just to be in her presence. The other women glance in my direction, but do not stare long, as it would seem they have gotten used to my making visits while she is working.

"It looks like we are going to be heading out soon. Tonight, possibly tomorrow," I tell her. "It's going to be difficult."

"I know, but everything will be all right." Her demeanor is cheery.

"Yeah. I will protect you from everything, even *falls*." I allude to the possibility that we will be forcefully pulled back to the house if our escape plan fails.

"How will you do that?" She continues to concentrate on her large needle and thread, but she is smiling.

"I'll find a way." I smile back, despite her attention being elsewhere.

With my feet rested, I stand up and massage her shoulders for a moment before leaving. The muscles around her shoulders and neck are tight, so I do what little I can to work a few knots out. She relaxes some, and I take my leave, heading down the ladder only to have Lady Eve intercept me.

"Rain, the only man I'm interested in seeing. Why don't you bed with me tonight in my tent?" She says it loud enough for Ami to hear, and winks.

"I will continue to stay with Ami," I respond in a normal tone.

"But she's no fun. I can show you the time of your life," she says in a sultry manner.

"Lady Eve, you know that Ami is my partner. I will not betray her."

"Being in charge here has its advantages. I can make people disappear if I want. She could be exiled without you, or perhaps even killed," Lady Eve says in a disturbingly excited manner.

"You would be unwise to do such a thing as it would only anger me," I cross my arms and scowl. "I promise if you hurt her I will unleash unbridled wrath."

"Ooh! Are you threatening me?" She giggles. "You know I like my men strong, and I definitely like it when they try to be dominant too."

"Laugh if you like. It does not bother me. Just keep what I said in mind."

"Don't worry. I will, honey." She slowly grabs for my crossed arms but I back away and turn around. "Aww, now don't be like that."

Leaving in silence, I move under the wagon where most of the people have begun to congregate, and mingle amongst them in the shade. Though tents have been taken down, many people have retained their cloth bedding and have begun to rest up for the journey. Looking for an open spot I find that between the two armored wagons there is minimal space for me, let alone for when Ami and I will need to sleep. Kohan finds me as I wander.

"Servant. Get some food and sleep. You're on point with Bezzel and myself tonight as the caravan moves."

"Who is Bezzel?"

"The superstitious guy you scared into thinking you're bad luck."

"You sure he's going to work with me?" I chuckle.

"Just keep your mouth shut and things will be fine," Kohan snaps.

"Fine, fine!" I proclaim loudly and throw my hands up in the air.

I storm out of Kohan's presence in an attempt to get people's attention, and make my way to the food tent. A few dozen others are already in line, and I wait to receive my gruel and water. When I take my bowl, I find there is a double portion of meat in it.

"What's this for?" I ask the cook, pointing to the meat.

"By orders of Lady Eve, you are to receive a double portion of meat from now on," she responds.

"Take it back. There are others here that need it more than I do." I shake my head.

"If I don't give it to you, Lady Eve will have my head mounted on a pike."

"Whatever," I sneer, and then in a boisterous voice I yell out. "Which one of you servants wants this extra meat?"

Surprisingly, it takes a moment for someone to speak up. A very skinny man with an unhealthy slouch stands. He appears to be older as his face is wrinkled and his hair is graying. His tattered clothing barely fits his body, threatening to slip off him, were it not held on by rope. I move toward him at the back of the tent, my bowl of gruel and two pieces of meat in my hand. I take one of the pieces of meat off, and stretch my hand out to him.

"Eat that food and you won't be eating again for a week, servant," Lady Eve's voice snaps from the opening of the tent, directed at the older man.

Lady Eve's cruelty angers me. I slam my bowl of food down on the table near the old man, slap the meat into his hand and spin around with the water cup still in hand.

"I will do with my portion of food what I like!" I yell across the tent.

"Make no mistake, Rain. I may like you, but I still make the rules around here. You will eat that extra piece of meat, or Ami won't get anything." I can see her anger flaring up, and I have struck a chord.

"You think you can manipulate me? You're wrong." I storm over to her and stop two to three inches from her, then whisper. "It would be easier for me to manipulate you than it would for you to manipulate me."

"Oh really?" She glares angrily.

"Yes, and I will prove it." I shake the cup at her voraciously. "The servants, the captured people, get one piece of dried meat, where all the trusted people get two correct?"

"Yes."

I have her hooked.

"If you start treating these servants better, starting with that extra portion of meat, I will willingly kiss you in private." I attempt to strike a deal for their sake.

"In public and you have a deal," she counters.

"*In private* or no deal."

Lady Eve crosses her arms, and a sly smirk appears. She stands there for a few moments, leaving me to guess at what she's thinking about, but she breaks the silence before I can.

"Make it a sweeter deal for me. Sleep with me before we set out tonight," she speaks loud enough for everyone to hear.

"Out of the question." I grind my teeth, and I can see where this is headed.

"Fine. I guess I'll just have to take away all the meat from the servants, and give it all to my trusted."

"You would not."

"I would, *and will*, unless you sleep in my bed with me, tonight," she rubs her hand across my face.

"You're a tyrant." I pull away in disgust.

"Now what was that about you manipulating me?" she whispers deviously. "Who has the real power here? I want to hear you say it."

"You...," I mutter.

"That's right. Now the deal is you kiss me in public *and* sleep in my bed, and they continue to get meat. Are we in agreement?"

"My morals to see these people treated better dictate one real answer to your proposal. I will do as you ask."

"Good. You'll come to like me eventually," Lady Eve winks and turns around to leave.

"What about your kiss?" I ask sarcastically and grab her shoulder to stop her.

"I said in public. I plan to hold an announcement before I take you into my tent, and that's when you can do it." She pulls away from my grip.

She is gone, and I am left humiliated in front of this lot. Returning to my bowl, the old man nods in thanks, but I am too annoyed to acknowledge him properly. Instead I slam my cup down, losing a little bit of water and eat while thinking to myself.

What have I gotten myself into? Outplayed, I have effectively sold myself so that these people can keep eating the same as they were. Ami and Kohan aren't going to like this either. I'm not sure who to tell first.

After my meal and a good deal of contemplating, I get up and slam my dishes down at the front, still irritated at myself for being so arrogant to think I could convince her to do what I wanted.

Leaving the tent, I watch people work for a few minutes while I look for Kohan, figuring he should probably know first. When I spot him, I move to intercept. He appears to be going over the inventory laid out, I assume for our trip tonight. When I approach, he looks to his side, takes notice of me, and then returns to counting out bullets on a cloth.

"Kohan," I start, while looking around to see if anyone is listening in. "There's something you need to know now before Lady Eve announces it."

"What is it?" He stops and turns his full attention to me.

"She has manipulated me into a promise I don't want to keep, but if I don't, the servants will have their meat privileges revoked." My nerves start getting the best of me.

"Spit it out, Rain."

"She has demanded I publically kiss her during an announcement, and then retire into her tent with her, to her bed, before we leave tonight."

"Decline her," he demands sternly.

"I cannot. Those servants cannot live off of that gruel alone," I say in a pleading tone.

"Listen here. I don't give a snake's tail about those servants. They're going to likely die in the upcoming battles anyway. I'll say it again, decline her." Kohan becomes very agitated, his face turning a bright red.

"I am sorry, Kohan. I cannot do that. Perhaps if they are fed better they will have more energy, and a better morale for the upcoming battles, and we will not lose as many people."

"You don't get it. They're all expendable. All of them. I will put it to you this way, decline her or our plan and deal is off," his voice elevates further.

A conundrum. I have two options. Decline Lady Eve and let them suffer while Kohan's deal stands, or help the people of the camp by agreeing to Lady Eve's deal and have Kohan betray me, likely resulting in mine and Ami's death. As much as I want to help those people, staying here is the worst of the options for Ami and I. I have to keep her safe, for Agatha.

"Create a distraction for me," I tell Kohan.

"What?"

"Interrupt her announcement with something. Anything."

"I can't just come up with something like that."

"You are going to have to," I point at him aggressively. "Otherwise I am going to be forced – against my will – to kiss her again and then be hauled into her tent. It is up to you to create a distraction."

"How about I just kill you now and that's the end of it." He grabs me by the wrist and threatens to break it like a twig.

"I would prefer to live, thanks." I wrench my hand away. "Just come up with something. I have to go tell Ami to be on her toes."

Sprinting toward the armored wagon where I last saw her, she is still there, pulling the cloth over the top of the framework. She and the others tie it down, making it enclosed, except for the front and rear sides of the wagon. With an opening to jump in before she starts something new, I find myself trying to catch my breath after running.

"Ami, we need to talk," I whisper and pull her aside.

I brief her on all that has transpired between Lady Eve, Kohan and I and I can see she is not pleased. Pretending to be a couple has undoubtedly brought us closer together, and she would be upset about Lady Eve's proposals and actions.

"Is he going to create a distraction?" she asks.

"I don't know. I hope so."

"Me too." She hugs me.

After sitting for a bit, the noise of a horn blasts across the camp, and everyone begins filing out of the wagon. Following them, Ami and I exchange glances and head toward the hill near Lady Eve's tent. Standing atop it she holds a large brass horn in her hand, and is having everyone gather around the front side of the hill. Her eyes dart around, and I just know that she is looking for me. When she finally spots me, she beckons me with her finger. I look to Ami.

"I guess this is it," I mumble.

She has a triumphant look about her as she stands tall and waves for me to come forward. I make my way through the crowd and up the hill, feeling the stares from these nomadic pirates on my backside. If I had not been nervous already, the hundred or so people staring would have done it. But my embarrassment has only begun. I climb the hill and turn around to face everyone. Lady Eve grabs my arm, and giggles.

"My clanswomen and men, my servants, our day has arrived after being exiled into the desert to retake our rightful place amongst the other clans in the mountains! And at my right hand will be your new Lord. Lord Rain! His compassion has stirred me to be more generous, and therefore by my decree, all servants now get the same amount of food as normal clanswomen and men! Take this gesture of goodwill and use it to strengthen your morale in taking back our home!" Lady Eve is boisterous and flashy with her speech, and tugs on my arm a few times.

"I want everyone to eat well if you haven't already, and get their rest before we head out because tonight is going to be a long night of travel!" She finishes up with a leader's words of kindness that I know are false. "Now to seal mine and Lord Rain's bond!"

She turns to me and grabs both of my hands while looking at me expectantly.

I hesitate and look at Kohan who stands off to the back. He is staring me down, eyebrows furrowed. With no distraction, I have no choice and begin leaning forward toward pressing my lips against Lady Eve's. My breathing becomes heavy. Sweat begins to drip down my forehead.

This is it. I have to risk Ami's life – and mine.

A flash of light catches my eye from the other side of the camp, beyond the caravan.

Bezzel, using a mirror to reflect what sunlight is left in the sky, is running full-speed toward the gathering, yelling heavily and unclearly. Lady Eve sees my attention is diverted, and turns to find out what the yelling is about. He leaps and bounds up Lady Eve's hill and comes to a dead stop, huffing.

"There is a large, heavily armed caravan heading this way! They're coming from the direction of the mountains!" he yells.

"Are they a supply caravan?" Lady Eve drops my hands and turns to him, her mood becoming serious.

"They are carrying mostly munitions. It's a war caravan," he coughs and sputters.

"How far out are they?"

"About two hours march."

"Well, it seems that we're not getting that rest." Lady Eve pouts and then yells at everyone. "Pack up the rest of the stuff! All able-bodied men pick up your rifles!"

Kohan turns to move off and I jump down the hill out of Lady Eve's grasp to follow. He does not acknowledge my presence as we walk toward where the rifles are stored.

"Good distraction," I whisper while people bustle about us.

"I didn't do it," he whispers back. "I had no intentions of creating a distraction. I wanted you to publically humiliate Lady Eve so that she would turn to me instead."

"Good. Glad to know I can count on you when I need it," I sneer.

"You'll have your help of getting out of here." He glares at me briefly as we push our way through a crowd.

When we make it to the cache of rifles, Kohan retrieves the life-saving vest from a hiding place. It is heavy, but it is neither metal nor wood. Crouching to hide myself from Lady Eve's sight, I pull my white top off and fit the vest over my head, putting my arms through and cinching it down with adjustable straps. I put my top on, and stand back up. Kohan loads me up with a rifle, a pouch of bullets and a bag to sling over my shoulder. Bogged down, I move sluggishly, but I am prepared.

Following Kohan to the front of the caravan, I notice that the air has begun to cool as the sun is nearly against the horizon. Behind and to the sides of me, the rest of the camp has been quickly disassembled and packed.

Lady Eve appears on the forward wagon at the front. She puts her brass horn into the air and blows. Kohan and the small army amassed, with rifles at the ready, begin to move. When I look over my shoulder, I see underneath the wagons the people slaving away to push and move it.

Kohan allows Bezzel to lead our group several hundred paces in front of the wagons, and like a sea of people, we wash across the sand. On the front line, next to him, I struggle to keep my footing with all the weight I am carrying. The shoe attachments catch little sand mounds, but I keep moving. On our way to plunder this caravan, I have the distinct sense that there is a familiarity about this, as if I have done this kind of thing in my past. I feel unclean.

I don't want to take someone's life from them, but no doubt I will have to fire to keep the charade up. I will have to purposely miss so I can keep my conscience clean. I may be willing to fight someone, even injure them greatly if I know they are doing evil, but I don't know if these people are good, bad, or somewhere in-between.

Walking about the distance Bezzel mentioned leaves us still moving at dusk. Black specs appear in the distance, and beyond them, past several larger mounds of sand, appears the top of a dark brown mountain. Bezzel corrects our course, and we move on an intercept path. Their wagons soon become distinguishable. Bezzel holds his fist up in the air and Kohan follows. Everyone stops marching and our wagons quickly catch up to us.

Kohan raises his rifle to his face to look through the scope, and addresses the immediate vicinity of rifle carriers. "As night falls, we will fall upon them! Their numbers appear to be small, and we will have the advantage! Take as many captives as you can, but don't hesitate to kill them if they resist! Spread out!"

With the sun gone and the moon just rising, our guide to their camp is a beacon of fire they have started.

Slowly at first we creep up toward the stopped armored caravan, and our group spreads out to surround them. Finally, when we are close enough to them, we charge toward their caravan with our guns pointed. I cannot tell where the first shot is fired, but it quickly begins the battle.

A yell from within their encampment calls for reinforcement. Dozens more pile out of the four wagons with their weapons, and begin firing. Ducking and dodging through the storm of bullets, I avoid being hit for the moment only to watch as our group begins to take casualties. From within the wagons, the reinforcements are tossed large, clear barricade shields. They quickly set them up, and fire in between the gaps, turning the tide of battle in their favor. Bodies begin falling on the ground around me and the iron smell of blood begins to fill the air.

With our forces being decimated by theirs, Kohan calls for retreat and we turn to run back to our caravan, finding ourselves soon out of range of their weapons. Expecting the whole time while running to get hit in the back with a bullet, I am surprised I have made it back alive, along with those who turned and ran when Kohan called it out. Disadvantaged by their shield wall stopping bullets cold, and now outnumbered, I am left wondering what the next move will be.

Following Kohan, he moves to the second wagon where the munitions were stored, and climbs up to the covered area. He tosses his rifle down to me, and I hold it while waiting. Scuffling can be heard, as well as a few protests from Kohan to whoever is up there. He reappears with something I had not seen before. Placing several large round objects in various pockets, he climbs back down the ladder and snatches his rifle from me.

"What was that?"

"Grenades. Those shields won't do anything for them now," Kohan mutters more to himself than me.

Returning to the first wagon, Kohan climbs up and I follow along. Making our way to the front where Lady Eve is precariously perched, he addresses her.

"Lady Eve, I am taking some of the plating from the wagons. They've constructed a bullet barrier and are picking off our men from behind it," he tells her.

"Do it. You have my full confidence," she tells him. Though it is dark, I can see this perks his attitude up.

Back down on the ground, we return to the group which made it back, and he begins bellowing. Though they are recuperating, some being bandaged up from wounds, they seem eager and ready to march off again to their deaths as Kohan begins directing them.

"All able hands, start removing the metal plating from the sides not currently exposed to the supply caravan!"

Kohan oversees the removal of the plating from the front, rear, and right sides of the caravans. They come off in sizes two to three bodies wide, and the group drags them along by handles I had not seen previously. I sling my rifle over my shoulder and find an open spot amongst two others to assist in moving the plating to our defense at the front. With the plating we need down and in place, we wait for something. When I hear the wagons moving, I look to see that the sides that we did not take plating from are being lined up to protect those still underneath.

Moving again, our wall of shields leaves little gap to be hit through. Kohan leads point with a single shield. Barely able to see Kohan through the gaps, I do my best to just keep up with the two others with whom I am carrying the large metal shield.

Gunshots ring out again, and this time it's clear that they are coming from the opposing camp first. The sound of the metal bullets ricocheting off our plating makes me feel a bit safer, but I know at the end of this I will be shot anyway. A new sound can be heard and when I hear a weapon being rapidly fired it strikes terror into my heart. With bullets pinging one right after the other in quick succession on several of our plates, I can't help but think that they set up a whole row of people just to fire. But the rate it pounds on us sounds inhuman.

"Chain gun! Band together! No gaps!" Kohan yells out over the noise.

Shuffling around, we begin to make our wall solid, and he joins us. No longer able to see him amongst the mass of people and shielding, I am left to wonder what comes next. He steps back from the crowd a few paces, and begins throwing things high above our wall and toward the firing, one right after the other. Yelling is heard briefly, followed by explosive vibrations shaking our shielding, and several fireballs torching the sky. Amongst the chaos, the bullets stop pinging our barricade, and Kohan hurls more grenades.

A large explosion rocks me to my core, larger than any of the others, knocking our plating out of alignment. One of their wagons has been enveloped in flames. It crackles and pops, with several smaller explosions. The opposing faction has scrambled to move the other three wagons away. Kohan sees this too.

"Charge!"

The metal plates drop, and everyone charges forward, rifles at the ready, except for Kohan who turns to me and trains his gun on my chest. A crack fills the air, and I am impacted directly in the chest. Knocked onto my back, I wheeze heavily, and I have difficulty breathing. My chest aches, but somehow I can discern that it is nowhere near the pain I should be feeling if one of the bullets had actually ripped through me. Kohan begins stripping my shirt and vest, and smears someone else's red sticky blood all over my chest.

"Stay completely still. The battle isn't over yet, and we will be returning to pick up the metal plates. You need to be convincing to anyone who sees you," he tells me while kicking sand over my lower half, and running some through my hair.

Peace finds me as Kohan leaves and the people from camp continue to wage war against the three wagons. The urge to look around is difficult to control as noises draw my attention, but needing this escape, I do as I am told, keeping my breathing shallow.

After having laid there for what seems like hours, the battle dies down and one side or the other has been victorious. There is shuffling around me. I stay motionless, save for my shallow breathing, and Kohan's voice can be heard.

"Everyone not injured start hauling these plates back!" he barks. "All injured report to the caravan for medical attention! Keep the prisoners secured!"

Feet stamp around me, and the metal plate that lies nearby is picked up. Bezzel's voice is heard not far off.

"He really was bad luck. Got himself killed," he says.

"Forget about him. He's dead, and we have living to worry about," Kohan snaps.

"Lady Eve won't like this," he continues to talk.

"I suggest that if you don't want to join him, you get to work, Bezzel!" Kohan's voice elevates.

Finally, the noise disappears in the far distance, and I am left to wonder if it is safe to move now. Cautiously, I open my eyes to find the stars twinkling like gems above me, and a cloud rolls over the moon. A breeze hits, but the burning wagon warms me. I turn my head from side to side slowly and look around the nearby area; not a living soul is in sight. Lying half naked, the sand chafes my skin, but I still don't know if it's safe to move.

I assume by now Kohan will have shown Lady Eve my blood soaked clothing, and told her some wild story about how he had to put me out, or maybe he blamed it on the other group. I suppose I don't care now, as long as he can get Ami out to me.

Becoming restless, I implement the next phase of the plan and flip over onto my stomach. Needing to stay low so as not to be noticed, I crawl along toward the smoldering wagon. Coming across a dead body I strip her of her shirt, slip it on, and continue moving past the first wagon heading toward the other three that were moved off and are not illuminated.

I need to circle around the back of our stopped caravan. Hopefully by the time I get there, Kohan will have found a way to pull Ami away and given her provisions.

Crawling takes a significant amount of time, but playing it safe I make sure to avoid detection. Out beyond the three other wagons, and away from the light, I feel it might be safe for me to stand up and at least crouch along. The moonlight illuminates nearby sand dunes, but I find that with the darker shirt I wear now I'm not as reflective. When I look to gain my bearings on Lady Eve's caravan I find that it too is not reflecting light. A shadowy speck in my sight now, I follow an arc far outside, and my mind begins playing tricks on me.

What if those are not the wagons? They could be hills, or something else.

With no choice but to have faith, I focus on them, and make a wide berth around to the other side, my legs carrying me swiftly while I hunch and walk. Needing to occupy my mind with something other than doubts I am heading in the correct direction, I focus on Ami.

Where does friendship end and something else begin? We had been enjoying each other's company before, but now what are we? Having to pretend to be a legitimate couple, including sleeping curled up together and being affectionate in public has to have changed something. When we get back to the house will all of that revert back to our friendship, or will that something else finally blossom?

I know we will have to talk about it. Could something develop so quickly? We have only known each other a few months and I am the first constant male contact she has had in years. And then there's the issue of who I am, or was before. I know nothing about me.

Turning my head, I find I have walked around so far that the caravan we attacked is barely a blip in my sight. I immediately turn left, trying desperately to catch sight of Lady Eve's camp. Finding a few dots that are between me and the orange glow I know is a small fire, I feel a little at ease. I move to place those dots directly in the line of sight of the glow, and head toward it little by little. Finally, I stop and sit in the sand having reached the approximate rear of their position, waiting for any sign of Kohan or Ami, but none comes.

Unable to properly discern time at night, I have no idea if an hour or six have passed, and not seeing either of them worries me. I resolve to get closer. At first I crouch and walk, but when I get closer to the wagons, I lie down in the sand and crawl along on my belly again.

A figure in the dark moves about, patrolling, and I stop completely until I notice that it's Kohan. I make a hissing noise to try and get his attention. It works briefly, but hiding myself against the sand, I am blending in too well for him to see. I hiss a little louder. This time I know he heard me. His attention turns directly to where I am, but he makes no direct advance. Instead he makes an about face and hastily retreats to the camp, disappearing from my sight into the wagon on the left.

When he does not return right away, my mind turns to the worst, thinking he might be telling Lady Eve I deceived them and deserted, or perhaps he is getting a weapon to silently kill me. Whether he will hold to his promise or not makes me anxious with intense anticipation, but as more time passes, I realize that if he was going to do something sinister it would be done by now.

Whether it is a trick my eyes are playing on me, or if the sky is actually getting lighter, I feel like time is running out. I wish with all my might that Kohan would hurry up, and lo and behold two figures emerge from the wagon. One is Kohan, and the other appears to be Ami.

Leery, they make sure it's safe before quickly moving away from the camp and straight out to me. Kohan stops about half way, while Ami continues on, crouching and moving directly at me. When I see Ami's face, I jump up and grab her by the hand, pulling her away without a second glance to Kohan.

Not a word is exchanged between us as we run across the plain, passing small dunes and dead brush. When we are a great distance away I allow us to slow to a fast walk as the light on the horizon threatens to reveal us. Looking over my shoulder, their caravan is but a dot now, and I sigh in relief. Removing a sack from her back while we continue to walk, she pulls out a water skin. We stop and take a swig from it. She caps it off and puts it into the bag before throwing her arms around my neck.

"I thought you might actually be dead!"

"Kohan played the whole thing out, didn't he?" I hug her back.

"Yes, he really made everyone think he killed you for attacking him." She drops down from hanging on my neck, and I let her go.

"Well, we are both alive, and now we just need to get back to the house. We will be fine," I tell her and begin walking again.

"You mean until Mother or Aunt Evalyn gets to us, right?" She laughs.

"I'll take the blame. I'll tell them that I was the one who convinced you to go, and then tell them the rest of what happened," I offer.

"No, I can't let you do that. Mother knows that I have a tendency to wander off when we reach a new time." She catches up and puts her arm through mine.

"Well, you don't have a choice. I am taking the blame."

"My noble knight," she whispers.

My stomach growls, and she opens the bag while we walk. Digging around in the predawn light, she produces a couple slices of meat, and hands me one. I gnaw on it, keeping a bite or two in my cheek to let the saliva pull the flavor out and soften it up. While we eat and walk, the sun rising into the sky quickly becomes a nuisance. Without a hood to block it, I am exposed to the sun's harsh rays, but I know moving in the daylight will provide us a greater chance to find the house.

Marching through the sand in the direction I think we originally came from, I try to take note of everything around us, but unfortunately the sand and occasional dead plant provide no assistance.

"Hold on a moment," I tell Ami.

I run over to a nearby patch of dead plants and drag my foot through the sand in a big arrow next to it, marking our passing through the area. Though it would only tell us if we had somehow circled back on ourselves, it gives me peace of mind.

"Good plan."

I search the horizon and determine by the rising of the sun in the east, by putting it to our backs we will align ourselves closer to the direction we want to head, hoping that any amount of good luck will help us find the house within hours.

~~~~~~

The sun had brought the heat out quickly. Now arching high into the sky, its rays are deadly, nearly unbearable. Having walked for at least a few hours now, and rested several times, one of the water skins has been emptied. Breaking for a few minutes, I work at the string tying the two halves together, and finally getting it open enough I place it over my head as protection. She laughs at me.

I pull the sack back up on my shoulder; my turn to carry it. We continue, but with the sun high above us now I do everything in my power to not stray from our path. Turning too far left or right might have a catastrophic effect. Our rations would run out far before the house were to yank us back. Climbing up to the top of a sand dune, I look around for any possible glimpse of the valley that the house sits in.

The desert stretches on. Though I cannot see anything which would help, I notice dark clouds moving rapidly in from the northwestern horizon. There is a haze underneath. Pointing for Ami to see she practically squeals in delight.

"Wow! It's really coming down!" Excitedly she jumps up and down.

"Should we head that way? It would not be going backwards."

"We have been traveling west for too long." She takes a moment to think before continuing. "It might be a good idea to start walking in that direction."

We survey the dunes and valleys where the rain is falling, and move to intercept. Directing us down into a valley, and back to the top of another plain, we make our way toward the heavy rainfall. Meeting us halfway, we find ourselves being pelted by the hard rain. I take the water skin from my head, and let it wash over me while filling the skin at the same time. Drinking heavily from it, Ami and I quench our thirsts. When I bring my head down from a healthy gulp, I notice Ami's white clothing is now clinging to her skin. I try desperately not to stare, but fail. She notices.

"We should huddle to keep warm and rest," Ami suggests, making my nerves worse.

"I don't...I..." I stammer, completely tongue-tied.

She grabs me by the hand and pulls me over to a nearby bank of sand. Sitting down, we huddle close together, our arms wrapped around one another. She leans her head on my shoulder and I try to shield us with the open water skin. But we both end up shifting several times trying to get comfortable and warm.

"This isn't working well," I mention.

"Yeah."

"Here, lie down on your side and face me. I will shield you from the rain," I tell her, trying to overcome my embarrassment.

"What?!" Her eyes widen and face turns red.

"I am not going to do anything. We are just going to share body heat like we did at camp."

She does as I request, and I pull her into me by her waist. We intertwine our legs together, and I tuck her head against my chest while resting my arm and the water skin over her head to create a pocket. My face is exposed, but I find myself uncaring as long as she is comfortable. I rest my head against the sand near the top of hers and breathe heavily so that the warmth of my breath keeps her from feeling too cold. She pulls in closer and rests her face against my chest. I struggle to keep my thoughts pure.

However, it's not long before my fatigue sets in, and I turn my face toward the ground to block the rain, taking comfort in the heat that Ami is providing through her curled up body and hot breath against my torso.

~~~~~~

Unsure of how long I was out, when I wake the rain has stopped, and the clouds have dissipated, leaving a clear sky above us. My eyes adjust, and night has fallen upon us while we slept. My body jolts with fear, realizing we slept through the rest of our daylight traveling time. My body spasm has awoken Ami, and she jumps up too. Eagerly I look around and try to discern the direction we need to head.

"What's wrong?!" she asks anxiously.

"We have slept too long. We need to get moving," I reply as calmly as I can.

"Food first," she says while digging into the soaked bag.

We devour two slices of meat each and drink from one of the water skins. Standing up, I grab the bag and hoist it over my shoulder as she puts the skin back in. Taking the lead we head in what I hope is the right direction.

The moon illuminates the land in front of us, and between hills and valleys in the near distance I wonder if we are anywhere close. Still we continue to move in a northwest direction.

After several minutes of shuffling along the edge of a sand dune, a howl pierces the night from behind us. Looking over my shoulder, a sinking feeling enters my gut. As a growling enters earshot, I find a beast of the desert is stalking us.

"Ami, run," I warn.

Letting her take the lead, we begin to move at a great speed, and another howl comes from near the mound where we had just been. Looking again reveals a four-legged beast dashing toward us in chase, overtaking us with ease.

"Run faster!" I yell at her.

Ami leads us along to the edge of the plain we are on, and turns abruptly, her foot slipping down the embankment. She cries out, and I lunge to grab her hand before she tumbles down the steep grade. But in saving her, the dog-like animal has caught up with us, and I place myself between it and her.

The beast lunges at my neck, and I sling the bag from my shoulder at it. It connects with the animal's head. Unyielding, as soon as it hits the sand, it lunges again. Instead of swinging again, I use the leather strap and catch the mutt by its neck. It struggles against me, but as I pin it to the ground I pull hard and begin to choke it. Thrashing about it tries hard to escape, but I am stronger.

Even if it was trying to kill me, this feels wrong.

It begins to slow its struggle and I remove the strap from its neck while pinning it down to the sand. This initiates a new fight within, and it chomps at me. Backing away, I drop the bag and wait for it to come at me again. When it does I duck, grab its legs, and swing it over the edge of our plain. Yelps and whimpering can be heard as it tumbles down the sand. I look over the edge, and it lies on the ground, still alive but wounded.

"He must have smelled us. That fresh rain washed away our desert smell," I huff.

"I'm just glad it was alone," she says picking up the bag, and returning to me.

"I had the chance to kill it, but I felt sympathy for it. It was probably just hungry." I take her arm in mine while watching it limp away.

"Just shows that you have good character, though maybe a little naïve." She giggles.

"Either way, we should move. We don't want that thing coming back with friends," I tell her while moving along the edge of the plain toward our original destination.

Walking arm-in-arm, I keep my ears perked for sounds of more beasts which I may have to defend against. For every minute that passes, I find myself more thankful to hear nothing of the sort. Following the plain by moonlight we come across a new valley, and a few hills and Ami suddenly stops. She turns around completely and looks about excitedly.

"What is wrong?" I ask.

"I know where we are! Hurry!" She darts off, and I follow after her as fast as I can.

I don't see what she sees, but I trust her judgment and hope she is leading us toward home. She disappears from sight several yards in front of me, dipping down into a valley, and when I reach the edge of it a familiar sight comes into view. The house is there, but there are no lights on. The moon's light reflects off of the solar panels, and causes the house to shine like a beacon in the night. Already nearing the bottom of the hill Ami darts into the grass and waves at me.

"Hurry, Rain!" She giggles excitedly.

I follow her down by sidestepping, though quite a bit slower for fear of slipping and falling. When I make it to the yard we tear the sand shoes off and race together toward the kitchen door. The door swings open with a loud creak, and Ami runs over to the light to turn it on. Digging into the fridge, I find a few pieces of turkey and pull them out.

"Ami! Real food!" I point out and begin to scarf down a chunk of it.

The comforts of Agatha's home return, and I feel at peace once more to have a solid roof over my head and delicious food to eat. As Ami joins me in devouring the turkey pieces, the swinging door to the living room bursts open. Spinning, we see Agatha wielding a large metal pipe.

"Where have you two been?!" She's frantic.

"Where we have been is a long story, but let me enjoy this turkey just a moment." I smile with a mouthful.

"I've been sick to death!" Agatha begins to bawl, sets the metal pipe on the table, and hugs Ami.

"It's okay, Mother. There was no need to worry because Rain was protecting me." Ami hugs her.

"Well, she did worry." Evalyn's voice comes out clear and angry from Agatha's throat, and she pushes away hard.

I can see in her face that she wants to strike Ami, but sees that I am ready to intercept. My brows furrowed at her, she sits idly by while I speak.

"If you are going to punish someone, punish me," I tell her.

"You? Your head is messed up and as far as we know your judgment was impaired too. Her judgment isn't," Evalyn retorts. "And you've gone and hurt yourself again."

"What?" I look down and find that at some point during the fight, the animal must have scratched me as there is a large gash across my forearm, and blood is dripping down my hand. "Wow. How did I miss that?"

"Oh dear." I see Agatha's face return to normal. "I will get some bandages. Go rinse that off in the sink."

Doubling back to the sink, I see I had left a trail of large blood drops. Putting my arm under the faucet, Ami turns the water on for me and gently rubs the wound to clean it. The more she rubs, the more the blood oozes out, and I find myself feeling nauseous. Agatha returns with supplies, and pulls my arm out to place closure bandages on the gash, followed by pads to soak up the blood, and likely the same elastic bandage which held my abdomen pads on. Feeling a little dizzy, I stumble and lean against the counter while my whole arm throbs with pain.

"Come on, sit down at the table."

Ami helps me over while Agatha cleans up. I sit in my chair and close my eyes, trying not to focus on the pain, instead paying close attention to Ami and Agatha's sounds. One of them comes over to me, and I open my eyes to see who it is.

"Here, take this." Agatha hands me a little white round item and a glass of water.

"What is it?"

"It's a potent pill that takes away pain. One of the things we used to keep you comfortable the last time you were wounded." She smiles.

"Do I chew it?"

"No!" Ami says excitedly. "That would taste awful. Just drop it under your tongue, take a drink of water and swallow it whole."

I follow instructions, but the pill hits the back of my tongue, and I gag. I throw my good hand over my mouth and nose, fighting not to spew my water all over the table. I try again and force it down successfully, but it leaves a lingering pain in my sinuses. After clearing my mouth of all the water, I begin to hack and cough violently.

"Are you okay?" Ami asks.

"I'm...fine..." my answer is labored.

"Okay. Just relax there as much as you can, and the pain should go away soon. It's going to make you loopy though, so when you're ready for bed I'll help you up to your room," Ami informs me.

Agatha sits down next to me while Ami cleans up my mess with the turkey, and it is not long before I feel a significant difference. The pain in my arms subsides and my head begins to spin. My thoughts become cloudy, and I obsess over apologizing.

I should have said no to Ami's little adventure. If I wasn't here she probably wouldn't have ventured out that far, not gotten caught, and wouldn't have been put to work as a servant.

"I...put you two through so much trouble. I...I should have pro...protected her better. Aggy," I try to stop, but my mouth has grown a mind of its own. "Aggy, I'm sorry. I will keep her home from now on. Keep her safe, and warm, with me."

Aggy? Where did I get that name? I've heard it before, right?

"Okay!" Ami says, rushing over to me. "Looks like the medicine has kicked in quickly! Time for you to go to bed!"

"But, I'm not done 'pologizing yet!" I slur my words as if I have become drunk with spirits and realize my eyelids feel like someone attached weights to them. "What's the fun in that?"

"What's the fun in what?" Ami grabs me under the arm that is not injured.

"Being drunk without drinking!"

I see Aggy smiling caringly at me, and I'm not sure why. I look at Ami and then at Aggy, and then back at Ami. "I can see where you get your good looks from."

Ami's face turns as red as a delicious red apple, and Aggy begins to laugh hysterically while I'm assisted out of the kitchen. We climb the stairs one by one.

"One...two...three..." I count.

"What are you doing?" she asks.

"Counting stairs." I smile at her, but realize it's dark and she can't see me. "Aww, you made me lose count."

"You can count them tomorrow when you're feeling better." I can hear in her voice that she's smiling.

That makes me happy. This pill makes me happy too. Hey look, my door!

Ami opens my door, flips on the light, and brings me inside. Before we get to the bed, I begin stripping off my clothes, sand pouring from them onto my already sandy floor.

"What are you doing?" she protests.

"I can't go to bed with sand all over me," I tell her.

She ducks out of the room and I continue to disrobe, throwing my dirty clothes unsuccessfully into the laundry basket. I wobble and collapse into my dresser while trying to brush the sand off of me.

Ami calls out to me. "Rain? Are you okay? Is it safe for me to come in?" she asks.

"I'm naked!"

"Get dressed already!"

Wiping off as much sand as I can, I pull out new undershorts and some baggy pants to wear to bed. With a great struggle, I am able to get them on without falling on my face. I sit on the bed and realize it feels so good.

"I am…I'm done," I tell her, and she reenters the room.

She's so nice. I can't let anything bad happen to her. I wouldn't be happy if something did. I would make someone pay.

"All right Rain." She sits down next to me and lays me on my pillow. "I will see you in the morning."

"Okay. Night-night, gorgeous."

Her face turns red again and it's cute. She jumps up and heads out of the room, flipping off the light and closing my door. Sinking into the bed, I find that I can't focus on anything.

Sleep time.

~~~~~~

The light from outside permeates my eyelids, and I am brought up from a dreamless slumber. I pull the covers up over my head and try to go back to sleep, but as my mind becomes fully aware, I realize I have a pounding headache and it's now impossible for me to do so.

I let out a moan when I try to move my wounded arm in a way that causes my body to protest. With a heavy sigh, I realize there is no choice now but to get out of bed.

I gently push the covers off and rotate my body so my feet hang over the edge of the bed. When I sit up, I see a sandy heap of clothing I apparently left in a pile last night, and I can't remember doing it. Searching my thoughts, I barely remember what happened after having my wound treated. I recall being given a medicine that made me light-headed, but everything beyond becomes hazy. Raising my good hand, I rub my face, wipe the sleep gunk from my eyes, and rub my cheeks.

With my desert top lost, and the pants filled with sand, I try to pick from my wardrobe something light and simple. I find a white t-shirt and tan cotton pants which look like they should keep me fairly cool today. Once I have changed, I make my way downstairs to the living room. The shades are closed and it's fairly dark in here, but I can tell no one is around. In fact I can't hear anyone at all. Peeking in the kitchen, everything is cleaned up, but no one is there either.

Could they still be sleeping? They were probably up later than I was. I should make them breakfast to show my appreciation for the care they give me.

Heading into the kitchen, I open the refrigerator and find Agatha has definitely been using food sparingly. A half-dozen eggs lie on the top shelf, and in the door I find a small amount of cheese. Setting them both out on the counter, I search the pantry for bread, but find none.

Perhaps in the storage room below?

Propping the door open, I find the light switch on my right, and illuminate my way down. Before me lies a large room underneath the house, with many racks lining the walls with food, most of them canned or jarred, and I understand our food situation is not as dire as I had been thinking. A wall runs across in front of the stairs, and about the middle, where I think the hallway runs, is a door to a second area. Peeking in reveals a multitude of tools, some of them even familiar, but I resolve not to let my curiosity distract me and return to looking for bread. Luckily I don't have to search long to locate a loaf, and head back up, turning out the light behind me.

With the eggs, cheese, and bread on the island counter I begin to prepare. Breaking several eggs into a bowl, I whip them with a fork, adding some salt and pepper sparingly. Setting it aside for a moment, I remove the thin plastic sheet from around the cheese and cut off a few slices. Returning the cold items to the refrigerator, and tossing the eggshells in the waste bin under the sink, I am ready to start cooking. Following what I had seen Agatha and Ami do several times, I turn the front left burner on by setting the dial to 'medium'.

Putting the eggs into the pan, they start cooking, and I grab a spatula from the large utensil drawer in the island counter, and return to start stirring it. When the eggs start to solidify and clump I throw the cheese in, and continue mixing vigorously. Working away at not burning the eggs, a noise from behind makes me jump. Turning around I find Ami in a light blue button up shirt, and loose pants, rubbing her eyes and yawning.

"Rain, what are you doing?" she asks while scratching her head.

"I am…I'm cooking breakfast," I correct myself.

"You shouldn't be doing that with your hurt arm," she halfway scolds me.

"It's okay. It doesn't hurt right now and you two deserve to be taken care of, instead of having to take care of me all the time."

"That's sweet of you, Rain, but—" She tries to stop me but I cut her off.

"Shush. I will rest after I finish this. Now sit," I smile at her.

She does as instructed by taking her normal seat, and I'm able to focus on cooking. The eggs and cheese have mingled together nicely. Turning off the stove and setting the pan on a cool burner, I get out three plates and dish them up equally. Moving quickly I slather some butter on bread, one slice for each of us, and then set the plates on the table.

Just as I set it down, Agatha walks through the kitchen door fully awake, dressed in one of her brightly colored sundresses.

"Ami, you let him cook?" She almost looks stern when she says it.

"Let him? He shushed me when I tried to stop him," she protests.

"Rain, you have to—" Agatha tries to mother me but I cut her off too.

"I know Agatha, I need to give my arm some rest." I wink and smile at her. "It'll be all right. Now do like your daughter, and let me take care of you a little bit."

Agatha hesitantly sits down across the table from Ami, and I provide us with forks. Sitting down together I take my place at the table, and grin from ear to ear. Finally back to having a nice meal together, I realize I enjoy their company and the comforts of civilized life, like I picture a family might.

Though I'm not sure what I am to the two of them, I know they are everything to me, and to be with them makes me happy. Making eye contact with Ami causes her to blush a little. My face responds in kind. She notices, and a bashful smile crosses her lips.

What are we to each other? I feel like we're becoming really close. More than friends. Could she be feeling the same way? Would it really complicate things so much if something did happen between us? We are together by force, but how can one not grow to like the people who they're constantly with?

Finished with her food, Ami stands up with her plate in hand, and before I know what is happening, she leans over and kisses me on the cheek, as if she had been reading my thoughts.

"Thank you for breakfast, Rain," she says and then puts her plate in the sink.

My face, if it was not already completely red from before, likely turns three shades darker. My heart skips a beat or two, and my hand has stopped moving food to my mouth. Agatha has a delighted look, and titters. As soon as she has finished breakfast, she does the same thing as her daughter. Embarrassed completely now, my face is so hot, and my eyes water so much, that I'm forced to hide my face by keeping it pointed away from them.

They clean up after me as I sit and let my bashfulness fade away. When I am done with my breakfast I bring my plate over to the sink where Agatha has filled it with water from a jug. She takes it from me and washes it before I have even moved away from the counter. Contemplating what I should do next I head to the back door to look out and see what work might be done. The grass has begun to wilt and brown in the desert heat, so I do not expect to find myself using the push mower any time soon.

"Where do you think you're going?" Ami asks.

"Outside?" I play coy.

"I don't think so. We are going to do two things today, which are studying and sewing." She crosses her arms.

I sigh, defeated, and relinquish control of my day to Ami's itinerary. She waves for me to follow, and we enter the living room, still dark from the shades being drawn. Rather than open the curtains and allow the sunlight in, she turns on the overhead lighting and grabs a few books from the left bookcase. Sitting down on the floor next to the table, she pats the wood, indicating she wants me to take a seat next to her. As I do, I can already feel that the days from here on out, until the end of our time here, are likely going to be slow.

~~~~~~

Looking out the kitchen window, I sit in Ami's chair and find she has the perfect spot for eating. There is ample lighting, and she has a view. Sipping on a cool glass of water I examine the dune as a gentle breeze flows past it, pushing along a drift of sand. I am antsy to do something.

Another week closer to leaving here, and I have been almost useless! Helping Ami in her sewing endeavors is not satisfying enough to feel like I'm being productive. I can't even sneak around and do some work, because by the time I think of it, they've either already done it or are doing it.

I close my eyes and lay my head down on the table, noting that the wood seems to like to absorb this arid heat. With a lot of time to reflect, I try to remember who I used to be, but am only able to come up with a few pieces; stone buildings, sharp weapons, sets of armor, and Drake. I start back at the woods, remembering the greens and browns of the dense forest, and hearing Ami and Agatha talking.

What came before that? The dagger through me. I remember looking down and being shocked. I can't remember even feeling pain, just that initial shock. But what came before that? There was nothing but woods out there. Running. I have a vague feeling of running and feeling out of breath.

Come on, come on. Just a little more. Where was I running from? The woods. There's nothing but woods. Why would I be out there with this Drake person? He was in armor, but I wasn't. Could I have been taken out there to be executed?

Struggling against the mental block I want to know what my life was like before, if only to quiet my own mind's questions but when the door opens I lift my head to see Agatha enter, and I refocus my attention. She dips her hands into a clean sink of water and then dries them on a towel nearby.

"Would you like something to eat?" Agatha asks politely.

"No, thanks. I'm not all that hungry right now."

"If I made you something and set it in front of you, would it get eaten?" she says with a grin.

I smirk back while stretching out my arm and rotating it. A little pain rings through, however it has begun healing up nicely. "Eventually. But you really need not worry about me right now."

After a few moments of silence while Agatha moves about the kitchen, she abruptly asks me a very sensitive question. "What are your intentions with my daughter?"

My face turns red, and I drop my arms to the table from my stretch.

"What...what do you mean?" I stammer.

"You know what I mean, Rain. She likes you." She makes her way to the table and sits down across from me, in her spot.

"Wow. I...uh...that's difficult to answer." I try to form an on the spot answer. "I like her too, but I'm in unfamiliar territory here. I admit that I'd like to think we're close friends."

"And if my daughter did end up liking you more than just a close friend?" She leans forward and rests on one of her arms.

"I...why the sudden interest?"

"We're going to be together for a long time. It's a precarious situation, and I don't want to see her heart broken."

"I see your point. I suppose I better be very sure and careful about the situation."

"I agree, but let me point out it's not entirely in your hands. Ami has a mind of her own and she could very well want to date you before you've come to your decision."

"Well if something more were to blossom, would I have your permission to court her?"

"Of course. You've proven to me that you are more than worthy. You can protect and provide for her in ways that I cannot." She smiles sweetly.

"Okay. Well, let's keep this hushed for now. I want to see what might or might not occur naturally."

"All right, Rain." She reaches over and pats my hand.

Agatha stands up and begins moving to the back door when Ami bursts in from outside.

"Rain! Mother!" Ami yells. "There's someone in the hills!"

Jumping to my feet, I run out the door, and find Ami standing near the clothing lines pointing up. Straining, I see him poke his head up. Light from the sun gleams off of his head. Without warning I begin running to the edge of the perimeter and quickly put the sand shoe attachments on my feet. Back out into the desert sand, I give it my all and push against the ground to get to the hill. Scaling it on all fours, I dig in and move like the wild dog that had attacked us, leaping and bounding up the dune. But when I get to the top of the hill he is no longer at the edge, and now running well ahead of me in the direction where Lady Eve's camp was.

If he gets away we are in serious trouble.

My feet tear at the sand, but he is faster than I am. I push hard, and my lungs burn as I breathe the dry air deeply, but he is still gaining ground away from me, becoming a speck in the distance. His endurance surpasses mine, and I become too winded to run any farther, my ribcage protesting with pinching in several spots. I crouch, placing my hands on my knees and coughing loudly. When I regain my composure, he is gone, and I am left to retreat to the house.

With a potential attack imminent now, I have to wonder if he was from Lady Eve's camp. She would no doubt be angry to find me alive, and Ami with me. How am I going to fend off an army?

Back at the ridge leading to the house, Ami and Agatha look at me with hopeful eyes. I shake my head and climb slowly down the sand dune. I sigh loudly, coming to a stop in front of them.

"This is not good," I say. "I think he was from Lady Eve's camp."

"Weren't they headed for the mountains though?" Ami reminds me.

"Hopefully they made it all the way there, and are busy enough that by the time she sends a group out here to take us, we will be gone. However, we had better prepare for an attack."

"How strong are these people?" Agatha asks.

"They have rifles and explosives. If they make it here, we are in serious trouble." I shake my head. "If they show up I want both of you inside at all times."

Back at the house, I leave my shoes outside, but still manage to dredge more sand into the kitchen. We sit at the table, and I stare at the wall, trying to brainstorm a way to provide us an advantage. Many ideas come to mind, but none seem feasible.

A trap in the sand would be nice, a hole to hold off several people at a time, but I would have to place them everywhere and hope that there are more holes than there are people. Even if that worked, they would quickly find their way out.

I let out a large sigh and reach out for Agatha and Ami's hands. They both look at me caringly, and take my hands into theirs.

"I know you will protect us, Rain. I have faith in you," Ami says reassuringly.

"I wish I had that same faith in myself." I shake my head. "I can't think of anything to do that though."

"Well, maybe something will come to you if you go rest a bit," Agatha suggests.

Shrugging, I slouch back in the chair, and stare at the white ceiling for a while before retiring to my room. Lying on my bed, I rest my head so that I can see the sky out of my window and stare into the blue.

I don't know what to do...

~~~~~~

Opening my eyes slowly, the room has gone dark. I feel a little refreshed, but my mind is too groggy to think about anything other than looking for Ami or Agatha. Standing up, I turn and find light seeping from under the sewing room door. Putting my ear to the door I listen for sound. When I don't hear any, I knock lightly. There is no response and I open the door to find Ami sitting in her chair, leaned over and asleep on one of her work desks.

I step lightly, trying to keep the floor boards quiet while I make my way to her. She's snoring lightly with her mouth open a little, and a drool puddle forming on a pattern she was apparently working on. Slinging her arms over my neck causes her to stir a little, but I keep going. I lift under her knees with my arm around her back. She clamps onto me, and I head toward the door.

I take the stairs one step at a time, and bring her to her bedroom. It takes some very careful maneuvering to not drop her, but I'm able to grip the knob and twist it open. With the blinds drawn open, and a little moonlight pouring in I can see her bed silhouette easily, and I set her down on it. When I attempt to remove my arms, Ami grips my neck tightly.

"Rain, sleep with me," Ami mumbles.

"No, Ami, I can't do that," I whisper to her, my face flushing.

"Why not? I'm cold," she mumbles more.

"I'll cover you up then."

"Thank you, Rain." She rolls over so I can pull the covers back, and then rolls onto the cleared area.

I pull the covers over her body and tuck them under her arms, which she has pulled to her chest. She smiles with her eyes closed, and I realize that she's not likely to even remember this in the morning. Heading out of her room, I shut the door behind me. Though I am doing my best to be quiet, my stomach growls. Heading to the kitchen, I find the light on, but Agatha is not there. Looking out the window I do not see her, or anyone else.

The refrigerator door gives little resistance when I pull on it. Looking inside, our cold supplies are running low. There is a little milk left, a jar of pickles is a little under half full, and there's not much for leftovers as we've been conserving what we make, and eating as much of it as we can. Closing the refrigerator, I decide on a peanut butter sandwich instead, and make and consume two sandwiches.

A trench? How big of a trench can I make in a couple days? Maybe a series of holes to slow them down? I would need a shovel.

After cleaning up, I wander down to the basement, and to the door which leads to the tool storage. There are a wide variety of tools, and I find two shovel toward the back, hung on the wall. Grabbing one I head back upstairs and out the door to the yard. It takes me a few moments to get my shoes on with the sand attachments, but I am soon across the yard and begin to dig, tossing the shovelfuls of sand toward the already massive dune.

Hours pass, and it feels like I am not making any progress, but I keep digging away at the border of our land, determined to do whatever I can to keep them safe. Finally, it seems I have started making a dent in the desert when I can only see the top of the house. Having left myself a ramp back up, I use it to escape and continue on with digging the trench.

Losing track of time, dawn creeps up on me. Stepping into the yard, I look at the work accomplished. Though I have made a dent in the ground I find that my work is nowhere near complete, and the sun is quickly going to turn it into an oven out here. Debating for a minute, I decide to rest and pick it up again at dusk. Making my way back inside I kick my shoes off at the door, and feel the cooler air washes over my sweaty skin.

"Where have you been?" Agatha asks with her motherly tone from the table.

"Digging a trench, or at least what I could for now." I get a tall glass of water from a pitcher in the refrigerator and chug it down.

"Are you sure you should be working alone? That animal wasn't too far from here, right?"

"Thanks for the concern, but you two need your rest at night. I will keep watch and work at night, and you two can guard in the day."

"If you insist, but I want you to promise that you'll be careful. You still need to heal too."

"I will try." I smile, setting the glass down.

Heading toward the living room, I grab a piece of bread and devour it. Just before I reach the swinging door it swings wide open, and I'm nearly knocked over. Ami has appeared with a large smile on her face and she throws her arms around my neck, pulling me in close. I hug her back.

"Morning, Rain!"

She's awful chipper. Must have gotten decent sleep.

"Hey, I need you to do me a favor," I tell her, releasing the hug.

"What's that?" She lets go and heads for the refrigerator.

"I need three long and wide sheets of material sewn together, and some stakes," I push the door open and stop to look at her.

"Okay!" She turns her attention to the refrigerator and rummages.

"Thanks, Ami."

I push through the door and head up the stairs. Upon entering my room I close the door and strip down to my undershorts. Taking a moment, I brush myself off before getting into bed, but I reach a point that I'm satisfied and lie face down, covering my head with the pillow.

~~~~~~

Standing atop the dune I scan the horizon, and am thankful to still see no sign of anyone coming. With the sun illuminating the yellow and brown landscape for miles, all that exists is sand, but when I look down behind me I see our little oasis in the desert, and the large trench that reaches half way around the perimeter.

I suppose I should have made it deeper, but I can only do so much. Maybe there will still be time after I finish digging these holes.

Turning my gaze back to the desert, I look into the holes I have begun to dig at the top, hoping that they come from this direction. I plant the shovel into the sand and lean against it while looking at the three holes that I have started. Though they are not as large as the trench, and will likely not be effective enough to stop an army, doing this gives me a sense of worth to the house.

He had to have made it back to Lady Eve by now, if he was in fact from her camp. What will she bring with her? How many?

Standing, I retrieve the ladder from the hole closest to me, and on my way to the house I pluck the shovel from the sand. Carefully, I make my way down the hill. Agatha is there removing clothes from the lines. Using the ladder as a bridge, I cross over into our territory and pull my bridge across.

When I reach the house, I place the ladder and shovel against the side, and shoot a smile over to Agatha. Concentrating on her work, her face looks neither happy nor angry. It's difficult to tell if it's Agatha or Evalyn. Looking around the decimated yard, the fourth clothing line is looking quite pitiful, knocked over by the sandstorm. The garden is ripped to shreds, and the apple tree a husk of what it was before.

We are going to have our work cut out for us when we enter a new time.

Kicking off my shoes and dusting off, I head inside. Ami is making breakfast. The delicious smells waft over me, and I inhale deeply. My stomach growls, telling me it wants this salty smelling food sizzling on the stovetop.

"That smells wonderful Ami. What is it?"

"Potatoes and bacon," she replies cheerfully. "It's almost done. Why don't you wash up and set the table."

"Okay."

I lather my arms all the way up to the elbows, rinse them in the sink filled with cool water, and then dry myself off with a nearby towel. Cleaned up as much as I am going to get for now, I set the table for the three of us and place some glasses.

"I made some orange juice," she mentions. "It's in the refrigerator."

"You *made* some? From what oranges?" I am confused.

Ami laughs. "We didn't have any. I made it from frozen concentrate."

"What is that?"

"It's where they take the water out of the actual juice, and what you have leftover is a compacted form of the original stuff. You just put water back into it and it makes it into regular juice again," she explains while dishing the plates up.

"Amazing. What will this world think of next? Or, I should say, what has it thought of in the future?"

I head to the refrigerator to retrieve the pitcher.

"A good question." She shrugs.

Pouring the juice, I watch out of the corner of my eye as she heads outside to retrieve Agatha for breakfast. I fill our glasses to the brim, nearly overflowing mine waiting for Ami to reappear. I catch myself just in time. They reenter the house, Agatha with a basket full of clothes, and they join me at the table. Agatha sets the basket on the ground and I wait for them to both sit before I do.

"Thanks, Ami," I tell her while taking a bite.

"Of course." She smiles at me. "I enjoy taking care of you."

I blush, but before I can respond Evalyn blurts, "Enough. You're making me sick."

Eating quietly, I eye Evalyn and she glares at me.

What can be done about her? Does she have the power to break this cycle at will and is just keeping it going out of spite? I wonder if there is a way to put her spirit to rest.

Shrugging it off, I return my attention to the food and find that I have already eaten most of it, but my stomach doesn't feel full yet. I know all of it has been divided between the three of us, and they too are nearly finished. Instead of wishing for more, I take one bite at a time, savoring the delicious saltiness of the bacon and earthy texture of the potatoes. When it's gone, I guzzle the orange juice in a few gulps. Upon placing the glass down on the table, I find Evalyn staring at me again. I sheepishly grin. She scoffs, and it makes me laugh.

Slouching in my chair, I let the food settle. It seems like it was enough after all. With my hunger quelled and my stomach heavy I let my eyes shut, and realize it's about time I should head to bed. Slowly standing up, I grab my dishes and turn to head to the sink. Two steps forward and my knees buckle. All I can do to keep from collapsing onto the dishes and injuring myself is to toss them out in front of me. Hitting the ground, I grunt, and Ami and Evalyn rush to my side.

"You're overworked, Rain." Evalyn leaves and Agatha begins to mother me. "It's time for you to rest and I don't want to see you out of bed until I say so."

"What about the bathroom?" I joke.

"We'll get it over with so it's out of the way," she says while grabbing me under my left arm, while Ami gets my right.

Though they haul me to the bathroom, the ability to move my legs returns, and they let me do what I need to. When I'm finished they assist me up the stairs, and half way up I can feel the bones and muscles aching all throughout my body.

By the time they get me into bed, I feel shooting pain welling up from inside, building up to something. Squirming around, I can't seem to get comfortable. Agatha puts her hand on my shoulder comfortingly, and heads back downstairs. Ami moves to leave too, and I try to stop her, but I can't get anything out. She heads into her sewing room, and I expect that she is going to work, but to my surprise Ami returns to my room dragging a chair, and a lot of folded up cloth. I look at her puzzled but she doesn't notice my gaze.

She sets the chair by the head of my bed, and acknowledges me by looking over and smiling. Footsteps make their way up the stairs again, and Agatha appears with a familiar tray. There is a silver bowl and a glass of water on it. Setting it down on the floor, she grabs a rag and dunks it into the bowl. Wringing it out, Agatha hands it to Ami and she puts it on my forehead. Though it does nothing for my pain, it feels good.

"Here, drink some water." Agatha grabs the glass.

Ami takes the rag while helping me sit up, and I take the glass. My hand shakes heavily, and the building pressure inside me intensifies, but I ignore it and push through to drink the water slowly.

"Thank you," my voice comes out raspy.

"Rest now. Ami will watch over you," Agatha says.

Ami lowers me back down onto the pillow, and I stare out the window while trying to get comfortable. Agatha leaves again, and Ami settles in after placing the rag back on my head. The pillow does nothing for the uneasy feeling, and my body can't take much more of the pain, deciding to remove me from consciousness to compensate.

~~~~~~

I'm surrounded by darkness. My feet appear to be on solid ground, but there is nothing around me; I'm unable to even see my own body. Bending down, I touch what I think is ground but feel nothing. There is nothing below where I am, even under my feet. I move to take a step, but my legs won't cooperate. Air, or what feels like air, rushes all around me like a whirlwind, but then switches to being directly from under me. Light appears and I find that I'm falling straight down into a forest. I try to yell out of fright, but my voice is locked up. Shutting my eyes, I expect impact any moment with the trees growing ever closer.

It does not come though. The air stops, and the fall hasn't turned my body to a crumpled heap on the forest floor. When I open my eyes, I am in the middle of the forest I was rushing toward, and the clearing where the house is supposed to be, but it's not there. Instead the clearing is covered in a purple aura.

Is the aura supposed to represent the house grounds? How is that possible if it isn't there?

I try to take a step toward the purple covered field, but before I can I am pulled away deep into the woods by an unseen force. My body stops suddenly, and I become a witness to a strange spectacle. Two shadows appear to be fighting, colliding multiple times. As I watch intently, pieces become more visible. There are swords involved. But I am mystified when I notice things are not flowing normally. Everything is backward; movements are in reverse. Swords clash together, but in such an abnormal way that it almost looks like a strange dance with over-exerted movements where the persons are trying to actually hit each other's swords instead of one another. However the shadows never become fully illuminated, and I'm unable to determine if it is who I think it is. I assume they are Drake and myself fighting.

Who else would be out in the woods?

They stop fighting and appear to be having a lively conversation, waving their swords at each other, and then they put them away. Attempting to move again, I discover I'm still stuck, paralyzed in place watching this scene. My body snaps, and I'm hauled back into the black above.

~~~~~~

I wake, startled, sitting straight up in bed and dropping the wet cloth from my forehead. My heart beats so heavily that I fear it will burst through my ribcage, and I breathe heavily to try and calm it. My body has become drenched with sweat and I feel like I am burning up.

"What's wrong?!" Ami asks, alarmed.

"I just had the strangest dream where I saw two shadows fighting with swords, but everything was moving in reverse."

"A dream? You've only been asleep for five minutes," she says while pushing me back down onto the pillow and replacing the rag.

"How is that possible? It feels like it's been hours." I am affected by vertigo as I close my eyes.

"I'm not sure. Just rest now, okay?" Ami touches my bare arm lightly for a moment.

I roll over, opening my eyes in an attempt to alleviate the spinning sensation, but I cannot get it to stop. Feeling nauseous, I sit up again, but find myself losing grip on reality. Completely restless, I feel like my body is on fire, and I cannot speak. Ami stands up and I see her trying to talk to me, but a ringing in my ears blocks her out. My vision goes black. When it returns, I am lying down. Agatha and Ami are hovering over me, placing cool, wet cloths all over my body.

I can hear them talking now, but their voices are muffled. Agatha looks directly at me, and I can read her mouth asking 'can you hear me?' but when I attempt to move my arm to respond, I am immobilized.

Panic sets in. My eyes begin to move left and right rapidly on their own. My body convulses, and I'm powerless to control it. Ami and Agatha do their best to keep me from falling to the floor by placing themselves on the edge of my bed and letting me convulse against their bodies. Sound comes in clearly for just a brief moment and I can hear Agatha.

"His fever is causing a seizure! We need to cool his core down now! Bring him to the shower!"

Picking me up by my feet and under my arms, I feel nothing except my body spasm against their hold. Carefully they bring me from my room and down the stairs. I fear for their safety, unable to control myself. Agatha stumbles and nearly falls back first down the stairs.

"Careful, Mother!"

"I am fine! We need to hurry or he is going to die!"

My vision goes black. And then I am in the shower while Ami soaks me, clothes and all. Agatha disappears through the bathroom door and soon returns with towels, draping them over my entire body, all but my face. The tub fills, and I become encased. I fade in and out. My body has ceased its convulsions, and my mind drifts away as I lose consciousness.

~~~~~~

When I open my eyes again, I have a slight sense of disembodiment and wonder if I died. But as my eyes adjust, I am just in a dark room. It's not mine though. A light briefly floods in from my immediate right when a door is opened, and turning my head I find that I am in Ami's room. Ami's silhouette moves over, and she comes to rest on the bed next to me.

Straining to sit up, every muscle in my body hurts as there is a residual feeling of that built up pressure, but I'm in full control of my body again. As I let out a large grunt, Ami places her hand on my shoulder and settles me back to the bed gently.

"Shh. Don't get up."

"Ami...Ami?" my voice comes out strained and hoarse.

"I'm here, Rain. You're going to be okay."

"What happened?"

"You had a fever and it spiked so high you had a seizure. But we got it under control with the shower. We are not sure why, but you should be fine now."

"How long have I been out?"

"Three days."

"No...this cannot be..." the realization that time is running out hits me and my work is not complete. "Has Eve come?"

"Not yet, but it's okay. Mother and I finished the traps together, and placed the cloth over them like I assume you wanted."

"It's not enough. That will only slow them down, I have to do something else."

I fear that I will not be able to save them in my current state.

"It will be okay. If it is Lady Eve we can try to appease her by giving her our supplies, and then we will just survive until we are pulled through time again."

"Why do you still call her *Lady* Eve? It's a self-imposed, undeserved title," I grumble.

"I'm not sure. Habit I guess." She runs her fingers through my hair.

"Why am I in your bed?"

"After we knew you were safe for the moment, we dried you off and brought you in here. We wanted to keep you near the shower in case you had another episode." She brushes my cheek with the back of her hand.

"Wait. You dried me off?" I ask, a little alarmed.

"I...uh...yes?" she says, understanding what I am getting at and looks away.

"You didn't take off my clothes, did you?"

"We kind of had to, Rain. But don't worry, I didn't look!"

"I am mortified. How embarrassing is it that I had to be stripped and dried?!" I turn away from her.

She says she didn't see me naked, but someone had to. If not Ami then Agatha.

"I understand. I would feel the same way, but I know if the situation were reversed you would do everything to make sure I survived first, and worried about embarrassing situations later, as well as not looking." She lies down behind me with her face in the nape of my neck, and her arm wrapped around me.

If she says she didn't look, I'll take her word for it. I would rather have Agatha, someone who's like my mother, have seen me than Ami who's more like a best friend or romantic interest.

"So what happens now?" I ask.

"You get better and save us," Ami says playfully, her warm breath causing the hair on the back of my neck to stand on end. I shiver.

"I'll try." I close my eyes and drift off again.

~~~~~~

"Rain! They're here!" Ami bursts in the kitchen door frantically.

Using the roof as a lookout while performing regular solar panel cleaning, Ami and Agatha have been keeping an eye out for movement, and it has finally come. I place my fork on the plate in front of me, having just finished my breakfast. I push up off of my chair, grabbing my newly sewn white cloak from the back of it and tossing it over my shoulders.

I was beginning to wonder if maybe they couldn't find their way here, or if they were even coming at all. I don't know if I can fend them off until the vortex takes us.

I exit the house quickly, flipping the white reflective hood up over my head, and put my feet into my shoes, making sure the sand attachments are snuggly in place. Ami follows me back outside, retrieving the ladder from against the side of the house and collapsing it to its compact form. Ami, Agatha, and I walk to the deep trench and we lay it across as a bridge. Once on the other side I turn back to them.

"Pull it back and go inside," I tell them firmly.

"Be careful. Don't over work yourself. And take this water bottle." Ami tosses me a bottle from the pocket of her pants.

"Do not come to my aid," I say. "If I have to die out there to make sure you are safe, I will."

"Don't talk like that," Agatha scolds me.

"I am not playing around." I frown. "I am going to do everything I can to keep you two safe."

"Rain, please…" Ami tries but I shake my head at her.

Watching, I wait for them to retreat into the house before I make the climb up the sand dune I have visited so frequently these past few weeks. With my eyes against the landscape, I cannot tell where I had placed the holes, finding that Ami and Agatha had done a tremendous job in hiding them with a layer of sand.

Beyond the immediate smaller dunes, on a plain just a little bit to the right of our original course, I see a single wagon making its way here and I can tell there are dozens of people with it. The people are split in half on the two sides of the wagon, as well as an uncountable amount underneath pushing it. I can see them, and I'm certain they can see me as my white cloak glistens in the sunlight.

Nothing says 'come get me' better than standing in one spot with my arms crossed, and tapping my foot impatiently. With every step they take my heart beats a little faster, and even more so when Eve pokes out from the front side of the wagon. Our eyes meet, and even at this distance I can see she is furious.

They come to a stop a few hundred yards out from the traps, and she stands perched on the edge of the wooden platform. I drop my hood, smile, and wave excitedly just to get her blood boiling. She makes a brief glance down to the group, and when I follow the direction of her gaze I find Kohan. Her voice rings out, but at this distance I cannot discern the words. Her attention reverts back to me.

"Come on, move closer," I mumble while crossing my arms again, having positioned myself so they will walk into the traps as they come for me.

Her arms begin flailing, and she motions for them to advance once again. They do as ordered and their speed picks up. As they get closer, I notice their rifles tucked in at their sides, likely loaded and ready to shoot. But they move forward instead of shooting, and Kohan leads the wagon and the small army right toward the traps. Eve stays steady through the bumping, leans forward, and crosses her arms.

Keep coming.

I put my arms straight out as if to embrace them as they near; they're so close now. As they approach the first two pits, my heart begins to beat faster. The wagon's wheel lines up to hit the first hole. A smirk crosses my face, one I know that Eve and everyone else can see. As it touches the cloth covered void my grin gets wider.

The sand sinks inward under the weight of the wagon, and starts to roll to its side. Eve screams in shock as she is thrown down into the pit. Several servants from underneath and to the side are pulled in as well. The wagon tips far enough that it falls completely onto its side, and the cries can be heard as people fall in, and the sand sinks around them. Several scramble to jump away while others are sucked down in. Attempting to rush me, more are caught off guard by the other two traps.

Now is my chance to strike.

I let out a bestial roar, and break into a sprint toward those left standing. In disarray they are either too distracted in helping those who fell in the holes, or are too shocked to notice me coming. Without any one to block me, I dart around the first hole and aim my right shoulder into a man who is trying to help another out of the pit. Connecting hard with him causes both of them to go tumbling to the bottom. Spinning around and slamming my foot into the stomach of one of Eve's bandits puts him back first into the sand. Before he can retaliate I grab his gun and lob it over a nearby sand dune.

"GET ME OUT OF THIS HOLE!" Eve bellows.

A few men mobilize against me with their rifles pointed, but I refuse them the opportunity to fire by sprinting into the middle of them, and throw my fists and knees around. I hammer one in the ribs with a quick succession of blows, and then spin to grab another trying to put the knife of his gun to my back.

Taking the barrel, I rip it from his hands and grab his arm, pulling it up behind his back and yanking hard to dislocate it. Another comes upon me and puts the butt of a rifle in my back, but I am able to ignore the pain easily enough. Reaching back, I grab the attacker by his shirt and head-butt him directly on his nose, shattering it. A gunshot rings out, and I protect myself with the man in my grasp. He arches, hit in the back.

Using him as a shield, I run in the direction of the fire, and lob the body. The dead man and the attacker tumble into a hole, but I am also caught off guard and shoved from behind. Tumbling down, I fall into a few men trying to get back out, and when we land I am on the bottom of the pile. Pushing hard with my arms, struggling against three men and the soft sand is too much. Captured, the three men hoist me out of the hole to another group of Eve's minions, and she too has made it out of her hole, finding her way over to me.

"Don't you move!" her voice rings with hatred.

Surrounded, guns aimed at me, I am held by my arms stretched out to the side for her to do what she will against me. She circles like a vulture, and though I have been defeated I speak smugly.

"Long time no see, Eve." My grin is wide.

"That's *Lady* Eve to you, worm." She punches me in the stomach.

Coughing while fighting back vomiting, I find an opportunity to goad her more. "Aww, is that how you treat the man you wanted so bad?"

"Shut your mouth. Did you think I wouldn't find out that you were still alive? How did you escape?"

I spit at her feet and give her a dirty look, provoking her to kick me in the ribs.

"Now, instead of being my lover and second in command, you're going to die, but not until I kill Ami in front of you," her threat is convincing.

"I won't allow it," I wheeze.

"You can't stop me! You are but a single man who thought he could outsmart and out-fight a small army. You had no chance of winning."

As I am under her control, I take her threat seriously and struggle against those holding my arms tightly. My mind reels in an attempt to thwart this situation from happening.

The two men holding me don't have their guns. The one on my left is large enough to be used as a shield if they do fire. I don't want to kill anyone, but I will to save Ami. In fact the only way this is going to stop now is if I get a rifle and begin firing.

"I can and will stop you, Eve," I calm myself and retort.

She slaps me across the face, then paces away. "No, you won't."

With a quick motion, I slide my leg to my right and wrap my foot around one captor's, pulling it out from under him while yanking with my arm. He loosens his grip. I'm able to get my arm free, swinging quickly to slam the other man in the gut. I jump behind him quickly, and shove him forward into Eve.

Another shot is fired, and it misses my head, whirring by me, and I dive to roll behind one of the men with a rifle. Under his legs, I jump back up just as another shot is fired and I use him as a shield, snatching his gun and opening fire. They scatter back a little bit, but return fire. My human shield is hit multiple times.

"Don't back off, shoot him! I don't care anymore!" Eve cries out.

I look down and train my sight on her. "Eve! If I get shot, you get shot too!"

As men circle around me, my shield no longer useful, Eve hesitates. She raises her hand to halt them, and glares at me.

"I don't want to do it, but if I have to in order to protect my family, I will," my threat rings out in the silence. "You can just turn around and head back to wherever you came from, and no one else has to get hurt."

"I can't do that. You have humiliated me, and you no doubt have supplies that we can plunder," she yells.

"If you want the supplies, you can have them, but my family stays out of this." I slowly stand, keeping the gun trained on her head.

"*We* could have been family, Rain. You could have been *my* husband." She crosses her arms and I can see her eyes well up.

"You didn't know me. You still don't. You couldn't possibly want me other than to be your trophy."

"I'm a woman who knows what she wants. If I can't have you, then no one will!"

I hear guns cocking. With my sight trained directly on Eve's face, I try to strengthen my resolve to actually pull the trigger if I need to.

Can I really do this? Am I destined to just be violent?

"Kohan. Go get Ami and the other woman. We'll execute them all together and take their supplies," Eve commands.

"Don't you dare. Don't you bring them into this."

"It's too late. When you rejected me, you brought this upon them too."

"Wait. Wait! I have a proposal! You could leave with me and the supplies we have, but you have to leave Ami and her mother alone," I bellow out, and Kohan stops to look at Eve.

"You would insult me further by pretending you have the power to bargain? You have lost! Why would I gamble on your proposal?"

"If Kohan moves, I will pull this trigger. You and I will die in this desert and Kohan can take the supplies and leave." I keep the trigger squeezed just enough to not fire the rifle. "He has no reason to harm them."

Looking back, Kohan waits for another command to move. Eve puts her hands on her hips and sighs, staring me down, and I can tell that she is giving it thought. She waves her hand at everyone to lower their weapons, but even though they have, I keep mine trained on her.

"What is your proposal?" she scoffs.

"You and I duel. No weapons. Just us. If you can defeat me, you get to keep me and take all of the supplies from the house that you can."

"How arrogant. Thinking I would still want you." She snubs her nose at me, but her eyes are still directly on me and she's buying it.

The tension in the air is high as she thinks about it, and I know with her overconfidence it is too good a deal for her to pass up. While I can acknowledge that I am being arrogant, if only to myself, I know that she will go for it. She's obsessive and won't give up until she has what she desires. Eve lets out a low growl.

"Fine, if I win I take you as my personal slave, and the supplies are mine," she says, a confident smile finally returning to her face.

"And if I win, you leave and we never see you again." I grin back.

"Sounds like a deal. Drop the gun and let's go now," she says, trying to coerce me from the only thing keeping me alive.

"I'm afraid that's not how this is going to work. As soon as I drop the gun I die, so here's what we are going to do. You will stand right there while your people retreat several hundred yards away." I let that arrogance shine, the tide tipped in my favor for a brief moment. "When I know that I will not be shot, then we can have our duel."

"And what's to stop you from killing me once they are away?" she honestly questions me.

"If I wanted you dead, you would be dead right now, even knowing that it would cost me my life."

"Fine," she says while moving around, and I keep my scope trained on her. "You heard him! Get out of here! Grab a few tents and some food from the wagon and go set up."

It takes several minutes, but as Eve and I stand off, her bandits retreat in the direction in which they had come from and begin setting up. Both of us stand in silence until I feel safe to loosen my trigger finger.

"Are we going to do this, or what?" she snaps.

Tossing the gun to the side I step backward a few steps on the soft sand and brace myself, preparing for Eve's attack.

Without warning she hurtles toward me. Her bare feet claw at the ground like a wild animal. She approaches, and when she thrusts her arm out to punch me, I suck in and arc forward, causing her to miss. Her balance is thrown off. I grab her arm and pull lightly in the direction she was already going. She trips over her own feet and falls to her knees. She growls, pivots, and lunges upward. Her fists fly. Uppercut. Right hook. Left hook. Right leg kick. I dodge the first three, and grab her leg. Pulling upward, I throw her onto her back.

"Stop being soft and take some hits. This is a duel!" she yells while standing back up and brushing her shirt down.

"And this is me dueling." I step back to put a few feet between us.

She runs at me and tries once more, but because of her lengthy arms and legs, reading her movements is simple. Throwing one fist after another, her aim is good. If she had a little more speed, she might just hit me, but my agility keeps me ahead of her blows. Her face turns red with anger, and she swings her left leg around, finally connecting with my ribs. I exhale sharply. A smug look crosses her face as I bend over to catch my breath, but she is relentless.

Taking advantage of my temporary immobility, she tries to kick me again. I weakly block it with my hands before it connects, but she hits my wound. Instinctively, I leap up and ram my shoulder into her breastbone. She hits the sand again, crouched this time with her hand pressed against the ground as a support.

She looks up at me, and the twinkle I see in her eyes tells me she knows that my arm is a weakness. From her position she leaps into a roll, and when her feet come back around to the sand she pushes up, launching herself into the air and coming down on me hard with both fists. I am forced to block with my arms. When she connects, pain shoots up. She hits it over and over. I halt her by grabbing her arm as it is coming, and pull her forward to my face. I sweep my leg behind her, place my elbow on her collar bone, and shove her to the ground again.

"If all you can do is push me down you're going to lose," she taunts.

"It's all I will do. You're a woman."

"Are you saying that because I'm a woman I'm inferior to you?"

"I'm saying I think you are fragile enough for me to break," I taunt to get under her skin.

Determined to take me down, she crouches, and breaks into sprint. She fakes left, and when I dodge, she catches me off guard. Eve jumps into the air from all fours, her hands and feet extended to claw at me. Unable to dodge, I plant my feet. She connects, wraps her hands around my neck, and lands her feet on my knees. Grabbing her by the waist, I swing her around and let go. The force sends her flying against a dune, but she is back up and charging me again.

Both her fists fly at me. When I block, pain screams through my wound. Stunned, she takes advantage, punching me in the ribs with quick successive punches. Before I can regain composure, Eve has wrapped her arm around my neck, and chokes me. Grabbing her arm, I try pulling it away. The blood in my vessels pulses, and I can feel my face turning red.

I swing my right leg back behind hers, and shove with my left side. We both fall. My shoulder blade hits her sternum. She exhales, and her arm loosens. In a brief second, I rip her arm away and jump off of her, but I'm tackled and turned onto my back.

"Why must you struggle?" Eve says, and slams two fists together into my chest. She pins my arms to the ground with her knees while sitting on me. "You're going to be my personal slave!"

I swing my legs up, and kick her in the back of the head. I don't want to hurt her, but I need to step it up if I want to stay a free man. She's stunned, and her knees come up a bit, but before I can get free she pins me again. I struggle. She readies to hit me in the face, and as she plunges her fist down, I yell out.

"Wait!"

She halts, "What could you possibly want in the middle of our duel?"

"Before you hit me in the face I think we should kiss. It's obvious you win and if you hit me, it might be awhile before you get another chance," I suggest slyly.

"You're offering to kiss me?" She looks at me puzzled, she pulls her fist back again. "I can just take one as I please."

"But, I am offering willingly. That's what you really want is it not?" It's a dirty tactic to stall for time, but it's all I can think of right now.

She does not hesitate and thrusts herself down on me. Our lips press together, and she turns it quickly into a passionate open mouth kiss. Her guard drops as her muscles relax. I seize the opportunity.

I manage to roll us over, and she lands on her back. I pull away, our kiss broken, and we tumble around. I finally get the upper hand by jumping on her back. With my knee in her spine, I pin her in place and she realizes I am not just playing rough, but that I've deceived her. Flailing to reach me, she cannot get a grip. I grab her arms and pin them behind her back, shoving her face into the sand.

"GET OFF OF ME!" she screams violently while struggling.

"Not until you forfeit," my voice comes out calm but I twist her arms harder.

"Never! You said I won!" She groans through the pain.

"Yeah, well, I lied," I snap at her.

She squirms, but with her arms pinned, and my knee in her back, she realizes she's been outdone. I wait for her fighting spirit to break, and I can almost feel it as she huffs into the sand angrily, knowing she's helpless. Finally, she quits.

"Holding you here takes no effort, and I could easily lock my arm around your neck to knock you out. Are we finished here?" I ask her.

"I give. You win," she grunts angrily.

"Kohan!" I yell out.

"Don't bring him over here. Please," she pleads.

"I have to have a witness that you are giving up," I tell her. "Otherwise how would I trust that you will leave?"

"You will just have to trust me," she tells me. But it's too late, Kohan is upon us.

"What?" he asks sternly.

"Eve is defeated. You will all leave now," I reply.

"Let me up!" The fire in her voice returns, and it rings of destroyed pride.

Doing now as she has requested, I relinquish my hold on her arms.

When I see no movement from her, other than to relax her hands to the ground, I lift my knee and return to a standing position. She lies there for a moment, so I offer my hand to help her up. She swats it away childishly. Pushing herself up, she takes a moment on her knees before standing. On her feet again, she looks at me with disgust, but says nothing.

Kohan takes her by the arm, and they promptly do an about-face, beginning to walk toward the stuck wagon and the tents. I watch them with suspicion, no trust for either of them.

Finally, maybe I can rest until we shift through time.

Turning around, I head toward the edge of the hill down to the house and I see Ami and Agatha standing in the door of the kitchen. Waving, I smile at them, and their faces are relieved.

"We will not leave empty handed!" A rally cry pierces the air, coming right from the mouth of a person so deluded by their own grandiose self-empowerment that I should have expected it. "Plunder the house and kill them!"

Eve has gone back on her word. When I turn, her battalion is already rushing toward me. Watching, time feels as if it moves slowly. A sense of helplessness falls over me. I feel the need to fight them rising, but I am frozen in place.

My body begins to convulse. I am forced to place my knee into the ground to keep myself from falling over. Fighting against losing consciousness, I cannot believe this is happening.

A seizure?! Now?! I have to fight! I have to be able to defend Ami and Agatha! Eve is nearing. I have to pull it together!

I fight my body as that pressure builds up inside me again. It feels like my body is going to burst. I struggle to focus, but my vision blurs. My arms shake violently. In some manner beyond my understanding, I find myself channeling the pressure through my body, and into my hands. My head, my torso, and my legs calm, but I cannot control my arms.

As they near, I push up with my legs. It is difficult to stay upright. Letting my body do as it wants, I help it push that pressure to rid the shaking of my arms and hands. Clenching my fists, my nails draw blood.

Past the slow motion lens I'm seeing the world through, Eve and her army have nearly reached me, and my body instinctively reacts. Turning my head, and shutting my eyes, I throw my hands out in front of me and open them, palms out.

"NO!" I yell at the top of my lungs.

The pressure begins to leave like a wave, sent from my toes, up through my body, and out through my arms and hands. Like thunder, a crack rips through the air. It sounds like the world itself has shattered in front of me. Screaming is heard from the multitude. I open my eyes to see the army has been knocked back several feet. Beyond them, I can see an almost visible ripple slice lengthwise through the air, and it destroys their wagon.

What was THAT?!

Eve moves amongst the pile, and she groans. They're all beginning to get back up, regaining their composure, albeit disoriented and confused. Taking a defensive stance I keep my hands out and try to do it again. My hands are tingling, but they are not shaking like before. Eve staggers forward, her face angry and determined.

How do I do it again?!

"Stay there, Eve!" I yell.

She grunts in response, and waves her hand from back to front to signal a second attack. Regaining as much composure as they can, they stumble forward, but as momentum builds they steady. I find myself bracing, but there is no sign of the pressure from before. I'm not seizing this time. Pointing my hands at the ground I see them hesitate, but Eve refuses to give up.

"STAY THERE!" I bellow.

I feel it again, and a rush flows through me. With my eyes open this time, I watch it happen. A fraction of a second before I hear the noise, I see that wave exit my hands, only made visible as it slices even the light particles in the air. The crack follows. When the wave impacts the sand, it sprays up toward the group. Eve staggers, and screams out. Her people either fall, or run the other way.

The earth shifts and everyone's footing is loosed from the ground. Familiar with the small quake, I look behind me to find that blue swirl kicking up around the house, cutting through the air. Looking back at Eve, I grin mischievously. The quaking gets heavier, and I turn to jump down the hill.

Side stepping down the dune, I head for the vortex. The blue mixing with the sand causes a marbling effect within the air, and were I not in a hurry to make it, I would be able to admire it. Reaching the bank of sand just before the trench I run to leap over it. Ami cries out.

I'm tackled from behind. Turning over I kick violently. Eve grips me heavily, and glares, but I shove and push away. Leaving her in the sand, I run and jump over the trench, landing inside the vortex. Looking back, I can see the new destination all around us. It is a lush green forest.

Could it be that we are going back to my time?

"RAIN!" Eve yells, barreling through the vortex, and tackling me to the ground.

~~~~~~

4 CONFRONTATION

Before any of us can realize, the quaking ceases, and the blue vortex dies down. As I struggle with Eve, I do what I can to put my legs between us while she swings wildly. She lands a solid blow to my temple. My vision goes black briefly, causing my head to spin. I am stuck in a daze, unable to defend myself as she hits me. Ami and Evalyn intercede. My vision returns, and they are pulling Eve off of me.

"Get off of him!" Evalyn yells.

"Rain! Are you okay?!" Ami cries out.

"Is it too late?" I ask looking out to the forest where there is no sand or bandits in sight.

"Where are my men?! Where have you taken me?!" Eve's shrill voice rings out, her head darting from left to right.

"It's too late!" Evalyn yells.

"What have you done?" Eve struggles against Ami and Evalyn.

"They're gone. Or I should say they're still there, and you're gone," I mumble and sigh heavily.

Rubbing my head, I blink several times to get my vision to right itself. Getting up, I watch Ami and Evalyn restrain Eve as best as they can. They finally cannot hold her any longer. She lunges at me. I am too tired and disappointed to care about not hitting her and I grind my fist into her ribcage, just below her breasts. She coughs and sputters while stumbling backward.

"What have you done, you vile creature?!" Eve coughs and cries out hysterically.

"This is not what we needed; another mouth to feed," Evalyn protests.

"I did not do it," I tell Eve calmly.

"You lie, fiend! First you hit us with an invisible shockwave from your hands, and now we're in some foreign place! What are you?!" Eve yells out, the spite in her voice piercing my ears like a knife.

"Invisible wave?" Ami asks.

"I'm not quite sure myself. That was the first time I had done that." I shrug.

"You think this is funny?! How do I get back?" she yells at me.

"You don't," Ami tells her snidely, moving around the side next to me. "You're stuck here with us, and us with you."

Eve's anger shifts focus to Ami, and she tries to hit a weaker target. I am on her before she can successfully connect, jumping in to take the full force of the side swing. It connects with my shoulder, and I shrug it off. She tries again, but I grab her by the wrist.

"You have a short memory, don't you?" I glare angrily at her. "I will not allow you to harm these women."

"Rain, I blame you for this. We didn't need another freeloader," Evalyn sneers.

While ill-timed due to the volatile nature of the situation at hand, Evalyn is right, and we now have another person stuck. Where I was at least welcome by Ami and Agatha, Eve has been dragged along unwillingly by all parties.

"Take me back! Now!" Eve yells.

"We can't. Where we go isn't controlled by us," I tell her, using soft tones to try and disarm her.

"Then tell me how *I* can get back!" She struggles to get away.

"There is no way back! You are stuck with us forever!" It just spills out. "If you'd have just left well enough alone, none of this would have happened!"

Whoops.

"What do you mean?" she asks.

"It's a long story. Eve is it?" Agatha is now in control of her body, and signs of sympathy appear in her face. "Perhaps we should sit down, have a glass of water, and we can bring you up to speed."

If only she really knew Eve.

Eve looks at us all cautiously, determining whether to trust us, no doubt. She rips her arm free of my grasp, tugs on the bottom of her cutoff top, and crosses her arms hastily. With no choice, she nods for us to lead the way. Agatha starts toward the door. Ami follows. Eve is behind her. But when I try to walk, my body stops responding. I feel it coming, and I'm helpless to do anything.

Another seizure?! Now?!

~~~~~~

I startle awake to find myself inside, lying on the couch. The table is at my side, with a bowl of water, and a washcloth is across my forehead.

Seeing the woods beyond the living room window, the familiar scene haunts me, and I quickly check my chest to make sure that my wound is still closed. The healed scar allows me to breathe a sigh of relief. Despite my mortal wound so few months ago, my body has nearly recovered, with minimal aches now and again. I tug on my shirt to pull it down while I readjust to a more comfortable position, and regain my senses.

A yellow shirt? Is this a fresh shirt? It has to be. It's not the one I was wearing.

Nobody is in the room, and I cannot see anyone beyond the drawn drapes. The door is cracked open though, and a warm smell of fresh vegetation drifts in. I feel a little nostalgic. Sitting up, my mind begs me to go look out the window at the dense forest, desperately needing to know if we have returned to my time. Drake enters my thoughts, and a sense of dread creeps up on me when I recall his evil form.

Why do I have the feeling he would murder Ami and Agatha just to spite me? Is that who he really is?

I lift myself off the couch and head over to the window. Peeking out, Ami and Agatha are pulling the cover off of the well. They are in conversation, but I cannot tell what it's about. When the cover is dropped, Ami moves her arms sharply. She is trying to get a strong point across, which would not be her demeanor if it were Evalyn.

Moving to the door, I am a little light-headed, which is unsurprising considering everything that has happened. I lean against the wall for support. The door creaks as I pull it open a little more to listen in, and I can hear Ami's side of the conversation.

"No, you can't go alone!"

Agatha says something that I cannot distinguish, so I pull the door enough to slip out and then crouch along the small porch to get closer. I catch the tail end of what she's saying.

"...to survive. It has to be done."

"Then let *me* go, Mother. I am faster than you. Besides it's been much more dangerous since Rain joined us. We need to be cautious."

It has? Have I somehow put them in danger by being here? I suppose I have been sort of an enabler for Ami's curiosity and need for exploration. Perhaps by that means I've just led her into danger – which I seem to be a magnet for. But from the way it sounded, it was almost like she was accusing me of doing it intentionally. I need to know if she feels that way.

"Has my being here caused it to be more dangerous? Are my actions somehow to blame?" I stand upright and ask without any negative undertone in my voice.

Both of them turn around, startled.

"Rain, I...I didn't mean it like that!" Ami tries to explain herself.

"You could be right, though. I seem to attract trouble." I shrug.

"No! Please don't take it that way!"

I try to respond again, but my head swims, and I get dizzy. Bracing myself against the side of the house, I look down and close my eyes.

"Do you...do you regret..." I force half a sentence out but end up collapsing to one knee.

Why is my body failing me?

"Get him inside and back on the couch!" Agatha tells Ami hastily.

They pick me up and bring me back inside. Laid down, the wet cloth is again placed on my forehead. Ami sits on the table next to me while Agatha hovers.

"Just rest, Rain," Agatha's familiar motherly tone soothes.

"I am a nuisance. Better that I work with Evalyn soon to break the curse so I can stop bringing trouble to your doorstep. You do not deserve the problems I cause," I mumble.

"You're talking nonsense. You aren't bringing us trouble," Agatha reassures me. "And to prove it, I will be the one to go search for any nearby cities and when I return we will have a big dinner to celebrate not being in the desert."

"Rain, I'm sorry. I didn't mean what I said. Your being here has been the best thing for us. Even for Aunt Evalyn, whether she'll admit it or not." Ami touches my shoulder gently.

"From the looks of it, and I'm sure you can tell also, that we're in a forest like the one we found you in. There's no way of telling yet if it's close to the original time we rescued you from unless we find a city," Agatha tells me.

"Head the direction I came from. West," I blurt.

"Why? Did you remember something?" Ami asks.

"No, I didn't remember anything. It's a choice based on my running path when I was trying to escape from Drake."

"Well, then that's where I will go," Agatha smiles.

She heads into the hallway while Ami switches from the table to the couch. She lays against me, her ear against my chest. Closing her eyes she lets out a sigh and it seems like she might be upset about what she said.

"It's all right, Ami," I comfort her, and stroke her soft hair.

"I didn't realize that it was going to come out that way. I'm sorry."

"I forgive you. Forget it happened, okay?"

After lying there for a while, Agatha emerges from the darkened hallway. She's in a very simple light yellow dress, with a white cloth belt around the waist. Draped over her shoulders is a tan cloak with a hood, marked with Ami's signature pink rose. She also has her straw basket.

Ami lifts and turns her head to speak to her mother. "Are you sure?"

"Yes. Rain needs you right now." She winks at me. My face flushes.

"Be careful, Mother."

"I will be back in no time." She makes her way to the door and quickly turns back around, waving her finger at us. "Don't go anywhere."

"Okay, *Mother*!" Ami says exasperated.

When Agatha has left, Ami rests her head back down, and sighs again out of worry.

If we are indeed back in my time, I can't blame her. Beyond the woods is unknown, and there may or may not be danger. However with Eve now part of the house we may be in danger regardless. Stuck with her, I don't think we have a choice but to find a way to cohabitate peacefully. Where is she?

"Where is Eve?"

"She ran off into the woods in the direction where the sand hill was. She didn't believe the story and insisted that this is just an illusion. It's been a few hours now."

I let silence fall over the room, comforted by it and the lack of immediate danger. With just Ami it's peaceful. Though I fear what is in the forest, I am glad we are no longer in the desert. Looking down, Ami's eyes are shut, and her breathing has relaxed. I figure a nap could do me some good against my aching body.

~~~~~~

A creak in the house wakes me up from a sound slumber. When I open my eyes, it's dark, and I cannot tell what caused it or where it came from. Sitting up, Ami is no longer near me. It could be her, perhaps having gone to the bathroom or upstairs to the sewing room. But now it's silent again.

Determining that I should go look, I head to the kitchen door, peeking in. The light is off, and no one is there. Down the hallway, her door is open. She is on her bed, cuddled up to a pillow and snoring lightly. My heart jumps a little, and the hair on the back of my neck stands up.

With her passed out, where could the creak have come from? Agatha or Eve? If Agatha were back she too might be asleep, but if Eve were back there would most certainly be more noise than a single creak.

Down to the last door on the right, I peek into Agatha's room. She is not there. The silence becomes eerie to the point that I become anxious about Drake sneaking up on me and finishing what he started. Feeling closed in and stifled, I head to the living room to leave the house. When I open the door, sweet air from the woods rushes past me. Though I suffered trauma there, the serenity about it is calming, and much nicer than the dry desert.

Barefoot, I walk to the edge of the forest where I directed Agatha to go. Circling the perimeter of the house, I cannot see far into the woods. The moon is but a crescent in the sky, and only two lights on the house illuminate the yard. I am trapped for the time being.

With no sign of Agatha, I begin to worry. My mind plays tricks on me. *Is she lost? Maybe an animal attacked her. Or maybe she tripped and is injured, unable to walk.*

Despite her specific instruction for us to stay put, I want to venture out to locate her.

I must find something to do with myself to keep from going stir-crazy.

Shifting my mind, I focus on the mystery of my absurd power, having created something from my hands which I cannot explain. Eve called it a shockwave, and it reminds me of the wave that hit after one of Kohan's grenades exploded, but there were no flames from my hands or body.

How can I wield such power? Am I like Evalyn, able to control some unnatural force? I'd ask her about it, but without Agatha I don't think Evalyn has an outlet to communicate.

Perhaps I can call it forth and use it at will.

Raising my hands, I stretch my legs apart, and put myself in an awkward pose. Straining, I attempt to call it up from deep within, only to have nothing happen. I try several things, including changing my footing, thrusting my palms out, and grunting while attempting to recreate the effect, all of which fail.

What were the conditions that caused it? My stress level was high, my body was fatigued and battered, and I was in immediate danger. None of those things I can recreate right now. I also yelled. It can't be that simple, can it? Yelling? Worth a shot I suppose, but what do I yell?

Deliberating for a few moments, I come to the conclusion that the first word I used was 'no' and therefore it must have power behind it. Deep breath in and...

"NO!" I let out the largest roar I can while thrusting my hands out together from my chest.

However, to my disappointment, or perhaps delight, nothing happens. No boom, no wave, no destruction. There is no sense of pressure and no borderline seizure welling up in me. I wonder if those two were the only ones in me, needed at a precise moment.

Footsteps approach from behind, silently padding along in the grass. Turning, I expect to see Ami, but find someone less friendly. Eve, seeing she's caught, breaks into a sprint, leaps, and pins me to the ground. Her knees dig into my hips, and I groan.

"Don't have it in you anymore, huh, Rain?!" She raises her fists, clasps them together, and attempts to slam them into my ribs. I block, grab her arms, and pull her in to me, face to face.

"Hey!" I yell in her face while scowling. "You need to let this go. We are stuck together, and I don't want to worry about being attacked every day."

"Those hussy women fed me their lie! I don't believe a word from them, or you, imp!" she snaps at me and struggles, while I hold her from hitting me.

"You will find it very hard not to believe when that vortex kicks up again." I laugh at her.

"Let go!" she screams and struggles. "I demand a rematch, and when you lose you take me back!"

"Eve, there is nothing you can say or do that will allow any of us to take you back." I laugh harder. "If you don't want to believe what you've been told then fine, don't. You'll learn the hard way, like I did."

"Why are you laughing? What do you mean?" Her struggle lessens for a moment.

I shove her off of me and stand up, but she comes at me again, swinging her right fist toward my jaw. Leaning down to avoid it, I ram my shoulder into her. When she is knocked back I grab her wrist, twist, and lock it in place behind her back. Pulling hard, I threaten to dislocate her arm, and then use my other arm to choke her.

"I mean that if you are outside the house's perimeter when it shifts through time, you will be pulled back and your landing will be a very painful one, like mine was," I tell it to her as it is, finding a violent urge well up in me. "Now, you can keep fighting me and I will snap your neck, as much as I would like not to, or you can stop attacking and allow me to relax."

Letting my arm slack from against her neck a little I give her an opportunity to speak. She's silent for a moment, likely hesitant to give up as has been shown by her actions, but I her muscles loosen against my body and I take that as submission. Slowly, I release my arm from around her neck and back up, waiting to see if she strikes again.

"So if we're not in my time, where are we?" Eve spins around while crossing her arms, her tone condescending.

"We are not sure yet. Agatha left earlier to find out but I don't think she has returned."

"Is there a way to fix this?"

"They don't know, and it's why I'm here. They saved my life and in return I am going to help them figure out how to break this curse."

"What happens when you break the curse?"

"I don't know! This all started way before I joined, so I'm completely in the dark! I don't even know if I am going to succeed!" I yell angrily.

Even in the dim light I can see the look of shock on Eve's face, and I can tell that underneath her brash and arrogant front that she is genuinely scared. With her reaction, I liken her to a little girl, lost and away from everything she knew that gave her comfort, regardless that they were despicable conditions. Her fiery red hair flows in a slight breeze, and I stare into her eyes, causing me to soften and rethink my reaction.

"Look, I'm sorry Eve. Between being in the desert, running short on supplies, dealing with you and yours, and trying to figure things out, it's all been a bit stressful. I haven't had much rest, and I have been ill a lot lately."

She snubs her nose at me and my apology, turning toward the forest. Tightening crossed arms, she acts like a child. Luckily, just beyond her, Ami comes into view in the doorway and I sigh in relief as I now have support. Rubbing her eyes, she slowly makes her way down the stairs and through the grass to us.

"What's going on out here?" she asks through a yawn. "You're being so loud."

"Nothing!" Eve sneers.

"Eve and I have worked through some things and I think she understands the gravity of the situation," I explain.

"I didn't say I believed you!"

"Okay, Eve." I shake my head and switch focus to Ami. "Anyway, your mother hasn't returned."

"That's not good. She's normally back within a couple hours." Ami becomes concerned, crinkling her eyebrows downward.

"Right, but for all we know she's had to travel a long way to find any signs of civilized life," I try and comfort her.

"Or she could be in trouble," Eve throws in rudely.

"Eve, can you muster even a little sensitivity?" My anger toward her flares back up.

"Whatever," Eve huffs while storming off to the other side of the house.

"Has she ever been gone this long before? Ever had to stay away from the house?" I ask.

"No, never. Until you, we've always stayed within close range of the house and never stayed out too long." Ami moves over to me and hugs on my chest.

"Then that settles it. I'm going to find her. Imagine how disorienting it was for us together. It has to be worse for her." I hug her back.

"I'm going with you." She looks up into my eyes.

"No." I shake my head. "Someone has to stay here and keep an eye on Eve. We don't need her eating all of the food, or trying to plunder the house and run off."

"But…" she tries to argue.

"No buts."

"Fine, but I'm loading you up with supplies. I don't want you caught out unprepared."

"What did you have in mind?"

She pulls away from me and grabs my hand, leading me into the house and pointing at the couch indicating she wants me to sit. "I'll be right back." She turns into the dark hallway and disappears into the shadows.

I sit as instructed and wait patiently for her. She returns, only briefly, setting down a black knapsack and folded heavy piece of cloth on the table in front of me, and disappears into the kitchen. Leaning back, I rest my head against the back of the couch and close my eyes, my ears picking up the sound of her moving about. When she returns I crack my eyelid just enough to see. Even in a disheveled state from having been asleep only a few minutes ago, she's still graceful and beautiful. I become fixated on her lips.

My lips know the touch of another, but not hers. What does her kiss feel like?

She bends over to put some food in the sack, and her shirt droops at the collar a little. Even in the dark, her chest is slightly visible. Though my male urges insist I look, I shut my eyes tight and wait until she's gone, not wanting to taint the relationship we have right now with thoughts of what could be. After hearing the swinging door, I open my eyes.

Is it wrong that I find myself attracted to her? We have bonded over these months, but would it be wrong for me to pursue her only because we have only each other?

Returning one last time she has a fancy lantern, and a sheathed weapon which looks like a dagger. Setting them down by the bag, she puts her arms on her hips and looks at me.

"You sure I can't convince you to let me go?" she asks with a pleading look on her face.

"I'm positive. You are needed here."

She moves around the table and sits on the edge, reaching over to take my hands in hers. My cheeks get a little warm, but it's dark enough in the room that she cannot see me blush. Impulsively I lean forward, moving to kiss her. Before I can the kitchen door bursts open and light floods in. Ami is assaulted by the core of an apple in the side of the head, and she jumps up to hit Eve. Grabbing her by the hand I hold her back and Eve stands there with a smug look on her face.

"What was that for?!" Ami raises her fist threateningly.

"Do you have anything else to eat? That fruit was mealy." Eve picks at her teeth.

"You'll be lucky if you get anything *now*, you tramp!" Ami wipes the side of her face.

"I'll just take it, you lying hussy!" Eve laughs.

"Hey!" I yell out, a little frustrated at the whole situation. "Eve, what did I tell you earlier? We're stuck together. That means get along!"

"You keep saying that..." She looks toward the stairs.

"Eve, shut up. If you don't believe me, that's your problem. Disappear for the month then." My voice raises a bit, and I glare angrily.

Eve does as she is told and the whole living room falls silent. Letting Ami go, I reach down to collect the items she has set out for me, starting with the dagger. Wrapping its belt across my shoulder so it hangs at my side for quick access, I cinch it in place and then hang the bag over so it partially conceals my weapon. Unfolding the heavy cloth, I find that it's a dark colored cloak with a hood. I wrap it around my back and button it at the neck. Lastly, I pick up the lantern and examine it.

"Is this electric or oil?" I ask, while dropping my arm to the side.

Ami giggles, and I feel like I've asked a question with an obvious answer. "Considering that we're likely in the past again, we don't want to draw too much unnecessary attention, so it's oil. There's an extra oil flask in the bag."

"Electric?" Eve asks with an attitude.

"Hah! Looks like you get to teach Eve what you had to teach me. I wonder if she's from farther in the past than my time and that's why she's so uncouth." I smirk.

"Not funny." Ami puts her hands on her hips. "Now, get out of here before I change my mind and I go with you anyway."

"What do we have for lighting the lantern?"

"Matches."

Pulling a small box from my bag, she slides it open, retrieves a small stick among many from inside, and swipes it across the side. It ignites and I remove the lantern's glass cover while she brings the flame down to the wick. It catches fire, and I replace the glass. She returns the box of matches to the bag under my arm and then spins me around and places her hands on my back to get me going.

"Be safe out there, Rain," Ami coddles.

"Yeah, be safe out there," Eve teases sarcastically.

I slip my shoes on and exit the house, once again heading to the edge of the property. Looking back, Ami stands on the small wooden porch, watching anxiously. I wave to let her know it will be okay, and she hesitantly waves back.

I pull the cloak's hood over my head, and tug on the sides to bring it over each shoulder to shut out the cool draft. Stepping nervously into the forest, its eerie darkness, and thoughts of what happened here, gives me pause. I strengthen my resolve to find Agatha and begin to stride into the unknown.

Even with a lantern, traversing the woods is more difficult than I thought it would be. Having become accustomed to roads or openness, I trip and stumble over the vegetation within the woods as if it had a vendetta against me. The forest throws everything it can muster, including tree roots, bushes and dips in the ground, all in the direction I need to go.

Even after adjusting my eyes into a habit of looking mostly at where I'm walking, rather than the direction, I still stumble.

My stomach grumbles and I stop for a moment to dig through my bag. There is a sandwich right at the top, and I pull it from its plastic container, eating while walking. Finding my attention divided between eating and walking in the dark, I choose to focus on not falling face first, leaving my food to be eaten slowly.

The woods seem endless, and were it not for a few random creature noises, it would be silent. Not even the wind seems to dare rustle the trees. Though I'm not sure how long I have been walking, my mind obsesses over just wanting to be home with Ami and Agatha safely, relaxing. But adventure seems to be in my blood, my very essence, and I cannot tell if I am subconsciously seeking it out, or if it's finding me.

It cannot be ignored that so far I've been stabbed, fought a crime ring run by a little boy, and fought against being a slave to an egotistical woman. And now I'm off to find what has happened to Agatha. Nothing may have happened to her at all. It's quite likely that she found some semblance of civilization and got stuck there simply because it got too dark to navigate the woods.

My legs ache from the walking, and my arms grow weary from holding the lantern, even with switching hands every now and then. Out of the corner of my left eye I notice a glimmer, and I'm not sure if my mind is playing tricks or not, but I turn to it anyway. I pick up the pace and begin a quick stride toward it. The light brightens.

Another lantern?

My quick pace turns into a jog, and I take greater care not to trip. In my haste I nearly barrel right into a large thistle bush. Turning to my left I try to find my way around it while keeping the light in my sight. It takes me a minute, but when the path is clear I increase my pace again. Closing in on it, I see a structure, a watchtower constructed with wood, and men in armor guarding it. One of them notices me and yells out.

"Halt!"

I stop a few hundred feet from the guard at the base of the tower. Upon closer inspection of his armor, it feels very familiar. *Have I been here before? I must have.* The most noticeable pieces are a cone tipped helm with a guard piece coming down over the face for his nose, chainmail on his chest, and large silver boots all marked with a crest that looks like two birds swooping down for the same kill. A wave of nostalgia hits me.

Do I know this person?

"State your business at this hour of night!"

"I'm simply a weary traveler looking for refuge," I explain.

He looks at me with his head half-cocked, and his eyes quirked. "The city gates are closed at night. You will have to wait outside until the rooster crows at the dawn."

He has a slight accent that comes from the way he moves his jaw. It's different from the way I speak, but it also has a familiarity to it. My own speech blends naturally to accommodate his.

"Tell me sir, how might I find the front gates?" The feeling of remembrance hasn't faded.

It's like the information is right there at the front of my mind, and I can almost find my own way down, but I can't get to it. I'm still being blocked by my own mind.

"Follow the path beyond our tower here. It will lead you down into the valley where Asta resides."

"Thank you, sir," I reply politely and bow.

"Long live Asta!" The guard snaps to attention and pounds his left fist against his right shoulder.

"Long live Asta!" My mouth and body react in the same manner instinctively.

Now I know I've been here, but does that mean Drake is waiting for me?

As instructed, I follow the dirt path from the guard's tower down into a valley. While mostly dark, I can see the whole city, a familiar city, illuminated by lanterns and lights in windows. There I recognize Asta. The crescent moon and starlight, now unhindered by any trees, provide little to help illuminate structures within the valley. What I can identify is that inside the city walls, deep beyond rows of buildings, sits a large castle surrounded by another much larger wall with archers towers all around it.

Finding my way down the curvy dirt path, making a gradual descent into the valley, I see scattered homes and farms. There is not a single light on within the farmhouses, leading me to believe that it's fairly late in the night. Slinking through a field of corn stalks, I find the main cobblestone path up to the gate of the city. From above everything looked small, but now in the thick of it I find the farms are actually quite large, and I am still at least a fifteen minute walk from the well-lit front gate.

Two large, stone fire pits burn intensely to illuminate two armored guards on the ground, and two in the archer towers on the wall. The feeling of familiarity hasn't faded. Though I still cannot remember, I know for sure that I have been to this place before.

"Halt!" The guard turns and puts up his hand.

"Yes, sir." I stand still.

"The city gates are…" the guard starts in with the same warning as the last one.

"…closed for the night. Yes, thank you. I will wait out here until they open in the morning," I finish his sentence for him and move to a fence that is bordering a farmhouse near the wall.

That is probably why Agatha never returned. With the city gates closed she would be stuck in there.

Sitting down with my back against the end post of the wooden fence, I turn the wick down in the lantern and blow it out. I set it to my side, and bring my knees up so I can wrap the cloak completely around myself to keep warm. Resting my chin on my knees is uncomfortable for a few minutes while the muscles in my back relax, but I get to the point that I can ignore it, and close my eyes. Waiting for the dawn which comes slowly, I am in need of a nap, and allow myself to drift to sleep, my hand on the hilt of the dagger.

~~~~~~

The sound of feet beating against the stones wakes me. I look up to see a smartly dressed couple arm-in-arm walking past me on the dirt road toward open city gates. Looking the man over, I find that I should be able to blend in well enough, as what I am wearing is in line with their fashion. Wearing a long-sleeved undershirt, covered by a thick vest, and loose pants with a slight bit of embroidery sewn near the seams of his breeches, I almost feel underdressed compared to him.

I remove my hand from the hilt of the dagger and grab the lantern instead. Using the fence to help me stand, I look into the now open gateway to the city of Asta, and my next move is unknown. Knowing the city is large, I wonder if I should wait at the gates to see if she appears, or if I should venture in and start searching.

I suppose I could at least look at any local inns, see if she had stayed there.

Swiftly I stride to the couple walking arm-in-arm toward the gate and lower my hood. "Excuse me."

"Yes, what is it? Oh…" The man turns to speak but looks at me with disgust. "We do not need any trouble. The guards are mere feet away."

Do I look like a bandit or something?

"No, you misunderstand. I'm simply a traveler in need of a little direction." I put my hands up to show him I mean no harm before he calls guards over unnecessarily.

"Be quick, we have somewhere to be." His deep voice intimidates me.

"I'm looking for someone who probably stayed here last night. Are there inns within the city?"

"There are at least half a dozen inns within," he offers.

"I appreciate your time." I place my arm at stomach level and bow slightly. "If I might borrow just a moment more, which way is the closest inn?"

Annoyed with my questioning, he answers brashly, "Enter the gates, go four streets up and take a left. Follow that down a few hundred yards and you will find yourself at 'Farstride Inn'. Now if you will kindly leave us be…"

He abruptly turns toward the city, and I follow. With the doors open, a massive iron gate is visible, drawn up between the two archer towers. Guards stand at the ready on either side of the entrance, and as my eyes meet theirs, I nod out of respect. Beyond the gates lies a city that nearly eclipses the castle. The buildings reach as far as I can see. I admire their simplicity compared to the monstrosities of Chas in little Emma's time. Stone stacked upon stone, wood nailed to wood. I am at home within this simplistic environment.

The streets are bustling, and it slows my progress to the inn, despite the short distance. Moving through the crowd I dodge and duck around people, evaluating the alleyways for shortcuts, but those too are filled.

Turning left at the fourth street, I delve deeper into the city. Farther off the main street, the type of people I find myself surrounded by quickly turns from classy to a bit untidy. Unsavory types lurk around every corner, and I am unable to imagine Agatha choosing this inn if she did in fact make it here, but I have nothing else to go on at the moment and cannot leave any place unchecked.

The wood door of the two-story inn is simple with a brass knob, and is in dire need of replacing due to rot. The building itself looks decent otherwise, until I step in and a nauseating smell hits me. I can't put my finger on it, but it could very well be the smell of death. The design inside is depressing, with dull colors and minimal lighting. There are a few heavily worn chairs strewn about, apparently for guest lounging. Stairs are off to my left. I spot a desk near the rear of the room and a stout, bald man behind it, not paying attention to me, with a ratty looking book in front of him. As I walk over the stench gets stronger and I realize that it's coming from him.

Oh, wow. When was his last bath?!

A fly buzzes my face as I reach the desk and wait for the man to acknowledge me. He either doesn't care I'm here, or is oblivious due to picking at a festering sore on one knuckle. The decrepit book in front of him is the guest logbook.

"Good day, sir," I announce myself, causing him to briefly glance up at me from his current endeavors. "I'm looking for someone who might have stayed here last night. Could I look at your guest log?"

"No one stayed 'ere last night, lad."

"Did a woman perhaps stop by here last night? She's in her early forties, wearing a dress, and tan cloak."

"I said no one stayed 'ere last night," he responds, continuing to pick at his knuckle.

"No one even showed up?"

"Tha's not what I said." He looks at me the same way the guards looked at me, as if there is something wrong. It's a little unnerving that people seem a little hostile here.

"So then, you didn't see the woman I described?"

"Nay."

"Thank you for your time." I nod and turn toward the door.

Leaving, I get the feeling he's staring at me. I can't explain it, but when

I reach the door I glance, and he *is*. I shiver and exit back out into the sunlight and fresh air. A cough of relief escapes my throat, no longer under the stench and tension in there.

One down. I need to find the ones that aren't rat-infested holes.

I find my way back to the street I came in on, and turn toward the castle. Walking with the flow of people, I reach what appears to be the city center, open and filled with many different things. In the middle lies an enormous fountain with a variety of bronze eagle statues on it. Each one has its beak open with water spouting out.

All around are people moving around, and performers and jesters entertain with dances and tricks. There are a slew of market shops built into buildings, and on carts, for people to patronize. I scan for Agatha. Wandering in circles around the fountain, I scour the crowds hopefully.

My track of time is lost, and I only regain it with the help of my stomach. While it is gurgling and grumbling, I seek food from my bag, and upon finding a jar of sliced apples I sit at the edge of the fountain to eat. Even stationary, I hope to catch sight of her amongst the masses.

When the apples are gone, I search the bag to see what else Ami packed; more apples, dried meat, another sandwich, and a little pouch. The pouch jingles when I pull it, and to my surprise, there are a couple dozen gold coins inside. Anxiously, I look around me to make sure no one is looking over my shoulder, and then close up the pouch, throwing it back in the bag.

Just another thing to keep me on edge. Carrying gold.

With the sun directly overhead, and having no inkling to Agatha's location I stand and move to find another inn. Needing directions, I look for someone a little friendlier than the last time. A brightly dressed jester passing by seems to be the ideal candidate.

"Excuse me," I stop him briefly. "Could you direct me to the nearest inn?"

"The nearest inn?" The jester gets a smile across his face and quirks his head sideways, making several bells jingle on his two-pronged hat. "Your mind will wear thin just sitting in an inn. Get out and mingle, you look like you are single!"

"Thanks. Nice play on words. But seriously, I need to find the nearest inn."

"Seriously?" The jester dances about in a circle in front of me waiving his fool's bauble around while laughing.

I should have known asking an entertainer would result in this. No doubt he will want payment too. I get the sense that even before my memory loss I despised jesters.

"Yes. Come here." I motion for him to come over waving my hand.

"I come, I go, running to and fro. We are all but dust for the wind to blow."

"Are you a poet or a jester?" My voice comes out snidely.

"A little of both my friend, and for a little coin I shall direct you to the tavern and inn of 'Day's End'," he points his bauble at me and sticks out his hand expectantly.

There was the pitch, both for his flippant display and his rhymes. At least I will get direction to yet another inn and hope it leads to Agatha. This would have been at least a little more entertaining if it were a harlequin.

Rummaging back in my bag I keep my hand hidden while I pull a coin from the pouch. The gold shimmers in the light, and the jester's eyes go wide, making me think that it's probably more than anyone usually pays him.

"For you sir, I shall lead you there!" The excitement in his voice confirms my suspicion.

"That's quite all right. Just direct me, and I will find my way there myself." Despite his newly found attitude to help, I don't care to follow or be followed by a jester.

"A map then, it's the least I will do! Nothing less for a man as generous as you!"

I trustingly hand the coin over to him, and he rushes off into a crowd. Waiting patiently at the fountain, I climb onto the stone I had just been sitting upon, trying to see if I can catch a glimpse of Agatha. Nothing. When the jester takes a few moments too long, I begin to worry he will not be coming back.

Could it have been a mistake to hand it to him first? He didn't seem dishonest, but for all I know he could be just a thief dressed up as a jester. One who, rather than reaching his hand into your purse to take the money, reaches into your head and makes you feel like you owe him something, and so you pay him.

Now looking for two people, I figure finding a jester with such a flamboyant hat shouldn't be too hard, but the crowds make it difficult. After a few minutes pass and I don't see him return, I step down from the fountain's stone rim and re-adjust the strap on the bag so that it's a little more comfortable. Just when I'm about to cut my losses and start walking, I hear jingling bells within the crowd and he emerges with a rolled up piece of parchment, making his way quickly over to me.

"As you can see you have nothing to fear, quickly let us open your map over here!" The jester points at the place I was sitting.

He kneels down and unrolls the parchment. Setting his bauble down next to him, he motions for me and I take a couple steps and drop to one knee.

"What you need to do is make your way to the east side, though you'll want to use the shadows to hide." He points to the map of the city and directs me with his finger through alleyways to get me to my destination.

"Why would I want to hide?"

Looking around he responds in whisper, "The city has people who cannot be trusted."

"That wasn't a rhyme."

"Whoops, it appears that my words need to be readjusted."

I quirk my eyebrows at him.

Something isn't right.

"What do you mean?" I ask but he jumps up and starts to dance away.

"It is time for me to flee and spread some more glee!" He bounces away.

Within moments he is moving along, spinning his bauble, laughing and mingling with the passing people as if he had not just given me dark words of warning. He disappears from sight and my muscles relax, no longer plagued by something that I have a strange apprehension about.

Could there be an actual danger, or is it just tricks from a jester?

Memorizing the route I need to take, I roll up the map and place it in my bag. Heading toward the nearest alleyway, my feet carry me as the map and jester indicated, pushing through a crowd to reach it. These alleys have significantly less people than the main pathways and it's as the jester said it would be, in the shadows. Due to the narrowness between the first two buildings, even the near midday sun isn't penetrating into the sliver of room between them. Moving quite freely, I find my way down until I reach a fork. Turning to the left fork I continue to head in a mostly eastern direction.

The new branch of the alley has a little bit more room than when I first entered, but the sun still doesn't come any farther than a few feet from the top of the buildings at most. The alley makes a right angle at the intersection of two buildings, and as I come around the corner I bump into a small-framed woman dressed in an elegant white cloak with gold embroidery. Though she has her hood up, I can see her face well enough. Her skin is fair and smooth. Blonde curly locks flow out from under the hood of the cloak, and her light amber-colored eyes seem to gleam.

"Pardon me," I excuse myself and step to the side to get around her. She blocks me. I move to get around her again but am intercepted yet again. "Sorry, I don't have time to dance, miss. I'm in a little bit of a hurry."

"I need your help," her voice is sweet and melodious.

"As much as I would like to help, I simply cannot detour from my current objective," I tell her as politely as possible.

"I know what your mission is, and I think you will find that what I need your help with coincides with what you are doing."

"How could you know of my mission?"

"I am a smart woman." She smiles innocently. "You have come here seeking someone."

"Could be. I could be seeking companionship with a beautiful woman." The urge takes over my mouth and I say things I don't mean.

Her innocent smile turns into a smirk. "You have the makings of a jester. But truly I know that you seek a woman who wears similar clothes to yours. Your clothes are different than the people of this city."

"A good guess."

"It is no guess. You wear an orange chrysanthemum on the right shoulder of your cloak. Hers had a pink rose."

"Now you have my attention." My mind clicks from being flippant to alert. Seeing I am now focused, her face becomes serious.

"She came into the city yesterday, but she has nay been seen since."

"What happened to her?" I ask, raising my voice quite a bit.

"Shh." She looks around and behind her before returning her gaze to me. "I am unsure what has become of her to this moment, but an awful thing is happening in the city, and unfortunately the king is blind to it."

I nod for her to continue while listening intently.

"Illegal slave trading has crept into the city and has been corrupting its citizens. Travelers who come in disappear shortly after, and are not seen again. I have been able to gather some information through my eyes and ears in the city but it has been limited due to his…we will say, jovial nature."

"Jovial? The jester?!"

"Yes, he was under my direction to find a fresh, young and strong looking traveler and direct that person to me. When he saw you and the flower you have sewn onto your shoulder, he knew you would be seeking your friend. He is very observant."

"Is that why he was gone so long?"

"He was reporting to a guard who then came to inform me."

"So is it your assumption that the person I seek has been taken into this slave ring?"

"Yes."

"How is this happening to me? Can't I just get a month of reprieve?" I mutter under my breath and cross my arms, speaking normally again. "I guess now is the time I ask, 'what do I need to do to help?'"

"Indeed. Since you will already be seeking your friend, what I am asking can be done along the way." Her sweet tone returns. "I need you to find evidence of the slave traders working in Asta and the nearby area. If you could, and bring that evidence back to me, I would be indebted. And hopefully you find your friend safe."

"What kind of evidence? How do you propose I do this?"

"Anything. Journals, log books, falsified indentured servant papers. Head to the inn that my jester marked on the map, rent a room and then go to the tavern and feign being drunk. They will no doubt target you, and from there you will be on your way."

"Were my friend not missing, I would just as soon sit this out. I have seen too much adventure lately, but because I am unlucky, *you* are in luck." I frown.

"Then it is settled. I will give you some coin now as a good faith payment and a full reward upon your successful return." She smiles, kneels down and removes a pouch that was tied to her ankle.

She holds out the pouch as payment. Hesitation enters my mind, and for a brief moment I wonder if I should just seek out Agatha and forgo the mission she asks of me. But that feeling dissipates. I take the payment and place it in my bag.

"Good, it is settled then. You find your missing person, I get my evidence, and we all live happily ever after." She smiles again.

"Hah," I let out a sarcastic laugh as 'happily ever after' seems to be a myth. "I would ask how I get in touch with you once I am finished, but you will be watching for me will you not?"

She smiles, pulls the hood down farther over her face, and turns around to head down the alley. According to the map, she's heading in the same direction I need to, so I follow. We reach a side alleyway. She turns one way while I'm to go the other. Curiosity stops me, and I call after her.

"Who are you?" I ask.

She turns back for just a moment, barely showing the profile of her face. "For now we shall just say I am someone who is concerned about the state of this kingdom."

I watch as she heads down the long alley, and disappears into the sun and bustling crowd. Continuing on my way down the alley, I follow the directions on the map, and a short time passes before I reach the street where the inn lies.

The sun hits my eyes, and I shield my face for a few moments. Turning to my right I follow the flow of the crowd and make my way to the inn.

A sign hangs out from the building on a post in front of me, clearly labeling my mark. The sign is wood, carved and painted white as a backdrop, while the words 'Day's End Inn and Tavern' are raised out of the wood and painted in a bold red. After the last inn, I'm reluctant to enter. When I do push through the heavy wooden door, a bell jingles softly above my head. It's cool inside, with a sweet smell. I am pleasantly surprised at the classiness of the interior.

The inside is well-kept. There are bright woven tapestries hanging on the walls depicting many different things; a bird's eye view of the city, the crest of the kingdom, a farmer standing in front of his farmland. At my immediate left is a counter, and a savvy looking man sorting rolled parchments.

To the front, on the left and right are spiral staircases that lead up to a second floor balcony. Past them is the tavern area with shellacked tables and fancy chairs with red cushions. Even further is a bar with brightly polished steins lined up in a row. Different colored liquor bottles glisten in the lantern light on shelves behind the bar tender who is cleaning an open space on the bar.

If Agatha wasn't kidnapped before night, this is definitely somewhere she would have stayed.

"Good day sir!" The man behind the desk turns from his parchments and greets me with a warm smile. His appearance is immaculate; his hair is styled, his clothes are clean and pressed and his hands appear to have no wear on them.

"Afternoon." I nod at him. "What is the going rate per night at this establishment?"

"Fifty silver pieces. This includes the room and the evening's meal. Drinks are extra."

"Sounds reasonable. What is the exchange rate of silver to gold here?" I pull out a single gold coin with Asta's crest on it from the pouch given to me by the mystery woman, and set it down on the counter.

"With that coin you will be well taken care of! You drink as much as you like! Let me show you to your room!" The man seems a little overzealous in his excitement to see a single gold coin, the same reaction I received from the jester in the city's center.

I push the coin his way, and he takes it and puts it in a coin pouch of his own strapped to his belt. From the wall he grabs a key ring of simple, long, one and two-pronged keys and then eagerly pulls a half-door open on the side of the desk, motioning for me to follow.

He leads me up the left staircase, taking two steps at a time. Not sharing his eagerness, I take my time. When I reach the balcony overlooking the lobby and tavern, he has already made his way to the back wall. Several doorways down on the left he is flipping through the keys for the right one to open my room. I hear the tumbler within the door as he slides the key in and then turns it.

It clicks and the door swings open to reveal a huge and fancy suite lit up by a chandelier with candles. The bed is on the left, and is sized for a king, with large pillows and a canopy. On either side of it are windows with dark blue curtains woven with such intricate spiral gold thread patterns that it amazes me. Tables sit under each window with lit oil lanterns. On the right hand side of the room there are a few paintings of boats on either side of a vanity with a large mirror. The room seems intended for women, but due to its size and extravagance it works well to cater to men too.

I move to the bed, setting my oil lantern on the table closest to me. Untying the strings on my cloak, I throw it onto the bed. The bag and dagger follow, though quite a bit more delicately. Turning around, the man from the desk is still standing there.

"Was there something I could help you with?" I ask.

"The chamber pot is in the corner. Just let us know and we shall dispose of it," he tells me.

I am slightly disgusted remembering that working plumbing doesn't exist now.

"Since you have paid so generously I wanted to make sure all your needs will be met while you are in our establishment. Is everything satisfactory?"

"At the moment I don't have any needs, thank you. When will the evening's meal be served?"

"In just a few hours."

"Sounds perfect. I'm going to rest in my room until then. Please let me know when it is ready."

"Yes sir!" He bows courteously.

As he leaves, I close the door behind him and return to the bed, lying down to think. While there are now technically four women in my life, as much as I would like to keep my mind focused on just the two I actually care about, I can't help but wonder about Eve's acclimation.

I hope Agatha is okay wherever she is at, and I hope Ami isn't worrying about us too much. What could Eve be doing right now? Annoying Ami by pretending she's still in charge? Or is Ami dominating now because Eve is in her territory? Eve pretends she is independent, but if she were truly left alone I wonder how she would do.

I shut my eyes and allow my body to relax a few moments.

~~~~~~

A loud knock on the door wakes me. Startled, I grab the dagger and move to the door.

The mysterious woman said that since I was new to town I would be targeted, could they have found me so soon? With the number of people in the city, the magnitude of this operation has to be huge, otherwise how would they know a new person from a regular?

I pull the dagger out with my left hand, while with my right I hold the sheath and reach for the knob. Yanking it open, I brandish the weapon at the knocker. The desk clerk's face pales. His body locks up. I had forgotten that I asked to be informed when the meal was ready. Sighing in relief, I sheathe the dagger and return it to the bed. When I come back to the man he stammers.

"Th-the m-meal is r-ready."

"Sorry about that. I am a little on edge," I apologize. "Please, lead the way."

"Yes sir!" He does an about face and strides toward the staircase.

I close the door behind me and follow him. He leads me down to a table near the bar where a stein and silverware have already been set out for me.

As I sit, I notice there are now a few women servers about, dressed in clothing which appears to be standard uniform for this establishment. The shirts are white, frilly. They hang off of the women's shoulders, showing collarbone and a few inches of chest, and they end only a few inches below the women's busts. Their pleated blue and white dresses hang off of their hips. The puffy style reminds me of something Ami might make and wear, though showier than her normal choices.

Do they dress this way for bigger tips? To get men to buy more alcohol?

A server brings my food, and it smells delicious. There is shredded meat, of which kind I'm not sure yet, cooked beets, and a small, dark brown loaf of bread. My mouth waters.

"What would you like to drink, love?" My attractive server asks in a sweet tone.

I wave her in close with my hand. Now is the time to enact the feigning drunk plan. "I want you to be my server tonight, you and you alone. There is a full gold coin in this for you, paid in full, up front."

"Such generosity! But I will have you know I am betrothed, so no funny business!"

"No, nothing like that," I whisper. "I simply need you to keep my stein full with small beer, but you must play it off like you are giving me actual alcohol and go along when I act drunk."

"Why?"

"Sorry, no questions. Can you do this for me?"

"I can."

"Good. Please bring me the first stein. I will be right back."

As she takes the stein and goes to the bar, I head back upstairs to retrieve my belongings. From above, I see my server setting my stein down on the table and waiting for me to return. When I get there, I promptly pull a gold coin out, and pay her. Back in my seat I take a sip from the stein to make sure she had done what I asked. She has.

While I'm eating, more people begin to trickle in, mostly for the alcohol. Every time I take a drink from the stein, I glance around, noting that the majority of the patrons seem to be of the middle to higher class based on their clothing. Men and women alike eat and drink, and the once quiet tavern has become noisy with chatter and laughter. I empty my stein and wave my server over. When she reaches me, I hold up my stein and say nothing. Taking it, she leaves and returns moments later with the small beer. I continue to eat and watch the people around me.

With my plate, and a second stein now empty, I begin to act slightly drunk. I sway back and forth a little and crane my head around, grinning like an idiot. I holler out holding up my stein.

"Wench! Another refill!"

She looks slightly embarrassed as she heads my way, which works quite well to call attention to me. Taking my stein she heads behind the bar, fills it and returns. I drink it sloppily, spilling a little on myself, then using the shoulder of my shirt, I wipe my mouth. Slouching in my chair and putting my arms behind my head, I look about noting no one suspicious. But people are still coming and going, so I must wait it out.

If I drink any more small beer my bladder is going to explode.

To take my mind off of it, I purposely slip off of my chair, falling to the floor hard, and when I try to get up I grip the chair tightly, feigning having a hard time doing so. When I get back into the chair, I drink again from the stein and slam it down. Knowing I'm getting looks, I look around and smile sheepishly.

"Free drinks for everyone in the house!" I yell out and pull a coin from my pouch, fumbling a bit, and then brandish it for everyone to see.

For some reason, I expected some sort of cheer from the masses, but only one or two men make any acknowledgement. I hand the coin off to my server, and all of the wenches start taking orders for extra drinks. Though not many cheered, the patrons of this business certainly take advantage of my generosity.

Needing to relieve myself terribly, my only options are the chamber pot in my room or the alley out back. Since I'm not likely to encounter kidnappers for this slave ring in my own room, the alley is my choice. Getting up, I make my way to the door and am stopped by my server.

"Sir, you forgot your pouch."

I turn to answer her in whisper, "Take two coins, one more coin for you and one more to the man at the desk to pay for the room. When this is done return the pouch to my room. If I do not return tonight for it, I will be back to claim it later."

Night has fallen, and though torches and lanterns are lit up, it does little to actually illuminate properly. Stumbling, I round the corner into a dark alley and make sure no one is around before relieving myself. When I'm finished, I turn back to the light coming from the street. As expected, there is someone there, waiting. I continue my drunk act and stumble toward them, propping myself up against the wall a few times. They make no move toward me however.

"'Scuse me! You are blocking my way," I tell him, slightly slurring my words.

Before I reach him, everything goes black when a sack is thrown over my head from behind and pulled tight against my face. Caught off guard, I struggle and grab at the opening of the sack that is cutting into my neck.

While I knew I was going to be attacked, I wasn't sure how, and I defend myself as best I can while blinded.

Swinging an elbow back, I hit the guy behind me in the ribs, but find that was a bad idea. I'm struck with something hard upside the head. My ears ring, and I get dizzy. I struggle harder as it becomes difficult to breathe while the sack tightens more around my throat. I am hit in the stomach, which causes me to exhale heavily.

I collapse to a knee.

~~~~~~

My head hurts. It's throbbing and when I reach up to scratch my head, there is a knot where I was hit. The fact that the sun's rays flicker on my face through the trees only causes the headache to get worse. My body jostles up and down rapidly, and I hear the sound of wheels.

Where am I?

Peeling my eyelids open a little bit at a time, I find myself in a wooden cage wagon being pulled by horses. Surrounding me are other people. Men, women, and one female child, all very dirty looking and in shabby clothing. None of them are Agatha unfortunately. My clothes have been replaced with simple, tattered and dirty ones as well, to match what an indentured servant might wear, with chain shackles tying us all together by the ankle. No one is talking, and most have their heads down instead of looking about.

Were it not for my need to find Agatha, I'd find a way out of here and make them sorry for attacking me. I just hope they are holding her wherever they're taking me.

Deep into the woods with no sign of a city around, we follow a dirt trail in an area that is unfamiliar. I attempt to turn around to get a good look of what is behind me, but a whip cracks against the side of the cage.

"Sit down and do not move!" A deep, raspy voice orders me.

I do as I'm told, but continue to look around at what's in front of me in search of anything that might serve as a landmark which brings any sense of remembrance. There is nothing of the sort. Just trees, bushes, and everything else woods usually have.

My head pulses with pain a little more and I close my eyes to try and relieve some of that. I listen to the clopping of the horses' hooves against the dirt. My perception of time is skewed, and I attempt to focus on anything other than my head.

When I get out of this predicament, these slavers are going to wish they had chosen another path in life.

We come to a halt and I hear a few men talking. From the back of one horse, a broad-shouldered, burly man in a white and yellow striped shirt pulls a black folded piece of cloth and unfolds it. I recognize him from the bar. He was sitting at the corner stool on the left side of the bar, and had barely ordered one drink before I was getting up to leave for the alley.

Did he slip out a back door into the alley? Is that how they got the jump on me?

The man from my side, whom I do not recognize, moves to help the first, and they pull a black cloth taut over the cage.

Do they not want us to see something? Or do they not want us to be seen?

I can now freely move and test the limits of the chain. As I pull with my hand, the man next to me protests.

"Hey!" he whispers. "You better not try anything funny. If you become more trouble than you are worth, they will kill you!"

"They can try," I whisper back, and test the lock around my ankle.

The wagon begins to move again, and I take the opportunity to feel things out. A metal band wraps around my ankle. It has a hinge on one half, and the other half has a hole for a key. There are solid loops where the chain links hook to the band. Though I might have a chance to break the links if I had a tool to pry with, I know I will not find one within here.

"Are all of you prisoners against your will?" I whisper.

"Listen, kid. Shut up or you are going to get us all in trouble," the man next to me scolds.

"Have you all been kidnapped?" I ignore him and whisper again.

"I…" a woman's voice starts in but the man interrupts.

"Shut up!" he yells and then becomes gravely silent.

The cart comes to a halt again, and the back of the drape is pulled up. The door of the cage is revealed, and the man I'm now referring to as 'Burly' appears again.

"Who is yelling back here?" he demands.

The man next to me is staring down, looking nervous. Burly pulls his keys out and unlocks the door. As he steps inside, the weight of the cart shifts and he moves in looking at all the shadowy faces. Quickly he snatches up the little girl sitting across from me by her collar. She screams.

"Tell me who yelled, or I take the girl out and lash her with the whip!" He shakes her a few times one handedly.

"I did! I did! Please, spare my daughter!" The man next to me confesses.

The slaver drops the girl, and she lets out a whimper. He turns his attention to the father, unshackles him, and begins to drag him out. The man begins to plead for his life.

"Please! I promise I will be quiet. Please! Lana! Lana!" The man reaches out for his daughter who clings to the woman next to her.

"Daddy!" She jumps up and reaches for him.

The slaver backhands the little girl, and she falls over, wailing. Anger rises in me, and I find it building to rage. Their cruelty of hitting a little girl causes my fists to clench and I attempt to harness my inner power. Breathing heavily I focus myself.

I cannot sit idly by!

I jump up, though still shackled, and yell in rage extending my hands out. When I am unable to manifest a shockwave, I grab the slaver by the hand, and attempt to pull him back into me. Finding I have no leverage within the small confines, I rip and claw at his fingers, but it does no good. When I release my grip, I attempt to punch him. He grabs my arm with his free hand, twisting me around and pulling my arm behind my back. He kicks me in the knees, and then I receive a boot to the head.

My face smashes into the floor, and I am dazed. Even with the pain, I struggle. He grinds my face into the hay. Unable to muster my power, or enough strength at the moment to do anything, I am forced to give up. He exits, and the cage door shuts with a creak and slam. Light fades as the drape is pulled back down. I can hear the man.

"No, please! It was a mistake! I was trying to tell him to be quiet! I promise I will behave!"

I hear a weapon being drawn from its sheath.

"No! No!" he cries out.

The swish of a blade cuts through the air, and silence follows. I grit my teeth and climb to my feet. Screaming in rage I charge the door and slam my shoulder into it, not caring that I am pulling at people's legs with my shackles. The first hit does nothing. I ram again anyway causing the cage to rock. Putting my hands in front of me I try to bring out a shockwave to tear the cage apart, but nothing happens.

"Murderers!" I yell out. "Filthy, stinking scum!"

The drape is lifted once more and he is back. The man who I stand no chance of defeating right now has returned for me. Pulling his keys he unlocks the door again and enters. I back up a couple of steps, and take a running start at him. Trying to misdirect him I feign a left hook to his side, but instead throw my right fist toward his throat, hoping to connect with his windpipe and fell him. He catches me, taking both of my wrists into the palm of one of his hands, and uses his free one to smash my face. My vision goes dark and I lose myself.

~~~~~~

When I attempt to open my eyes my right one is swollen shut. My head throbs, and everything aches. With my one good eye, I see the cover is no longer on the cage, and the light from the sun causes my already throbbing head to hurt even worse.

Laboring just to keep my eyes open I find that it's difficult and give up, closing them to rest. A nightmare has fallen upon me and, try as I might, I know it's not one I can wake from. The man who had sat next to me, the father of that little girl, is dead and it's my fault. I shouldn't have said anything, but my desire to help others got him killed.

Why couldn't I just keep my mouth shut? The girl is fatherless now because of me. How was I so powerless to stop his death? When I get free and find Agatha I will make them pay. I will make all of these slavers pay!

I adapt to my pain and open my good eye again. No longer in the woods, we are now on a much wider path next to them instead. On the other side of the cage are farmlands, and an upcoming city. My vision is blurred so I can't make out how large the city is, but it does look to have some taller buildings. Two, maybe three stories tall each.

We bump along, and as we hit a hole the little girl whimpers. Everyone else is silent still until the slavers begin to speak. They mumble at first, but their voices quickly turn to a normal tone and volume. I can barely hear what they're talking about, but nothing seems to stand out as information I could use. My ears perk up however when I hear them talking about me.

"Is the profit we are going to make from him worth the profit we lost on the old man?"

"He better be. It was your idea to keep him alive. Let us hope that he can behave himself during the auction."

"Just make sure we get our money as soon as possible. Once the sale is done we need to split."

I could make their work harder for them. Do exactly as they don't want me to do, but my hopes of finding Agatha and taking the slavers down would drop significantly. I will have to do as they say for the time being.

"Shh, we are almost there."

More voices can be heard, and my interest perks up. We're moving into a populated area. Few of the people take notice of the slave cage passing them, but the ones that do have a look of disgust in their eyes. They pass over me like I am nothing but dirt. This doesn't bother me however, because I know better.

As we near the city, I notice that there are no walls like there were around Asta or its castle. The building types vary in style quite a bit, and are close together, leaving hardly any walking room between.

We find our way onto a cobblestone street, and beside our wagon people from all walks of life make their way about. Though they are all dressed quite nicely, you can tell who is a servant, who is commoner, and who is of importance. Tunics and breeches seem to be the common theme among men, and long, puffy dresses for the women. The women servants and commoners seem to keep their hair simple, with braids or ponytails. Those of status have their hair elaborately done up with loops and small braids, or neat, tight buns, or all of the above.

The cart turns down a street and begins heading toward an open area filled with grass and a few trees, where in the center a wood platform sits. A red curtain is being used as a backdrop on the platform, and there are already people up on it. More slaves. Surrounding the stage, people are already gathering for the auction mentioned by my captors, but it appears that it hasn't started yet.

The cart pulls up alongside the platform, and Burly comes around to the door, jingling his key ring. When he unlocks the door, my mind argues with my plan. It tells me to jump up, hit him and cause a scene, but the will to carry out my plan wins over my impulses. I stay silent.

He grabs the chains which lock all of us together, and tugs on them, pulling on the legs of the first two people in the cart. They stand up and the rest of us follow their lead. There is enough slack in the chains that he is able to turn around and throw them over his shoulder and not trip the first person in line. He leads us out and down one by one to the ground, and then right back up a set of stairs on the platform, moving us all the way to the end.

It's not long before things begin to really heat up as the crowd grows, and a few more groups of slaves show up and are led up to the platform. My eyes hurt, and I still can't get one hundred percent vision in my damaged eye, but I do my best to scan the slaves for Agatha. There is no sign of her.

I am going to be rather irritated if she wasn't kidnapped at all. Maybe this was all just a setup to capture me and sell me as a slave instead.

Looking back I can see it all fitting together now.

What a cleverly concocted story to lure me in! How could I have been so dumb? That's it. As soon as my shackles are loosed these slavers are going to feel my wrath.

"Ladies and gentlemen, we are about to get under way! The debt of each servant here has been collected! Their service times vary based on the debt! See the clerk upon winning an auction for their certificate!" A man yells out.

I bide my time as the auction starts. There are rows of chairs down from the stage, all full, and beyond that, a large crowd forms like a swarm, leading me to the conclusion that slaves are either very big in this city, or people come from other cities to this one to purchase. It would make sense since I didn't see anything like this in the brief time I was in Asta.

One by one, shackled people are sold by a man with a speaking trumpet. When the man calls the end of the bidding, the slave's leg is unshackled, then new shackles are placed on their wrists to be led down to the winner. Some slaves sell for as little as a couple copper pieces, which makes me sick to my stomach.

How can a person's life be valued that little?

When the auctioneer gets to our lot, I'm first to be sold by Burly. It's as they said, they want their money for me now, and I am all right with that. I couldn't care less about being sold, as the moment my shackle is removed I plan to kick Burly's teeth in and make a break for it, hoping that I can just push through the pain to complete that plan.

"Next up we have a lad just acquired! He is fit, he is young, and he has spirit! His debt term is long! Now who will take the first bid at, we will say, fifty silver pieces?!" The auctioneer hollers into his trumpet excitedly.

Immediately, I see a paddle go up with the number 'five hundred seventy four' on it, and I squint to see who is interested. Due to the distance, and my eye, it's difficult to make out the figure too well, but I can tell it's a woman and she is dressed well.

"Fifty silver pieces! Do I hear seventy-five?"

The woman is outbid by a man in the front, and a bid war ensues. Flurries of arms begin to fly up while the auctioneer continues to raise the price each time. Some holler from the crowd indicating bids while others wave their paddles furiously for theirs.

Are young men in such short supply that people would want one so much as a slave?

Several people bid on me over and over until the price is outrageous, though the same woman, the first one, comes out on top each time. The auctioneer's mouth moves a mile a minute as he garbles his words and only spits out numbers. The bidding slows and eventually it's between 'five hundred seventy four' and the man in front. The woman has the leading bid and the auctioneer is calling out for last bids.

"Sir, do you want to go to fifteen gold and twenty five silver pieces?"

He hesitates.

"Going once!"

I can see him deciding.

Hurry up so I can be unshackled!

"Going twice!"

He shakes his head to the auctioneer, indicating he won't go any further up.

"Sold to number five hundred and seventy four! Please have your gold ready upon collection of your servant!"

Burly moves over to me, his keys jingling while he walks. I do my best to stand still, but the urge to act is growing. My impulse is to make him pay for what he did earlier, for everything that is going on here. Rage builds. I clench my fists down tight to the point which my fingernails dig into my palms. He kneels down to unlock the chains, and I can feel my opportunity almost upon me.

In an instant though, it's all gone. The rage disappears as I see a friendly and familiar face walking slightly behind the woman who has purchased me. Agatha is safe, and from what I can tell, unharmed, better dressed than when she left the house, and her hair fancied up even. From the way the woman who bought me holds herself and is dressed, I figure she is well off.

She's a good-looking woman who appears younger than Agatha, but older than Ami. Her short brunette hair falls over her lightly powdered face, coming only to the bottom of her chin. Her light green dress is fancy, with an uncountable number of frills and pleats.

I let Burly unshackle my leg, and shackle my wrists, despite still wanting to hit him. For now, I let the opportunity to strike pass me by, resolving to take care of it later. Burly leads me down a set of stairs to the winner.

She promptly hands a bag off to him, and he counts out the currency. Satisfied, he hands the chain and key to her, and I'm led off to the side and into the crowd. Glancing back one last time I give Burly a look I hope sends the message that I will return for him.

The woman retrieves her paperwork from a person to the side of the stage, and then we begin walking into the city. Agatha is strangely silent. She's acting the part of a servant, but doesn't seem to be doing anything for our captor. I want to speak, but I will wait until we are in a less crowded area.

Down a small walking path, we find our way toward a set of connected two and three story buildings which remind me of a maze. Looking up, most have balconies or overhanging windows, making it a very shaded place. I turn my attention back to the woman and Agatha, and still neither has said a thing.

What is Agatha thinking? Is she actually content with this situation? As soon as I'm free, we're leaving here so I can get her safely back to the house, and then I will destroy this slave ring for my own peace of mind.

"Okay, we are away from the crowd. You can unshackle me now." Out of impatience words escape my mouth.

"You will not be unchained until we reach my home." The woman's words come out cold and flat.

"Agatha, tell her there has been a mistake." I tap on her shoulder.

The woman who has bought me turns around and, with a sharp glance with her dark eyes, barks at me, "Servant! You will be silent until we are at my home!"

"Listen, miss, I am nobody's servant. My being sold as a slave was a mistake on the slaver's part."

Agatha elbows me in the ribs, and I look at her with a brow half-quirked in question. She pays me no mind. My new 'master' ignores my rant, and pulls me along.

Were it not for Agatha, I would have bolted by now, but since she's part of the equation I have no choice but to go along.

Making our way around a few corners, our path comes to an intersection, with more row homes in front of us. We turn left, and follow the street to its end. Houses enclose around us on all sides except the way we came.

The building directly in front of us at the end is where we stop. It is two stories tall, and its length is at least double that of the other buildings around it, indicating that this woman is probably of more wealth than those around her. A large brass lion-head knocker hangs in the center of the marble brown door at shoulder height, but she doesn't use it. She pulls a key from a pouch at her waist, unlocks the door, and pushes it open.

She yanks me in by my chains, and Agatha follows behind us, closing the door once we're all in.

To my immediate left is a wall with a metal door, padded around the frame. In front of and to the right of us is a large den and dining area. The dining area is on a raised step where a table and eight chairs sit. There is a small but elaborate and elegant chandelier above it. Down from the step, and a few feet away are a couch, a few chairs and a brick fire place against the far right wall in the middle of the furniture.

Vases of many different sizes line the walls on pedestals, going from small to large to small again, around the room. Portraits of very noble looking men and women line the far wall of the den, except on the left side where a door and an open section in the wall to the kitchen exists. If the paintings are any indicator of her heritage, she could be someone of importance, as each one looks distinguished.

"Here is the key to unshackle him. Take him upstairs, and get him cleaned up and into a nice set of male servant clothes."

The woman turns to Agatha with her hand outstretched, instructing her as if Agatha was actually her servant.

"Yes, Duchess." Agatha complies, taking the key and chain from her.

My mouth opens to speak out against this 'Duchess' woman, but Agatha moves quickly and pulls on my hands with the chain. The comment I was about to make is redirected at Agatha.

"Hey! Why are you being so rough?" I pull back a little bit.

"Silence!" the woman speaks harshly. "Evalyn, while you are up there, instruct the new servant in my rules."

"Evalyn?!" My mouth drops, and I stare in shock. She grins impishly.

"Yes, Duchess."

She pulls again on my chains, and leads me around the corner on our left. There is an opening, and set of stairs to the second story. We climb the first flight, and turn around to a second. On the second story, we make a right to a long hallway with several rooms on either side. At the end of this hall is another leading left toward the back of the building. Evalyn pulls me down to the far hall, which is much shorter, and at the end she pushes a door open.

The room is neither elaborate, nor bland. There is a fair-sized bed with a small dresser next to it, a window with pulled back blue curtains, and a bathtub surrounded by tile toward the right-hand side of the room. It's illuminated well enough by the light coming in through the window. As I'm taking in everything, Evalyn unshackles my wrists. Instinctively I rub them to get rid of the residual feeling the constraints leave behind.

"What is going on here, Evalyn? How are you even here?" I ask.

"I'm not confined to that house as long as I'm in Agatha's body. I jumped into her as she was leaving," She lets out a cackle. "I needed some time away from you all, but it looks like that did no good."

"I bet you're regretting it now, being the servant of some strange woman. You got Agatha into trouble, and I had to come looking," I snap at her.

"You're the one who looks like he got into a bit of trouble. That smart mouth of yours cause that?" She pokes at my swollen eye.

"I got it because I had to get captured to find you." I swat her hand.

"How did you know I was taken?"

"I was approached by someone who I think set me up to be captured as well. Described you, gave me some story about how people had been disappearing, and that my help was needed to find information on the slave ring while I was trying to find you."

"You fell for that?" Evalyn crosses her arms and frowns at me.

"I was just worried about Agatha, and I wanted to get her back safe to Ami. I had no other leads."

"Thanks for the consideration," she scoffs.

"I had no idea that you had taken Agatha's body. Now that we're together, we're going to get out of here, and I'm going to find those slavers."

"Why? If it was a setup from the start, isn't it pointless?"

"It's personal. Evil like that needs to be destroyed."

"Aww, did Wain get a widdle hurt?" Evalyn sniffles sarcastically and talks at me like I'm a baby.

"I don't have to explain myself to you. We're getting out of here and I'm exacting justice upon them."

She's silent for a moment, then retrieves servant's clothes from the dresser. Throwing them in my face, she smirks. I catch them and wait a moment for her to turn around, but instead she stands there with her arms crossed, as if waiting for me to change in front of her.

"I'll leave when it's closer to time," she says.

"For what reason?!" I get a little loud with her.

"Shh!" Her eyes widen. "It's not as easy as just sneaking out. Runaway servants are dealt with pretty harshly. Lashings, starvation, death. I am patiently waiting for the right moment."

Reluctantly, I am forced to follow along with Evalyn's plan, and place my own on hold. While I have no intention of staying here long, I have to convince Evalyn to follow me.

"A little privacy, please? Turn around," I instruct.

"Wash up a little. There is cloth and some cold water in the tub." She points.

I look at her questioningly, but if I want to clean up I need this. Moving past her to the tub, I look over my shoulder to make sure she isn't watching. I drop the clean clothes to the side, and strip my shirt off. Inside the tub is a little bowl hooked to the side, a cloth lying across it. Soaking it in the water, I clean myself off the best I can.

"You know…" she starts in and I quickly look to make sure she's still facing away. "Your help wasn't needed."

"Don't be ungrateful. I thought I was saving Agatha." I wash quickly.

Throwing on the dark pants provided I reach down and grab a white button up, long-sleeve undershirt and a black vest.

"I think it's me who did the saving back there. You would have been sold to some creep if I hadn't convinced Duchess to buy you."

"And how did you do that?" I question her.

"I told her that we shared a previous owner for a short time and that you were a hard worker." She laughs with what sounds like a snide tone.

"Is that right?" I pull an embossed leather belt on, pushing it through all the loops.

"And when that didn't work I told her you were a stallion in bed," she snorts and laughs.

My eyes go wide and I spin around, cinching the belt on my pants to a comfortable notch and raise my voice a bit, "You what?!"

"You heard me *lover*," she laughs maniacally, clearly getting a kick out of my discomfort.

"No. We're going out there right now and explaining that this is all just a mistake."

"What mistake is there? That she saved you from those awful slavers or the creepy man who was bidding on you for unknown nefarious purposes? Or that she has provided you with clean clothing and you now owe her a small debt, same as me?"

Thinking for a moment, I know she's right. And without my belongings, I have nothing to repay this woman with. But I still have to set the record straight, that Evalyn does not know me in that manner.

I glare at her. "You should have tried harder to convince her of my work ethic rather than resort to a gimmick of giving her hopes that I am going to get into bed with her."

"Your work ethic stinks, Rain," she crosses her arms and looks down upon me. "You're a burden, having being incapacitated a number of times from doing idiotic things, and Agatha and Ami are picking up your slack!"

"Oh, so now you care about them? You who despise their very being? Or is it that you just dislike me more?" I snap.

"I'm not having this discussion with you, peon! Go meet with Duchess Tamiell!" Evalyn throws her arms down to her sides, huffs, and storms out.

I tug on my shirt to make sure it looks wrinkle free, and head downstairs. Duchess Tamiell is waiting for me. Her elegance, the building, and the possessions indicate that she might just hold that official title of Duchess. If so, then either her Duke isn't here, or he is no longer alive. I won't bother asking the question, however, because it's none of my business.

"This will be your new home, servant," Duchess Tamiell says abruptly.

"Duchess Tamiell, with all due respect, I am no servant…" I try to explain to her.

"Silence! You will speak when I need you to, and no more."

"Duchess Tamiell, I understand your position. You spent money to obtain Evalyn and me. I will gladly pay you the gold you spent to free us."

Without warning, she reaches up and backhands me across the right side of my face. My face throbs not only because of the blow, but because it's already swollen and hurt. Had it been Evalyn, I wouldn't hesitate to blow up at her, but since this woman doesn't know me, I bite my tongue.

"My name is Duchess Tamiell Benite. You will address me as Duchess or Duchess Tamiell. As my servant you will do what I need you to do. I will not tolerate laziness or talking out of place. As you acclimate here, you will find that I am a strict but fair person."

While she continues to ramble on about her rules, which I ignore, I focus on not letting my mouth run me into the ground. Instead I think of her potential nobility, and the possibility that I might acquire information about the slave ring through her, or the people she mingles with. The only issue really needing resolution is that Evalyn is here in Agatha's body, and Ami is back at the house, no doubt worried for us both now.

"Your duties are going to include all of my heavy lifting, whether that be bringing food from the market, to chopping wood. You are at my beck and call. This bell here is for when I am calling you." She lifts up one of two bells from a sash around her waist and rings it heavily. It has a deep tone to it.

Rather than risk a smack to my face again, I point at the second one on her sash.

"This one is for Evalyn," she tells me blankly. "If you hear yours, come immediately. Now follow me and I will show you around."

She leads to a sliding door, and to the right of it I see the kitchen through the breakfast nook. Evalyn has snuck in, and is chopping something up, paying us no attention. Duchess Tamiell slides the door open, and upon entering, I notice that the kitchen is drab compared to the rest of the house. While still very clean, everything is metal or wood, causing the room to look dull in the light of the lit lanterns and daylight seeping in from the window on the back wall.

The heat and smell of wood are coming from a medium sized, iron stove with enough room for two to three pans for cooking on. There are two doors, one at the back wall directly across from us that leads to another alleyway, and the other is on the back side of the right hand wall, and I can only assume it is storage or a pantry.

"This is the kitchen area. It is Evalyn's area since she can cook. Whenever you're not assisting me, this is where you'll be to help her."

"Might I speak...Duchess?" I ask, cringing at having to address someone as my master yet again.

"No, you may not," she answers abruptly then continues on. "That is the pantry and wood store room. Normally we have wood delivered, but their fee has been steadily rising, so you will fetch wood from the market instead."

Duchess Tamiell turns around, and motions for me to leave with a wave of her hand. I follow her command and head back to the empty space between the den and the stairs.

"As you have already seen, the den and dining areas are combined. I take my meals whenever I feel like eating. Whenever you are not doing heavy work, you are to make sure there are clean dishes on the table at all times." I pay attention only to pick up essentials. "When I have company over you are to make yourself available for whatever need arises."

I resist letting out a huge sigh to show my discontent for this whole situation, simply because she technically freed me from the slavers.

Would it be right to not repay her in some way for the money she was swindled out of? I wonder if I had such moral guides in my past life. Was I as soft-hearted then as I feel I am being now?

Looking around the room I try to tune her out, but as she continues my attention is recalled to her.

"...cleaning out the chamber pot room." I catch the tail end of her sentence and hesitate to let her know I wasn't paying attention.

"What now?" I ask, practically admitting that I was ignoring her.

"I said that another of your responsibilities will be cleaning out the chamber pot room!" She shoots me a sharp glance.

"Where is that, Duchess?"

"Were you not listening to me? Do you think that you can mock me and get away with it?" Her voice raises and she becomes animated.

"Honestly? I was beaten in the head a bit today and I am having trouble concentrating. I mean no disrespect."

"I should not have paid so much for damaged goods," she mutters under her breath. "Well then, we will see how you fair later after you have rested. Retire to the room that Evalyn took you to previously."

"Yes, Duchess," I say it with disgust at the title.

Turning, I head up the stairs and through the hallways to 'my' room. When I enter, I begin pacing back and forth while looking out the window to that alleyway behind the house. Farther down it opens up to a lush and green courtyard with a simple water fountain, and more buildings beyond it. Finding myself wanting to berate Evalyn for getting us into this, there's no telling when, or if, she will show her face in the room.

Beginning to feel light-headed, whether from the stress, or from my injuries, I decide that lying down sounds pretty good right now. When my body hits the mattress, my muscles feel like they're turning to jelly because of the softness of the bed. Sinking in, I can't help but think that it's more comfortable than my own bed which I haven't had much opportunity to enjoy sleeping in lately. Shutting my eyes feels good too.

~~~~~~

The sound of a heavy bell permeates my sleep. Rolling over I pull the pillow over my head to muffle the racket, but it only gets louder as time goes by. When the fog from my mind clears I realize that it's the Duchess calling for me.

Can I just ignore it?

As unlikely as that seems, I wait it out, but over the bell I can hear footsteps coming down the hallway. The door flies open without warning and slams against the wall.

"Servant, it has not even been a few hours since I told you what this bell was for, and you seem to have forgotten it!" By her tone she seems quite irritated. "You are needed downstairs, and I will not have my guests waiting for their meal because my newest servant decided a nap sounded better."

"You remind me of Evalyn," I mutter.

"What was that servant?" she snaps at me.

"Nothing."

"Nothing what?" Looking at me with expectant eyes, she waits for me to say something again.

"Duchess?"

"That is right. Duchess! Widow of a Duke! Status symbol among the community, and I will not be mocked!" She waves her finger angrily at me.

To me it appears that it wasn't just a first impression issue, but that she has an entitlement mentality.

This is Eve all over again.

"Yes, Duchess," I reply.

"That is more like it. Now, I need you to serve while Evalyn is cooking." Her voice calms down, and as quick as her temper flared up, it's gone.

She turns around and exits the room while I stand up from the bed, stretching and groaning. Feeling quite a bit better, my muscles feel rejuvenated, and my face doesn't hurt as much as it did before.

Downstairs, I feel an opportunity is near to confer with Evalyn, and quietly plot a way out of this situation while the Duchess is busy. She is greeting guests, an older man and woman, but I pay little attention to them. As I head for the kitchen door, I am beckoned over.

"Servant, come here so that my guests may get a better look at you," she calmly instructs.

While I could disobey her and likely have her get angry in front of her guests, I play the part of the obedient servant, for now. I approach with my arms crossed.

"Do not be rude. Offer to take their coats." She smiles at me and motions with her head. "I must apologize. I just purchased him and he has not been broken in yet."

Not only am I a slave, but I am apparently just an animal to be 'broken in' to this woman. It is difficult for me to sit idly by while being degraded, but I do as she asks and hold out my arms for them to lay their coats across.

"Yes, Duchess," I reply with just a hint of a sour tone.

"It is quite all right Duchess. We have had to break in our fair share of servants over the years," the man responds, while taking off a fur overcoat and putting it on my arm. The woman follows his lead, but says nothing.

They're both short and a little plump, but have nothing really of interest about their characters. Rather, they are just more faces that will fade into nothingness when I am out of this predicament.

"Where shall I put these coats, Duchess?" I ask sullenly.

"Upstairs, the door immediately in front of the stairs is a closet. Now hurry on and return so we can be served our evening meal." She waves me off and proceeds to lead them to the den area where a fire crackles in the fireplace.

Doing as I am told, I make my way upstairs and hang the coats on hooks inside a very roomy closet. Returning to ground level, Duchess Tamiell immediately addresses me.

"Servant, some wine for my guests and me," the Duchess commands. "Evalyn knows where to find it."

I head to the kitchen door, but when I slide it open the Duchess stops me again.

"I think you forgot something," she laughs snidely.

"Yes, Duchess?" I hesitate a little while turning to her.

"'Yes, Duchess' is right. Remember to address me properly when spoken to." She laughs with her guests.

Entering the kitchen, the smell of delicious food hits me, and my stomach gurgles heavily. There is a small black kettle and iron frying pan on the top of the wood stove. Evalyn is moving back and forth quickly from the counter on the right wall, taking chopped vegetables, and throwing them into the pot, then proceeds to flip what looks like small round slabs of beef in the pan. I close the door behind me.

"Evalyn, I need to know where the wine is."

"Why? Going to drink your problems away?" she says with a flat tone. I can't tell if she's being snide or if she's just playing.

"*The Duchess* required me to get her and her guests some wine."

"Fine glasses are in the top right cupboard by the door, there, and the wine is in the cabinet below where I was chopping." She keeps her back to me while she pokes the meat with a fork and then stirs what's in the pot.

I approach her side and whisper, "We need to figure out how we're going to get out of here and back to the house."

"I'm quite enjoying myself here, actually." She looks at me through the corner of her eye.

"You're kidding, right?"

"No, I am away from the house. This is quite nice."

"Being a servant isn't *nice*!" I whisper harshly.

I hear the low ringing of my bell, and realize if I don't get out there soon, Duchess Tamiell will become suspicious and come looking for me. I obtain three short wine glasses, and proceed to get a bottle of wine from under the counter. Uncorking the dark green bottle, I pour. A dark, red liquid sloshes out of the small bottleneck into each glass. As it settles, the aroma of the wine mingles with the smells of the food cooking. My stomach grumbles more. Evalyn takes the bottle from me, and puts a little in the kettle, and the pan, for her cooking.

"This isn't over, Evalyn. We'll talk about this later," I tell her while picking up the glasses, maneuvering their thick stems between fingers so that I can carry two in one hand and one in the other.

Using the hand with only one glass in it, I'm able to grip the door's handle with my pinky finger, and slide it open with only a little difficulty. In the main area again, the Duchess and her guests are enjoying a conversation in front of the fireplace. Their laughter is quiet and distinguished. When they see me carrying the drinks, it becomes a little louder, like I've done something socially unacceptable.

"Servant, next time use a tray. You look quite silly carrying those in your hands," Duchess Tamiell titters, then looks at her guests and shrugs.

"Yes, Duchess."

I provide each of them with their drinks and cross my hands in front of my body. They begin conversing about matters of little interest to me, a family business of some sort. I'm unsure if I should stay or go, but they ignore me as if I ceased to exist the moment they obtained their drinks. Shifting my weight nervously, I wait.

Evalyn said she likes being away from the house, but I have a feeling she's staying here to torture me instead. She wants to make me miserable because she's always miserable. If the Duchess doesn't need me, I'll go have another little chat with Evalyn.

"Duchess, I am going to see if Evalyn needs any assistance," I tell her, waiting for some snappy remark for speaking without being spoken to.

"Fine, fine. When you come back, bring the bottle of wine and another piece of wood for the fire," she says, waving me off, not even looking.

This is going to be yet another long month. I can feel it.

When I re-enter the kitchen, Evalyn is tasting the soup. Apparently finding it lacking, she begins adding spices from a nearby spice rack. I head to the door on the right wall, and open it. The light from the kitchen lanterns only slightly illuminates the inside. A few pieces of chopped wood are stacked on the left, and shelves of food are on the right. I grab a single piece of wood and close the door.

"So when do we get to eat?" I ask Evalyn.

"Later, when her guests are gone. We get whatever is left in the pot."

"I guess it's better than Eve's gruel," I whisper more to myself than to her while grabbing the bottle of wine. It's empty. "Did you use all of this in the food?"

Evalyn looks at me and smirks deviously, telling me that only some of what I left was used in the food. Shaking my head at her, I obtain another bottle, uncork it, and head out to the den once again.

I find the three having a mildly serious conversation based on the looks of their faces and their lower tone voices, but upon seeing the bottle the Duchess's eyes light up once again. Instead of me refilling it for her, she snatches the bottle from me, and offers her guests more, then pours some in her own glass, leaving me free to put the wood on the fire.

When I'm done I return to her and wait to see what else she wants, but again she ignores me. Their conversation turns to talk of hosting a party at her house to find her a suitor. I am bored nearly to tears.

Why can't they talk about what I need to hear about, like the slaves or slavers?

I find myself slipping into a daze and think about this time that I'm in.

No one has seemed to recognize me, so this likely isn't my time. But due to the familiarity of it all, I can't be far off. Perhaps I'm a child right now? Would it be possible to stop the time vortex here and live out my life in at least a familiar setting? It would stick Ami, Agatha and Evalyn here though.

"Servant, go and tell Evalyn that we are ready to eat." I snap back to reality at Duchess Tamiell's voice.

"Yes, Duchess."

Entering the kitchen, Evalyn directs me to a tray which has three bowls of soup. While I take that one, she plates up the steaks on another tray and garnishes them with parsley. Evalyn follows behind me while I bring the soup out, and cuts me off to set the plates out. As I am setting down the bowls directly next to the plates, Evalyn corrects me.

"Bowls go to the top right of the plate."

I shoot her a glance out of the corner of my eye, and fix it as she says. The Duchess and her guests make their way from the den to the dining table, and stand there waiting for something else. Evalyn frowns at me, and shows me by demonstration that I need to pull out the chairs and seat each individual. As she seats the woman guest, I pull out the Duchess's chair and force a smile. I push the chair in and walk to the man and follow the same procedure.

"Thank you, servants. You are dismissed for now," the Duchess waves us off and begins to eat.

Finally, we have a chance to escape. As Evalyn walks by me, I follow, putting my palm in the arch of her back and pushing her along to the kitchen.

First thing's first, I'm hungry.

When we enter, I shut the door and Evalyn giggles. The pot is on the stove with a large ladle sticking out, but no bowls are on the counter.

"Where are the bowls?"

"Cupboard, next to the wine glasses."

It's vegetable soup, and the smell is mouthwatering. Dishing some up, I move as if in a frenzy to eat. It can't have been more than a few days since I've eaten, but my body is acting like it has been weeks. When I turn around to ask for a spoon, Evalyn has already retrieved one for me. I grab it from her and begin to eat ravenously.

"Thanks," I do my best to talk with a full mouth, practically choking on my food and breathing heavily to cool it off. My tongue burns but I don't care.

Evalyn laughs and proceeds to get her own bowl. We eat in silence. Her in a sophisticated manner, taking a spoonful at a time and blowing it off, and me while I take bite after bite. When I've successfully consumed three bowls of the soup, my stomach is satisfied. Letting out a sigh to reflect that condition, I get a disapproving look from Evalyn.

"What?" I ask.

"Your manners are awful."

"Right now, I couldn't care less." I shrug at her.

"If you have any thoughts of dating my niece, you better straighten up. She may like you now, but if you act like a slob, that could change."

I blush, not sure what to say at this point. She makes a good argument, but the whole idea of dating Ami is still very back and forth in my mind. One minute we're just good friends, and the next we're on the verge of something more, but I can't read her well enough to decide when, or even if, I should make an advance.

"Why? Do you think that there is a chance of me courting Ami?" Looking through the corner of my eye, I wait to see what her response is.

"Well, I can't expect an oaf like you to understand a woman, so I'll explain it. She likes you, whether you know it or not." She crosses her arms and frowns.

"Okay," I turn to her and give her my full attention. "What about the complications of that kind of situation? We're stuck time-traveling together, and I've only been with you a few months. Would it be wise to enter into a formal relationship so soon after knowing one another?"

"A valid point, but the heart wants what the heart wants, and I'm afraid that hers is set on you. Whether it's infatuation because you're the only man in her life, or because she has actual feelings for you is yet to be revealed, but make no mistake a woman's feelings are on the line."

"I'm not sure that it would be prudent to try until we find a way to stop the curse on the house. While it's easy to let one's emotions control them, if it comes down to it, I think that I will have to let her know that."

"All right, 'Mister Sensibility'. We'll see just how it goes." She smirks.

"What do you care anyway?" I ask abruptly. "You are the one that cursed them to this life. Just a few months ago you were trying to slap Ami, treating her like she was nothing."

"I admit, I let my anger get the best of me. I've been condemned to this existence just as much as they have, and it's grating." She gets a little agitated and begins glaring at me.

I let the subject drop, needing to keep her open to the idea of escape. Through the silence that follows between us, I hear the sound of slightly raised voices coming through the wall, and laughter, but even with open wall area I can't make out what is being said.

"We need to figure a way out of here," I tell her.

"Why? I'm enjoying this." She continues eating.

"You're enjoying it because I'm being treated like a servant, and you know the only thing holding me here is you."

"Exactly. I do this kind of stuff on a daily basis, so staying here is simply to watch you squirm. Ami can take care of herself, and Eve."

"And what about Agatha? You're holding her hostage too, aren't you?"

Evalyn's face turns sour and she gets defensive. "That's none of your concern."

"It *is* of my concern. Agatha is like a mother to me. When you possess her, she's still there, isn't she?"

"Yeah, so?"

"Isn't it unfair to her to suppress her? I know why you don't like me, but what do you have against her? What do you have against them at all?" My mouth gets the better of my best intentions.

She clams up and turns her head away. Before I can get anything else out, my bell rings. Despite having every intention of being out of here within another day, I feel that nagging compulsion to at least somewhat repay the woman who 'purchased' me. When I stand and move to the door, I turn and talk at Evalyn's back.

"Be stubborn, Evalyn, but really think about it. It's been how many years and you're still holding some grudge?"

I leave her with that thought. While I have no clue what it is that she's harboring or why she is so angry, I have a feeling that it's going to drive us all insane eventually. I am amazed that somehow Ami and Agatha have managed to deal with it for as long as they have.

Coming to the dining table, Duchess Tamiell and her guests are quite tipsy from the alcohol. All of their cheeks are a deep rosy red. Their plates and glasses are empty, and the bottle that was once full is tipped on its side as if it had been sucked dry.

"Servant, come here." The Duchess waggles her finger in a beckoning manner to me, and then giggles. A shiver falls over my spine as I get a bad feeling.

"Yes, Duchess?" I slowly move over to the side of her chair.

To my surprise she reaches up, and runs her hand across the muscles of my right arm. Jerking away, appalled, I realize what she's doing. While I'm not sure I believed Evalyn at first, she must have actually told the Duchess I had prowess in bed to get her to purchase me. So beyond getting physical labor done around the domain, to her I'm a plaything.

I have to find a way out of this!

"D-Duchess, do you require more wine?" I stammer a little.

She looks at me, smirking. I can't tell what she's thinking, but by the almost strained look on her face I appear to have given her a serious question to ponder. Taking a moment before answering, she rubs her cheeks and looks across the room at the fire for a moment.

"No, our guests will be leaving shortly. Please clean up the dishes."

"Yes, Duchess," I breathe a sigh of relief.

While her mind has been distracted for the moment, there is no doubt that the longer we stay here, the more possibility there is of finding myself in an even more awkward position.

It doesn't take long to clean up. I bring the dishes to Evalyn for washing, and then return with a cloth to wipe the table. While I'm doing this Duchess Tamiell and her guests have returned to the fireplace, standing in front of it this time.

"Servant, when you have finished with that, please retrieve our guests' coats."

"Yes, Duchess."

Considering the labor around here is what I would be doing for Ami and Agatha at home, this isn't terrible. But much like with Eve, I will have to do everything in my power to avoid being bedded by some strange woman. My only option is to anger her when it comes to that.

Obtaining the coats, I return to the guests. The man holds out his arm, but when I try to give him his garment he shakes his arm expectantly. I slide the coat over his extended arm, and then move around to his other side to assist him with his other sleeve, where he proceeds to get his elbow caught and struggles a moment to shove his arm in. The woman's goes smoother, with no catches or snags.

This is a little much. Putting on people's coats for them? Are they children? Oh, wait, they're drunk.

Duchess Tamiell shows her guests to the door, with me following along to open it for them. The Duchess kisses their cheeks while they say their farewells, and I close the door.

"Servant, go help Evalyn finish cleaning and then retire for the night," Duchess Tamiell tells me while yawning.

"Yes, Duchess."

She must have forgotten about her previous notions from when she was caressing my arm, as she shows no further interest in me. Instead she opens the metal door next to the front door, and I'm assaulted by the smell of urine. There is a lantern lit inside, and something similar to a toilet in there, however the seat is attached to the wall and underneath is a removable pot. It seems so unclean compared to the modern toilet I'm now used to, but this is what I have to deal with for now. When she shuts the door behind her I quickly walk to the kitchen to find Evalyn already has everything under control and mostly cleaned up.

"Evalyn, we have a problem. The Duchess got a bit too friendly out there and I'm not sure whether it's the alcohol, or that notion you put in her head, but I am apparently a target of physical affection."

She snorts as she bursts into a fit of laughter. Finding nothing funny about it, I cross my arms and frown. Seeing me this way causes her to laugh harder, having to put her face in her arms on the counter.

"Why is this funny?"

In between laughs she finds a response. "Because I can't tell what's funnier, the fact that she bought my story, or that she actually took the initiative with you, or that you're taking this so seriously."

"Seriously? I'm being held here against my will by you, and for all I know she's going to try and bed me! That's serious in my book!"

"Why?" She calms, wiping tears from her face.

"I...I don't know. It just doesn't seem right that two people should be intimate unless they're married."

"So noble and old school!" Evalyn clasps her hands in front of her chest and sways back and forth mockingly.

"Pick at my moral guide, sense of chivalry or gentleman's ways, whatever you want to call it, I don't care, but you need to help me out here. What can we do to dissuade her?" I take a moment and think of a way to jolt Evalyn into helping. "What would it take if it was you?"

My statement catches her completely off guard, and she blushes. She covers her face and turns away, giggling a little, acting like I had asked her to be the Duchess, rather than just put herself in the Duchess's position.

"Oh, Rain! Why would you ask me that? How would I know what it would take?! What makes you think an old lady like myself would even find you attractive?!" Her speech is elevated and fast. I remember she's also been drinking.

"Evalyn, cut it out. You know what I meant. I need you to get in the mindset of the Duchess, and figure out what it would take to put her off."

Her laughter kicks in again while she still faces away from me. "Well if it were me, just be yourself!"

"Har har," I sarcastically laugh. "If you don't want to help then I'll do something drastic."

"You could try telling her you're taken," Evalyn turns back around, her face normal again.

"I tried that with Eve, and it just made her try harder, especially because Ami was there."

"I'm afraid you are just going to have to figure it out on your own, Rain. This old lady has no wisdom for you."

"Thanks for nothing. I'll avoid her as best I can." I turn and walk out on Evalyn and head upstairs.

Her attitude is all over the place. Angry, sarcastic, jovial. I don't understand what drives her mood or emotion. How irritating.

I'm tired once again, and when I run my hand over my face it's still swollen. Having forgotten about it because I was busy, it's now at the front of my mind, and I feel a headache coming on. Heading upstairs to my room, it's dark, only partially lit up by moonlight shining in through the window. My mind is fuzzy and my eyes are heavy. As soon as I rest upon the mattress it feels like the muscles in my body are being sapped of their energy. When I close my eyes, I can feel myself sinking into the cushioning of the bed and it's comfortable.

I wonder what Ami is doing. Or rather, how she's doing with Eve.

~~~~~~

My bell rings again, and it hardly feels like I have slept, but upon opening my eyes I can see why. It's still dark out, and I can't tell if it is still night or early morning. Grumbling and turning over on the bed I think to myself.

Do I get out of bed and find where the bell is ringing from, or do I anger Tamiell again?

Coming to the conclusion that I don't really care to be yelled at so soon after waking up, I stand and make my way out of the room. When I follow the sound of the ringing, it leads me back down the hallways toward the stairs and to the last room on my left before them.

This must be the Duchess's room then.

It begins ringing louder, as if she's shaking it to death, so I knock on the door. Silence falls and I hear her speak.

"Enter."

As I enter the room, it's lit up by several lanterns. Her room is far more luxurious than the one I'm in, being intricately painted fading blues from light to a medium in a gradient going from top to bottom on the walls. In just the right light, the blues seem to sparkle, as if there are gems embedded in the wall, reflecting light around the room and illuminating the objects quite a bit more.

The bed, a nightstand, and a very large dresser seem to be finely carved and polished with their swirling details jumping to the attention of the gazer due to the special lighting. But as nice as the other pieces of the room are, she has a similar plain bathtub to mine sitting on tile toward the far wall, and a wooden bucket by its side.

She is sitting on a canopy bed, its see-through pink curtains down, slightly obscuring her figure. But I can see her legs outstretched and she's wearing a dark red, provocative nightgown. I stand at the door and wait for her to acknowledge me from the book in her hands.

"Is it morning, Duchess?"

"No," she puts her book open and face down then looks at me with a look in her eyes I've seen before from Eve.

"What can I do for you then?" I begin to get nervous.

"Come over to my bedside." I can hear a hint of glee in her voice.

"Duchess?"

"You heard me, servant." She pats the bed, indicating that I come over.

Walking slowly, I try frantically to think of a way out of this situation that Evalyn has put me into.

What can I do? What will stop her advances?

When I reach the side of her bed she pulls a drawstring, and it brings the curtain to the top of the bed's frame. A smirk crosses her face as she pushes herself up from the sitting position. Pulling her short hair back from one side exposes her neck, and I notice just how low her nightgown hangs.

"Servant, your friend has told me about your skills in the bed. Are they true?"

"I am afraid that Evalyn has misled you, Duchess. Neither she nor anyone else has bedded me. I am celibate, waiting to marry." I look away, keeping focused on the bed's curtains.

"Well, that is unfortunate." She catches me off guard with her assertive tone, and I see her out of the corner of my eye maneuvering herself around, sitting up on her knees at the edge of the bed, grinning seductively.

Unwilling to accept a verbal 'no' for an answer, I back up a few steps, hoping that by outright refusing her I will be able to anger her and push her interest to at least disciplining me rather than trying to be intimate with me.

"Duchess, I cannot."

"Cannot, or will not?" Her grin turns to a frown.

"Cannot. I have told you that I am waiting to marry, and since we are not married I cannot," I tell her as boldly as I can muster against this emotionally intimidating woman.

A long, drawn-out moan comes from outside the room, and down the hall, a moan that sounds like someone is in pain and suffering.

Evalyn?

Turning to leave the room, despite the fact that the Duchess is probably burning holes in my back with her eyes, I go to find Evalyn down the hall. One room farther than the Duchess's, groaning comes from inside and it gets louder when I open the door.

"Evalyn?! What is wrong?" I ask.

Another moan escapes her lips. She's lying in the fetal position on the floor, lit up by a single lantern. Moving quickly to her I kneel down and place my hand across her forehead to check for a fever. Her skin feels normal.

"Evalyn? Can you hear me?" I ask.

She looks up, smiling deviously, and I realize that she just saved me. Letting out another moan that almost convinces me that she's actually in pain, I look behind me to see if Tamiell is there, but Evalyn catches me off guard and wraps her arms around my neck while whispering in my ear.

"You owe me."

"What is wrong with her, servant?" The Duchess's voice comes from behind me.

I have to play into it or else the Duchess will become suspicious. "She is ill. What food did she have before I got here?"

Evalyn moans again.

"I am not sure. She served me potatoes and eggs, but I could not tell you if she ate any of them. As you can see I am fine."

"I need to get her some water. Where can I get some?" I ask her while fluctuating the tone of my voice to mimic worry.

"Out the back door there is a water pump…"

No sooner than she's spoken, I lay Evalyn down carefully, run out of the room, and make my way to the back door. When I'm down the stairs, out of earshot of Tamiell, I let out a chuckle under my breath. Despite Evalyn telling me that there was nothing she could do to help me, she found something anyway.

But if she thinks I owe her, she's wrong. That was just payment for getting me into this mess in the first place!

In the kitchen I look around for something to put a lot of water in. The glasses in the cupboards won't hold enough to make this believable. Searching the wood and food closet, I find a bucket on a shelf next to a sack of potatoes. I pull it down and head out back, finding the pump just as the Duchess mentioned. It doesn't take long to pump up a bucketful, and I return inside.

Grabbing a wooden cup from the cupboard, I cautiously make my way back upstairs. The water sloshes, and like waves crashing against rocks, it springs up and splashes. Around the corner at the top of the stairs, Duchess Tamiell still stands in Evalyn's doorway.

"Excuse me." I push past her. "Here, Evalyn, I have brought water!"

Kneeling down, I dip the cup into the bucket and put one arm around Evalyn to elevate her. Playing the part of the worried friend, I put the glass up to her lips and she begins to drink. While she does, an evil thought crosses my mind, and I wonder only briefly what kind of repercussions that it will have.

Would playing a prank on Evalyn right now be prudent?

When she looks at me I furl my eyebrows in a menacing manner, and show a very toothy grin while whispering as quiet as I can, "I spit in there!"

Evalyn's eyes go wide and she chokes. She's hurled into a violent fit of coughing in reaction to my statement. Leaning her forward, I slap her back a few times.

"Evalyn! Evalyn! Are you okay?!" I ask with artificial fear in my voice.

With watering eyes she looks at me angrily while continuing to cough rapidly. Taking a breath in through her nose she lets loose a large cough through her mouth in my face, spittle and all.

"Just breathe, Evalyn! You'll be okay!" I tell her. "Here, we will get you up onto your bed!"

Getting up, I move behind her and place my hands in her armpits. When I try to help her up, she drops all of her weight on me and I stumble, nearly collapsing into the bedpost.

"I am too weak," Evalyn's voice comes out soft and innocent, just loud enough for Duchess Tamiell to hear, but under her breath she whispers to me. "The war is on."

Her arms flop over my back as I hoist her up by the waist, and fling her over my shoulder like an oversized bag of potatoes. Moving to the bed, I roll my shoulder and let her fall off onto the mattress. I pull back the covering, help her into it, and then tuck all of the blankets under her so that she's cocooned and can't move, even going so far as to sit on the bed so she can't get free easily.

"Do not worry, I will take care of you all night if I have to, Evalyn. You are like a *grandmother* to me." I smile from ear-to-ear while she grimaces. "Duchess, she needs my care. I will have to stay with her through the night to make sure her fever doesn't go up!"

She stays silent for a moment but then responds. "You will tend to her here, but I expect that you will take care of your duties tomorrow, and should she be well enough, that she also be up and tending her duties as normal."

"Yes, Duchess," I reply. "I will make sure to take good care of her and have her in good health again!"

The door is shut as Duchess Tamiell leaves, and I grab the spare pillow from the bed, plant my face into it, and laugh hysterically. My sides begin to ache, and my tears wet the pillow. Evalyn squirms against the blankets trying to get out, but with me sitting on one half of them it makes it quite difficult for her. She grunts and writhes. Feeling her get free, I think nothing of it until she smacks me upside the back of the head. Even though it hurts, my laughter continues into the pillow.

"Your grandmother?!" she whispers exasperatedly. "I saved your hide tonight and this is how you repay me?"

I calm down and take deep breaths. Turning to her, sitting with her arms crossed and leaning against the bed's headboard, I show her my ear-to-ear grin. "You forget, you got me into that mess: you owed me anyway."

A whispering battle ensues.

"Owed you?! You still owe *me*! I saved you when you almost died!"

"You saved me?"

"That's right! I saved you! If it wasn't for the vortex you'd be dead in the woods!" Her voice begins to rise up. "Besides, I had a large role in getting you healed up! So you owe me twice!"

"Calm down!" I put my hands up trying to shush her, while looking over at the door to make sure that the Duchess hasn't snuck up on us. "Why would you save me?"

She glares at me and slouches onto the pillows of the bed.

What isn't she telling me?

"I saved you because I wanted to." She shifts her gaze from me to the window.

"You saved me because you wanted a man around, didn't you?" I jest.

"No, I saved you because I *wanted* to!" She looks back at me quickly with hostile eyes. "You haven't even said 'thank you'!"

"Thank you, Evalyn," I honestly reply.

Relaxing the muscles in her forehead, her wrinkles nearly disappear, and she looks out the window again. I scoot over to her, stretch my legs out, and we sit together in silence for a moment.

"Do I really remind you of a grandmother figure?" she asks meekly.

"No, it was just something to get you riled up. You're not that old."

"'Not *that* old' huh?" I feel her jab me in the side with her elbow, but it isn't hard like I would have expected from her.

"You know that's not what I meant." I jab her back. "I think of Agatha as a motherly figure, therefore you'd have to be an aunt figure to me."

"It's too bad we met under these circumstances, you know, me being dead and all."

"Why's that?"

"Because I think we could have been *really* good friends." She jests.

Not quite sure how to respond to what might be Evalyn making a pass at me, I just go with an honest and simple answer. "Well, if you hadn't done what you did with the house, I'd have died and none of us would have ever met."

"Strange how that works isn't it? Time is a funny thing."

My eyes are getting heavy, and my mind begins to shut down once again. As I contemplate the odd bond I seem to be forming with Evalyn, I can't help but wonder why she chose to save me over letting me die.

What would have given her motive to keep me alive? Did she know that I would stay with the house? She's been so hostile toward me that she's given no indication she actually wanted me around. But now her actions are conflicting.

When I close my eyes I can feel myself drifting, and I let go, soaring into my sleep state where I rarely seem to dream. It's my silent reprieve from the world.

~~~~~~

My bell rings, and I'm woken from my nothingness to light pouring in through the window. Evalyn is leaning on my shoulder, still asleep, surprisingly.

Gently, I move her by the shoulders so that she's sitting up in a sturdy position, and then move from the bed to the door. As I walk down the hall toward the ringing, I find it coming from the Duchess's room. When I knock lightly I hear her sigh loudly.

"Come in!" She sounds annoyed with me already.

I open the door to find her standing in front of a full-length mirror in her dark red nightgown, her hands holding her hair up in a messy fashion. In the mirror I can see her full form, revealed by the tight nightgown, and I avert my eyes.

"Yes, Duchess?"

"Is Evalyn well enough to perform her duties today?"

"She has recovered."

"Good...Servant, why are you looking away from me while I am addressing you?"

"I'm sorry Duchess. You are indecently dressed and I figured it was only respectful."

"Indecently dressed? What is indecent?"

"I..." I honestly don't know how to explain to a woman that I can see her full figure through her clothing. "It is your nightgown, Duchess."

"Is there something wrong with my nightgown?" I hear the inflection in her voice peak curiously. Through my peripheral vision, I can see her turn around and drop her shiny brown locks of hair to fall across her face.

"It is a bit too revealing for me to be in your presence."

She sighs loudly. "Fine, leave. Go get Evalyn up and prepare my breakfast."

I'm quick to leave, shutting the door behind me and returning to Evalyn. As I look at her, I see another woman who, despite her outspoken dislike for me, seems to need me in some way as well.

What is it about me that attracts these lonely and desperate women? What could I possibly have that they need so terribly that they assault me, keep me captive, try and force me? Perhaps when I figure out how to stop the curse I will settle down in a quiet town away from these types of people. Did this happen to me in my past?

"Evalyn, wake up." Leaning over the bed I shake her shoulder gently.

She startles awake and swats away my hand as if she wasn't expecting to see me. Looking around, I can practically see her realize she's not at home, that she's still in some random woman's house as a servant.

"So, what's our plan?" she asks.

"Our plan for what?"

"Getting out of here," she grumbles.

"I haven't thought it out. All I know is that we're taking you home, and I'm finding those slavers, so I can take care of them."

"You're really going after the slavers?" She sits up and quirks an eyebrow.

"Yes. They kidnapped us, and they've wronged others. I was witness to the murder of a man who was probably innocent. And what's worse is they did it with his daughter there. This is unforgiveable."

"Your sense of justice is misguided. As deplorable as their acts might be, you will likely end up dead, and we can't have that."

"You can't talk me out of it Evalyn. We'll discuss an actual plan later. Now let's get downstairs before the Duchess comes looking for us."

I abruptly turn and leave, slightly agitated. Through the halls and down the stairs, I realize that Evalyn is just looking out for me. But something inside me is urging me to right this wrong. When I reach the bottom of the stairs, I find Duchess Tamiell wrapped in a robe and sitting at her table.

"Where is Evalyn?"

"She is waking up. I am getting the fire started for her to begin breakfast."

In the kitchen, it doesn't take long to get the last few pieces of wood from the closet into the stove, and get it lit with some flint and kindling that were with the wood pile. As it roars to life, Evalyn enters the kitchen and finds an apron to put on.

"She's not likely to let us out at the same time," Evalyn says while I pass her to exit the kitchen.

Turning to her I whisper, "Yeah, I figured as much. We need some way of keeping her attention off of us and then sneak out."

Pulling the kitchen door shut I head to Duchess Tamiell. She's writing with a quill and ink on parchment, and hardly notices me. She glances in my direction, and returns to what appears to be a list. After waiting for a minute or two, she folds it up, then hands it and a coin pouch from her belt to me.

"I want you to head down to the market and find 'Renald's Lumber' and pick up two bundles of chopped wood, and one bundle of moss and kindling. That should equal fifteen silver pieces. Then when you have returned all of that to the house, you need to take the remaining coin and pick up some meat from the market.

"The list I have given you has everything on it. I am not particular about which butcher you get it from, but the closest one is farther down the way from Renald's. Return any leftover coin to me after that."

"Yes, Duchess. Which way is it to the market?" I study the list she hands to me

"Follow the route back to the auction stand, then make a left and head into the heart of the city. Stay on that main street until you reach the fountain and take another left. It is not far beyond there you will see the market places."

"Yes, Duchess." I tie the coin purse on my belt.

"Oh, and do not think you can run off either. Runners are killed, and I have eyes throughout the city," she warns me sternly.

"What makes you think I would run?"

"You are too free of spirit, still. I know your type."

I choose my next words carefully so as not to arouse suspicion. "Well you can rest assured that because Evalyn is here, I have a reason to come back."

She nods and I turn to leave. Upon exiting the house, I'm hit with a wave of warmth created by the sun reflecting off of the buildings, and it feels good. Following the Duchess's directions I make my way toward the market. Passing by the auction stage, I find it, and the area around it empty. No slaves, no slavers, and no auctioneer.

I grumble, fearing the slavers more than likely skipped town shortly after settling up with the auctioneer, and that means they have a head start on me.

While I move with the flow of people on the streets, I pass many different stores, stalls, and sellers, each of them hollering at passersby trying to get everyone they can to purchase their wares.

Passing by a side street which doesn't look like it has much besides a few randomly placed shops and housing, I see a tavern a ways down. I catch a glimpse of a large man who resembles the man I labeled Burly heading inside.

There's no way it would be this easy. To find him still here would be a stroke of ridiculously good luck, considering they said they were going to leave with haste.

The opportunity to get some information out of him is too good to pass up, despite my current directive from Duchess Tamiell. Diverting, I head to the tavern, look around, and enter quickly. The place is stuffy with what smells like sweat and cheap liquor. It's not as dank and rundown as the nasty inn back in Asta, but this one certainly isn't high class either.

Shifting to the side of the doorway, I scan for Burly while trying to get my eyes to adjust to the dim lighting. There are several larger men in here who are about Burly's size, but his clothing is unmistakable. He is sitting at the bar, in the same clothing as he was the other day. The yellow and white stripes stick out.

What now? Walk up to him and say 'Hey, how's it going? I'm doing great with the woman you sold me to!' Think, Rain, think!

Despite needing some sort of plan, the only thing I can think of is to lure him outside and into an alleyway.

I need the information he has. If I can get him alone I just might be able to get it from him.

My feet carry me over to the seat next to his, and I sit down, placing my elbows down on the counter with fists clasped together. I rest my weight forward and glance in his direction.

"Hey," I start.

He glances at me, seeming to show no sign of emotion, then returns to his tall glass of ale.

"Hey." I raise the tone of my voice a few notches.

"I have nothing to say to you, servant."

"Do you remember all of the faces of the people you kidnap?"

"Get lost."

"I'm going to make you pay for what you did."

"You are lucky you are owned now. It might look like I was trying to cheat the person who bought you if I killed you only shortly after their purchase."

"You can only kill the defenseless. How about you and I step outside and see if you *can* kill me?"

In one big gulp he swallows the rest of his swill from his half full glass, and stands up. Standing, I head to the door and motion for him to follow me. I exit the building, doing my best to show no wavering, no fear, no emotion, but inside my rage builds against this abomination of a person.

By instinct, I quickly scout out a secluded alleyway. Looking back, I see he has accepted my taunt and is following me. His size is intimidating, but I'm confident that now we are one-on-one – and I am not shackled – I can take him.

Steadily I walk into my scouted alleyway, and find a few vagabonds. They take no notice of me until Burly darkens the entrance to the alley. They all double-take.

"Move along," I shoo them off.

They're quick to do as I suggest, with Burly behind me acting like a scarecrow. When they're far enough away, I step farther into the alleyway until I reach the intersection of another alley. Nothing else is in my mind but taking him down and making him talk. Freezing in place for a moment my thoughts scream.

Fight dirty!

I turn around to find him reaching at me with his bear-sized hands. When he gets close, I let my rage loose, charging from only a few feet distance. I jam my knee into his groin. Giving him no time to retaliate as he begins to double over, I kick his left knee out from under him, and he collapses to all fours on the ground. Stepping toward him, I yell.

"You're going to tell me everything you know about the slave operation in this region, or I'm going to stomp your jaw until the only thing you can eat is mush."

His response is to retaliate rather than talk. He swings his arm out trying to catch my legs, but I jump back in time. Standing up, he wobbles a bit, his head likely still spinning from the pain in his groin.

Pulling out a blackjack, he attempts desperately to hit me with it, waiving it around wildly. Ducking and moving, I keep close to him so that even if he does hit me, it won't be at full force due to the limited space he has to swing. As I do so, I find I am able to shift to the side and pound his ribs.

While I want to beat him unconscious, I keep enough sense to hold back so he'll be able to answer my questions. When I throw a punch at him, he gets a lucky shot in. While my guard is down, he hits me with the blackjack in the shoulder. It fazes me for a moment, enough to allow him to grab me and squeeze.

I don't think so.

With my feet still touching the ground, I bend my knees, drop my weight, and then slam my feet on the ground. Springing up, I angle the top of my head toward his jaw. It cracks loudly as it slams together, and his grip loosens enough for me to wiggle out. As he rubs his jaw, he attempts to defend himself with his weapon.

I charge again, slamming both fists into his sternum. When he bends over, I jump up, grab the back of his head with both hands, and let my weight pull him and me over. As my feet touch down, I pull hard and slam his jaw on my knee. I hear teeth break. When I let go of his head, he collapses onto his side, grabbing his jaw and moaning in pain.

"You think you can kidnap just anyone and not have repercussions eventually? You picked the wrong person," I lash him with my words.

Kicking him in the side, he winces, and spits broken teeth and blood out. It takes a moment, but he pulls himself into a sitting position and scoots backwards to the building adjacent from me.

"Isht jusht buthineth," his speech is slurred almost to the point that I can't distinguish what he's saying, but I can guess.

"Business? What you do is despicable. I want information about your 'business,' and you're going to give it to me, or I swear I will end you," I yell at him, letting loose the rage I pent up when he killed the father from the wagon.

"I wiww nawt thawk."

"Then you choose death!"

To show my anger, I kick him several times. Grabbing him by his mangy hair, I yank him around until he is face down on the ground, and then stomp on his neck once.

"You have one last chance to talk and tell me about the slave ring. Save yourself, worm, and give up your friends. I already know you have no honor."

"Thine! Thine!"

"Is that supposed to be 'fine'?"

"Yeth."

"Do it and I'll let you up."

"They are too largthe thor you to thake. Our leadther ith a neihhboring king."

"Do you have bases? Hideouts?"

"Yeth."

"Where?"

He hesitates, but when I grab his blackjack and stick it into a soft spot in his spine, he winces and talks. "They are thpread out."

"Which direction?"

"North-wetht. A cave carved into a hiwwthide."

"Hillside?"

"Yeth."

"Any operatives left in the city besides you?"

"An inthormant. I ownly know him ath the man with the owang bewet."

"The what?"

"Owang bewet. A thlat hat."

"A hat? That's what you're giving me to go on? No, you will take me to your hideout."

"No. You might ath weww kiww me."

"Fine."

Before I know what I'm doing, I bludgeon him in the back of his head as hard as I can with the blackjack several times, until I can no longer hear his labored breathing. I toss the bloody blackjack aside. Though I should be appalled at my brutality, instead I feel vindicated by the justice served to him.

Did I really just kill him? I know he murdered a man in my presence, but is that why I feel no remorse for this action? He had it coming, but was I really the one to do it?

I suppose it's moot now and I need to find the man with the orange hat, get Evalyn out of Tamiell's house, and find the slavers ring.

Checking his body before I leave the alleyway yields his coin pouch, and I confiscate it. When I open it, I find a couple gold, silver, and copper pieces. Exiting the alley reveals passersby who seem to either not notice what happened, or they just don't care. The sun feels nice as it beams down on me. I close my eyes and soak it up for a minute.

Returning to my original path, I follow the flow of the city's inhabitants, making my way to 'Renald's Lumber' without further incident. The business, which occupies a booth built into the corner of a building, is busy. I'm forced to wait for several minutes before I'm even addressed.

There is only one man inside the booth, which I assume is Renald, and he is a very plain merchant. His prices are listed on a sign, carved in, and the letters painted white. The Duchess mentioned that what she sent me here for should cost fifteen silver pieces but he apparently has raised his price since she last bought. The total for all three added together is eighteen silver pieces.

I wonder if I can haggle with him.

"Next!" the man calls out.

I move up and answer his call, "I am next. I need two bundles of wood, and one of moss and kindling."

"Eighteen silver."

"Duchess Tamiell said that it should only cost fifteen."

"Yeah, well costs rise as I have to go farther and farther out for my supply. Eighteen silver or get out of my face."

"Sir, I implore you to reconsider. Does the Duchess not bring you good and constant business?" Though I'm not sure if she actually does, I do what I can to bluff. From the look on his face, it's working.

"Fine, since you are working for her I will give you a discount. Seventeen silver coins and you have yourself a deal."

Better than no discount, I decide to take it. "Done. The Duchess appreciates it."

He hefts out my three bundles from the back of his cove in the building, setting them down harshly on the cobblestone street. The bundles of chopped wood are the size of my torso, and I'm not quite sure how I'm going to get them back to Duchess Tamiell's place.

When I attempt to pick them up by loops in the rope with one arm each, they're so heavy I struggle to lift them. Setting them down, I sling the bundle of moss and kindling over my shoulder and tie it underneath my armpits with a bit of excess rope so I don't have to fuss with it. Making my way back is grueling work.

At least this will keep me fit.

When I reach Duchess Tamiell's house in its little dead-end street, I set down the bundles, grab the knob, and open the door. One after the other, I drag the wood into the house and to the wood room, and then unload the kindling and moss. But my job is now only half over. The Duchess still needs me to purchase the meat cuts for her. Back outside, I begin making long strides toward the market.

I stay alert for any men with hats. If I took Burly's slurred words right, it's an orange 'beret'. While I'm not familiar with that style, I can't imagine many men around here would be wearing an orange hat at all.

At the street with the bar where I confronted Burly, there is a crowd gathering around the alley. Not wanting to be fingered as the culprit by anyone that may have seen me, I move on quickly. Turning left on Renald's street and following it down leads me into a larger market area.

The first butcher shop I come across has a wooden sign hanging out from the doorway that simply says 'Butcher' in white paint. I enter and join a line of half-a-dozen people waiting to either drop their orders off, or pick them up. When my turn comes, I step up to a slightly pudgy butcher who looks like he probably eats a bit too much of his own product. I hand him Duchess Tamiell's list, and after he studies it carefully he nods at me.

"This will come to fifty eight silver," the man says.

Pulling out the coin pouch given to me by the Duchess, I count out the silver pieces and hand them to the butcher. He writes on my list and then on a piece of parchment and hands the parchment to me. When I examine it I find that all he wrote was a number, thirteen, and it's the same as what he wrote on the list.

"Come back when the sundial in the nearby courtyard reaches one and bring that with you. I will have your package waiting."

Exiting, I shield my eyes and look up at the sun. It's nearly midway through the sky now, so if the sundial is accurate to local solar time, then I have an opportunity to look for the man with the orange hat.

Wandering with the largest flow of people going further into the city, I hope to randomly find my way to the courtyard with the sundial. As I scan the crowds, I find very few people wearing any sort of headgear, and certainly not any orange ones.

Having turned several times, I keep track of how to get back by memorizing stores. One particular one stands out because it reminds me of Ami. It's a cloth store, with vibrantly colored woven cloths hanging over the shop's doorway, acting as flags. Looking in the windows, I see bolts neatly stacked one next to another. It reminds me of the sewing room.

I hope she's not getting too worried.

Continuing my quest for the orange hat, I locate the courtyard with the sundial. The chances of me finding him without help are slim, and I will likely have to enlist the aid of others to find him, perhaps even finding a way to coax the Duchess into looking too.

At the sundial, I examine the metal, octagonal plate. In an arc across the top are raised numbers for the hours in local solar time. The triangular gnomon stands about five feet high, and the shadow it is casting is nearly pointing to the number one already. Doubling back, I return to the butcher, with no sign of the man with the orange hat. In a city this large, I fear it might take the whole month just to find him, and by then it will be too late.

~~~~~~

Having acquired the meat from the butcher, I make my way back to the Duchess's home. Evalyn waits for me at the door, tapping her foot impatiently.

"What took you so long?" she enquires, though not in an unfriendly way like she might have previously.

"Well, I brought the wood back a while ago and—" I try to explain myself but Evalyn cuts me off.

"Duchess Tamiell has been looking for you. You should give me the meat and go find her."

"I'll put it in the kitchen and wash off before I go find her. I'm a bit dirty."

"You're going to make her angry."

"Good, maybe she won't try to assault me tonight then."

She sighs, "You don't know how lucky you are. Now get moving."

I bring the packaged meat to the kitchen, and set it on the counter. Out back, I remove my shirt, shake it several times to get dirt off, and hang it on the knob. Pumping water, I quickly bathe my arms, face, and torso, and then put my shirt back on. Returning to the kitchen, Evalyn is already portioning out the meat.

"So, I'm working on finding info on the slave ring. I ran into the guy who took me from Asta, and coerced some info out of him. Be on the lookout for a man with an orange beret hat," I tell her.

"So how much longer are we staying here?"

"Not sure. I am letting my moral compass guide my actions right now, and that means finding out what I can to stop those slavers from hurting more innocents."

"Rain, you're simply delusional if you think you can take it down by yourself."

"I'm not alone. You're going to keep an eye out for the man with the orange hat for me, and let me know if you see him."

"Oh, am I now?"

"Yes, because the sooner we gather information, the sooner I can take you home." I glare at her.

All she does is smile playfully at me, and I can't understand why, but I ignore whatever mind game she's playing and exit the kitchen. Duchess Tamiell isn't downstairs, and I'm hesitant to head up to the second floor because I don't know what she has in store for me.

She could attempt to seduce me yet again, and I would have no way out of it this time.

I climb the stairs and find my way to her door. Rapping on it lightly yields no response from inside, so I knock harder. Still nothing. Twisting the knob, I push the door open. The room is mostly dark, save a little light peeking in through heavy closed curtains and the light I'm letting in. She is lying on her bed, facing away from me with the canopy down.

"Duchess. Evalyn told me you wanted to see me."

"Come in and close the door." She's so quiet I almost don't hear her.

"Duchess, there's something you need to know."

"I do not care. Come in and close the door," she demands.

"I will, but you will hear me out."

I begin to close the door, but before it is shut, she has jumped up. Without time to react, I'm left frozen in place as she attacks me. Throwing her hands around my waist she pulls me in. I push her away.

"You're as bad as Eve!" I yell out at her.

She stops. Her brows are turned downward in a questioning manner.

"Who is Eve?" Tamiell comes off as territorial. "Why do you speak so strangely? Are you from another land? Is Eve your betrothed?"

"I am a traveler, and we will leave it at that. Eve is nothing more than a narcissistic woman who thought she could throw herself at me, just like you, and failed."

I can tell I've lost her completely by the bewildered look and awkward silence, so I switch topics and get down to the real issue at hand; my being her servant.

"Look, since you purchased me, I've been trying to tell you that an error was made. I'm not a slave. I was captured illegally."

"No one ever called you a slave. You are a debt servant."

"It's the same thing, because I owed no debts to anyone. Neither did Evalyn, nor probably any of those other people who were being auctioned. There is a slave ring kidnapping travelers in the region, and I was investigating. The day I arrived in Asta was the day I was captured."

"Where is your proof?"

"I'm trying to obtain some. I tracked down the guy who captured me in the city, and obtained some information from him, but I need more."

"How can I trust that you tell the truth, other than your word?" She comments while releasing me from her pin and backing up a step.

"Go ask Evalyn. She's my friend's aunt. We all live in the same house in the woods outside of Asta. Or better yet, we could take you there and give you the proof that you want."

After a few moments of silence she speaks again. "Is it because I am unattractive?"

"What?" Now it is I who am confused.

"That you make up all of these things just to avoid sharing a bed with me."

"Look!" I shout exasperatedly and throw my arms up in the air. "It has nothing to do with you! Are you so self-absorbed that you would rather think this whole thing is about you, rather than accept that I might be telling the truth?"

She begins to sob, and turns around, walking to her bed. "All I want is for someone to give me attention. I picked you because Evalyn mentioned that you would be a good bedmate."

"I'm sorry, but Evalyn lied to you. My attention is on Evalyn and three other women in my life right now. I simply don't have any more to give out."

I realize now, after the fact, my statement came out sounding like I'm quite free with my body, but only with specific women. However, before I can fix my mistake she pounces on my slip.

"So it *is* about me then." She spins around being dramatic, as if I personally insulted her. "If you can give *them* your attention, then they must have something that I do not!"

"It's not like that. The attention that they receive from me isn't physical. It's a symbiotic relationship. I support them and they support me."

"So you love four women?"

"Well, two of them at least, but one is like my mother, Evalyn is like an annoying aunt, one is my friend, and the fourth is a pain in my rear."

"You receive no physical love from them at all?"

"If Eve had her way I would, but I won't let her."

"I have been so lonely since my husband died, and—"

I cut her off before she makes herself sound even more desperate, "I am not what you're looking for. Even if I were willing, I would be a very temporary solution to your circumstances. What you need is to find someone you connect with, someone to actually love."

"If you stay here you can learn to love me!"

"I cannot stay," I tell her bluntly. "Whether you like it or not, I am tied so deeply to these other women that wherever they go, I must go too, and they will leave in less than a month."

The air is thick with tension. I can't tell what she's thinking as she sits down on the bed and puts her face in her hands. She cries, and I can't help but feel sympathy.

To be unwanted, unloved, would be a terrible thing to go through, but I cannot cure her loneliness. Still, perhaps something can be done to help her.

"Did you not say you were going to throw a party?" I lean against the wall and cross my arms.

She continues to sob almost uncontrollably. Between the sniffles and hiccups, I can't tell if she is actually listening, but I continue anyway.

"Sitting in this house alone with servants will get you nowhere. If you're looking for attention, have that party you were talking about. Evalyn and I will help."

Dropping her hands to her lap she snaps with exasperation. "You speak as if it is easy!"

"Honestly? It's not that hard. You tell Evalyn and me what you want, and we will do our best to make it happen. We'll invite the whole city if we have to, and you can pick through them to find one that will suit your needs."

This could be very good for me. A party means people and that could lead to finding the mysterious man with the orange hat rather than having to scour the city for him.

"You would do that for me? Despite your claim of being a free person?"

"I won't lie to you. I have ulterior motives, but if it helps you not be lonely, then I will willingly help. Evalyn might protest, but I will deal with that."

"Motives?"

"The slave ring is going to burn for what they've done. I want to lure in a person of interest in connection to them. I might be able to use your party to do that."

"And what if you cannot?"

"Then I will continue to work for you while I look for him, and hopefully, I find him and his cohorts before I have to leave."

"I paid a hefty sum for you and you want to leave after less than a month of work?"

"Must leave. And I can repay some of that now," I retrieve the coin pouch tied at my waist. "I took the coin pouch of the slaver who captured me."

"You mean you stole his money after he gave you information?"

"'Stole' is a harsh word. He didn't need it anymore." The feelings of vindication and justification rise up again.

"Do I want to know what happened to him?" she asks.

Shaking my head, I take both coin pouches from my belt, hers and his, and set them in her hands that are laid across her lap. She doesn't reject them, so I assume she has accepted my plan of action. When I turn to leave she grabs my hand.

"I'm going to need my hand, Duchess Tamiell," I tell her without turning back around.

"If you have been obtained illegally, I apologize for my actions. I am not that kind of person and I will let you go," she tells me sorrowfully.

"It was not your fault that I was captured." I shrug and change the topic. "For my sanity, can I just call you Tamiell?"

"Okay." She sniffles.

"I am going downstairs to plan with Evalyn. We will need your help," I head to her door.

There's no telling how Evalyn will react to the news that we're staying here to help Tamiell with a party, in the hope we may find my next connection to the slave ring, but she did state she was enjoying her time away from the house.

Will she continue this line of civility toward me, or will she revert to being hostile when we get home?

When I enter the kitchen I find her cooking. Moving closer, I find that in one pan is some ground meat, and in a pot of water, chopped vegetables are boiling. She moves back and forth, and at one point takes the pan of meat and drains it into the pot of boiling water.

"These smells are making me hungry," I tell her.

"The Duchess wouldn't be too happy with you if you ate her lunch."

"First, she's not going to eat all of that. Second, Tamiell and I have come to an understanding."

Evalyn turns around and looks at me wide-eyed, a look of shock on her face. It's quickly replaced by anger and the wooden spoon in her hand becomes a weapon, as she assaults my arm with it several times.

"How could you do that to Ami?! I thought you had more integrity than that!"

"Wait! Stop! It wasn't anything like that!"

She stops. "You were up there an awful long time!"

"We were talking, you *dirty* old woman!"

"About what?"

"About how I'm going to stay here and be her love slave," I slather on a large amount of sarcasm and grimace at her, before turning to a serious note. "About how we're getting out of here after we help her out with one thing."

After a moment's thought she blurts out, "I'm not going to apologize for hitting you."

"That's fine. I will find a way to get you back. Now are you going to hear me out, or am I getting a frying pan to the head next?"

"Do go on." She leans one elbow on a counter, flashes a smile, and flutters her eyelashes at me in a mocking manner.

"Finish prepping Tamiell's lunch and we will sit and talk with her."

I exit the kitchen into the dining room and sit at the table in the position farthest from Tamiell's seat. She comes downstairs, her face cleaned up from smearing her makeup and sits in her spot. Evalyn appears with a bowl and sets it down in front of Tamiell with a fork placed to the side.

"Evalyn, sit down," I instruct her and she glares at me evilly. "This is the plan. Tamiell, we will coordinate with a local crier and anyone else you deem necessary to call together this party. Make it semi-prestigious, as the slave ring leaders are likely to be of higher status than the rabble they employ to kidnap."

"Is this your moral compass?" Evalyn jests.

"Yes. Now we need to prepare for a party, let's say at the end of this current week. We will give people enough time to prepare for the event and that will give us time to gather resources. A good deal of alcohol will be needed to loosen up some tongues, for both of us." I smile slightly at Tamiell.

"What of the expenses of this party?" Tamiell asks.

"There is quite a bit of coin in what I have given you and I'd say that it'd be a good investment for you if you find a partner."

"You've agreed to find her a mate by getting them drunk?" Evalyn laughs. "Where's that moral compass now?"

"Bigger picture here, Evalyn. You and I are using this party as a guise to hopefully gain intelligence on the ring while Tamiell's chances of finding a companion increase with such an event."

"So we're sticking around for your personal vendetta?" she sneers at me.

"Leave then, Evalyn! Tamiell will let you go right now if you choose. You'd be a liability anyway," I bite her head off, not quite meaning to, but nonetheless the action is done.

She becomes silent, her face blank, and I can no longer gauge her mood. Looking back at Tamiell she stares intently at the meat in her bowl.

"I have no appetite today," she states as a matter of fact.

"Pass it this way then, because I am hungry," I tell her.

No sense in letting it go to waste.

As Tamiell brings it down to me I nod at her politely. "Thank you."

I eat quickly, my stomach quiets.

"When you are done shall we go out?" Tamiell asks.

I nod and she sits and patiently while waiting for me to finish. Evalyn gets up and returns to the kitchen without saying a word, and I feel bad for snapping at her.

Perhaps I have been too brash. I really need to stop thinking about apologizing to her and actually do it.

~~~~~~

After lunch, I help Evalyn clean up, relieve myself, and take the chamber pot to a designated pit beyond the auction stage. With a lid on it, the chore is manageable, and when I have returned I wash up out back. Following Tamiell outside, I feign my status of being her servant, walking a step or two behind her. She leads us into town several minutes from her home to a local winery, and upon entering, I notice a rich and slightly bitter aroma permeating the air. Tamiell pulls me aside.

"What should we get?" she asks.

"Some wine should get people started, but then we should switch to ale. It's best not to waste too much on expensive stuff."

"Very well then." She abruptly turns around and heads to the man behind the counter.

As they work out their transaction, I wait patiently. It's not long before Tamiell returns and hands me a basket filled with half a dozen bottles of wine. The basket is quite heavy, but putting it in the crook of my elbow makes it easier to carry. She leads the way out, and I am left to assume that the ale will be delivered later.

When we return to the street I tap her shoulder. "We need to get someone to spread the word."

"We do. Can you arrange that?" she asks, while handing me eight silver coins.

"That should not be a problem." I nod while taking the coins. "Can you take the wine?"

She holds out her arm, and I place the basket in the crook of her elbow. We head our separate directions, and I begin my search for someone to take on the job of spreading the word. A half hour passes as I wander aimlessly before finding a young man leaning against a post of a fruit stand, relaxing in the sun. He looks to be barely over the age of sixteen, but is dressed well enough, and appears to be free of any current responsibilities.

"Hey, how would you like to earn some extra coin?" I ask him.

He redirects his attention to my current position from his lofty gaze into the sky. "How much?"

"Eight silver. Four up front and four after the job is complete."

His eyes light up, "What do you need me to do?"

"Hey! I will work for eight coin!" A scruffy man passing behind me exclaims.

"Sorry, I offered it to this young man first," I barely turn to tell him.

"Give me the coin and I will not have to cause you any problems."

I feel him step right up behind me. Without thinking or hesitation, I jab an elbow into his stomach, and he buckles over coughing and wheezing. Turning, I put my foot behind his heel and push. He collapses to the ground.

With my attention back on the young man, I reveal four coins.

"So the task at hand," I start. "How well do you know this city and the more sophisticated folk?"

"Well enough to know who to avoid on the streets, and who will tip extra for delivering to their home." He crosses his arms and grins.

"Duchess Tamiell is hosting a party at the end of the week starting at dusk. Think you could handle making a few rounds through the city and inviting the upper class?" I raise an eyebrow at him in a questioning manner.

"That will not be a problem." He nods and holds his hand out.

"Good. Make sure that there are some single men in the mix," I whisper and drop the four coins into his open hand. "When you have told all of the people you can think of, stop by Duchess Tamiell's place and you will receive the other half of your pay. Will you need directions?"

"No, I have delivered to her before."

"Then be off." I wave my hand expectantly and turn to walk away.

As I start back to Tamiell's home, I hear him tell the person at the stall that he will be back, and he runs off into the heart of the city.

Taking my time walking, I admire the simple lives people lead compared to my overly complicated one. While times may get tough, they plug on doing what they know and do best. The farmers grow, the merchants buy and sell, and the politicians know how to keep everybody beneath them. The only major complication is slavery.

"Hey," an unfamiliar man's voice comes from behind me. "Hey wait up!"

It takes me a moment to realize that he is addressing me.

"I saw what you did back there!" he calls out.

"Then you will know not to attempt a theft," I tell him while I continue my stroll.

"No, no. What you did was amazing!" He finally trots up next to me then matches my pace.

Glancing over I notice that he is well enough dressed to not be a commoner, but not finely enough to be anyone of serious stature. Then the color of his clothing hits me. Orange. He wears puffy orange clothing, and a flat beret hat hangs off the side of his head. He looks like a musician of some sort, but no instrument is on his person. I do my best to hide my surprise that my one lead in the city has found *me*, rather than the other way around.

Is this even possible? First I find Burly without any special searching and now this guy practically falls in my lap? Is my luck changing?

"Your clothing is a little out of sorts for this region. Are you a musician?" I point out in a nonchalant manner.

"And your accent is the same. Are you a scholar from far away?" He fires back with a friendly smile.

He has to be the informant. How many other people would wear something so gaudy, and in bright orange?

"I overheard your conversation with the boy. Would your Duchess be interested in hiring a band?"

Stopping my stride for a brief moment, I contemplate his question.

That would kill two birds with one stone; atmosphere to the party and a better opportunity to overhear something. Perhaps I will be able to get him drunk and not have to torture him to divulge something.

"We haven't hired anyone else yet, so that would work well. What are your rates?"

"Sixteen silver, four for each of my band members."

"Sixteen it is. Follow me, and I will show you where to be, and when."

"Thank you! You will not regret hiring us."

I'm sure I won't.

The walk back to Tamiell's house is quiet, and upon reaching the front door, I turn to the man.

"This is where you will play. Be here about midday on the last day of this week and we can discuss setup, music, and provide payment."

"Thank you." He bows and removes his hat in a showy fashion then turns around and heads back down the cobblestone road.

~~~~~~

The end of the week finds us quickly, and I make my way around Tamiell's house doing menial chores. As guests begin to arrive, I bring out a fine silver tray of wine glasses, and place them in their hands.

The man with the orange hat has arrived and his band begins to play a soft, yet upbeat piece which dramatically lifts the room's normally dull atmosphere. Conversation fills the air as the guests sip their wine and eat from trays of bite-sized foods Evalyn and I prepared and laid out.

Breaking off into their own groups, for now many of the women attendees gossip with Tamiell about her lack of public appearance lately, and she plays the hostess, while the male attendees sit in the den discussing unknown topics, as their voices are out of the range of my hearing.

One of the women makes a comment about "Tamiell's handsome new servant," and I take that moment to leave the area and stand over in the den by the music and the men. While I can still see the women peering at me every once in a while, I try to avoid catching their gazes, and instead attempt to focus on the conversations.

The last thing I need is more attention.

I shift anxiously from one foot to the other, hoping to hear something worthwhile, but they all talk about things of little interest to me: taxes, local leadership, their favorite taverns, servants, and wealth. While I can't relate to any of it, I am a little more at home near the men and musicians than standing near the women who chat and titter.

Evalyn moves from the kitchen to the dining area and back, keeping a constant eye on the food and replenishing the platters as necessary. She doesn't even glance my way, which for now is fine as I am out of the line of fire of snarky remarks.

Even so, we have been getting on better than the first few months. Perhaps she is growing a little more accustomed to me.

"The auctioneer will be back soon likely with another shipment of servants. Maybe I can get as lucky as you!"

My ears perk up, and while I thought the men would be the ones to initiate conversation about servants, it was instead a woman talking with Tamiell.

"I am not lucky. My servant…only had a small debt and he will be leaving my service soon," she replies solemnly.

"Maybe I can hire him to work for me then!"

"Dear, you do not need any more servants," replies another woman. "I have seen how many you keep around to do your bidding."

"No, he has made it quite clear he will be leaving the area," Tamiell tells them.

"That is unfortunate. I guess I will have to rely on the next auction." The first woman makes a face at the second.

"Do you know anything about where the servants come from?" Tamiell asks them for my benefit.

"Who cares?" another woman speaks.

"What if, say, they did not have a debt but were sold as slaves instead of servants?"

"Impossible," one of the men chimes in rather quickly. "They are screened by local officials as they enter town, and papers are provided to prove their debt."

"Is that so?" Tamiell replies. "I wonder if they are forged papers."

"Stupid woman. What do you know?" he replies and turns his attention back to the male guests.

Interesting way to speak to the host of the party.

I resist the urge to pop the guy in the face with my tray of wine glasses, and instead gauge the reaction of the musician with the orange attire. He focuses on his playing, and shows no sign he has any more information than the next person.

As the wine on my tray runs out and fills with empty glasses, I head to the kitchen. Before I can refill them, quick raps on the front door indicate more guests arriving. Answering, I invite the new faces in, and shut the door behind them, taking their coats upstairs. Back in the kitchen I notice the house has gotten louder, and I can't keep track of any conversations at this point. The groups reintegrate with each other, and my ears only catch every few words. I stop trying.

The night drags on, the wine disappears, and the first keg is opened. Mugs are already set out, thanks to Evalyn, but she is still ignoring me for unknown reasons. Filling up mugs, I take four at a time out to the dining table. Before I can even set them down, men snatch them from my hands. Several trips later, many guests have mugs in their hands, and the table is taking the rest. During a break in the music, I offer the band ale. While they give me puzzled looks, I smile and urge them to take it. They drink, and I am pleased.

One down, many to go.

By the end of the night they are all drunk, and many have left while others have drunk themselves into such a stupor that they sleep in random locations. The musicians have toned their playing down to softer levels, and my point of interest has had his fair share of ale.

Tamiell looks at me, knowing my interest in him hasn't dwindled, and moves to the band. She pays them each two additional silver coins, and while dismissing the others she pulls my suspect aside. They talk, and she laughs, though I can't tell if she is feigning or if it is real.

They sit idly and chat while I clean up the mess which has been made. I hear her giggle, and their low tones can be felt as vibrations in the air, but I can't make out anything they are saying.

Heading into the kitchen, I assist Evalyn in washing glasses and setting them out to dry on the countertop. I sneak a few crackers and pieces of cheese into my mouth. The moment my lips are sealed I hear some movement come from the dining area. Turning around, I see Tamiell enter, the door closing behind her.

"Rain, in about five minutes head up to my room. I will have him ready for your questioning," Tamiell says quietly with a solemn smile, and then promptly leaves.

I hurry to finish chewing while I dry my hands off. Evalyn glares at me, and I know she's likely going to be irritated at cleaning up without me, but I cannot miss this opportunity.

Swiftly moving through the kitchen door and up the stairs, I find the door of Tamiell's room. I hear them talking and laughing. There is some shuffling around and movement on her bed as the springs creak ever so slightly.

Please…please still have clothes on.

"I'll be right back," I hear her say, muffled by the solid wood door.

More movement. She approaches the door. It opens, she steps out, and before he knows what's happening, I burst into the room. As he lies on the bed, I move to the side of it and hover over him with a vengeful gleam in my eye.

Startled, he scrambles to cover himself with a blanket, though only his shirt is currently removed. Filled with bewilderment he looks as though he wants to ask what is going on, but is petrified at my sudden appearance.

"You're going to give me what I need," I snarl at him.

"I…I…" he jabbers.

"'I' is a good start. Follow it up with 'know how to find or get in contact with slavers' and we'll be off on the right foot." I cross my arms.

"What?"

"Slavers. The people who move from one town to another kidnapping people, and selling them falsely as 'debt servants' to people in other towns."

"I know nothing like that," his voice trembles.

"I have it on the authority of a man dying that you have information I can use to hunt them down," I yell at him. "It must be mighty convenient for the slavers if they send a group of musicians ahead of them to the next town to scout."

"What? No, I…"

"No, you? You what? Did you not think it would catch up to you?"

"You are mistaken!" he pleads.

"About what?" I lean over the bed, propping my hand against a nightstand, and get in his face.

"I have not helped any slavers."

"Lies. You were fingered as an informant by one of the slavers. Tell me what you know!"

"I know the people you speak of! We have run across them on occasion since we are well traveled. They are the sort who will extort you for money if they think you have it. We, the band, have had this misfortune."

"You're not telling me anything I care about. Where is their hideout?"

"I do not know!"

"Never seen the direction they travel?"

"Only once did we see them, but we wanted nothing to do with them so we jumped off the road and let them pass."

"Where?"

"North by north-west of here. A day's journey."

"That's nothing I don't already know."

I sense that he is holding back. While I can't see her, I know Tamiell is still there.

"Tamiell, a dagger please."

"Under the mattress where he lies." She stands there with her hands over her mouth.

"Convenient!" I reach under him and he tries to scramble.

Finding the sheathed dagger, I pull it out. The blade glimmers in the dim light.

"You're holding back!" I lunge at him from across the bed and stick the knife to his throat, my rage builds against him and the slavers.

"I am sorry! I am sorry! I am only a new recruit to their guild! I *was* sent here to find people for them, but I really am a traveling musician!" he cries out. "They threatened to take *us* if we did not cooperate! Their operatives are keeping an eye on us!"

"May your death be slow and painful." I swing my arm back, positioning to thrust it into his neck.

"I can lead you to their cave!"

Finally, a spineless fool, unlike Burly.

I smirk and re-sheathe the dagger. "Good. We leave at first light. If you try to run you will start losing pieces of your body."

While I head out of the room, I look at Tamiell and shake my head.

Holding out my hand with the dagger in it, I wait for her to take it from me. She puts her hand on the handle and I release it to her.

"I'm sorry I had to ruin that one for you, but you wouldn't want to be associated with him or his ilk," I say while looking over my shoulder at him.

The look of sorrow on her face tells me she found nobody tonight, and I can offer nothing to console her other than hollow words at this point. While she continues to lean against the doorframe, I head down the hall to my designated room.

While my intent was to sleep some, my mind is too anxious. It stirs with thoughts of what I will do when I get there, what I hope to accomplish, and if any of it will make any difference. I pace back and forth on the hardwood floor, playing out imaginary scenarios in my head in hopes for some peace of mind, but it's useless.

The hours pass by, but time feels like it is at a standstill. The best plan I can come up with is sending Evalyn on her way back to the house while I head to the slaver cave. The lack of knowledge of how many I will be facing, and the lack of weapons to use against them seems to be the only hitch in the plan.

The element of surprise against an unknown number of enemy combatants is the only thing I have going for me.

Finally, I cannot stand being alone anymore and head downstairs. Evalyn is in the kitchen, bustling about the stove, and I hear the whistle of a kettle. Two cups are set out. She prepares a hot drink and drops a spoonful of sugar into it, then stirs. After she takes a sip she acknowledges my presence.

"So, now what?" she asks, holding her cup about the middle of her chest.

"You'll head back to the house tomorrow while I follow the musician to a cave which the slavers are using as their base of operation."

"You can't go alone," she looks at me with scornful eyes.

"I can't take you with me and risk Agatha's body getting hurt."

"You underestimate my abilities."

"Maybe, but it would still be better to not take any chances. I don't need the responsibility of explaining to Ami why her mother got hurt." I frown at her.

"This is my only outlet. Do you think that I would let something happen to Agatha?"

I sigh, fall silent, and cave in.

"Rain," Tamiell's voice comes out softly from behind me. "Oh, I am sorry, I did not realize that you were in conversation."

"It's fine, Tamiell. What is it?"

"I want you to have this. It is not much, but I want to help," she hands me a small purse with a few gold coins in it.

"Thank you. I will make sure it goes to good use. I'll need to buy something to defend myself with."

"Take care of yourself," she says with sadness in her voice.

"I will. And don't lose faith that you'll find someone. Just get out more and I am sure that someone will find you." I smile at her.

Tamiell makes herself a cup of the tea, no sugar, and takes it upstairs. The spy, for lack of a better word at the moment, finds his way downstairs. I glare at him. His head hangs in shame and I'm not sure if it's because he's feeling guilty about his dealings, or if it's just because he was caught. Neither matter to me though.

"What is your name?" I ask him.

"Lester," his voice comes out in a low tone.

"Lester, tomorrow is the day you redeem yourself and start anew."

"I—" he starts, but I cut him off.

"Go sit down in an open chair out there." I point for him to leave the kitchen.

Following him out, I leave Evalyn to herself again. He moves to an open chair by the dwindling fire. Taking a seat on the hearth, I warm myself and cross my arms while stretching my legs out. Staring at him I find myself drifting.

"Get some sleep. We're going to be walking non-stop tomorrow," my tone is harsh. "If you move from that spot I will break your fingers."

He nods, fear in his eyes, and I find a brief bit of peace.

~~~~~~

My head jerks and my eyes snap open in fear that Lester had absconded while I dozed. But he sits there in the chair, asleep, as I had commanded him. I sigh in relief. Heading into the kitchen, it's empty, but a sack is there with a note on it. Written in a difficult to read, fancy handwriting, I can tell it's from Tamiell. She wishes us well. Looking inside, I find an assortment of food, enough for at least a couple days.

Footsteps come from behind and startle me. It's Evalyn. She laughs, takes the bag from me, and slings it over her shoulder.

"Are you ready to go?" she asks.

"As soon as I wake Lester." I nod.

Moving back out to the living room, he's where I left him, still asleep. I kick his foot to wake him. He screams and jumps to his feet. Evalyn scoffs. Silently, I direct him to the front of the house, and out the door.

While walking to a blacksmith I remember seeing on my treks through the city, my thoughts turn to imaginary scenarios of what could happen, of how far outnumbered I am going to be.

The odds will likely be heavily in their favor, and I will need to stay on my guard.

Dawn has not yet broken the sky, and the blacksmith's window is still closed, but that doesn't stop me from pounding on the wooden window panel until a scruffy man pulls it open.

"Not open yet," he mumbles and rubs his eyes.

"I just need a sword."

"Come back later."

"I cannot. I need it now as I am leaving town." I plink down the few coins in my possession on the windowsill.

He grunts, takes the coins, and fades into the dark shop returning only moments later with a rather boring looking sword in a cheap leather sheath. Before I can say anything, he shoves it in my hands and proceeds to slam the wood panel in my face.

Turning to Lester, I use the sword to motion for him to move and lead the way. He leads us from the city, and to the road heading north. The silence between the three of us is lessened by the sounds of nature as the sun comes up, and birds begin to chirp and chatter while fluttering about underneath the roof made by the forest trees.

Lester keeps to himself while leading, and I take a moment to nudge Evalyn and point to the sack she's carrying. We trade, sword for bag, and

I rummage for something to drink. Tamiell has packed a small jug of water, and I ration it by taking a few small swigs, and place it back in the bag. Evalyn and I exchange again.

After hours of walking, Lester suddenly stops and looks around. I listen for anything that might be coming, but hear nothing of interest. No hoof beats, no feet marching. Lester points to some bushes.

"I need to…um…relieve myself," he states clearly embarrassed.

"Go, and hurry up. And if you attempt to run…" I point at him with the sword and trail off.

He nods and stumbles down off the path, and hides behind the bushes. Evalyn turns away, and sits on the opposite side of the road.

"You should have gone back to the house."

"So Ami and I can sit around and wonder if you've died on your fool's errand? At least if you do, I'll be able to break Ami's heart with a first-hand tale of your idiocy."

"You'd be safe," I tell her, while keeping an eye on the bush Lester is perched behind.

She sighs. After a few minutes, and some rustling, Lester reappears. We resume our trip in silence. Lester's pace is slower after restarting, and I notice him checking around frequently. After following the winding road for several more hours he stops again, and looks to his left at a well-traveled offshoot.

"This is where we have to veer off." Lester points, his voice nervous.

There are clear wheel marks from carts on this new path and they seem quite fresh, a good indication that Lester isn't lying, but through all of the trees I cannot see any place which would hold a cave. Though the end destination is not in sight, my drive pushes me forward, and I allow Lester to lead the way.

To break the awkward silence that plagues us, I ask Evalyn a difficult question, touching on sensitive matters.

"Why did you do it?"

"I suppose I can't claim it isn't any of your business anymore, since you're stuck with us." She knows what I refer to without any prompting. "I was angry."

"Angry about what?"

"Agatha. Miss perfect-life. It wasn't fair."

"So you did it completely out of spite?"

"I was dying, and I just wanted her to feel some sense of the despair I was feeling. When you're dying, things just seem like a dream."

"Yeah, I know that feeling."

"So you do." She glances at me, then returns her eyes to where she's going. "At the time, separating Agatha from her husband, and leaving her spinning through time seemed to be enough to drive her mad."

"Why can't you stop it now?"

"In hindsight, I realized that my power was too much. Using it to jump through time as much as I did took a very heavy toll on my body, leading to my death. If I tried any such thing in Agatha's body, it would surely kill her, and I think I've punished her enough."

"Isn't possessing her body punishment?"

"Perhaps she feels that way, but she's never expressed it."

"If she did, would you stop?"

Evalyn becomes silent, not to say that she would or wouldn't, but she appears to be actually contemplating it. Though I cannot tell what she is thinking, it is apparent on her face that she recognizes it as a legitimate question which requires answering. But no answer comes from her, and silence falls between us.

~~~~~~

Night has fallen, the sun seeming a distant memory. After hours of walking, several rests for various reasons, including having to jump off the road to hide while a slave wagon passed, we decide to sleep for a few hours. With the base not far off from our current location, I decide a fire might attract the slavers before I am ready. Huddling together in the woods we attempt to keep warm, and I close my eyes.

I wonder what Ami is doing. She's not likely to let either of us out of her sight again for a great while. And what has Eve been doing? How much fighting has gone on between the two of them?

Thoughts plague me. Ami must be worrying. Eve has to be annoying her quite a bit, assuming that she didn't run off and get herself into trouble. Ami though, despite our lengthy absence, would stay put in order to keep a presence at the house.

Caught in a state between awake and sleep, I dream about the ominous character Drake, but not in the woods as I have seen and remembered. It's in a room made of stone with a large banquet table. Paintings hang on the wall. One of them is of a family of four; a man, a woman and two children. It is familiar and might even be my family. My attention is redirected and my vision turns to Drake sitting at the end of the table. He's casually eating a meal, and looks in my direction. As his lips move, I notice I can't actually hear him.

My eyes snap open as Lester stands up, and my hands immediately unsheathe the sword. Even in the minimal light, I see his eyes widen as large as a doe's. I'm on my feet and ready to cut him down.

"I just need to relieve myself!"

"What a coincidence. Me too." My instincts kick in and, while it may be an overreaction, I decide not to take the chance that he's simply telling the truth.

Was I this cynical in my past? This violent?

He walks off from where Evalyn continues to rest, and leads the way for us both. He heads off behind one tree, looking over his shoulder to see if I'm following. I nod at him, and head behind my own tree while putting the sword away. When done, I return to where I last saw him and wait for him to reappear. I don't hear anything behind where he disappeared and I begin to get suspicious.

If he ran off, he could head right for the slavers…

I tap my foot impatiently. Just as I am going to head for the tree, I see Lester reappear, fixing his pants. I breathe a sigh of relief, and we return to Evalyn. Noticing the sky beyond the trees lightening, it seems we rested longer than it felt like.

I tap Evalyn on the shoulder. "Hey, we're going to get going."

"You're going to have so many chores when we get home, Rain," she grumbles.

"I know." I hold my arm out for her to grab, and hoist her up.

She brushes herself off and grabs the bag of supplies. Lester shifts his body weight nervously. Out of pity, and perhaps guilt over almost attacking him, I address him.

"Lester, if we keep following this path we will find them, right?"

"Yes," his voice quivers.

"Good, get out of here. If I hear about you back in the slave business, I'll spill your insides." I wave the sword threateningly at him.

"Are you serious? I can go?"

"Yes."

He hesitates by walking slowly back toward the path, looking over his shoulder a couple times, likely to see if I am being honest. When he's several hundred yards away, I start in the direction of the carriage tracks, Evalyn at my side.

A little rested, my pace is quickened. As the sun begins to illuminate the forest around us, I see the terrain is changing. Entering an area of hills this secluded seems ideal for the slavers operations. The hills begin to tower over us as we move closer to them, and I constantly check our sides and back for any potential threats. The path ahead is hugged by two hills enclosing it like a small valley. It appears to be the perfect place for an ambush. I put my hand on Evalyn's shoulder, shaking my head, and lead her off the path before we reach the bottleneck. The hill is steep, but we slowly make our way up it in order to better position ourselves.

Using the bushes and trees to aide our climb, we reach the top only to find that it's more of the same. Trees as far as the eyes can see, with the exception of being able to see down into the pathway, which branches off a few times into different directions, any of which could lead nowhere. Or perhaps right into the camp of the slavers.

There's a rustling several yards away, and Evalyn and I instinctively duck and hide. After a moment, a lone man appears with the appearance of a bandit: scruffy, dirty and armed with a dagger on each hip. I give Evalyn a look, and point to where she's crouching hoping she will take it as an indication to stay put.

While I move off quietly, ducking from one bush to another, I look back and see her get into a prone position. Circling to flank the man, I find him at a disadvantage while he appears to be relieving himself with his eyes closed. Swiftly and quietly, I move only to snap a twig mere feet from him. He wheels about but it's too late, my hand is upon his mouth shoving him against a tree, my sword unsheathed, and aimed at his heart.

"Not a word until I say, and if you try anything, you die," I whisper while pushing the tip of the sword in between two ribs. "Take your daggers and toss them on the ground."

He does, and returns his hands to a surrender position about shoulder height. I kick the daggers away from him. I let my hand off his mouth and put it to my lips.

"Very quietly, identify yourself."

"INTRU...!" He tries to cry out, but I shove my hand back over his mouth and jam my sword into his right leg.

His eyes widen, and he sinks to the ground, crying out in pain through my hand. I cover his nose too, blocking off his airways for a short time until his wail dies down. I release my hand from his nostrils.

"Not very smart of you. If you want to get out of this alive you'll do as I tell you and answer my questions. Which way to your camp?"

He hesitates, and I twist the sword still dug into his leg. Letting out a yelp through my hand he points to my left, and makes an arcing motion to indicate going around a fairly large tree in the distance which stands out from the rest.

"Then what? Around the tree, and..?"

He points down. I nod, and as a reward I draw the blade from his leg, swing it back, and put the pommel into his temple to knock him out. Standing up, I wave Evalyn over and she follows me through the forest.

Keeping as quiet as we possibly can, we move toward our first goal, the aged tree. Reaching it, we duck behind and look beyond down into a little cove with two things of interest: a slave cart, and the other man who was with Burly when I was kidnapped. He and other men are leading chained slaves into a cave carved out of the side of the hill. When he cracks a whip against the back of a man to get him to move from the cart, my rage begins to build.

"You need to stay here, no matter what," I whisper to Evalyn.

"I've come this far. I'm not sitting here."

I turn my gaze to her, and give her a very angry look. "You aren't going to like what I'm about to do, and I'd rather not have Agatha's see what is about to transpire. We'll talk about it later."

"But—"

"No!" I whisper harshly, but quickly reconsider my tone with her because of the peril I am about to put myself in. "Look, Evalyn, I want you to know I'm sorry. I know I have been a nuisance to you and I've said some rude and harsh things. I am sorry for the misfortune and pain you've had to endure."

"Stop talking like you're not coming back." She hits me in the arm, frowning.

I smile, and leave her behind. While I move around the back of the cove where the entrance is, I make sure to stay hidden, utilizing mostly bushes for cover. I keep an eye on the man who stands guard near the carriage while it is emptied. No one seems to be alerted to my presence as I reach the edge of the hill leading down to the cave. Squatting, I take a moment to listen. Voices disappear down into the hole and Burly's accomplice crosses his arms, watching as they leave the open area.

When I feel they've gone far enough for me to be undetected in my descent, I choose the accomplice as my first target of retribution. The hillside is steep, and I position my legs along the slope. Pushing up with my arms, I offset my balance by leaning back, but as I begin moving down the hill, my feet carry me into a run. The hill becomes a cliff at the mouth of the cave, and nearing it I slide the sword out of its casing, leaving the sheath on the hill. When I reach the edge, I leap forward.

That blood smell enters my nose, as if I'm about to impact something very hard. In midair, I bring the sword up with both hands, and his eyes go wide. Before he can call out for his fellow slavers, I have landed on him. I thrust the sword down. His arms are up defensively, but it provides no protection from my velocity and the downward force coming at him.

He stumbles backward, and then collapses onto his tailbone. My impact causes him to fall the rest of the way to the ground. A muffled thud is heard, and I lie on top of him. He stares at me for a moment, great pain in his face, and he attempts to speak. Nothing but a gurgle comes out. His eyes roll back, and no more movement is felt from him. Rolling off of his small frame, my sword found a home through his arms, and at a severe angle down his ribcage.

That's two. What would Ami think of me if she knew I had killed two men? How many more will I kill? Should I feel remorse over their deaths, or should I chalk it up to dealing justice, and ridding the world of a little evil?

My resolve strengthens once more. Standing, I pull the blade from his chest and turn my sights to the cave's entrance. Slinking over to the darkened corridor, I peek inside to find it poorly lit with torches every ten or so feet. With no one in the initial passage, I slide in, hugging the wall, and step quietly.

A faint sound of cracking of whips can be heard further down the cave. The hairs on the back of my neck stand on end as I slowly make my way toward it. All doubt about whether I did the right thing or not is quickly dispelled, and replacing it is the urge to kill the rest of them when I hear their harsh voices and laughter echoing upward. The sound of a woman crying can be heard very faintly and I grit my teeth.

Reaching a branch off from the main passage, I stop and wait for anyone to emerge, but when no one appears, I contemplate my options.

Take the safe route and detour into it, and make sure no one comes up behind me? Or the somewhat reckless route and keep moving headlong on the main path into the cave, and hope that I'm not prematurely discovered?

My mind urges me to take the safe route, but I am feeling impulsive. Down the main path, I hear the voices of the slavers get louder. Rounding a corner, light pours in down the way and I find a natural doorway leading into what I assume is the main cave. When I approach, I crouch and move slower so as not to attract attention.

Down from the doorway are stairs carved in a spiral around the side of the cave. Cages are built into the rock walls, with barred doors reminiscent of a dungeon, just past the rock stairway. I count three slavers there, but hear others across the cave out of my vision.

Switching to the other wall of the opening, I can see down into the rest of the cave. There are crude wooden tables set up, with stacks of gold and silver coins spread out. A few flour sacks sit on the floor near the tables, and I can imagine that they too are filled with coins. Four more slavers hover around a separate table. While I can't see what it is they're looking at, they seem to be discussing plans.

A whip cracks, and a woman cries out. The slaver who assaulted her grunts and laughs. While I move back to the left side of the opening to get a better look, I settle in time to see him crack it once again at a pair of hands clasped around the bars. Blood immediately oozes out, and a man groans. My rage builds.

I can't wait here much longer. Do I rush in, or do I force them to come up the stairs and fight me in the tunnel?

Before I get my answer, one of the slavers begins to climb the rock stairway. My only choice is to take him down as he stumbles upon me. Grabbing the torch from the wall right behind me, I hide it behind my back, holding it at an angle away so I don't catch my clothing on fire.

The slaver is moving slowly. I take two steps back from the opening so he doesn't immediately notice me. He reaches the top of the stairs. My heart beats faster. I can see it in his eyes. He knows something is wrong, and still he edges toward the darkened opening.

My sword gleams, but before he can get a word out I arch my arm back and pitch the torch at his face. He screams in pain as it burns him. While he stumbles, rubbing his eyes, I lunge and put my sword upward through his torso. Subtlety is out, so I lean back, put my foot on his hip, and kick him off my sword, causing him to fly backward off the top of the stairs, landing with a thud and a gurgle.

The other slavers seem stunned for a moment as I stand there baring my teeth, and staring down at them in a taunting manner. They have no choice but to come up the stairs, or so I think until two of them pull swords and quickly disappear into a sub-passage I was unable to see until now. Three of them head up the stairs, and one hangs back by the gold.

The sub-passage must attach to the one I chose not to go down. They'll be upon me in a moment.

My only option is to jump into the three heading up before the other two get to me, and I do just that. Taking a step back, I rush at them and jump. The closest one readies his dagger, expecting me to come at the upper half of his body, so instead I shift my weight downward and plant both feet into his right shin. It snaps. Before he can bring his dagger down, I put both feet on his chest and shove. With a broken leg and no balance, he has no choice but to go where I've directed him, falling into the others. They tumble to the bottom.

In hindsight, I realize I shouldn't have drop-kicked him. Returning to my feet, I rub my tailbone. A noise from behind alerts me to the two who have circled around, and I turn to address them, finding myself now at the disadvantage of being lower than they. Looking down behind me, two slavers are getting back up while the other one lies on the rock floor wailing. The body I had thrown over the edge lies there motionless, and an idea comes to me.

I jump. It's stupid, but I do it anyway. Aiming for the dead slaver, I point my feet in his direction. When they impact his soft flesh I drop my sword, tuck, and roll forward. When I'm finished, I jump up, stumble a few steps, and find myself face to face with the one who was sitting back. His fist connects with my jaw. It hurts, but I retaliate with a right hook toward his ribcage. He deflects, and pounds me in the temple. Blurry vision plagues me briefly, and I stumble.

He doesn't let up, and aims an uppercut at my jaw. Moving slightly to the left makes him miss. I take the opportunity to bring my knee home to his gut. When he steps backward, he coughs and bends over. Not unaware I'm being closed in on, I grab his dagger, move around his back, and put it to his throat. They stop.

My mind races, and I try to decide what to do next. Justice must be exacted, but something inside hesitates to draw the knife across his jugular. They begin creeping toward me, surrounding me.

If I want to get out of this alive, I have to act before they form a circle.

Clenching the muscles in my arm, the knife gets tighter against his neck, and a trickle of blood runs down the blade. He attempts to throw me over his shoulder, but I grip him, and dig my heel into the back of his knee. As he lunges up and bucks against me, my hand slips. The knife in my hand has drunk his blood, and he collapses to his knees.

"Kill…him…," he gargles while grasping his neck.

They rush at me, four on one, and I pulse with energy. No hesitation, I rush into them, swinging the dagger to deflect incoming attacks and to hit them. Dodge. Parry. Strike. Spinning around, I attempt to keep them all at least in my peripheral vision, and while looking one direction, I attack in another.

They parry, and I try again, only to divert halfway through to dodge a sword. Nearly making myself dizzy trying to keep an eye on them while being circled like weak prey, I feel the hair on the back of my neck stand up. When they all swing at once, and close in, I dive through one of their legs. Back on my feet, my sword is only a foot to my right. I try to quickly grab it, but one of them rushes at me, planting his boot in my chest. I exhale violently, and roll to the left to avoid a sword coming down.

Struggling to regain my composure, they circle again. Closing my eyes I focus on breathing. My instincts tingle, nagging at me. I take a deep breath in, and open my eyes. A sword is coming, with no way to dodge.

"No!" I yell and extend my hand, as if to deflect the sharp instrument.

My latent power kicks in. It feels like every nerve in my body reverberates, and a visible shockwave blasts from my palm, impacting this assailant. The others, unsure what to do, stand there in awe as it pushes him into the bars of a cage with crushing force.

While still on the ground, I point my hand and use the still built up energy to do it again. Flying across the room, a slaver crashes into a table, and causes it to flip, sending treasure scattering everywhere. Glaring at the two still upright, I stand up.

"What are you?!" one screams out in terror.

They begin to scatter.

Too late, justice will be done.

I throw the dagger at a slaver fleeing toward the sub-passage, hitting him in the leg. To my disappointment my dagger throwing isn't great, and it hits him flat bladed. I grab my sword and bolt after him.

My eyes adjust to the darkness as I pursue. In an attempt to slow me, he grabs a torch and tosses it at me while continuing to run. Deflecting it, I catch up, and he tries to turn around to face me. As our swords clash in the confined space, I hold him in a deadlock, place my hand on his chest, and unleash. The shockwave tosses him like a ragdoll against the winding cave wall, and he bounces to the ground.

The cave shakes, and I run uphill to the main passage to attempt to head off the other one no doubt trying to escape. When I reach it, he is already well above me, about halfway to the entrance. He tries to outrun me, to no avail. I overrun him, and give him zero chance to fight back.

Thrusting my sword in between his legs while we both run, I put it against his inner thigh and draw back. Collapsing onto his hands and knees he cries out in pain. In two quick motions, my sword is buried between his shoulder blades.

A sense of vindication fills me. I feel powerful. Gloating, I hover over him as he dies, and when I pull my sword from his back, I kick him over so that he can see my face. He heaves and coughs, with fear in his eyes, and I feel something that I'm not sure I should right now: elation from their deaths.

Shaking my head, I break free of the evil, satisfying feeling taking their lives has given me. Turning around, I head into the heart of the cave again. As I reach the opening to the sub-passage, I glance in it and listen for any movement, any noises. Nothing.

Continuing down, I reach the doorway into the main cave. The slaver who hit the table tries to bolt past me. Throwing my arm out, I clothesline him. He falls back and hits the ground with a thud.

"Please, do not kill me!" he pleads.

"I bet that's a familiar phrase for you. How many people has your band of merry men killed?" Glaring at him, I put my foot on his chest and press.

"It was never me!"

"Did you stop them?" I point my sword at his throat. "Did you ever even try?"

"I…" he breathes heavily.

"Get up." I wave my sword upward.

He does, and I motion with my hand for him to turn around and head back down the stairs. With him facing away from me, I point my sword at his back, the tip pressed to his spine. He whimpers, though I take no action to kill him. The captives cry out for help, and I nod at them. At the bottom of the stone staircase, I survey the room more fully this time. No keys are in sight.

"Who had the key to open the doors?" I demand.

"Him." He points to the slaver whose throat I unintentionally slit.

"Get them and unlock the doors. If you run, you will die."

He does as I command, and the doors of the cages are opened one by one. Following him, I stop at the man whose leg I broke. His face is wet with tears, snot, and drool. The most he can muster is a whimper. A rush of people swarm outward. Several captured men begin to beat the slavers.

"Wait!" I holler over the yelling.

They stop and turn to me, and I now have an audience.

How shall I address them?

"I want these two alive to spread the word to any of their brethren who will listen that slavery will be punished with severe prejudice."

"Who are you?" a young man asks.

"My name is Rain, but let's save the questions for later. I need everyone's help to haul them and the coin up out of the cave."

The people rush to grab as much gold as they can, while I search the area around the collapsed table. A map lies next to it, and on it are routes and areas marked with ink I presume they've hit for people as captives.

Their reach is far, stretching over several cities and countrysides, but I note no originating kingdom. Flipping it over I find a detailed list of gold taken in over the course of a few years, but I find both the markings and the gold nothing more than circumstantial evidence. Leaving my sword behind, I fold the map up and stick it under my belt.

I wonder if I should go see the mystery woman. It's still unclear whether she set me up, or if this was what she actually wanted. I suppose if she requires anything else, she can do it herself.

As the cave clears out of both captives and coins, I'm left with the surviving two slavers. The one who had let loose the slaves lies on the ground with a swollen face. He groans when I move to him, bend, and yank on his arm to pull him up.

"Move." I shove him toward the staircase while pointing to the man with the broken leg. "Pick up your friend."

Rising back up out of the cave, I see the freed people have already torn the cage off of the cart, and at the head of it all is Evalyn mounted on one of the horses which will pull it. People gather on it, the gold in the middle, and they seem ready to depart. Pushing the slavers toward the cart, I receive glaring looks from the folk who harbor ill feelings toward them, but I ignore them and allow them both up onto the cart.

Turning back around, I face the opening of the cave. Like stretching and working muscles makes one stronger, and things become easier, I find that I am gaining the ability to control my power at will. I raise both hands. The hairs on my neck stand up.

Though it takes a significant amount of concentration, the energy builds within. It starts from the bottom of my feet and the top of my head, and converges through my torso, and out from my arms. Releasing the energy into the belly of the beast, the shockwave spreads outward, hitting the rock face, causing it to shake. It continues downward, causing a howl through the tunnel as it pushes the air rapidly into the main cavern.

The cave rumbles, and I hear it begin to collapse. Heavy thuds come from deep down, getting louder and closer, finally coming to a conclusion as the mouth rumbles and collapses in on itself, kicking up a massive wave of dust. I cough. Satisfied that the slaver's den is beyond repair, I turn to the cart and pass the dead man to address the two surviving slavers.

"If you move, if you talk to these people, if you try to run, I will kill you and I won't make it as easy as your friends. You will suffer." I point at them.

They avoid eye contact with me, ashamed, and I head for the second horse. Reaching it, I'm rewarded with a quip from Evalyn.

"That poor cave. What did it do to you?"

Smirking, I mount the horse and put my heel in its side to get it to move. Evalyn's horse matches mine, and we follow the path out of the hills. The ride is bumpy, but there's not much I can do except keep a steady pace.

Evalyn breaks the silence. "So...about back there..." She looks forward, her tone casual.

"I killed several, evil men," I tell her nonchalantly. "But Ami can't know."

"Understood. What you did was terrifying, but in a way, necessary."

"How badly will this affect time?" I ponder out loud.

"Considering things haven't looped back on themselves in a paradox, I'd say either not very much, or not at all," she says with a certainty.

What took us a day and then some to get here seems to be flying by quickly, and with ease, thanks to the horses. A few hours pass and nothing eventful happens, that is until a bush alongside the road yells at us.

Slowing the horse, I see a familiar face. Lester has apparently not made it very far, and I stop the cart. Motioning for him to get on, I see his eyes go wide when he notices the two wounded slavers. With none of the freed persons making any acknowledgement of knowing him, I take it that they do not know he was associated with the slave ring. Once he has settled, sitting away from the other two slavers, we resume our journey back to the city in which we left.

The sun gleams through the forest's roof, and the temperature is quite pleasant. I close my eyes for a few moments, thinking of Ami.

Soon enough I will reunite her with her mother, and we can relax for a few days before the time bubble whisks us away to yet another unknown time.

While focusing on the sunbeams warming me up, I can't wait to have my own bed, warm food cooked by Ami, and maybe even an embrace by her. Wrapping the reins around both of my wrists so as not to fall from the horse, my head droops and I doze off, exhausted from using up so much energy.

~~~~~~

Waking to Evalyn prodding me, I open my eyes and rub through the blurriness to see we are coming up on the farmland outside of Tamiell's city. As we pass through, many people tending the farms stop what they're doing to look at us with puzzlement. The town is abuzz as usual, and the sight of a cart rolling in with more than a dozen people on it piques the interest of a few people. Coming to a halt, I dismount. Some of the captured people begin to disembark, and grab at bags of gold.

"Hold a moment," I state as a request.

They stop and give me their attention.

"We're heading to Asta after this stop, so if anyone wants to stay on for that journey, you're welcome. Those that are staying here are welcome to take some of the gold to get your lives restarted, but I ask that some is left for those going to Asta."

People bustle about the cart, separating the gold out into portions. They seem to come to a fair settlement of what to give each person, and how much to leave. Most leave after taking their share. A little girl who couldn't be any more than ten years old, stands next to the cart and looks at me expectantly. It seems like she is looking for guidance as to what she should do, as no one claims her as theirs. Moving over to her I kneel down.

"Are you from Asta?" I ask.

"I was on my way there with my daddy, but then we were taken. I miss him."

"Wait, I know you. Lana, right?" I recognize her. It's the girl whose father was killed right after I was captured. His death was my motivation.

"Yes. How do you know me?"

"Dear, I'm sorry. I was there and I saw them hurt him. I had to pay them back for what they did," I say softly and put my hand on her shoulder.

"Thank you." She begins to cry.

I tear up and hug her, holding tightly as she weeps into my shoulder. After a few minutes, she calms, the tears reducing to a trickle, and she's left with hiccups. Letting go, I help her back up on the cart where I can see one other woman sitting, the only other remaining former slave. Thoughts plague my mind of what will become of her, and what could possibly be done since her father is no longer able to take care of her.

"Do you have family in Asta?" I ask her.

"No, my daddy and I were going to start a shop there, but we cannot do that now." She looks down.

"Well, it's not the same thing, but maybe we can still help you out with that. Some of that gold behind you is yours. We will get you situated, I promise."

"Okay." Lana smiles weakly.

Turning my gaze to the other woman on the cart I engage her, "Could you please look after little Lana here for me until we reach Asta?"

"Yes, sire," she says with a comforting smile and scoots over to her, putting her arm around Lana.

Lester looks at me, no doubt wondering if I will go back on my word about letting him go. With no intention of hauling him around, or making an example of him right now, I pick up twenty gold coins and put them in a pouch.

"Take this to Duchess Tamiell," I tell him sternly.

He nods, fear in his eyes. Before he turns around, I point to my eyes and then to him with a hard glare. Getting my hint, he nods at me, and hastily jogs off into the crowd toward Tamiell's place. The other two slavers look at me, and I stare back for a moment.

Not realizing it until I see her, Evalyn had slipped off and acquired more provisions for us. Three leather water skins, and a sack that probably contains enough food for all of us to get back to Asta. She tosses them up near the leftover gold, and mounts her horse, looking back at me impatiently.

Smiling at her, I glance at our four passengers, and then move to my horse and hop up. With a flick of the reigns, and putting my heels gently into the horse's sides, it starts off. Reaching the main road which travels between the two cities, we begin the journey home.

~~~~~~

After three days, I sigh when Asta comes into view in the light of the dawning sun. The castle towers over the city below, standing tall and proud. While I was able to save a few people, there's no telling how many have been taken from here, or anywhere else for that matter, and no way to get them all back in the time I have left. I am hard on myself for not being able to do more.

The horses trot along at a steady pace, and we make our way through the fields just outside the city walls where a few people have started working. When we get to the gate, it is conveniently just opening for the day, allowing us passage. The guards look at us strangely while we enter. I smile knowing we're oddities, and will likely attract more attention squeezing the cart through some fairly narrow streets.

Closer to the castle, I feel anxiety kick in. Not knowing whether the woman is friend or foe, I wonder if returning might mean more trouble. I hear a rustling, and the woman and child on the cart scream. Wheeling around I expect to see the slavers trying to escape, but instead they are still there. It's just a common thief trying to make off with the bag of gold. Jumping up, I leap to the cart, and off of it. Aiming my hand, I unleash a shockwave at the thief. It impacts him in the back. He trips, and smacks his face on the cobblestone, dropping the bag.

Gold and silver coins scatter. When the townsfolk begin to scramble for it, I yell out, "Anyone who touches that is dead. I won't discriminate!"

They stop in their tracks, and any coins picked up hit the ground once again. Glaring at the people around until they back off. The thief who is collapsed on the ground turns over, and attempts to scoot backwards away from me.

"Imp! Fiend!" a woman cries out of fear.

A hand comes to rest on my shoulder, and I lower my hand allowing the thief to scramble to his feet and run away.

When I turn around, it's not Evalyn as I expected, but the woman who sent me off in the first place. With no hood up this time, her blonde curly locks hang freely down the length of her body, and her amber eyes glimmer in the sunlight. The white robe she wears nearly blinds me as the sun hits it just right. She smiles warmly. People kneel, and it's then I understand that she must be royalty of Asta.

"Do I address you as 'Queen' or 'Mystery Woman'?" I ask with a grin.

"I am not the Queen. I am the daughter of the King of Asta." She motions for people to get back up and go about their business.

"Well then, Princess, I have some things you will find of interest," I tell her, while from my belt I pull out the map.

I hand it over to her and she immediately unfolds it. She finds the log of money, but has a look of disappointment and bites her thumbnail. Closing it back up, she looks at me.

"This is a start. Am I to assume these areas marked are the ones frequently hit?" she asks.

"That's my assumption. One of the slavers indicated the leader of this ring was a king, but did not specify from where. Why don't you ask the two men over there, though? I kept two from death so that I might turn them into the authorities."

"Indeed!" Her eyes brighten, and she looks at me with delight.

"But, before all of that I need your help now. This young lady's father was killed by them, and she has nowhere to go." I point at Lana on the cart, and she looks at me, scared.

"Do not worry." The princess smiles. "We will assist her as a citizen of Asta."

She straightens herself, places the map in a satchel on her side, and fiddles with the sword at her waist. Unlatching the belt straps, she takes it off and holds it out to me.

I look at her, puzzled, and she insists I take it by waving the pommel at my chest. Hesitantly reaching out for it, she places it in my hand, and I let my arm drop to my side.

"What is this?"

"An heirloom of the kingdom. It was forged by a master blacksmith several centuries ago, and given to the king at that time. It has been passed down since then."

The pommel is round one way, and flat on two sides, featuring two different colored gems opposite each other; red and green. The leather-bound hilt of the sword is long enough for me to make two fists overlapping on it, and could be wielded one or two-handed. When I remove it from its scabbard, I notice the different style the blade features. Instead of a straight sword that eventually tapers at the point, this one starts out wide beyond the simple guard and makes a continuous taper down, rounding together to make the point. While it seems like an unintuitive and bulky sword, I hold it straight out in front of me single-handedly with ease. The weight is actually manageable.

"So why give it to me? If it is the kingdom's, then it should stay with the kingdom." I sheathe it.

"It will, but I will have to tell you about that later," she says looking behind her, toward the cart and at Lana. She waves to the little girl, and Lana slowly raises her arm and waves back.

"I'm leaving the city as soon as my companion and I pick up some provisions."

"Tragic. I was hoping that you would be able to stay for dinner." Her gaze returns to me, and her smile persists.

"No, we have someone at home worried about us. It would be better to not keep her worrying any longer than she needs to."

"Understood. Nothing is worse than a woman waiting and worrying, but I will still come to you later as I have some things to share."

"We are outside Asta in the—" I start, but she cuts me off.

"I know."

"You do?"

"Yes. I will explain when we meet again."

She turns and heads to the cart. Extending her hand out to the little girl, she seems genuine enough to keep her word. Lana hesitates, and looks at me to make sure it's okay. I nod, and the lone woman releases her to the Princess.

Standing up, the woman turns, collects her share of the bounty from the ground, and proceeds to head toward me. With a quick arm around my neck, she pulls me in and hugs me briefly, then disappears into the crowd.

"Guards!" the Princess barks out. From the alleyways several guards appear, apparently having been waiting quietly for the Princess. "Take these men into custody under charges of kidnapping and forced slavery."

They do as they're told without hesitation, and both the Princess and Lana begin to follow the guards through an alleyway.

"Princess," I stop her. "Lana has a share of gold from the slavers on the cart."

"Take it as a gift from Asta. Lana will be more than well taken care of, and will not need it." She flashes her white smile at me.

I bow, as I feel a gentleman should, to both a kind woman and royalty. When I return to the upright position she is gone. Evalyn looks at me with weary eyes, and I know that it's time to head home. We gather up the spilt currency, and place it back on the cart.

Moving around the front of the horses, I attach the sword belt to my right side, grab the reins, and lead us through the narrow streets. Stopping at several shops, we find we cannot spend all of the money, even with buying provisions for four people, two bales of hay, and two saddles. When our shopping is done we make our way out of the city of Asta, and toward home.

It takes a bit of maneuvering and coercing of the horses to find a way through the woods, as there is no set path. Having to sidetrack several times due to obstructions, we manage, and the house in the field comes into view within a few hours. Evalyn slips off of the horse, and walks alongside as we bring the cart into the yard.

The door swings open, and Eve steps out in clothes that make me blush. She is wearing a top which looks to be two sizes small for her, and shorts that could easily double as underwear. She appears extremely lethargic until she notices we have supplies, and her eyes light up. Bolting for the cart, she squeals with delight.

"You guys have food! I'm so hungry!" She begins to sift through our provisions, and Evalyn slaps her hand. Eve scowls.

"How can you be hungry?" I ask.

"She almost ate everything," Ami says in a calm, joking voice from the doorway.

"Ami wouldn't *let* me eat everything! She rationed us!"

"I used it to bribe her in cleaning up some of the sand against the house." Ami laughs.

"Smart." I laugh and retort. "How does that feel, Eve?"

Ami smiles, wiping her hands off with a towel. She is disheveled, and looks as though she hasn't been taking care of herself very well. Throwing the towel down on the inside of the door, she steps off the porch, and heads over to us, taking a direct path to Evalyn.

"Mother, I was so worried about you!" She hugs Evalyn.

"It's okay, dear. Rain came to save me," Agatha's voice comes out. "We had a bit of adventure, and we'll tell you about it while we eat."

I'm taken aback, as I've been with Evalyn the whole time. Not expecting her to leave Agatha's body so willingly, I figure it was exhausting for her, and she must need a reprieve. Ami lets her mother go, and throws her arms around my neck. Her grip nearly chokes me, but I manage to put my arms around her back and return the gesture of affection.

"She wouldn't shut up about you," Eve sneers and looks away.

"Don't be jealous, Eve," Ami snaps back at her.

Eve and Ami's eyes meet for a moment of hostility before Ami returns her attention to me, letting her death grip go from my neck. Eve rummages through the cart again, and is struck across the back of her hand, this time by Ami.

Ami grabs one of the baskets we acquired full of fruit, and begins to take it inside. Agatha follows her. To make things easier, I try to head them off by moving the cart around the other side, but Eve steps in my path and stops me.

"Don't think that I've given up on you. Just because we had a little tiff before doesn't mean anything." She runs her finger down my chest. "We could run away together, here and now."

"Except we're stuck here," I tell her.

"I'm not convinced of that." She rests her palm on my face.

"Well, then step outside of the boundary of the property when the time comes, and see for yourself." I brush her hand away and try to move. She blocks me.

"Even if I *am* stuck here, at least I'll have you."

I sigh. Under normal circumstances, any man would relish this kind of attention, but coming from Eve, it's awkward. As attractive as she is, I know her true personality. Despite the impossibility, if I had met Eve first things might be different, but I find myself focused on Ami.

~~~~~~

After a long day, I rest in my room. Between traveling, and unloading everything from the cart, my body is exhausted. On top of that, I am mentally worn down by the lively conversation over soup and sandwiches about the whole adventure, carefully edited to omit my part in the slavers' deaths, and Evalyn being in Agatha's body.

Both Ami and Eve had shown a proper amount of disgust for Tamiell's advances, though for slightly different reasons. Thinking about it, I chuckle at Ami's overreaction to *Agatha* having suggested it to Tamiell in the first place.

Peacefully, I drift closer to sleep while lying in my comfortable bed, and it feels like the adventure is winding down, finally. Though I enjoyed the feeling of power, I realize that if I don't get control of myself, I could become the type of person who allows himself to be corrupted. My resolve to do some good in the world is strong, but I feel it, deep inside, that seed will grow and decide who I will be. I cannot let it become dark.

Just as I close my eyes, a whisper tickles my ear.

"Rain, come forth!"

I ignore it.

"Rain, it is urgent! Come!"

As I open my eyes, I see nothing but black. Lying there and letting my eyes adjust, I look around and see no one. Yet the voice calls again. It's coming from outside the house.

"Rain, come out! We must speak."

Making my way downstairs, I move through the kitchen, and look out the window. A slender figure stands in the shadows, and I turn on the porch light.

"Rain, thank goodness you did not leave here yet," the Princess of Asta addresses me hastily.

"What do you mean?" I play coy.

"I am a seer. I can see certain things of the future. It is how I knew where to meet you for the first time, and it is how I know that your house will vanish in thin air."

"If you could see the future, why not tell me to give me an advantage? I could have changed things!" I ask, slightly upset.

"It does not work like that. What I see comes to pass, that is all."

"Why are you here?"

"I have seen two visions of you, but it makes no sense. The first is of my future, but your past. The second is of your future. In one you are the King of Asta in the plentiful kingdom of Astid."

"The King of Asta? What do you mean?" My interest is piqued.

"In a time in the distant future, generations away, you are the king. You are my descendant, which is why I gave you the sword. It is rightfully yours to inherit, though I do not understand any of this."

"Well that person you see, your descendant, is a different person than I am. I have no memory of being a king, or ruling a kingdom."

My past? I was a king? This leads to far too many questions.

"But it is so. My visions are never wrong."

"After I am gone you will have to forget this whole situation as I can't explain it to you," I tell her. "What about the other vision you had?"

"Nothing."

"No, tell me," I insist.

"I mean a literal nothing. I cannot see anything, just you and nothing."

"How can there be nothing? There has to be something," I am thoroughly perplexed.

"I do not know. I have never had any vision like this before. All I know is that it will come to pass."

"I'm not sure how I ask you to describe nothing, but is there really nothing at all? What does nothing look like?"

"There is no sky, no sun, no ground, and no forest. It is simply nothing. Your future is bleak, Rain."

"Your vision is wrong then."

"I…wish you the best of luck. I must return to the castle now." She walks over and hugs me. Awkwardly, I hug her back. "Please take care, Rain."

She releases her hold on me, and disappears around the side of the house. Watching her go, I cannot begin to process the things she has told me. Knowing nothing of my past and having someone tell me I was a king is quite strange. On the other hand, her telling me that my future is bleak and she sees me in nothingness is also quite disconcerting. Closing the door and turning the light off, I sit at the table as questions haunt me.

Why, as the King, would Drake want to hurt me? It would explain the setting of the dream I had the other night, but doesn't explain how I came to be attacked in the forest. I had to have a reason to meet Drake, or whoever, out in the forest alone and feel comfortable doing it, else I wouldn't have gone, right?

Questioning myself leads nowhere, and I realize as the sun is rising I have stayed up through the remainder of the night. With little sleep, my eyes become heavy, and I move to the living room. Eve is sleeping on the couch. Though I had wanted to sleep there, it is not an option now.

I drag my feet going up the stairs. The comfortable bed calls out to me, and I collapse on it, quickly called off to my own form of nothingness. Sleep.

~~~~~~

Being back at home, the days pass slower, and I am bored with no adventuring. Planting seeds has kept me busy long enough, but revitalizing the garden was halted by rainfall. Looking out the window from the kitchen, the horses are huddled together under the destroyed apple tree, and it seems terrible to leave them like that.

If we are going to keep them, I will have to build a stable.

Ami appears through the swinging door, and presents me with a new shirt to make up for the one stolen from me. Smiling, she shoves it at me and turns around. I take that as an indicator that she wants me to don it now. Removing my current one, I quickly pull the new one over my head, and as I tug on the end to straighten it she twists back around.

"Hey! What if I was still changing?" I proclaim in jest.

"It's not like I haven't seen it before." She pokes me in the stomach.

"True enough. Thank you. I promise to *try* not to have this one stolen from me."

"You better fight them for it, and win." She laughs.

After a brief pause in our conversation I redirect, "I was just thinking. What are we going to do with the horses?"

"Well, horses would prove valuable," she shrugs.

"It could have saved me some time finding your mother, and we could have gotten away from Eve before we were taken hostage." I chuckle.

"No, my men still would have captured you," Eve's voice rings out from the living room.

I shake my head and grin. Ami nods, agreeing with me.

"I'd like to make them a stable. I could break the cart down and use the lumber from it to at least make a frame. Would you put some paper and a writing utensil in my room later?" I ask.

"Sure. I bet we could put it right up against the side of the house, but we should ask Mother."

"Okay," I wave my arm past Ami toward the door to indicate for her to lead the way.

She grabs me by the hand and pulls me through the kitchen door. Entering the living room gains Eve's attention. She looks over and glares at us from the couch, but Ami either doesn't notice, or doesn't care. Walking into the dark hallway, I hear Eve sit up.

"Hey, where are you going?" Eve asks.

"Maybe to my room. Not that it's any of your business!" Ami retorts and pulls me down the hall faster.

Eve gets up and follows. Ami glances behind, grinning, and I realize that she's purposely piqued Eve's interest. Moving down the long hallway, Ami quickly pushes into her room, pulling me with her, shutting the door and locking it. Eve bangs on it.

"Hey, come out here!" Eve hollers.

"No, go away. I'm going to spend some time alone with Rain!" Ami taunts her.

"What makes you so special?!" Eve yells, clearly upset, while she bangs on the door and jiggles the handle.

"Rain, sit down on the bed," Ami says loudly to provoke further response from Eve. "How would you like a shoulder rub?"

"Don't touch him! Come out here and fight me for him like a real woman!" Eve shouts and bangs on the door.

Ami giggles, and pulls me to the bathroom. She releases my hand to sneak over to the door. Slamming it shut she locks that one as well, and proceeds to antagonize Eve more by turning the shower on.

"How about a shower together, Rain? I could wash your back for you!"

This actually makes me blush, despite knowing she's kidding. Eve becomes infuriated, and beats heavily on the bathroom door.

How much can that door withstand before she breaks it down?

"Oh no you don't!" Eve yells. "If anyone's going to shower with Rain, it'll be me!"

Blushing even more, I feel the joke has reached its limits. I turn the shower off, and proceed to unlock the bathroom door. Eve bursts in, ready to fight Ami.

Grabbing Eve by the shoulders, I put my weight into her and hold her back from hitting Ami. Ami laughs and walks out of the bathroom while I restrain Eve. She struggles against me, attempting to grab Ami's hair, but misses when I put my shoulder into her sternum.

"Calm down Eve, she was kidding."

"It doesn't matter." She stops struggling. "She deserves a beating."

"We're not your captives, Eve. You don't get to beat us," Ami bats back while heading down the hallway again, presumably toward Agatha's room.

Feeling Eve no longer struggling, I pull myself away from her and exit the bathroom. Eve grabs at my hand, but I avoid her grasp by pulling it in front of me. While it may be cold, I don't want Eve getting the wrong idea by me allowing her to hold my hand.

I follow in Ami's footsteps. She has already reached her mother's door, and is knocking. A faint voice can be heard from inside, and Ami opens the door, turns to me, and holds her index finger up. She closes the door behind her. Leaning against the wall, I hear their voices behind the thick wood door, but it's muffled. It doesn't take long, and Ami returns, shutting Agatha's door behind her.

"She says against the house is fine, but not to start until tomorrow as she is still recovering."

"Sounds good to me."

~~~~~~

The next day comes and goes, as well as a few more with me keeping busy building the framework of the stable out of wood that I've torn from the cart.

Only having a rough idea sketched out of what the stable should look like, and how big it should be, I have to improvise as I move along. It doesn't look completely terrible. Using the thicker pieces as the outer bracing, and the thinner planks as supports, it is coming together fairly well.

The only problem will be the roof. When I am through tearing the cart up, there won't be enough. We'll have to pick some more wood up after we shift through time again.

Wiping the sweat from my brow, I lean against my handiwork, and look out into the woods, half wondering if the Princess will return. Her claim of being my ancestor is a little mind boggling due to the whole time travel factor, but I am able to comprehend it slightly. Wondering about paradoxes, and if meeting her has created one in some way, I suppose I won't know unless my memory returns.

Eve wanders through my vision out in the woods. She has been pacing out there for hours, determined to prove us wrong on being stuck with the house. Her thickheaded ways are not deterred by our attempts to convince her that she is stuck with us, despite neither of us really wanting that. Noticing me, she waves fervently. I nod in her direction.

"I'm not sure what would be funnier," I yell out to her.

"What do you mean?" she hollers back.

"The look that *would* be on your face if we actually disappeared and left you sitting there in the woods all alone, or the look that *will* be on your face as you hit the ground when the vortex pulls you in."

"Yuk it up, Rain. I will be grinning from ear-to-ear when I no longer have to tolerate Ami. You should come sit out here with me, and wave to them too!"

"I know better than that," I laugh at her.

"Please come out here. I will miss you if you disappear!" She pleads playfully.

Shaking my head and heading for the well, I draw the bucket up and take a large drink out of it, and then splash some on my face. As I dump the rest back into the well, I feel that familiar rumble. But something new happens. The house shudders, and I can hear a faint moan, though I cannot tell if the moan was from someone, or if it was the house.

Quickly looking over, I see Eve, and a swirl of air circles the house quickly. Her face turns sour and she screams.

As the world begins to change around us the horses neigh in distress from the tree, and I watch as Eve is picked up and launched, or pulled rather, into the side of the house. Into my stable. I hear the crunch and snap of wood as she hits it. As I rush to check on Eve, a bright white light blinds me, and I have to shield my eyes. Running around the house, I slam my shoulder into the corner as it becomes unbearable to open my eyes against the brightness. I can't see where I am going. Moving by running my hand against the siding of the house, I try to make my way to Eve. The horses neigh wildly, and I can hear them thrashing about.

"Rain!" Ami calls out from the back yard.

"Ami, I'm on the side of the house! Eve, are you okay?"

Silence falls as the wind dies down, no response from Eve. But it is not a normal silence. An eerie quiet falls around us, and I squint to see what is happening.

"Rain." Ami's voice is closer. "Can you see anything? I can't open my eyes without being blinded."

"Ami? Rain?" Agatha calls out.

"We're on the side of the house, Agatha. Stay there, we'll come to you," I answer to let her know we're okay. "Ami, I am being blinded by whatever is going on as well. Eve, can you hear me?"

A grunt comes from a few feet in front of me, and straining to see through the blinding light, I move slowly so as not to trip over anything. Finally finding the stable, I face the house and open my eyes a little more. Eve is collapsed in a heap of wood, and likely injured, but I can't see any apparent blood. Ami grabs my shoulder.

"Eve, grunt again if you can hear me."

She grunts. I bend down and grab Eve's hand, and tug a little to show her that she can use me to pull herself up. As she does, she complains.

"My back! What did you guys do to me?! What is this light?"

"We don't know," Ami snaps back.

As Eve hobbles into me, it appears that minus a back injury, she isn't wounded too badly. My eyes adjust a bit more to the light flooding in, and I cannot comprehend what I am seeing.

There is nothing beyond the green boundary of the vortex line. White is all that surrounds us. No land, no sky, no sun. White nothingness engulfs the house, and we are the last bastion in nowhere. We are utterly alone in a quiet void...

~~~~~~

~~~~~~~~~To continue in REsolve! ~~~~~~~~~

ABOUT THE AUTHOR

Thomas W. Everson loves spending time with his wife, Brandi, whom he adores, and their amazing son, Thomas (Bubby). They indulge in the fantastic and stretch their imaginations with books, shows, movies, LEGOs, and video games. Thomas is inspired by much, and loves to test the boundaries of fiction.

Like what you read? A review on Amazon would be appreciated!